Geanna

Crisanta Knight

Protagonist Bound

GEANNA CULBERTSON

BQB

Georgia

Published in the United States by BQB Publishing
(Boutique of Quality Books Publishing Company)
www.bqbpublishing.com

978-1-60808-154-7 (p)
978-1-60808-155-4 (e)

Library of Congress Control Number: 2016933377

Book design by Robin Krauss, www.bookformatters.com
Cover concept by Geanna Culbertson
Cover design by Ellis Dixon, www.ellisdixon.com

Other upcoming books in the Crisanta Knight series

Crisanta Knight: The Severance Game
Coming December, 2016

Crisanta Knight: Inherent Fate
Coming Spring, 2017

Dedicated To:

This book, like everything I shall ever accomplish, is dedicated to my mom and dad. You are my heroes, my coaches, my best friends, and I am thankful for you every day for more reasons than there are words in this book.

Special Thanks To:

Alexa Harzan Carter

Dear friend and big sister, it means a lot to know I can always count on you. You were one of the first people to read this, and for good reason. I am grateful to have you in my life.

Terri Leidich & BQB Publishing

Thank you for this (for all of this). Thank you for believing in me, and Crisanta Knight. And thank you for being the Fairy Godmother that made it so this protagonist's wishes could come to life.

Alex Padalka & Pearlie Tan

I am eternally grateful to you for all of the hard work you have put in to make this book the best it can be. Whenever I describe my experience working with you both, I always say, "They pushed me to be better," because I know it is the truth.

Gallien Culbertson

Brother, I appreciate your tough love, shrewd opinions, and the insult-laden banter that is our way of talking. Thanks for keeping me sharp.

I also want to thank Elise Fabbro, Claira Dieda, Erica Fine, Mary Roberts, John Daly, Ian Culbertson, & Kat Galindo/Paul Cassidy of Kinkos for their support of this project.

Bonus Dedication:

Since this is going to be an eight-book series, each book will issue a bonus dedication to individuals who have significantly impacted my life or this series in some way.

For this first book, I want to thank two of the greatest professors I ever had at USC—Aimee Bender and Geoffrey Middlebrook. Professor Bender, I loved learning from you. The work you exposed us to in our "Classic & Contemporary Fairytales" class inspired me tremendously, as did you. Professor Middlebrook, your Writing 340 course is one of the best classes I have ever taken. You helped me develop my own voice and ideas—you didn't force anyone else's on me. The work you allowed me to produce on "The Hero-Princess" archetype went on to be the foundation of my USC Discovery Scholar distinction, and enhanced my understanding of the characters and world I was already in the midst of creating.

PROLOGUE

What most people think of when they hear the phrase "Happily Ever After" is the romance, excitement, and adventure that led up to it. Very few people think too much about the "after."

That's me by the way . . . I'm the "after."

My name is Crisanta Knight, but I go by Crisa. You probably haven't heard of me, but I'd bet anything you've heard of my mother. She goes by Cinderella.

Okay, don't freak out.

The back-story is that I live in a world called "Book." Book is an enchanted realm, and certain stories about the lives of the people here filter into our neighboring realms, like Earth, in the form of "fairytales."

One year in my home world is equal to, like, twenty years on Earth, though. So, while you may know Prince Charming and Cinderella as characters in a four-hundred-year-old story, we know them as the current king and queen of Midveil, a.k.a. my mom and dad.

The thing is, not everyone in Book is what you might call the "main character" of his or her own fairytale. My parents and teachers tell me this just makes sense. Not every person is meant to be an epic-worthy protagonist, they claim, because the world needs supporting characters, and love interests, and antagonists too. Personally, I think it's a pretty messed-up system. I mean, the idea that we can only live up to whatever archetype is assigned to us—never able to aspire to be something more or even something else—just feels wrong.

I don't know, maybe it's just me.

Anyways, as the daughter of Queen Cinderella and King Jeremiah Knight (Midveil's former Prince Charming turned King Charisma), I am a princess. So, unlike many other people in Book, I'm actually guaranteed to be the main character of my own story one day.

As a result, I attend a special, extra-snooty private school for girls who are destined to be the next generation of female protagonists. My school, Lady Agnue's, and the school equivalent to it for future male protagonists, Lord Channing's, are geared toward grooming and preparing students for their impending fairytale fates.

Just so we're clear though, the children who are chosen to attend these academies are not all royals like me. Nevertheless, they all do know for certain that they are going to have their own stories.

How, you may ask?

Good question.

A portal is said to appear in an area of the Forbidden Forest near the kingdom of Harzana. It is guarded by a group of Book's most powerful Fairy Godmothers known as the Scribes.

Every so often this one-way portal regurgitates an actual "book." And each of these volumes, though initially blank on the inside, always has the title of the story—the name of a citizen of Book—engraved on its cover (e.g., *Snow White*, *Sleeping Beauty*—you get the gist). Ergo, that is how each school knows which children of the realm to take in.

Talk about living life paying attention to the fine print, am I right?

If you're having trouble processing all of this, by the way, don't worry. We ourselves do not even really understand the higher power that decides who we are. All we know is that somewhere in the off-limits part of Book, the Indexlands, a sort of prophet who has never been seen is responsible. We call her the Author, because it is said that she spends her life writing and nothing else. The words her enchanted quill pen into parchment become the realities that Book's people live by. And *bing, bam, boom,* our fates are assigned and our identities are cast. We're put into these perfectly neat little boxes of character development that the Author has picked out for us and the world goes on ticking to its succinct rhythm of calm and tidy conformity—tradition (tick), order (tock), convention (tick), sedation (tock).

The Author works on the original copies of our books wherever she is, and then a twin of each one appears in the Forbidden Forest for the Scribes to share with the schools.

However, since these books begin blank, chosen protagonists, such as myself, must train and prepare for indefinite fates at the academies. We are cursed to wake up each morning not knowing when the Author intends to set our stories in motion, and, more importantly, not knowing what those stories will be.

Given that they have no control over what the Author writes or when it will be written, the people of Book have completely embraced the idea that who they are is not something they can decide for themselves. Those roles, it would seem, have already been cast . . .

On that note, I believe that's just about everything you need to know about my home world before you endeavor into it.

Wait; hold on a second. There's something else I should

mention, something important that I've left out about my realm's rules, my princess-ness, my school, and so on.

I can break it down for you in five words.

I absolutely can't *stand it.*

CHAPTER 1

Once Upon A . . . Well,
You Know the Rest

was going to be a great protagonist; at least that's what my mom, Cinderella, kept telling me. She assured me of this that sunny morning in September as she did every day. I, however, continued to have my doubts. Honestly, I was as much princess material as a wolf was grandmother material.

Alas, my mother did not find this fairytale comparison witty or amusing. Instead, she was convinced that someday all of my training and breeding would kick in and I would become the pinnacle of poised princess perfection.

A lot of alliteration and expectations for one girl and one sentence, I know.

But, well, them's the breaks.

Anyways, my complete lack of appropriate princess demeanor was only one of my problems. The other was that I really hated the whole "pre-chosen protagonist" idea. While everyone else in Book might have accepted the notion that they had no say in who they would be in life, I did not. It infuriated me to know that at some point the things I would do or say were inevitably not going to be my doing or saying; they'd be the Author's.

The icing on the cake, of course, was Lady Agnue's. As if having the Author's will to constantly worry about wasn't enough, I had to live at a pretentious boarding school that reminded me every day of the lack of control I had over my life, and that reinforced my celebrity-child syndrome.

I supposed I would have to try harder to get used to it this semester. Mind you, I'd been trying to get used to it for the last six years, since I'd started attending Lady Agnue's at the age of ten. But maybe my mom was right. Maybe one day I would wake up feeling totally content with the invisible shackles on my life.

Cue eye roll.

For now, all I knew for certain was that I was dreading where this carriage was taking us, and that my feet hurt. My mother had insisted that I wear heels, despite my protests about their discomfort and the short presentation I'd given her on the benefits of orthopedic footwear. Of course, neither of these efforts convinced my mother—the queen—that a princess should be allowed to wear combat boots on her first day of school.

"Mom, these shoes are killing me," I complained yet again as I examined the glittering pumps.

"They are supposed to, Crisanta dear. The pain reassures us of how lovely they look," my mom said as she patted my hair affectionately. "Trust me, Pumpkin, I speak from experience. The prettier the shoe, the more painful."

I sighed and decided to abandon the argument and my hopes for proper blood circulation in my toes. I would never be able to convince a woman who once waltzed in glass stilettos that my three-inch heels were unbearable. I turned my attention back to the window and watched the green blur of trees that continued to whizz past us.

We were getting closer.

My staring match with the local foliage was interrupted by the abrupt stop of the carriage. Several plainly dressed kids ran across the road in front of us. When they got to the other side, they took off toward a nearby field and continued whatever game of tag and chase they'd been playing. I observed them through the vehicle's rear window as we started to move forward once more.

It must be nice, I imagined, *to not be assigned a role. To not have to worry about being a "main character" and just be. I wonder if—*

"Dear, put on some lip gloss. Your lips look dry," my mom nagged, disrupting my train of thought.

"Mom," I huffed. "I'm fine."

"Crisanta," she said evenly.

"What?"

"What does Lady Agnue say is princess rule number twelve?"

I groaned. "Never leave the house without applying lip gloss?"

"No, dear. That is rule fifteen. Rule twelve is never use contractions, and you know how your headmistress feels about that rule in particular. So please, tell me you will try harder to work on that this year?"

"I *can't* make any promises." I smirked deviously.

My mother smiled, but shook her head. She handed me a tube of wild-orchid lip gloss that I begrudgingly took and applied.

"I am helping, not hurting, sweetie," Mom chirped.

Suddenly, our carriage made a right turn and entered a driveway. The hedges began to stretch higher and higher around us, progressively blocking the outer world the further we proceeded down the path.

Savoring my last few moments of peace, I closed my eyes and took a deep breath. A mere minute later, my Zen was lost as our carriage approached the gates of the institution we'd been journeying toward for the last several days.

We'd arrived.

Guards minding the gates opened them inwards. They made it look effortless, but it took three men on each side to get the job done. The gates were massive, after all—constructed from a combination of iron and bronze, and measuring at least fifteen feet in height. They must have weighed a ton. In truth, the only thing about them that didn't exude a sense of heftiness was the light-hearted nature of the golden leaf design, which decorated their exterior.

As we drove across the threshold, I couldn't help but cringe in anxious anticipation.

Sensing my stress, my mom took my hand and squeezed it.

I really had to give her credit. She did hassle me a lot, but she knew how difficult this was for me. And I guess it must've been rough on her too—having a daughter who was so different from her and all.

The carriage came to a sudden halt and I grabbed the velvet seat cushion as if bracing for impact.

We were parked among a wave of other carriages and a sea of girls in chiffon and lace being pursued by attendants carrying their designer luggage. Our carriage doors were opened from the outside and a large, white-gloved hand offered me assistance out of the vehicle. I took the hand and was pulled into the sunshine.

The day was perfect (atmospherically at least). Blue birds were singing in anticipation of our arrival, and the sun was reflecting light off every bejeweled bobble in the crowd.

I gazed at the building before me. It was crème colored, covered with purple flowering vines that climbed its walls. On the balconies a selection of silk, violet, and mauve curtains caught on the breeze, fluttering above like giant butterfly wings. The richly shaded purple flags with our school's golden crest emblazoned on them flew proudly overhead from tightly twisted bronze turrets.

From an architect or a tourist's perspective, I imagined the sight might've been quite beautiful. But to me, it was just daunting. For I knew that each of the majestic compound's tall ivory towers came with the price of equally tall expectations.

"Your Highness . . ."

I winced at the irritating title.

Why couldn't our staff ever just call me Crisa? "Your Highness" was such a precocious term. The only way I remotely associated with it at this point in life was in relation to the height I'd achieved with the pumps my mother was making me wear.

"Would you like me to carry your bags to your room, or would you prefer to check them in with the school's regular staff?"

I forced the annoyance down and plastered a pleasant smile across my face before turning around to address Jacque, one of our family's long-time attendants. After all, it wasn't his fault that I felt disconnected from the title. He didn't know he had the wrong girl.

"You can take them, Jacque," I said. "But I'll carry the satchel myself, like always."

Jacque nodded and went off to the trunk of the carriage. He reached inside and presented me with the bag in question. I grasped it protectively and thanked him just as my mom came over to join me.

She looked perfect today, just like she always did. Her soft peach sundress glittered, matching her strappy satin heels. Her short, strawberry-blonde hair bounced off her shoulders as she walked.

"Come on, Pumpkin," she said. "Time to go."

I sighed. "Yeah, I know."

My mom brushed a loose strand of hair from my face. "*Yes*, Crisanta. Please try to remember that a princess always says 'yes' and not 'yeah.' I cannot . . ."

She cleared her throat slightly—swallowing down the un-queenly public display of emotion I could hear in her voice.

"I am not going to be with you for some time to remind you."

I gave her a big hug. "I'll miss you too, Mom."

She hugged me tightly and warmly for a moment, in the worried way that only mothers could. Then she recomposed herself, sucked in her concern (the way she so often reminded me to suck in my stomach at royal functions), and sent me off.

I turned my attention back to the building ahead—the building that would be my home (or prison, depending on your outlook) until the summer returned. With a deep breath, I reluctantly proceeded through its arched entrance under a great, gold-encrusted sign that read:

Lady Agnue's School for Princesses
& Other Female Protagonists

CHAPTER 2

We Meet Again

lowery perfume and giggles filled the air, and the combined clicking of a hundred high-heeled shoes against the marble floor resembled a sound that was best described as a fancy stampede.

Lady Agnue's foyer swarmed with girls. Like the others, I found myself awkwardly trying to navigate my way through the crowd to get to the sign-in area to no avail. We all just kept bumping into one another like semi-formally dressed croquet balls.

"Crisa!" someone yelled from the other side of the room.

I spun around, trying to find the source of the voice.

"Crisa!"

There it was again—closer this time, but still muffled in the crowd.

"Crisa!"

I whirled around and saw my best friend squeeze past a disoriented Princess Marie Sinclaire to reach me.

"SJ!" I shouted happily.

The two of us embraced as if we hadn't seen each other in ages. It'd only been a few months since we were last together—since Lady Agnue's had let out for the summer. However, a few months apart from my best friend SJ Kaplan might as well have been an eternity.

"Come on!" SJ said as she linked her arm with mine and motioned toward the stairs.

"I still have to check in," I protested.

"I signed us both in. Thank me later!" she replied with a wink.

We made our way over to the grand staircase at the far end of the chaotic room. Thankfully, the sea of girls thinned as we ascended the stairs to the sixth floor.

First-year students at Lady Agnue's had their roommates assigned, but after that we were free to pick our own. SJ and I met when we were assigned to Suite 608 during our first year, along with Mauvrey Weatherall, another princess.

As far as roommates went, I was pretty lucky to get SJ. She was uncommonly kind, always calm and rational, and a rock-solid person to turn to when times were tough. Mauvrey, on the other hand, well . . . there were a lot of words to describe a girl like her. Unfortunately, none of those words were considered very ladylike, so I kept them to myself when in mixed company.

Mauvrey was the daughter of the world's most famous coma patient, Sleeping Beauty. The three of us were initially matched as roommates because we were all considered "Legacies."

In other words, our parents were both royalty and the main characters of their own stories so we, being their offspring, were expected to live up to their preset standards of greatness.

In an attempt to help us—and all other Legacies—cope with our celebrity-child woes, (a.k.a. the "our parents were awesome, so now the world expects us to be awesome" woes), we were bunked together our first year at Lady Agnue's. As a result, some girls like SJ and myself formed strong bonds and became the best of friends. Others, like Mauvrey and me, became the opposite. Needless to say the girl couldn't change roommates fast enough the following September when we returned for our second term.

But, you know, that's enough on Mauvrey for now.

Especially since there'll definitely be more on her later.

It's inevitable.

SJ and I arrived at the familiar door of Suite 608. She pulled out an unnecessarily ornate silver key from her purse and slid it into the lock.

"Home again," she practically sang as she opened the door.

The room was exactly as I remembered; after five years of living here I even had the smell memorized. Mandarins and freshly washed sheets were the room's natural scent. But, a few years ago SJ had added a third element to the aroma when she'd insisted that we keep lavender incense in our suite so as to try and help me with my unusual sleeping problems.

Don't worry; I'll tell you more about that later too. For now, though, back to the room.

After all, what's a story without a proper setting?

Suite 608's floors were wooden and its walls were the palest mauve. The edges of both the floor and ceiling were encrusted with a thin gold design that mirrored the vines climbing our balcony outside. The gold edging also matched the frames of the three identical canopy beds spread out across the room. Each one was decorated in various shades of maroon and purple and had corresponding desks and nightstands constructed of richly dark mahogany on each side.

SJ opened the doors that led to the balcony, which we

always kept open during the school year. Meanwhile, my first priority was to kick off the demon heels that had been crushing my poor feet. Thankfully, the blood flow started to return to my toes.

I sauntered over to my bed and set my precious satchel down next to the rest of my luggage, which, somehow, had managed to beat me here.

I opened the largest of the suitcases and dug around inside in search of one of my many pairs of beloved combat boots. But, just as I was elbow-deep in miscellaneous clothing, I stopped short. My hands suddenly felt like they were burning, as if I had stuck them in a lit fireplace. They appeared fine, but my palms were inexplicably pulsing with pain and felt like they were getting hotter.

"Oh no," SJ gasped from outside.

I tore my attention away from my painful problem at hand (no pun intended) and hastily made my way onto the balcony. SJ was standing at the railing with her shoulders stooped and her head down. When I got closer, I saw why she was upset. The lush green vines that normally decorated our balcony had all died. They were now brown, dry, and in desperate need of some serious mercy from Mother Nature.

"I hope they grow back." SJ sighed as she held one of the withered blossoms.

"Don't worry," I said as I rubbed my hands against my dress, trying to keep calm and keep the escalating burning sensation under control. "All they need is a little water and a little motivation."

"You think?"

"Definitely," I assured her. "Watch, I'll even get 'em started."

I cleared my throat, ignoring the fire-like pain emanating

from my fingertips, and forced a smile as I held one of the dangling blossoms.

"Come on, flower! Live, darn you! Live!" I shouted overdramatically.

My theatricality having successfully pulled SJ out of her funk, she turned her attention back to the reason she'd come outside in the first place. She sang a happy melody and in seconds several blue birds flew over to us and joyfully finished the tune with her. SJ hadn't seen these birds since we'd left for summer vacation, and they seemed extremely delighted to harmonize with one another again. I, however, did not join in so as to spare the birds the agony of witnessing my inability to sing in key. While SJ's voice could've hypnotized a siren, mine could've easily driven a canary to commit suicide.

SJ stood for Snow Jr. by the way. As in, *Snow White* Jr.

Unlike in my family, the apple didn't fall too far from the tree in SJ's family. Or maybe in this case it was the poisoned apple that didn't fall too far from the tree.

Ha-ha, fairytale humor.

Seriously though, SJ was the spitting image of her mother. For starters there was her appearance: skin as white as snow, hair as black as night, blah, blah, blah, etcetera, etcetera. The only notable physical differences between the two were their eyes; SJ had massive dark gray eyes while her mother had dark brown ones. SJ also preferred to keep her long black hair in a tight French braid, as compared to her mother's chic, shoulder-length bob.

In temperament my dear friend was also very similar to her mother. She was graceful, poised, polite, and had great vocal chords and a natural bond with animals. SJ Kaplan, in short, was everything I was not—a proper princess.

Once in a while I would get a little jealous. Having a best friend who embodied princess perfection was a constant reminder that I was nothing like I was supposed to be. It usually didn't bother me all that much that I was nothing like SJ, or my mom, or any of the other princesses at this school. I was just me. No matter how hard I tried, I could never seem to be anything but. And someday I would have to try to make peace and make sense of that.

After being sufficiently reacquainted with her winged friends, SJ waved good-bye and we returned inside. As I approached my desk I realized that my hands had stopped burning.

Weird, I thought, as I examined them. They seemed completely normal—no burning sensations, no pain. Whatever had been causing the problem had been taken care of, it seemed. So I brushed off the odd experience as SJ and I continued with our unpacking.

While my bed and desk occupied the center of the long room, SJ's inhabited the left side. There were dozens of glass animal figurines perched on her desk, which she'd been collecting for years now. Mounted on the wall behind her desk was a rendering of an old woman in a checkered apron.

Originally, I'd assumed the picture was of one of SJ's relatives. Although the elderly woman did bear a striking resemblance to the lady who sold churros two blocks away from our castle back home. They were really good ones, too—crispy, always fresh, and covered in enough sugar to make your teeth hurt . . .

Dang, now I want churros. Why didn't Mom and I stop there on our way over here?

That's a seriously major oversight on my part.

But I digress, as that is so not the point right now.

The poster lady was neither a relative of SJ's nor a local churro vendor. She was actually Madame Curio, the realm's most famous potions master and SJ's total hero. You see, SJ was an amateur potionist herself. Well, *she* would say amateur to be modest. The truth was, she had a gift for it and had been at the top of every potions class we'd ever taken. It was, without a doubt, her favorite and best subject.

Our third roommate, Blue, had her desk and bed on the right side of the room. To my surprise, a super girly unicorn poster with a rainbow was taped on the wall just above her desk. I was about to point this peculiarity out to SJ when a large hunting knife suddenly flew across the room and nailed the unicorn poster dead center.

Blue.

Our dear friend Blue Dieda stomped into the room and headed straight toward the poster.

"Ugh!" she groaned. "They can never leave up my normal stuff, can they?"

Blue proceeded to remove her knife, which was firmly indented into the wall from the force of the throw, and take down the unicorn poster. Then she reached into her duffle bag, pulled out a folded-up poster, and taped it to the wall in its place. This one had a picture of a knight mercilessly stabbing a giant black dragon.

She sighed with relief. "That's better."

At that, Blue whirled around and gave us one of her classic, giant grins.

"Hi guys!" she said, the annoyance in her voice replaced with happiness.

"Hi, Blue," I said as we gave each other a huge hug.

"Blue," SJ lectured, "I know I cannot stop you from

throwing knives in our room, but a warning would be nice. You gave me a small heart attack."

"Nice to see you too, SJ," Blue responded as the two exchanged hugs.

Blue's book had appeared courtesy of the Author almost four years ago, but at the time it was already the middle of the school year. With few free spaces available, SJ and I had subsequently volunteered to let her have the empty bed in our room. A fateful and rewarding choice since it wasn't long before she became a true best friend to both of us.

To put it in its simplest terms, I totally loved her.

For starters, it was refreshing to meet someone at Lady Agnue's, or anywhere really, who wasn't afraid to be completely frank about their strengths and weaknesses.

A second admirable quality of Blue's was the way she carried herself. She walked around every day with complete confidence. She never doubted herself, never hesitated, and never cared about what anyone else thought of her.

I glanced at my friend as she started to unpack the suitcase she'd dragged in. Unlike us, Blue was not a princess. Even so, she was still a Half-Legacy because someone in her family had experienced a fairytale and protagonist journey of their own. Blue's older sister, Rachel Dieda, was the main character in question, though most people probably knew her as "Red" from *Little Red Riding Hood*.

Blue was just a baby when the whole thing with the wolf and trip to Grandma's went down, but she had grown up with the story at the forefront of her mind. Not in the sense that she aspired to be like Red. Actually, it was the opposite. She absolutely hated the story that made her sister famous.

It wasn't that Blue didn't love Red, because she did.

But the way Red had been so easily tricked, so gullible and defenseless, and so in need of someone to save her, sickened Blue. And I totally understood why.

I mean, come on, anybody who would mistake a talking wolf for his or her grandmother seriously needs to get it together.

Because of Red's weakness and lack of admirable protagonist qualities, Blue spent her life striving to achieve something quite different. She wanted to be nothing like her sister—nothing like a damsel in distress. She wanted to be a hero.

This, sadly, was a dream that most of our teachers (particularly our headmistress, Lady Agnue) regularly tried to discourage.

Our school broke down its students into two separate categories: princesses and common female protagonists. The princesses were supposed to be princesses and nothing more. Meanwhile, the common protagonists had the option of either being damsels who got themselves into perilous situations that heroes had to save them from, serving as feisty sidekicks to boy protagonists, or winning the heart of a prince or other male main character. Being a *hero*, in short, was not even up for discussion. It was a career opportunity reserved for the male protagonists in our land. And the matter was sternly, cold-heartedly non-negotiable.

I have a few thousand things to say about that, but I'll keep it to five words:

What a bunch of malarkey.

Blue's feelings on the subject were equal to my own and, ever the gutsy one, she spent every day trying to defy the restrictions that people like her sister had always been bound by.

In my opinion, thus far she had been truly successful. She was one hundred percent nothing like Red. Honestly, the only thing the two had remotely in common was the fact that they were both nicknamed after the color of cloaks they constantly wore. Other than when she was asleep or at one of our school balls, Blue was never spotted without the powder-blue cloak that hung from her shoulders like a fashionable security blanket.

That, however, was where the sibling similarity ended.

Unlike Red, Blue was fearless, bold, and rebellious. She loved taking risks just to test her strength, which both physically and emotionally was unyielding. Above all else, she had devoted her life to becoming the fiercest of fighters. A big believer in the importance of warrior versatility, through a combination of her own self-teachings and the athletic electives our school offered its common protagonists, like Runaway Carriages 101 and Charm and Death, she'd become skilled in a myriad of combat forms. Sword fighting, archery, hand-to-hand combat, jousting—you name it, she'd mastered it.

But Blue's favorite form of kick-buttery, by far, was her knife. Rather, her hunting knife. She usually kept several tiny throwing knives on her at all times, but the hunting knife she'd been given when she was eight years old was like an inanimate best friend. She almost always kept it in a sheath that hung from her belt. And she polished it constantly; despite how frequently she practiced with the weapon, it gleamed like new silver.

That was the knife we'd seen sail across the room minutes ago. And, as per usual, Blue was now wiping it off against her pants leg in preparation for returning it to its sheath.

SJ was not as fond of it—or the various other weapons Blue utilized—as I was. In her opinion, ladies did not play with knives, especially not in such close quarters. But this was precisely another reason why I loved having Blue around. While SJ's princess decorum was habitually my norm fifty percent of the time, Blue's warrior persona impacted my other half. The most obvious way she influenced me being in the area of combat.

I loved the challenge of combat practice as much as Blue did; however, before she'd come along, it had been quite difficult for me to find anybody to train with. None of the other princesses would've ever been caught near the practice fields where many of the common protagonists worked on their fighting skills. And even though they were usually very nice and relished any opportunity to practice, the common protagonists typically felt awkward fighting me *because* of my princess-ness.

Basically, it was a lose-lose situation no matter how you spun it.

That was why it worked out so well that Blue was probably the most skilled fighter in school, and that she did not feel awkward in the least coming at me with a knife . . . so as to push me to improve my skills, I mean.

Blue unpacked several new long blades and a fresh set of throwing knives. I grinned at the prospect of the training-related fun that awaited us in the days to come. Although Lady Agnue's was far from my favorite place in the world, I felt happy to be back in this familiar room with my two very different, very best friends.

It was funny how well we worked together—them being so dissimilar and all. I mean, one aspired to be the model princess and the other to be a scrappy female hero. But, personality contrasts aside, it just felt right when we were together. We were like the Three Musketeers—the beauty, the brawn, and the—

Wait. What was I exactly?

Time passed quickly that first afternoon.

We spent most of it lounging around telling stories of our summer ventures. SJ gushed about the various upper level potions she'd successfully brewed in the basement of her castle without getting caught by her parents. And Blue was excited to talk about how she'd joined a pub fight club in her village and emerged as its summer champion.

Unfortunately, I didn't have much to tell when my time for sharing came along. My mother had kept me pretty close by her side all summer in the hopes that her example would rub off on me. And, truly, she also hadn't wanted me to waste my days getting into mischief as SJ had predicted and as Blue had, well, suggested.

The sun finally began to set as half past five approached. We all knew what that meant—time to get ready for dinner.

Evening meals at this school were never anything but formal. Like, so formal that a normal utensil would have imploded self-consciously around the stunning silverware that set our tables.

The reason for this was that Lady Agnue's used dinnertime as an unofficial class period to test its students. At the beginning of the meal, Lady Agnue would give announcements and usually some sort of little lecture. Then, throughout the meal, we were reminded and expected to employ formal eating etiquette (lest we want to be deducted marks from our overall class standing).

It made it a bit stressful to be honest, trying to remember

what fork to use and which direction to pass the bread when your stomach was growling and your teachers were hovering over you like vultures with lipstick.

But I digress.

At least the food was something to look forward to, even if all the table-manners rubbish prevented me from eating as much of it as I would have liked. Furthermore, I did keep in mind that I had it pretty easy in comparison to Blue. We princesses were trained in this stuff since our sippy-cup days. So, even for a princess like me, having been raised around this royal, fancy-shmancy nonsense allowed me to adjust a lot quicker than the common protagonists who weren't as accustomed to it.

My friends and I changed speedily and headed down the grand staircase toward the win-lose feeding situation.

When we arrived in the foyer I was struck by how quiet it was. The grand marble-tiled foyer, which had been bustling with activity just hours before, was now empty. The only sounds were my boots pounding against the floor and the subsequent echo they caused to bounce around the room's redwood-sized pillars.

The three of us headed down the hall. Chatter and clinking glasses became more audible as we walked on. Soon enough, we reached the entrance to the dining room where the sounds were coming from.

Describing it as a dining room was a bit of an understatement. It was more of a massive banquet hall—five long tables on the right, and one long table on the far left elevated atop a stage for the teachers to watch and judge us from.

Tonight all the tables were draped in raspberry-colored silk tablecloths with sparkling silver runners down their centers.

Interspersed across the tables were crystal candlesticks and bunches of white lilies that sat in tall, slender vases.

A warm glow from the dozens of candlestick chandeliers filled the air, their light reflecting off the flatware, glasses, and impeccable china. I practically had to squint in order to adjust to the shimmering light.

I didn't know what the school staff planned on serving in the hall that evening, but food around here was usually fairly fantastic. And they typically went all out for the first dinner of the semester. Accordingly, thoughts of prime cuts of meat and freshly baked pies filled my head like glorious, hopeful daydreams. It seemed my stomach got overly excited by the imaginings though, because it growled super-loudly.

"Classy as ever, Crisa. Did you spend your summer with trolls?"

Perfect timing as always.

I turned around to address the source of the familiar venomous voice. Mauvrey Weatherall was standing behind me in a magenta peplum dress with black, sharp shoulder pads that matched her glittering dragon-scale necklace and equally harsh stilettos. Her arms were crossed, and her pale blue eyes were fixed in judgmental amusement.

"Or maybe you just spent your summer with Blue." She smirked as she looked my friend up and down. "Same difference I suppose."

Mauvrey's usual posse stood behind her. This group consisted of two girls. First, there was Princess Jade—the oldest and least favorite daughter of, ironically, one of our realm's most favorite underdog protagonists, Aladdin.

Jade's younger brother and sister (twins Eva and Lawrence) were the sweetest and most humble kids, so I could never quite figure out why their so-thin-she-vanished-when-she-turned-sideways older sister was such a self-absorbed, self-entitled beauty queen. Nor could I figure out why in all the years I'd known her I had never given in to the urge to smack her across the face like she so justly deserved.

To sum up, Miss Jade was a shallow, conniving priss. And I (like so many other girls at school who she regularly tried to make feel inferior) really hated her. Even so, I still preferred her to the second member of Mauvrey's entourage: Girtha Bobunk, the little sister of Hansel and Gretel Bobunk.

Little was a relative term by the way, considering that Big Girtha was massive. Like, seriously. Unlike her older siblings, I gathered starving to death was never an issue that she'd had to face growing up in the forest.

I rolled my eyes at my nemesis. "Very funny, Mauvrey. At least I eat like a normal person. Unlike Miss Size Negative-Four on your left." I gestured to Jade. "And the teenage mountain range on your right." I gestured at Girtha.

Blue snorted, trying to hold back a laugh.

Girtha's dense forehead creased beneath her crooked, mud-colored bangs. She took a step toward me, but Mauvrey held up her hand and the lackey restrained herself obediently.

"Bold move insulting my friends considering the company you keep," Mauvrey replied. "*Really*, Crisa. Even you could do better than the she-man with knife-throwing action"—she nodded toward Blue, then angled on SJ—"and the daughter of the most gullible princess in fairytale history. I mean honestly, SJ, I have always wanted to ask, did no one ever warn your mother not to take food from strangers? Any fool with half a brain knows that. It is practically rule one."

"Oh, and I guess only a genius would willingly stab her

finger on a clearly poisoned spinning wheel spindle?" Blue snapped in SJ's defense.

"Blue," SJ said calmly, putting her hand on Blue's shoulder. "Calm down."

Blue was clearly annoyed that SJ was taking such an insult in stride, as was I. Mauvrey was such a . . . *witch*. (More than that really. But no one ever taught us any curse words around here so witch was about all we had to work with.)

I didn't care what Mauvrey said about me, but harassing my friends was crossing the line. SJ was too nice a person to deserve insults like that, and Blue was still on probation for punching a classmate last semester. If Mauvrey pushed her too far, Blue would surely knock the princess's pearly teeth in and might well be expelled for doing so. I had to direct Mauvrey's venom back in my direction to protect them both.

"Leave SJ and Blue alone, Mauvrey. What's the matter, run out of insults about me all of a sudden?"

"Never," Mauvrey scoffed, easily taking the bait. "How could I when you provide so much material?" My nemesis gave me one of her signature golden-blonde hair tosses, and she and her entourage pushed their way past us into the banquet hall.

Ah, nothing says, "Welcome back to school" like a toxic exchange with an archenemy, am I right?

"You did not have to do that, Crisa," SJ said when the prissy posse was out of earshot. "I appreciate the sentiment behind it, but Mauvrey already has it out for you. I can handle myself."

"Really?" Blue countered. "Well, if you can handle yourself then why don't you ever get upset when Mauvrey insults you?"

"Mauvrey is an unkind girl; it is true. But the best way

to deal with such a person is to remain even-tempered and be the bigger person by still showing kindness. After all, you catch more flies with honey."

Blue rolled her eyes. "That's a horrible saying. People don't want to catch flies; they want to swat them down dead."

"I agree with Blue," I added. "You really should react more to stuff like that, SJ."

"And you, my friends, need to react less," SJ chided. "You cannot allow your tempers to control you like this. You have to evaluate the situation carefully so as not to cause further damage or escalate a situation unnecessarily."

The princess part of my subconscious knew she was right, but that didn't make Mauvrey or the advice any less irritating.

Maybe I really should listen to SJ and learn to—

The scent of turkey wafted up my nostrils. I started walking in the direction of the banquet hall, my friends in tow. Most of the students had already taken their seats, so we scuttled to a few available chairs in the back. A couple more girls who'd arrived even later than us trailed behind.

"Hi!" Princess Marie Sinclaire said as she approached an empty seat across from SJ.

"Hi, Marie," we all responded in unison.

Our friend Marie tucked a strand of long, platinum hair behind her ear before thoroughly brushing a hand over her chair and checking the seat before sitting down. Watching her, I concealed a small smile. This tendency of hers was funny to observe. But it was a natural habit, I supposed, when your grandmother's fairytale was about the intense injuries received from lying down on a bed with a magic pea hidden underneath a hundred mattresses.

The enormous doors to the banquet hall closed then,

signaling that dinner was about to begin. A tiny glass bell on the stage rang and we immediately quieted down like well-trained show dogs.

From behind her tall-backed chair at the teacher's table, Lady Agnue rose. She was wearing a fuchsia dress with a high collar. Her brown hair was pulled back tightly in a regal bun. Her copper eyes shone like the ring around a solar eclipse and the sequined pretense around our place settings.

"Welcome back, ladies," our headmistress cooed in a honey-coated voice. "I hope you are all as excited about this new school year as I am. Just a few reminders before we begin dinner this evening. The In and Out Spell will go up around the school tonight at ten o'clock sharp. From then on, the campus will once again be concealed within its wonderful, protective barrier that shall only be lowered for field trips and preapproved events with the boys from Lord Channing's. On that note, this month's ball will be on Saturday night. But, as a special treat, the In and Out Spell will be lowered during the afternoon so you can socialize with the boys for a majority of the day beforehand. I trust you will all behave accordingly."

This announcement sent up a flare of animated whispers among my classmates. Usually we only socialized with the boys from our sister school, or rather, our brother school, Lord Channing's School for Princes and Other Young Heroes, at our monthly balls or occasional tournaments. A fact, by the way, I was totally okay with. Most princes and assumed heroes tended to act like invincible idiots, so the less time I spent having to make uncomfortable small talk with them the better.

There were of course *some* boys who were semi-interesting to talk to. Like our friend Jason and his roommate Mark, for example. Jason was a Half-Legacy—the younger brother of the famous Jack who once climbed that overgrown beanstalk. Mark, on the other hand, was the prince of Dolohaunty and a full Legacy like me and SJ. They were both good guys—two of the few good guys out there—and I didn't mind considering them my friends.

Thus, I conceded that this Saturday might actually be fun. Blue, Jason, and I would spend the day battle-royaling in the practice fields, and SJ and Mark would probably sit and watch us while discussing boring prince/princess stuff like the economy or trade routes.

I drifted out of my mental tangent then to discover Lady Agnue was still talking. She addressed each table in turn. When she glanced over at our table, I thought she shot me a slight glare. It might've just been my eyes playing tricks on me, but I wouldn't have been surprised if she did.

To put it simply, Lady Agnue did not like me. It was no mystery why. After all, she was traditional, proper, and all about the rules, while I was a bold smart-mouth who enjoyed breaking said rules. Her loathing of me was no skin off my nose though, given that the feelings of animosity between us were fairly mutual.

Eventually, and not a moment too soon, our headmistress finished her speech and the much-awaited food was finally served.

Speaking candidly, it was probably for my own good that proper dinner etiquette kept me from eating as much or as fast as I would've liked to. Because I seriously *love* food. And tonight's meal was definitely something to write home about. The main course was turkey, and the aroma of the roast and all its side dishes could've turned a vegetarian into a carnivore on the spot.

Needless to say that while catching up with the other girls around the table throughout dinner was great, what was really satisfying was shoveling way-too-large amounts of food in my mouth when my teachers weren't looking.

Mmmm . . . mashed potatoes!

Hours later, SJ, Blue, and I were standing on the balcony of Suite 608 in our pajamas.

Supper had ended long ago and it was nearly ten o'clock, but the air was still warm with the remains of summertime. We waited in silence—SJ brushing her hair calmly, Blue munching on a roll she had stashed in her cloak from dinner, and me just staring out into the dark quietude that felt like it would last forever.

Then, right on cue, the clock struck ten and our school's shield came down without hesitation.

The purple force field descended from the sky and encased the property like a giant snow globe. When it reached the earth, silver sparks splashed upwards from the ground like sea-spray. The dome's erratic, quilt-like patchwork of light flashed in clusters as the magic settled, glinting between different shades of indigo and translucent white. Then, after a minute, its color gradually fizzled. The whole dome faded to a paler shade of lavender until it blended in with the night completely. As the final sparks dissipated into the air, the entire thing turned invisible—out of sight, but most certainly not out of mind.

In and Out Spells did exactly what their titles suggested.

They kept anyone from going in or out of the locations they protected.

Created by the combined magic of dozens of Fairy Godmothers, these were the most powerful spells that could be cast. Moreover, they had proven to be impervious to any attempts at breaking them in recorded history.

As far as we knew, there were four continuously active In and Out Spells in Book. One was around the entire realm and had been cast in the before times. This enchanted barrier protected our realm from the others—keeping us safe and completely separate from the various worlds that existed beyond Book.

The second spell was around the Indexlands (the forest where the Author was said to live). Meanwhile the third spell encased the kingdom of Alderon.

We didn't talk about Alderon much—not here or anywhere. Lying on the eastern outskirts of the realm between the Indexlands and the Valley of Strife, it was the kind of place people feared. And, as with anything they feared, instead of facing the issue head on, people tried to push thoughts of it back to the farthest corners of their minds.

Unlike the other versions of the enchantment, Alderon's version of the In and Out Spell was unique in that it was only designed to work at half capacity. Meaning that people could go in, but no one could ever get out. The reason for this was that, while our realm's rulers did not want any of the kingdom's residents to escape, they also wanted the freedom to regularly add to its population if need be.

See, most of the monsters and antagonists in our realm used to come from Alderon. So, long ago, Book's

Godmothers decided to block it off from the rest of the realm preemptively and use it as a vast prison. This way all newly captured villains, monsters, witches, magic hunters, etc. could be sentenced to one place from which they could not escape. And the rest of us were proactively protected from them, as well as from the horrible people and creatures that were said to be born there every day.

Talk about nipping a problem in the bud.

The last In and Out Spell in Book was the one around Lady Agnue's. It was a full version of the spell like the others, but it was also a bit more basic. Not needing to be as strong, it only prevented people (and the occasional detrimental flux of weather) from penetrating its borders, while animals like birds, frogs, and deer could pass through at will.

Personally, I thought it was both stupid and insulting to have such an intense form of protection surrounding our school. Because, first of all, I highly doubted any of us actually needed to worry about threats coming to eliminate us. We were princesses, for goodness' sake. As much as it pained me to admit it, the closest we ever came to mortal peril around here was when we wore heels on the lawn just after it'd been watered.

Furthermore, if we actually *were* in the amount of constant danger our severe security system warranted, Lady Agnue's should've been teaching us how to protect ourselves against it, not hiding us from it like children in a lightning storm. We were princesses, not daisies. Just because we often came wrapped in gowns and glitter didn't mean we couldn't pack a punch. Frankly, I believed that we all had the potential to. That underneath the tiaras and the makeup, we could be just like the diamonds so many of us wore around our necks—a rare combination of shining and hard to break.

Alas, the school's staff evidently disagreed with that sentiment and felt its "defenseless damsel" students needed to be constantly guarded from the threatening folks of the outside world.

Meanwhile, the boys' school had no such magical prison around it because, unlike us, they were trained to fend for themselves.

Cue second major eye roll for the day.

The spell around Lady Agnue's was activated when each school year began. Once it was, no human being could leave or enter the school grounds unless the barrier was lowered by a team of Fairy Godmothers. And that only happened for our monthly balls, other social events with Lord Channing's, such as tournaments or similarly competitive sporting events, and the occasional heavily guarded field trip to somewhere off campus.

I watched the force field's last spark merge into the night and wondered what my friends were thinking. It was impossible to tell. They both gazed out at the cloudless sky with blank expressions that made them appear much more solemn than teenage girls ever should.

After some time, the wind began to pick up and the three of us returned inside to prepare for bed.

SJ combed out the last few waves in her long black hair. Blue gently tucked her hunting knife into its sheath like a young girl tucking a precious doll into its bassinet. And I took off the pumpkin-shaped earrings I wore each day—a special gift from my mother that I'd worn since I was young.

The earrings were tiny and silver, and consistently reminded me of her. "Pumpkin" being what she'd always called me.

It was a cute pet name. Once, when I'd asked her why

she'd selected it, she told me that it was because pumpkins, like so many things in life, could become more than people give them credit for. An idea she believed she'd learned from personal experience.

I didn't argue that this was a nice thought. However, it was also one that perplexed me. After all, the people in our land submissively lived by the oppressive mandate that they couldn't be anything besides what the Author had chosen. Ideas like change were beaten out of us from the very beginning. Example: in preschool I once told a teacher that when I grew up I was going to be a swordsmith who made blades by day and fought crime by night. And she'd responded by making me sit in the corner in a tiny throne facing the wall for the rest of the day—no recess, no talking, and tiara on at all times.

That was just one of the more mild forms of punishment I'd endured over the years for my resistance to the norm. Everywhere I'd gone in life the idea of a static existence had been banged into me. Our rulers had perfected a world of safe, stable, tried and true standards of conduct. Thus, they insisted that change was a concept we should never humor, much less believe in.

Still . . .

Despite all of this, and the backlash I'd gotten over the years, I held on to the hopeful idea proposed by mother's nickname just as firmly as I did the notion that it might well be false. Both thoughts hung from my head on a daily basis, just like the very earrings that represented their duality. And I concurrently dreaded and looked forward to the day when one of the two sentiments would reveal itself as truth.

Placing the earrings on my nightstand, I kicked off my slippers as I hopped into bed.

"Well, here comes another exciting school year," Blue said sarcastically from across the room. She proceeded to bury herself under her comforter like an animal burrowing into its den. A moment later, SJ turned out the last light illuminating our room.

"Sleep well, all," she added.

As if, I thought in response to both their statements. With that, I closed my eyes and wished for some peace of mind that I knew would never come.

CHAPTER 3

The PITs
(Princesses-In-Training)

"She could be useful."

"Perhaps. But as it stands she poses too much of a
threat for us to take that risk."

"So how do you want to play this then?"

"Simple. I want her removed from the game entirely . . ."

 shot up in bed as the voices in my head faded back into the shadows.

Thankfully awake, I rubbed my eyes vigorously, as if to drive away any residue of the vicious dreams I'd just woken from.

Exhausted and tense, I leaned my head back against my headboard. Morning had arrived far too quickly and way too suddenly—the shock of it coming head on like a beam bursting through my subconscious.

That had not been pleasant.

It'd been a few weeks since my last nightmare and, truth be told, I'd sort of hoped the restful streak would continue. Deep down, though, I'd known that it wouldn't. Over the summer I had periods without horrid dreams, but for whatever reason, they came almost every night when I returned to school.

As I sat there and mentally buried the anxiety produced by the strange visions and voices in my head, I saw that SJ and Blue were still asleep. While Blue's face was barely visible beneath a pile of tangled sheets, SJ lay perfectly tranquil—a true sleeping beauty with not a wrinkle on her pillowcase.

The peacefulness did not last much longer. A moment later, the mockingbird SJ employed to wake us up each morning flew through our open balcony doors and landed on her nightstand. He proceeded to make a high-pitched sound that filled the entire room like an alarm.

Blue groaned—displeased at the arrival of morning—but SJ's eyes simply fluttered open. "Good morning, little friend," she cooed as she stroked the bird on his head. "That will be all. Thank you."

The mockingbird chirped happily, then took off back through the open doorway into the morning sunshine. SJ rose out of bed and stretched. She seemed way too well rested and had a calm contentment plastered on her face . . . That is, until she glanced over at me.

"Are you all right?"

She came to my bedside and instinctively put her hand to my forehead to check my temperature.

"Do you want to tell me about it?"

I swatted her hand away and forced a smile. "I'm fine."

It was sweet of her to worry, but when you suffered from nightmares as often as I did, you got used to the side effects. Honestly, it was a much more rare morning that I didn't wake up looking all sweaty and disoriented from being tormented while I slept.

Like it did on most days, resiliency quickly swept over me and I took a deep breath. There was no time for sulking. I needed to get ready for school.

I made my way into the bathroom as SJ went outside to greet her bird companions.

"Crisa!" she suddenly shouted from outside.

"SJ," I groaned, "I said I was fine."

"No, no, come out here! You simply must see this!"

"Stop yelling," Blue grumbled as she burrowed further beneath her blankets.

I yawned and made my way out onto the balcony to see what SJ was fussing about.

"Look," she said, gesturing all around us.

I blinked, adjusting to the light, and then realized what she was so taken aback by.

The vines—the same vines that had been in their last throes of death yesterday afternoon—were alive again. More than alive, they were practically emanating life. Each one was strong, thick, and full of vitality. Their bright green coloration contrasted beautifully against the magnificent lavender blossoms that flourished from the practically glowing, golden stamen sprouting along them.

I couldn't believe it.

"What do you suppose it was?" SJ wondered aloud as she marveled at the sight.

"Magic," I mumbled.

"What was that?"

"Uh, magic," I stuttered, gathering my thoughts. "It was probably the In and Out Spell. All that magic coming down over the grounds probably affected them."

"Yes. You must be right."

I shrugged. "It's the only thing that makes any sense."

"Breeeeakfaaast. Now . . ." someone growled from behind us.

We spun around and saw Blue—half-asleep, hair tangled in a giant fluff ball—with one of her sheets wrapped around her like a cape.

"Blue, look," SJ said, showing our groggy friend the amazing plants.

Blue glanced right, glanced left, then yawned. "Yeah. Great flowers. But you know what'd be better? Waffles."

Ten minutes later, Blue got her wish and was delighted as ever when we sat down to breakfast in the banquet hall and found ourselves surrounded by a grand morning feast, including waffles.

Between the strange miracle of the flowers on our balcony and the homemade blueberry scones I was now stuffing my face with, I was in a pretty good mood too. Actually, we all seemed to be back in our element today. Blue continued the reenactments of her action-packed summer ventures using forks and knives as visual aids, I ate too many pastries, and SJ casually read a copy of the *Century City Summit Review* from last spring.

The Summit was an epically important meeting that the ambassadors of the twenty-six kingdoms in our realm (not including Alderon) held biannually at the realm's capital, Century City. These two meetings were the only times of year when all of Book's ambassadors were in one place. Thus, the purpose of the Summit was to give updates on each of the kingdom's activities, discuss issues, form solutions, and then sign a treaty that renewed Book's overall laws and its peace.

The *Century City Summit Review* was the only news periodical allowed in our realm, and studying it before our first day of classes was very responsible and conscientious of SJ. For me, though, reading a newspaper from several months ago was definitely not my breakfast time cup of tea. Instead, I focused my attention on Blue's colorful stories, the heavenly blueberry scones, and a cup of coffee.

It was, in summation, a surprisingly lovely morning. Even more surprisingly, the rest of the day went just as uncharacteristically smoothly.

First up in our schedule of classes was the total snoozer known as "D.I.D." a.k.a. Damsels in Distress.

Our teacher for D.I.D. classes had been the same every year. Her name was Madame Lisbon, and she was a short, robust woman with rosy cheeks and blue eyes. She scuttled about excitedly wherever she went as if every room was a party and she was its hostess. And she seized every opportunity to correct unladylike behavior. Which, unfortunately, tended to emanate from my general direction.

D.I.D. was one of the mandatory classes that all students had to take (not just the princesses). While I wouldn't have ever inflicted this kind of torture on anyone, I was secretly glad that Blue was trapped in there with me so that later on she and I could mock our lessons together in the ways that SJ always restrained herself from doing.

Since it was just the first morning of the semester, today Madame Lisbon actually decided to mix things up a bit from her usual didactic presentations. Instead of lecturing us on the basics of ladylike fainting, the whole class practiced fainting exercises for the duration of the period. This proved to be a sincerely nice change of pace, as my friends and I had a great deal of fun falling dramatically backward onto air mattresses for the better part of an hour.

Potions class came next.

We were a touch late getting there due to hallway traffic, but we managed to take our seats just as our instructor, Madame Alexanders, was distributing the last of the *Potions: Level Six* textbooks.

"Now remember, ladies," Madame Alexanders lectured, "potions are not a substitute for magic. They are a great deal like knock-offs—they are more of a gamble, not as strong, and do not last very long. But potions can still be quite powerful on their own and are extremely effective when combined *with* magic."

Madame Alexanders strode to the front of the room and picked up a piece of chalk. She wrote a paraphrased version of her statement on the blackboard, which the other students busily wrote down.

Instead of taking notes, I used the moment to admire all of the glittering lab equipment and miscellaneous substances displayed across the room.

The potions lab was one of the most colorful, fascinating places on campus. Walls were lined with shelves upon shelves of jarred ingredients—pickled this, freeze-dried that, bat fangs, white chocolate chips, rosemary sprigs, scorpion spit—basically a whole mess of weird stuff that was as diverse as it was grossly intriguing.

Large crystal vats fashioned in the form of punch dispensers were spaced out along the back wall of the room, ready to dole out any number of fragrant liquid ingredients. Small cauldrons, mortar dishes, and wooden cutting planks filled the translucent cabinets behind Madame Alexander's desk at the front of the class where the grand, floor-to-ceiling windows resided. And our own lab desks were always stocked with glass beakers, vials, and personal Bunsen burners of the highest variety.

The tools of today's experiment were lined up in front of us. One flask was filled with chunks of raw meat, another with cinnamon, another with dead moths, and the list went on randomly from there. Additionally, there were also vials filled with beautifully colored liquids that looked pretty enough to drink. Of course, there was a fairly good chance that half of them were toxic, so I didn't test the theory.

When our teacher finished writing she spun back around to face us and continued buoyantly pacing the room. "Ladies, who can give me a famous example of an extremely powerful combination of a potion *with* magic?"

Various hands went up across the class in response, but not SJ's.

"The water lily that turned Prince Egot into a frog," said Bonnie Rathers, a common protagonist from Harzana.

"Very good," Madame Alexanders responded. "But, bear in mind, class, that the majority of the enchantment in this case originates from the potion. It was the potion poured over the blossom that made the prince turn into a frog. The magic the witch used was only to preserve the blossom and keep it from ever wilting. Now then, can someone give me another example of magic combined with a potion?"

"The apple that poisoned Snow White," Mauvrey said smugly, shooting SJ a snide look from across the room.

I gave her a death glare on behalf of my unresponsive friend.

"Correct, Miss Weatherall." Madame Alexanders nodded without noticing our tiff. "Though here we find a case opposite that of the Frog Prince's water lily. Snow White's apple was magically poisoned via the powers found at the Valley of Edible Enchantments. And it was a *potion* that enticed the princess to eat it, not the other way around. On that note, who can tell me the *most* famous and powerful combination of magic with a potion ever recorded in Book's history?"

None of the students raised their hands. After slight pause, SJ at last resigned to raising hers.

I had to give her props for showing restraint for as long as she had. Although my dear friend did actually know it all when it came to potions, ever the polite one, she never assumed the role of a know-it-all. Until that instant, today, like all days, she had been kind enough to repress her urge to answer every question so as to give the other girls in our class a chance to impress the professor too.

"The Sleeping Capsule spell," SJ stated confidently when Madame Alexanders called on her. "A team of Fairy Godmothers created a complex sleeping potion to put the land of Tunderly to sleep when its princess, known today as Sleeping Beauty, fell victim to the bewitched spindle of a spinning wheel. The concoction not only kept Tunderly's inhabitants asleep, but it also made time temporarily stand still so that when everyone awakened, it was as if nothing had happened. The Godmothers, meanwhile, used their combined magical powers to amplify this potion's reach so that it would be projected indefinitely around the entire kingdom versus expiring after a few short hours."

I gave Mauvrey an additional snarky look that said, "Eat that, princess," while the rest of my classmates scribbled in their journals.

"Excellent, Miss Kaplan," Madame Alexanders gushed.

"Class, take note. As mentioned, many enchantments like the Sleeping Capsule spell would have still been possible without the use of magic; they just would not have been anywhere near as powerful or permanent. Potions this complex, however, require skill, time, and knowledge that few are ever able to possess . . ."

From there, Madame Alexanders's lesson continued for about another half an hour. Most of the info was pretty dry, and I would have been lying if I'd said I paid attention to all of it. Conversely, I was more than happy to participate in the hands-on lab exercise that followed.

The assignment our professor had given us was to create a potion that changed the tones of our voices. Blue and I ended up concocting ones that made it sound like we had inhaled a very potent form of helium. We thought this was funny until SJ made one that caused her to sound like a middle-aged man and we almost died laughing.

When our voices had tragically returned to normal, and our class had thankfully concluded, the three of us were halfway out the exit when Madame Alexanders asked if SJ would stay behind for a moment to speak with her privately. Our friend nodded respectfully and headed back inside, closing the door behind her. Blue and I waited outside the room. When she emerged a few minutes later, the smile on her face was so big it caused a glare.

SJ was holding an extremely worn, compact book with a leather cover and weathered edges. She told us that it was a book of the most famous and complex potions ever brewed, like the ones we had been talking about at the beginning of class. Madame Alexanders was one of the few people authorized to check it out from the restricted section of our school's library. And she had done so this morning so that she could lend it to SJ, her best and most promising student.

"She said she wants to encourage my love of potions. I still cannot believe she gave it to me," SJ whispered. "No one outside of the faculty is supposed to have access to restricted books; it is against the rules."

"You want to turn yourself in and give the book back?" Blue asked.

"Are you mad?" SJ hugged the book protectively as if it was the most precious thing she'd ever held, then carefully hid it inside her bag.

Blue and I smirked and then the three of us proceeded to part ways. Blue was off to Creative Rope Use 101 with some of her common protagonist friends while SJ and I were to attend Singing with Nature class along with the other princesses from our year.

Personally, I thought a class where you learned 101 ways to use a rope would've been way more interesting. Then again, my naturally out-of-tune vocal cords colored my opinions on the subject a bit.

Even Singing with Nature class was unusually enjoyable today, though. SJ's perfect voice attracted the attention of the cutest woodland creatures, and I was content to pet them as we listened to her and the other princesses sing the loveliest of songs in the soft afternoon sunlight.

The day ticked on with ease from there. After Singing with Nature class, my friends and I had lunch, which consisted of a variety of cheesy pastas and accompanying meat sauces, all of which were finger-licking good. (Not that I would've ever licked my fingers, mind you, as Madame Lisbon surely would've sensed a disturbance in the princess universe and then tracked me down to punish me in person.)

After lunch I had my math and finance course for the semester—Balls on a Budget: How to Maximize Your Happily Ever After without Bankrupting Your Kingdom's Economy. I assumed later in the semester this class would involve a lot of spreadsheets and graph paper, the likes of which would probably suck out my soul. But today there was only a short lecture, and some brief brainstorming about the pros and cons of floral versus candle-based centerpieces for semi-formal summer night galas.

This pleasant itinerary left me in a good mood when dismal came around. Of course, truth be told, we could have taken a hundred pages of notes and spent the hour trying to crack algebraic equations and I still would've been chipper when we walked out the door because next, I was heading to my absolute favorite class in the world.

It wasn't so much a class, really; it was our free period to pursue individual study. And the form of studying I chose to dedicate myself to during this daily, blessed hour was as close to my heart as it was compelling to my spirit and personal growth.

SJ typically returned to the potions lab during her free periods. Today she went with an extra hop in her step due to the gift Madame Alexanders had given her. Blue and I, on the other hand, went down to the practice fields situated at the east end of the property by the river that separated us from Lord Channing's.

The practice fields consisted of a small track by the forest area, a rock-climbing wall, a pole vault pit, a bunch of obstacles for the horses, and about an acre of raw field.

The stables, the barn, and a small weapons shed were also located on the practice fields. In sum, this area surmounted to the closest thing I knew to paradise.

Blue and I made use of the other areas of the practice fields from time to time, but normally we stayed hidden in the barn or the stables for our designated "individual study."

Currently, Blue was moving bales of hay out of the way to make the barn's floor space wider, as I picked up a broom to brush away some clumps of horse "leftovers."

Out of the corner of my eye, I noticed a rusty bucket sitting in one of the barn's windowsills. It was turned on its side and calling to me. In an impulse of childish mischief, I took aim with my broom and smacked a clump of dung I'd been cleaning up toward it. The small, smelly mound sped across the thirty-foot distance and flew directly into the bucket—a flawless, figuratively clean shot.

Blue was initially startled by the noise, but then she grinned at my weird genius. "Bet you can't do that again," she challenged.

"Oh, you're so on," I responded.

One after another I swiftly scooped and heaved the dried wads of excrement high into the air. Then, even more speedily, I spun the broom around in my hand, brought it up as the dung fell, and struck each wad with a powerful swing.

I sunk four more perfect poop goals, adding an extra bit of flourish to the last shot with a spin and giving the broom a bonus twirl.

It was odd, really. The feel of the broom flowing and rotating through my hands felt so . . . natural. Way more than most things around here typically did.

Fantastic. I finally find something that comes easily to me at this school and it involves horse dung.

Just perfect.

"Well done." Blue laughed. "That was both impressive and disgusting. I approve on both counts. Now you keep finding ways to entertain yourself; I'm going to go get a sword from the weapons shed. Be back in a minute."

Blue opened the barn doors and strode out. Once she'd gone, I opened my brown satchel, which I'd been carrying around all day like I always did. The spacious bag contained my ordinary school supplies—a notebook, quills, ink, hairbrush, etc. But the weathered bag was not special to me because it had a lot of pockets for holding my junk. I loved this bag because it was where I kept the most precious object in my possession.

My fingers found what they were looking for within the satchel and wrapped themselves around the cold, sleek weapon that I held so dear.

My magic wand was one of a kind and the most useful enchanted object I'd ever seen. It was standard Fairy Godmother issue—about a foot long, silvery off-white, and thick as a potion vial. More importantly, it was all mine.

My regular godmother, Emma Carrington, was also my mother's famous *Fairy* Godmother. She had given me the wand on my seventh birthday, nearly ten years ago. Naturally, I had thought it was just a toy wand at the time, but a couple of months later she'd sent a letter explaining the wand's hidden abilities and that the reason she'd gifted it to me was to ensure my own protection.

Regrettably, I hadn't seen Emma since that birthday. She sort of dropped out of contact with my family a long ways back for some unknown reason. I'd tried reaching out to the Fairy Godmother Agency she worked for many times since then in an attempt to track her down. But each time

I did, I received a not so passive-aggressive reply from the Godmother Supreme herself, who insisted such contact with one of her employees was not regulation and, therefore, *not going to happen*.

In truth I didn't know what was more frustrating about the situation. The mystery surrounding Emma's disappearance bothered me, certainly. However, getting condescending, vaguely threatening follow-up letters from some Godmother named Lena Lenore—who even had the nerve to tell me in our last correspondence that it would be "in my best interest" to leave the matter "lest I wish to suffer the consequences"—was not that fun either. In fact, the whole thing thoroughly ticked me off. Fairy Godmothers were supposed to help princesses, right? So why was their leader so dead set on thwarting my good intentions?

Sigh.

Even after all these years I really couldn't guess what Emma's reason for losing touch with us had been. Nor could I understand why this Lena Lenore woman seemed so consistently and maliciously set on stopping me from finding out.

Still, I remained thankful that I could at least be reminded of Emma every time I used this special, secret gift of hers (which, by the way, was very often).

Aside from my long-missing godmother, Blue and SJ were the only two people who knew about the wand and its true nature. It was vital that we kept it that way. While we did have access to the occasional enchanted knickknack (whether for designated use in one of our classes, or by accident in the real world), a wand was something special.

Only Fairy Godmothers were supposed to have them because they were only meant to be utilized in the practice of Fairy Godmother-brand magic. Granted, it was true that this wand had no such magic. Wands were just conductors, not creators of power after all. So, without a Godmother to operate it, this thing might as well have been a fancy stick.

Nevertheless, for whatever the reason this wand (*my wand*) had a special enchantment over it that made it far from useless in ordinary hands.

Moreover, between that and the nature of the thing in general, underserved Godmother-specific purpose or not, I knew that if anyone ever saw me with the wand it was as good as confiscated.

Lady Agnue once made me give up the roller skates I'd built as a final project for my Calceology (the Study of Shoes) class because she told me princesses were never intended to move on their own at more than eight miles per hour. I could only imagine what she'd do if she found out about my wand. She'd probably return it to the Godmothers and have me put on academic probation for the rest of my life.

As such, the wand had to remain a secret. Which was why I always had to be super careful about where and when I practiced with it. Here, that was normally limited to the barn, the stables, and our room during our free period or after school. Meanwhile, when I was at home in Midveil for the summer I had practically no such windows of opportunity. Castles were always bustling with activity. My parents regularly made sure to keep me busy with what they deemed "princess-appropriate" endeavors. And, in the rare moments I was alone, I was always too nervous to whip out the wand due to worry that someone might find me with it.

This past summer I had tried to get out of bed in the middle of the night to at least get some after-hours training in the privacy of my room. But even that proved to be difficult, as the guards assigned by my overprotective parents to repeatedly check my chambers deterred me from ever practicing for more than a few minutes.

Other than the brief hour or so of messing around with it yesterday afternoon in our room, it had been several weeks since my last good session with the wand. Ergo, I decided to warm up a little before Blue returned.

I grasped the familiar weapon in my hand with confidence.

Shield, I thought, commanding the wand to morph.

No sooner did I think the word did the wand transform into a thick handle, which sprouted a shield that opened up like a large metallic flower.

Knife, I thought.

The shield retracted back within itself as fast as it had expanded. The handle hardened and changed its shape at the same time. Barely a blink of an eye later it became a silvery leather grip from which extended a glistening eight-inch blade that looked so sharp it could have cut a person who stared at it too intensely.

I ran the wand through several more tests after that—morphing it into an archer's bow, a boomerang, a crowbar, and then my usual weapon of choice, a sword—before returning it to its original shape.

My magic wand was enchanted to transform into whatever handheld weapon I willed it into. Which, in a word, was awesome. The enchantment was also extremely handy, versatile, travel-sized, and user-friendly.

The only forms I regularly changed the wand into were the shield and the sword. The archer's bow was pointless in a close-range fight and completely useless unless I happened to have arrows on me. And the other weapons I'd tried morphing it into (the crowbar, axe, boomerang, etc.) were neither as helpful nor as practical as the sword was in my hands.

Then again, if I was to be totally honest with myself, I was not exactly a natural at swordplay either.

Okay, that was a vast understatement. The fact was I *naturally* sucked at it.

Between Blue, my brothers, and my own individual practice, I'd been honing my sword-fighting skills for a long time. As a result, I had genuinely managed to become pretty good.

But this understanding did little to bring me comfort. For no matter how you spun it, "pretty good" was just not that impressive when you had been training hard for nearly ten years.

What can I say? Practice apparently does not always make perfect.

A sword in my hand always felt awkward, unbalanced, and seriously lacking in harmony with my person. Frankly, that dang broomstick had felt way more at home in my hands than a sword ever had. And that was just depressing. I had this powerful, magical object at my disposal, and I continually did it injustice with my lack of fighting talent in any of the weapons I'd ever tried to change it into.

And yet, call me stubborn or unyielding, I was determined to keep at it. I trained, I worked hard, and I fought on despite my inherent hindrances. Because, one way or another, I had faith that I would get better in time.

Blue was that extra encouraging force I needed along the way. She not only helped me in pursuit of my combat-related goals, in our time together in the practice fields she also pushed me to further test my limits. It was difficult, often bitterly exhausting work, but I relished it and appreciated her every day for the skills I'd developed, and the drive it fueled in my heart as a result.

In that moment, my fearless friend returned to the stables. After slamming the door shut behind her, Blue tossed me an armored breastplate and a set of protective arm shields that I strapped on. The things were bulky, but I'd rather have worn twelve extra pounds of bronze than have risked Blue accidentally stabbing me if I was unable to block one of her strikes in time. The girl was my friend, but she took fighting drills super seriously, and she was not immune to losing some of her restraint due to an adrenaline rush.

Out of courtesy Blue also put on her own armored plates, even though I severely doubted she would need them against the likes of me.

All fastened up, I picked up my wand again and morphed it into the blade I was so used to.

Sword.

Blue twirled her own normal sword casually in her right hand as she paced the floor before me like a military sergeant. "Now I realize that since you and I haven't practiced together since last semester, you have not been properly challenged for some time and may be a bit rusty. Regardless, I will not insult your skills or my own by going easy on you. This way you can get back into shape quickly. Understood?"

I nodded and drew into a fighting stance.

Blue charged.

My friend was fast and precise with all of her strikes, coming in hot at every instance. I was kept on the defensive most of the time, as she was usually able to anticipate any strike or countermeasure I attempted.

The first fifteen minutes we fought were really rough for me. Accordingly, I found myself feeling grateful to be wearing armor and having the ability to morph my weapon into a shield within a split second.

Eventually, after a decent match, our swords clashed against one another, neither refusing to yield. My arm, however, started to quiver under the weight of Blue's superior position. I began to lose my footing and knew that my best bet was to break the clash abruptly and go for a low strike before she could stop me. I went for it. Regrettably, I miscalculated the reach of my blade and was unable to stretch my arm out far enough.

Blue saw her opening.

When my elongated jab failed to reach her, she forcefully underhand blocked with her sword, knocking mine out of my hand. Then, with a powerful thrust-kick, she sent me flying backward into a cushion of hay.

"You all right?" Blue asked as she picked up my sword from the ground.

"Fine," I sighed, spitting some straw out of my mouth.

Blue extended her hand to help me to my feet, but I waved it away and got up on my own.

"Not bad, Crisa, but you're overreaching with your strikes again. You need to learn to stop overestimating the length of your sword and quit doing so many of those swooping motions. They aren't effective and leave you wide open."

"Right. Got it." I nodded as I swallowed my ever-injured pride.

Blue and I practiced for another half an hour and evidently I did not "get it." I made the same mistakes over and over again throughout our drills. As a consequence, I found myself repeatedly landing on my butt in that same pile of hay.

I could not describe how frustrating it felt to not be as

skilled as I would've liked to have been at this. Overall, it just really burned on the inside to not be good at something you loved.

You know?

Still, even if I was not the best at sword fighting, I was at least fairly skilled at it. And (my low level of raw talent aside) I adored the practice. I didn't care how unladylike or non-princessy it was; fighting was fun. If anyone disagreed, well, I would have been more than happy to fight them to resolve the issue.

Wand.

I restored my trusty, magical friend back to its original form and placed it in my satchel. I had a couple more classes that afternoon and it was time for me to make my way back to the main grounds.

It was always a bit disappointing to leave the practice fields but, as it turned out, the second half of my classes went just as smoothly as the first. As a whole, it truly did end up being a productive and unusually pleasant first day of school. Frankly, it was an unusually pleasant day at Lady Agnue's in general.

Too bad unusual things aren't known for lasting that long . . .

CHAPTER 4

Unexpected Unpleasantries

or most people, sleep was a time of rest and rejuvenation. To me, sleep was a time of exhausting burdens.

Every night I went to bed wondering what fresh torment the night would bring. And in the mornings, I found myself feeling slightly jealous of Mauvrey's mother. What I wouldn't give to sleep like a rock for a hundred years. For maybe in the depths of a Sleeping Beauty-like slumber, I could finally find some peace, a break from the otherworldly visions that haunted me on this night like they did on so many others . . .

The air was cold and dry, and the wind was blowing hard without repentance. Such weather made it feel like I was standing in a barren desert in the throes of wintertime. However, in taking in the surroundings, it soon became obvious that the atmosphere did not correlate with the setting. Despite its deteriorated state, it was evident that the place housing these environmental conditions was not some sand-covered wasteland, but a sort of cynicism-laden metropolis.

Cement sidewalks everywhere were riddled with plastic

wrappers and lined with dirt and sewage. Streets were packed with metal, horseless carriages that honked angrily at one another. And the only sign of nature was a limp tree planted by a gray building. This tree was skinny, dusty, and enclosed by a fence feebly trying to protect it from the outer world. The poor thing was so badly withered that I didn't know what kind of tree it was supposed to be. I wondered if maybe it didn't remember anymore either.

On the stairwell adjacent the tree, sat a girl. Her hair was a curly, maple-colored mess, put up in a haphazard bun. She wore black pants and a white collared shirt that needed washing. Her shoes arguably had more scuffs on them than the aged strip of sidewalk between us.

The girl sat motionless at first—her brown eyes lost in some distant nothingness. There were two slips of paper in her hand. One was pink and official-looking, and the other was a piece of notebook paper. After a few moments she shoved the pink one into her pocket and re-opened the white one, which read:

"Natalie, let this be a lesson to you. Get in my way again and a job won't be the only thing you lose. —Ever Yours, Tara Gold."

The disheveled girl wiped a stray tear from her eye with the back of her hand. Then she grabbed a tan backpack sitting next to her, got up, and went inside the building she'd been crouching in front of.

The worn yellow hallway she walked into was cast in looming shadows. Sounds of babies crying and the aroma of burnt pasta filled the space, but they faded away as she made her way deeper through the corridor. Eventually she came to a door marked "3C" and entered by means of a rusty key pulled from her pants pocket.

Wordlessly, she entered an apartment in such a horrid

state that it would have made grown men cry had it been forced to be their home. The carpet was worn green shag, which may have been elegant once but now looked like the fungus between a giant's toes. Shelves of books and faded paintings in cracked wooden frames lined the walls, collecting time in the form of filth.

There was no natural light, except for a few streaks that came in from behind a boarded-up window in the back. But even those rays offered nothing but dreariness, as they simply allowed you to more vividly recognize the lint dancing in the humid airspace.

The girl, whose backpack had the name "Natalie Poole" sewn into it, stopped when she arrived at a ragged bedroom at the rear of the apartment.

The thick maroon curtains of this room were drawn shut and there was dust collecting on the few knickknacks decorating the shelves—among which was a picture frame made entirely from popsicle sticks. The frame held a worn photo of the girl, a man in his early forties, and the woman lying on the bed in front of her. This woman looked old and tattered like the apartment around her, but she had the same vibrant shade of hair as Natalie did, give or take a few gray streaks.

Natalie sat on the edge of the bed, but the woman did not open her eyes. She was asleep, but breathing slowly and with great difficulty. Her eyes were scrunched up tight like a child kidnapped by nightmares.

Delicately, Natalie took the woman's hand in hers. The two sat in silence for a few minutes while Natalie traced the pale red flowers on the crème-colored bedspread with the fingers of her free hand.

Eventually, Natalie stood up. She walked closer to the

aged, wooden headboard then bent over to give the sleeping woman a kiss on the forehead.

"I'm sorry, Mom," she whispered into the fading woman's ear. "I got fired today. But I'll get another job. I promise."

Natalie began to head for the door of the room, but stopped short just before leaving.

"I love you," she said, her voice shaking.

The tears built up in Natalie's eyes, and she dashed out of the apartment just as they became too much for her to hold back. Sadness streaming down her face like rainfall, she ran down the hallway and collapsed to the ground under the weight of the world.

"Time to get up," someone called to her from a distance. She didn't respond.

"Time to get up!" the voice shouted louder this time.

The whole room abruptly began to tremble and for a second it felt like it might crumble right there with the tormented girl trapped inside it. But then, just as suddenly, my eyes burst open and I re-entered the world of the living.

Blue was standing next to me in her turquoise bathrobe, shaking my arm.

I bolted upright and gasped for air like I had been underwater. "Where? What?"

"It's time to get up. It's almost eight o'clock. Classes start in, like, twenty minutes," she said.

Comprehension clicked in my brain and I jumped out of bed to head for the bathroom. I guess the rush was far too sudden a movement though, because I stumbled almost immediately and had to stop and lean against my desk to regain balance. The whole room seemed to be spinning. My head felt like I'd left part of it on the pillow somewhere behind me. Only then did I notice how cold I was despite the fact that my pajamas were soaked with sweat.

"Crisa, you okay?"

I turned slowly and stared at my friend hard—willing my vision to return to normal. Thankfully, after a few seconds she came into focus again and my dizziness faded away as quickly as it had come on.

I stood up straight and surveyed the room as if I was only now properly awake.

"Which dream was it this time?" Blue asked plainly.

"Natalie again," I sighed.

Blue nodded. "Sorry, that's rough. But hey, at least that's better than one of your, you know, darker dreams, right?"

"Yeah, but those are at least vague. The Natalie dreams feel so much more resonant, and lately . . . I don't know it feels like she, like *they've* been getting worse," I grunted, shaking my head.

They're getting clearer too, I thought, but kept myself from saying it out loud.

"You want to talk about it?" Blue asked.

"No," I responded like I always did. "I'm fine."

My friend nodded once more and then patted me on the shoulder as she returned to the bathroom to finish getting ready.

When she had gone I closed my eyes and took a few deep breaths.

SJ and Blue knew all about the vivid nightmares I had suffered from for years now. Even so, I still didn't let them see just how great an effect they had on me, or share too many of their details.

The broad perspective, which they were aware of, was that my dreams could be broken down into two categories:

The first half of them took place in a world that was strange and that I didn't recognize in the slightest. It was nothing like our realm, or anything else I had ever seen before either. Most of the buildings were gray and metallic and stretched to the sky like iron giants. The people in these dreams dressed plainly—fading in with the background that surrounded them. And there were all these tiny, shiny devices that made noise constantly and never seemed to leave people's sides. Overall, it gave me the creeps.

The subjects of these dreams were always suffering at the hands of horrible people and circumstances. None of them had ever made a second appearance, except that one girl. Natalie Poole. Over the years she had become a far too frequent and unwelcome visitor to my subconscious— especially lately, given that dreaming about her was like watching a private performance of a tragic play with absolutely zero comic relief to get by on.

While I didn't know what kind of place my imagination had intended Natalie Poole's world to be, it seemed that the second type of nightmares I suffered from consistently chose more traditional areas of Book for their subconscious settings.

It was true that I had no way of verifying this as I never saw the visions clearly enough to guess at specific locations. But every once in a while, I would register buildings or forests or mountains that struck a chord of familiarity.

Furthermore, it just felt like Book. I wished I could have explained it better than that, but after years of trying and failing to articulate a more acceptable reasoning, I found that beyond gut instinct, there was none. I just knew these dreams were based in Book as surely as I knew that the ones featuring Natalie weren't.

In retrospect, this second type of nightmare I was tormented by should have been a lot less off-putting than those of Natalie's gray world. These dreams were in places my brain understood. And since they were way blurrier than my dreams of that metallic city, they shouldn't have bothered me as much. After all, how could I be upset by fictitious, nocturnal glimpses of people I didn't know saying and doing things I didn't understand?

Despite this logic, there was still something unsettling about them. Not as unsettling as other Book dreams I'd had a few times. Those were . . . Well, let's just say Blue was right. They were a much worse kind of nightmare.

Nevertheless, these frequent, fuzzy visions of Book gave me the shivers in a way I couldn't quite explain but couldn't well deny either. They gnawed at me continuously—threatening to take up the attention of more than just my dreamscape if I ever let them get a tight enough hold.

Like I said before, SJ and Blue were the only two people that I had told about these, and all my other dreams. Although, to be perfectly honest, even with them I tended to be vague and elusive about the details.

Occasionally when I was really rattled I mentioned the content of certain visions. However, even in those cases, the specifics I chose to share were limited at best. For, despite being best friends with Blue and SJ for so many years, I still didn't feel comfortable letting them in on this completely. It just felt . . . wrong somehow.

For the rest of the morning, I was in a funk.

I did not enjoy the pancakes at breakfast even though there were twelve different types of homemade syrups to accompany them. And I didn't even make a single sarcastic comment during D.I.D.

Which is no easy task, by the way.

Today, Madame Lisbon was going on about Fairy Godmothers, avoiding confrontations, and the importance of waterproof mascara in today's society. I think SJ was listening, though it was hard to tell. She had her eyes glued to the teacher like she always had during our lectures. Then again, she was not very fond of this particular subject either, so she might've just been having a really focused daydream. Blue, on the other hand, was carving her initials into the desk with her hunting knife, in cursive. A bit of a bold move, but I respected the quality of her penmanship, or knifemanship, as it were.

Me, I was in no mood for daydreams or shenanigans. I simply stared absentmindedly at the chalkboard while my frazzled subconscious simmered like a fried egg.

While it was true that over the summer I had dreams much less frequently, as a whole, over the last year they had been becoming progressively more lucid. As a consequence, they were really starting to bother me.

It used to be that I could just push them all away at sunrise. However, as they'd grown clearer, more eventful, and more consistent, it was like their images had begun to loom over me like ghost memories.

My friends could tell I was being affected, but they knew well enough to leave the matter alone since, as mentioned, I wasn't too keen on sharing. As a result, I was left to my own devices for sorting out these feelings of unease and trepidation.

When morning classes finally ended and lunch came round, I found myself uncharacteristically lacking in hunger.

So, instead of joining Blue and SJ in the banquet hall, I spent the hour wandering the school hallways, reflecting privately on the matter of my dreams.

Most other sections of Lady Agnue's were deserted during lunchtime. That is, aside from the traditionally armored guards who constantly patrolled its red-carpeted corridors. Every nine minutes on the dot, one would predictably pass whatever area of the school I happened to be strolling through and raise a metal-covered arm to his helmet to salute me as I went by.

It was pretty much as close as a girl could get to being left alone around here, so I ignored their presence and allowed myself to get fully lost in my thoughts. Specifically, the unpleasant ones that I so often tried to evade but could never seem to utterly escape.

I shook my head and groaned at the frustration.

For the life of me, I couldn't understand why my dreams were so messed up. I mean, what kind of person even had reoccurring characters in their dreams anyways?

Ms. Natalie Poole had been a regular visitor to my sleeping consciousness for some time. She'd even aged over the years as my dreams about her had progressed. More disconcerting still, she had begun to appear in my dreams more frequently as I got older. While I used to average one dream about her per month, in the last year they'd begun coming on a weekly basis.

Natalie aside, my weird, indiscernible dreams taking place in Book were eating away at my peace of mind. These shouldn't have bothered me as much—being so fuzzy and all—but this notion was offering less and less solace in recent months because they, too, were beginning to get clearer.

I was starting to make out faces and conversations more

easily as if I was witnessing them firsthand. The sharper these visions became, the more I felt like I was suffocating from an irrational form of claustrophobia each time I woke from them. Which was just exhausting.

To make things worse, these dreams were a walk in the clouds in comparison to the more unsavory nightmares I had of Book—the ones Blue had been referring to earlier this morning. Those were about death.

Such ominous dreams had always been way blurrier, so it was difficult to make out many details. But let's just say that the main event of what was unfolding within them came across very clearly and very permanently.

Beyond that, even in recollection I didn't want to get into it.

Believe me, I'm doing you a favor.

The victims I envisioned in these nightmares were different each time; despite the general haziness within my subconscious, I could ascertain that. Strangely, though, these nightmares (like my dreams of that odd, *other* world) also had reoccurring characters. Two if we're being specific.

The first was a girl. She was much harder to make out than Natalie Poole. But from what I could gather, she had tan skin, dark hair, and a laugh akin to a serpent's giggle.

If you're trying to imagine what that sounds like, by the way, think tinkling bells mixed with the sadistic hissing sound a rattlesnake might make just before lunging for your throat.

The second member of this chronic duo I kept dreaming about was a boy. Judging by the sound of his voice, I garnered that he was in his early twenties. Alas, past that I was unable to make out a more detailed description.

My visions of him (and his counterpart) were always characterized by vague flashes or snippets of dialogue like I'd had the night before last; not full scenes. Moreover, his very essence seemed to be cloaked in shadow. No matter how hard I tried when I was conscious, my memory could only grasp at fragments of darkness when I attempted to recall him more finitely from my dreamscape.

It didn't quite make sense to me how he or the girl fit into my dreams. Like I said, neither one was a victim (as the victims of such dreams were new each time). I just kind of sensed phantom-like auras of them interspersed throughout the greater picture—usually surrounded by a backdrop of bronze and a lot of darkly colored stained glass.

Ugh, could I be any weirder?

How was I even able to imagine such things? I was a teenage girl and a princess, for goodness' sake. I should've been dreaming about unicorns and rainbows, not assassinations.

I sighed with frustration.

Like it's not enough that I don't have control over my real *life; I don't even get a say in what happens in my subconscious one either?*

That's just terrific.

I had been so consumed in my own head up 'til that point that I hadn't noticed just how far I'd managed to walk. Lo and behold, I now found myself coming upon the majestic Treasure Archives at the other side of the school.

Giving my mind a break, my eyes wandered from trinket to trinket.

Housed right here in Lady Agnue's for nearly two decades, the Treasure Archives contained the most historically significant relics in our realm. Each display held a variety of treasures, from Aladdin's chrome genie lamp to the tiny enchanted pea that had messed up Marie Sinclaire's princess grandmother while she slept on a hundred-plus mattresses. They, like the rest of the objects in these cases, gleamed under the rays of sunshine currently bathing the incredibly vast hallway intersection.

Suddenly, a dark figure blocked out some of this light and cast the treasures I'd been looking at in pompous shadow.

"Taking in our realm's ancestral history, Miss Knight?"

I turned around and saw the source of the darkness, Lady Agnue herself, standing behind me. Today she was wearing a navy-velvet dress. She carried a clipboard with her and—I suspected—a hidden agenda in talking to me. We weren't exactly gal pals after all.

"Something like that, Lady Agnue." I shrugged innocently. "Can I help you with anything?"

"I hope so, Miss Knight," she replied. "I was going to call you into my office later this afternoon, but as you are here I might as well tell you now."

"Tell me what?"

"The usual, Miss Knight. It is a new school year—the time for a fresh start, if you will. You are getting older. And as you enter into your second-to-last year at this institution, the clock until the Author begins writing your fairytale is rapidly ticking. Although, despite this, I assume you are still entertaining the delusion you have had since you were a child that you can rebel against the natural order and try to determine who you are fated to be on your own, correct?"

"Well . . ."

"Just as I thought," she said, cutting me off sternly. "Listen carefully, young lady. I have been very tolerant of you and your inappropriate behavior thus far, but my patience is wearing thin. You graduate next year and it is high time you swallow your pride and that silly idea that you can be something more than what you are. It is not possible."

"Lady Agnue, I know you don't want to hear it, but I don't agree. I think—"

"Female protagonists are not supposed to think, Miss Knight," Lady Agnue interrupted. "How many times must I tell you? They are supposed to be beautiful, charming, and poised. Things like thinking and fighting are for the heroes. And in case you have been neglecting your studies, I challenge you to open any fairytale and discover for yourself that the heroes are always male protagonists. Also, it is 'do not', not 'don't.' Princesses are not supposed to use contractions either—rule twelve, I might remind you."

I knew Lady Agnue was our headmistress, and talking back to a person of that level of authority was ill advised, no matter what type of school you went to. But this woman was the most narrow-minded, old-fashioned crone I had ever met, and she was really getting on my nerves. People lectured me about this stuff all the time, but she seemed to consider beating down my deepest hopes and messing with my self-image some sort of sport.

I'd never been completely sure whether this disaccord between us had been my fault or hers. More often than not, I ended up conceding that it was neither. Instead, I chalked it up to the natural order.

Lady Agnue was the old, the conventional, the tried and true timeless archetype of a woman that our world deemed young ladies should aspire to be like. She was, in an essence, so much like the worn classic books we were forced to read in school—full of wisdom, but also dust. For while the beliefs and ideals she represented contained certain amounts of worth, they were also out of date. Moreover, they were too proud to admit it.

I was not like those books. I had never lived to model myself after the past. As constrained as it may have been, I was compelled to live for the future. I took chances. I was not afraid to be different. I risked the respectability and security that came with sticking to the norm in the hopes of turning the pages forward in my life.

As such, it was only inherent that Lady Agnue and I were meant to be at odds. Since that first day of school five years ago when I'd arrived at orientation in my child-sized combat boots and went for the snack table before the program commenced, she'd pegged me for what I was. And I—since that same day when she'd made me wash all the windows in the ballroom as punishment for the transgression—had known what she was too.

With this understanding whole-heartedly absorbed, throughout my schooling I had ardently, stubbornly refused to back down to the tyrannical traditionalism she tried to force upon me. And she, in response, had kept me in her merciless line of fire as punishment for the impertinent behavior.

Over the years she'd dropped in on lectures to randomly call me out, ordered surprise inspections of my room in the hopes of finding unauthorized contraband like sports mouth guards or playing cards, and had on more than one occasion altered my school schedule so that my chosen electives like Archery or Advanced Horseback-Riding were swapped out for something she knew I'd hate like Sewing or Advanced Banquet Planning.

In spite of all such interference though, the worst of her treatment had always been moments like this.

When there were no classmates, no friends, no teachers around to witness her harassment, it took a turn for the psychological. Irritating things like room inspections or even a semester's worth of stupid coursework I could handle, shrugging them off as I refused to allow her ridiculous tactics to get the better of me. But this kind of oppression—targeted specifically at my heart and the innermost doubts and beliefs that dwelled there—that was hard to take. Especially given how direct these hits of hers had become over the years.

As much as Lady Agnue resented me, after being under her roof for the majority of my adolescence, she'd come to know me well. Thus, she'd fine-tuned her malice in a way that made getting inside of my head a legitimate possibility. And when she had me cornered like she did at this very moment, she'd become shrewdly skilled at unleashing it.

I, in turn, had to do everything I could to keep my guard and sass-levels up, and stand my ground despite it. Like now, for instance.

I reined in my anger at her last comment as best I could and crossed my arms.

"Scold me if you like, Lady Agnue, but I *don't* know if I believe that's true. Why *can't* female protagonists be heroes? Look at my friend Blue. She is just as strong and brave as any of the boys at Lord Channing's. She can be the hero of her own story one day. I just know it."

Lady Agnue paused for a moment and seemed to mull over my comment.

"Blue might be an exception to the common rule," she said slowly. "I will give you that."

Wait. Did she just concede my point?

"So you agree then, that an ordinary girl could be a hero?" I asked hopefully.

"Do not get excited, Crisanta. I do concede that, even though the odds are slim, your little friend Blue might be able to become some kind of heroic character. However, you must realize three things. First, Blue is a tomboy—a breed all on its own that is much less valued. Second, there is a difference between being a hero and being *heroic*. And third and most importantly, *you* are not an ordinary girl. You are a princess. Although you are as poor an example for one as there can be found, that is what you are, that is all that you are, and, ergo, that is all you will ever be. Your role, unlike hers, has already been assigned."

"What if it hasn't, though? I mean, who says I can't be both?" I asserted much less confidently. "Maybe a girl can strive to be more than what she is. Maybe I could strive to be more than what I am and someday become a good princess and a good hero?"

Lady Agnue emitted a precocious snicker and shook her head as if I had just told her the most amusing of jokes.

"Oh my dear child, no. I am sorry, but you cannot be both. No one can be both, as the roles are contradictory by nature. That point aside, even if they were not, this dream of yours is still foolish for, as I have just explained, you are not even a good princess to begin with."

I opened my mouth in retort, but nothing came out. And in my hesitation, Lady Agnue took that as her cue to drive home the vicious point with resolute sternness.

"Overall, Miss Knight, while your gumption was once cute, it is truly high time you stop mistaking rebellion for strength and individuality for free will. You must accept who you are and realize that this girl cannot be erased. She is you; she will always be you. All your wishing and denying and fighting will not change that. So please, for your own sake, do stop filling your head with such dangerous, empty ideas and fall in line where you belong. I do not want any more trouble from you this year. Understood?"

"Yeah, Lady Agnue," I huffed indignantly. "I got it."

"*Yes*, Miss Knight. A princess must always say 'yes', and not 'yeah'."

I narrowed my eyes at her. "*Yeah,* so I've been told."

Oh goody, the boys are coming.

The rest of the week went by in a blur—causing Saturday to arrive faster than expected. Now, mid-morning on the day in question, our entire floor and several others had become uninhabitable. Different perfumes clouded the air, extra traces of glittery eye shadow rested on every bathroom sink, and high-heeled shoes that girls had thrown about lined the hallways like colorful, strewn spikes.

It wasn't just the princesses behind this feminine tornado either; the common protagonists were in just as bad a tizzy. Yes, it seemed without a doubt that the majority of the student body had gone completely mad.

That, in a word, irritated me.

Seriously, what was it about boys that made teenage girls all riled up and desperate to please with tight dresses and mile-high footwear? Who cared if some shallow prince thought you were cute or not? It was all utter lunacy in my opinion—wasting time like that trying to impress them. If you were going to devote countless hours a day to making yourself better in some way, you should've been doing it for *your sake* not some boy's.

Case in point: in the amount of time Jade spent in the bathroom mirror this morning making sure her eye makeup was perfect so that her crush (Prince Theopold) would notice her, I'd finished my research paper for my Animal First Aid elective, completed a full workout on the pull-up bar Blue and I kept hidden in our closet, and learned how to make an inverted fishtail braid from SJ.

Thankfully, both my friends had also deemed it unnecessary to participate in "Mission Makeover" this morning. SJ didn't have to because she was just naturally the prettiest girl around and could put on any outfit in her closet and be the best-dressed girl in a room. Blue and I, on the other hand, just didn't care about turning the boys' heads. We weren't like grungy or whatever; we took pride in our personal appearances like every girl should. But we definitely didn't find it necessary to jump through any extra hoops for our so-not-prince-charming's.

As a result, when noon came around, the three of us marched confidently past our frazzled classmates—unaffected by the frivolous preoccupation with garnering the attention of the heroes from across the way.

SJ, Blue, and I journeyed to the area of the practice fields where we usually met up with Jason and Mark. I had my satchel, Blue some weapons, and SJ her new potions book. That worn-out thing hadn't left her side since Madame Alexanders had gifted it to her at the beginning of the week. In part, that was because she read it whenever she had a spare second. But it was also because she was worried that something would happen to it if she let it out of her sight for more than a few minutes.

This might have seemed like overkill, but I could understand. I had the same type of relationship with my wand-bearing satchel, after all.

Our group stopped walking when we reached the river

that separated our school from the forest surrounding Lord Channing's. The In and Out Spell should have been going down any minute, and I wondered if maybe it already had.

A gnome statue on our side of the river marked the exact border of the spell's barrier. Stupidly, I decided to test if it was still active by sauntering up to the water's edge and extending my finger to touch the air where the force field would have been.

This was a bad call.

No sooner did my index finger make its way into the air space above the gnome's head did I receive a substantial purple shock.

"Ow!" I squeaked as I jumped back and rubbed my hand.

"Crisa, you should know better than that," SJ chided.

I rolled my eyes. "Yeah, yeah. I got the message."

Residue particles of magic dust fell from the barrier where I'd touched it, floating around my nose and making me want to sneeze. I blew the glittering ash out of my face.

Some might have thought the sparkly substance pretty. But since it was useless to anyone outside of the realm's transportation department who harnessed magic dust for fuel, I just found it irritating and, also, a bit patronizing at the given moment.

I crossed my arms in annoyance and waited, glaring at the gnome with his judgmental, pointy beard and unnecessarily big overalls.

A few ticks of the clock later, we watched as the In and Out Spell was actually taken down—the purple color of the force field temporarily returning to view while it lowered into the ground.

Satisfied, my friends and I began to pass the time until

Jason and Mark arrived. I took out my wand and changed it into a sword—planning to keep it in that form for the rest of the afternoon since I very well couldn't risk any boys seeing it morph. Blue, meanwhile, emptied out her bag of weapons. She had brought a sword, her hunting knife, and some climbing rope to entertain herself with for the day.

You know, typical stuff a girl keeps in her purse.

After a few minutes the two of us engaged in a casual sword fight—our blades glinting in the weekend sunlight each time they clashed. It wasn't exactly an epic battle; nevertheless, ordinarily not even an earthquake would have been enough to shake Blue's focus away from a duel. However, when we heard a familiar voice yell "Hey guys!" from somewhere in the near vicinity, she immediately stopped fighting and whirled around.

Her face lit up. "Jason!"

Blue high-fived our friend with excitement.

Jason Sharp hadn't changed much since the last time I'd seen him. His hair was perhaps a bit blonder from being outside all summer, but it retained its normal boyish style— the vague shape of an upside down salad bowl with slight bangs. His eyes were blue as ever, and he wore his typical "game-face" as well as his weapon of choice (an axe holstered within the sheath on his back). Like Blue and her knife, he rarely went anywhere without this favorite tool of his.

Jason's trademark impish grin gently set the dimples into his face as he greeted us and we began to exchange pleasantries. As we did this though, I suddenly took notice of another boy about twelve feet behind Jason who was heading our way.

It was not Mark. Frankly, I couldn't recall ever having

seen this boy at all, which was strange because most students at Lord Channing's and Lady Agnue's had been going to school together for years.

Jason saw my surprise and introduced the stranger who joined our group in the next instant. "Everybody," he said, "this is Daniel."

In response to Jason's introduction, Daniel gave us one of those obnoxious cool guy head nods and a sorry attempt for a smile.

I stared at him with intrigue, but also hesitance.

Daniel wore a leather jacket that was rugged and ill taken care of. Despite its coverage, I was still able to notice how strongly he was built beneath it. (*Which was* very, *in case you were wondering.*)

The majority of the rest of his ensemble was unexceptional, except for the golden pocket watch I saw half-concealed within his pants pocket.

As for the man himself, he was a couple inches short of six feet tall and had chocolate brown hair that set off his deep, oak-colored eyes. His chin was strong, much like his other features. Moreover, he had a tan as noticeable on his face as the boredom in his expression, which he tried to mask with cordialness.

I didn't know why, but seeing him made me take a slight step back—like his presence knocked me off balance somehow.

"Where's Mark?" Blue asked bluntly as she eyed Daniel and looked around to see if our other friend was somewhere behind.

"He's not here. Actually, he's taking a temporary leave of absence," Jason replied. "Lord Channing made the announcement on move-in day. I guess Mark is sick or something and will probably take the whole year off. Daniel here is my new roommate."

We were sad to hear that Mark was sick and weren't sure how to process the news. So, our attention turned to his so-called replacement instead. The three of us studied Daniel momentarily to decipher how we felt about this.

SJ and Blue seemed to decide to give him the benefit of the doubt. They shook his hand and introduced themselves.

I was a bit more reluctant.

Daniel had a way about him. I couldn't quite place what it was, but I got weird vibes from the way he looked at me—like he already had me figured out and was enjoying the fact that the familiarity was not reciprocal. It was now my turn to introduce myself though, so I was forced to swallow down this aversion and try to be congenial.

"Um, hi," I said. "I'm Crisa."

SJ elbowed me.

What was that for? I wondered, perturbed.

Oh, right, princesses give formal introductions. Duh.

"Crisanta Knight," I added to please SJ.

He nodded as if he knew, and shook my hand. When he did, I received a small static shock—like a low-grade version of the one I'd gotten a few minutes ago from the In and Out Spell.

We both pulled away.

An awkward beat passed before SJ broke the ice by bidding us adieu. Since Mark was not there, and swordplay was not her forte, she was going to spend the afternoon reading in the garden. She waved goodbye, told Daniel it was a pleasure meeting him, and headed back toward the main grounds. A second later, before I had the chance to choose how I would spend the rest of my own day, Jason inadvertently made the decision for me.

"Hey, Blue," he said excitedly. "You wanna go climb the big fig trees in the orchard? I bet I can beat your best time from last year."

Now I realize that to most girls this might not have sounded like that great of a Saturday plan, but Blue could not have been more delighted by the idea. And she agreed to it so fast that she did not stop to think what the turn of events would mean for me.

I couldn't go climbing. See, normally I was totally gung-ho for almost anything action-packed. But intense climbing and I just did not mix well. This wasn't because I lacked the strength. Like I said, I worked out in the practice fields almost every day and could even do a decent amount of pull-ups on the bar in our room.

Which, let me tell you, is no easy task.

Don't believe me? Give it a try. Pull-ups when you're a girl are nuts!

No, when it came to tree climbing what I tended to fall short on (pun most certainly intended) was the dexterity. Between the rough, yet slippery feel of a branch within your hands, the difficulty of clinging to that branch while your shoes blindly searched for footholds, and the persistent, realistic threat that both might snap at any given moment, it never tended to end well. Every time I tried, I severely injured myself and/or those around me. The last time Blue and I had gone climbing together, for example, I'd broken my arm and knocked her out of the tree as I fell—causing her to sprain an ankle and one of her wrists.

We'd just gotten back to school and, needless to say, I was in no mood to put either of us out of fighting shape so soon. This, unfortunately, didn't register to Blue until I huffed, "Great, now what am I supposed to do?"

"Oh, right. Sorry, Crisa," Jason said, backtracking. "We could do something else if you want?"

"Well . . ." I started to say.

Then I caught a look at Blue who was shooting me a sort of silent *"please."*

"Thanks, Jason. But you two go on ahead," I conceded.

It was nice of Jason to offer; dude was always putting others before himself. But he and Blue were really good friends and were no doubt excited to catch up. I wasn't about to hold them back. Jason still seemed to feel guilty though. So, in his innocent, yet misguided attempt to remedy the situation, he made an even more horrible suggestion than tree climbing.

"Crisa, Daniel's an awesome sword fighter. Why don't the two of you hang out and practice?" he said, gesturing to the sword in my hand.

Suddenly I lamented bringing my wand. The sheath swung across Daniel's shoulder apparently had a sword in it as well, so neither of us had a plausible excuse for rejecting Jason's proposal. As consequence, we were both victims of our friend's good-natured idea and the unwritten rules of social decorum that dictated we go along with it.

After some unenthusiastic "yeah okay's" from both Daniel and myself, Jason and Blue headed off toward the campus orchards and left us alone together.

At first we stood there facing each other wordlessly. I didn't hang around with boys one-on-one very often, so I wasn't sure if I was supposed to initiate the conversation or if there was some secret code word to get his attention or whatever. Eventually, after shifting the weight back and forth between my left and right foot for a bit, I cleared my throat in an attempt to start a dialogue.

"Soooo . . ." I began.

"Yeah?" he responded.

Ugh. This was going to be like pulling teeth.

"So do you want to fight or what?"

Daniel eyed me up and down like he was calculating something. "Sure," he finally responded. "Could be interesting."

"What do you mean by that?"

"I mean it'll be like a test of my control."

He removed his sword from its sheath and spun it confidently to add flourish to the point. "I'll have to go against my instincts and hold back. Practice restraint."

I gave him a really skeptical brow furrow to hint that I needed further elaboration. He, in turn, went on to provide it and thus affirm what my instincts had been telling me since I'd first laid eyes on him. I did not like Daniel.

He drew into a fighting stance to signal he was ready.

"Have you ever had a pet dog?" he asked.

I mirrored his stance and raised my sword. "Yeah, what of it?"

Daniel delivered the first strike across my right side and I parried and endeavored to counter. He blocked it easily and went on offense, slowly pushing me back as we continued the match.

"Well," he explained calmly as he blocked one of my strikes after another, "a hard trick for a dog to master is balancing a treat on his nose and not eating it until the command is given. It's a pretty big challenge because he has to be strong enough to restrain his natural instincts."

The comment, and the little toadstool I almost tripped over, caught me off guard and filled me with annoyance.

"Am I supposed to be the treat in this anecdote?" I asked.

"Yup."

He swung at my left arm and I sidestepped just in time.

"And you consider yourself strong because you are such a great swordfighter? And resisting making me your dog chow is a challenge?"

Daniel smirked. "In a manner of speaking."

"All right then," I said as I calculated my next move. "Let me ease your troubles. I give you permission not to hold back, because *I'm* definitely not planning to."

At that, I broke my sword away from where he'd previously been blocking it, swung around underneath his arm, and came back toward his head. The down and up move caught him by surprise. He ducked just in the nick of time and the shock was evident on his formerly smug face. The humility didn't last long, though. A second later he recovered and grinned like the impressiveness of the move was more amusing than threatening. And then I realized why.

Not that I would've ever admitted it out loud, but he was right. Holding back was a feat for someone of his natural talent.

Daniel moved with both force and agility. He was much better at sword fighting than me, or even Blue, and it was all I could do to avoid getting sliced by his swift strikes.

It killed me to acknowledge it, but the fact was that he was just plain incredible. I had been practicing for most of my life and was not nearly as strong as him. The scary thought also occurred to me in that moment that I might never be. I mean, I was used to trying a bit harder than most people with the sword because the ability did not come easily to me, yet in the broad perspective I'd always considered myself to still be fairly skilled. But the way Daniel confidently fought me without even breaking a sweat—smirking all the while—made me feel a lot less sure of it.

Amazingly enough, five minutes later I was still in one piece.

"You're pretty decent," Daniel said at that point. "For a princess anyways."

I wasn't sure if he was being serious or sarcastic; either way the remark was unexpected and irritating enough to distract me for half a second. Half a second, however, was all Daniel needed. He came at me so fast I couldn't even half parry his strike. The sword was knocked out of my hand and I was left standing there defeated. To add injury to insult, the universe also picked that particular instant for me to trip over a large rock when I took a step backwards—causing me to fall on my butt.

"You overextend your strikes. It's like you think the blade is way longer than it actually is. And you make these weird swooping motions that don't work with a sword," Daniel lectured as I sat on the ground awkwardly. "If you ask me, sword fighting isn't really your thing. But hey, you should be proud of yourself. For a minute there it was like I was fighting an actual opponent."

"Thank you, Daniel," I snapped.

"You're welcome," he replied.

Daniel reached out his hand to assist me, but I scowled and picked myself up. I did not want or need his help.

In a huff, I went over to collect my sword from the ground. When I turned around I saw there was a smirk on Daniel's face, but also a bit of previously unnoticed coldness—making me wonder if maybe he didn't naturally like me either.

I was too angry and embarrassed to say anything more, so I just marched past him, shooting a massive death glare in his direction as I did so.

"It was nice meeting you," Daniel said sarcastically as I stomped off toward the school grounds.

"Likewise, I'm sure," I called back.

CHAPTER 5

The Prince & The Hero

gave Blue and SJ an earful that afternoon, sparing no expense in telling them that while they had both had wonderful Saturdays I had been stuck with the most obnoxious boy in the history of time.

My re-telling of the story was very theatrical and not lacking in colorful adjectives, so the two of them were thoroughly entertained as we readied ourselves for that evening's ball.

"He was so smug-looking I just wanted to smush his face," I continued as I searched my desk drawers for some kind of necklace to match the dress I would be wearing tonight.

"Smash," SJ corrected as she fastened the straps on her shoes.

"What?"

"'Smush' is not a word. You mean you wanted to 'smash' his face."

I rolled my eyes. "SJ, I'm in the middle of a rant here. Focus, please."

"Right, sorry." She looked at her sleek, silver watch. "Can we continue this later though, Crisa. Not that I do not love your stories, I just—"

"Yes, yes, I know. Go ahead. You have work to do. Blue and I will meet you there when we're done."

SJ smiled and nodded before hurrying toward the door.

"Do not be late," she called back as she shut it behind her.

I sighed and made my way into the bathroom, and then to our adjacent closet. There I found the shimmering silver gown I would be wearing for the next few hours. It had a bodice twinkling with crystals and a skirt that poofed out in the shape of a pound cake. I tersely removed it from the hanger and inspected it closely. å

Whenever we had a ball the school seamstresses made each of us a custom gown. In anticipation of this, I always went to see the seamstresses earlier in the week to request that they sew a zipper into the back of my dress instead of making it in the normal, loathsome corset style.

Like forced socializing with irritating boys wasn't painful enough, our professors expected us to do it while barely being able to breathe?

Not me, thank you very much. Tiny waist be darned; I happen to be very fond of not having my diaphragm crushed.

Zipped up, now all that was left were my shoes and I would be ready to go.

Tonight's main event was being held in Lady Agnue's grand ballroom, which was on the opposite side of the school. Given that, I laced up my trusty and comfortable black combat boots beneath my dress instead of putting on sparkly high-heels like a proper princess would.

Had SJ not already left for the ball a few minutes ago, I was sure she would have nagged me about the choice. But nothing she could have said would've swayed my decision. I loved my boots almost as much I hated corsets. And anyways, it wasn't like anyone was going to see them beneath the massive skirt of my gown. Heck, I probably could've smuggled three dwarves across state lines under there without getting caught.

Boots secured, Blue and I left the suite and made our way downstairs. From there we commenced our walk through the dimly glowing, heavily tapestried hallways of Lady Agnue's.

In order to get to the ballroom we had to pass through many corridors lined with dozens upon dozens of regal columns, precocious oil paintings, and hollow, armored knights dressed similarly to the live ones consistently patrolling the school.

Overall, every one of these hallways was pretty similar to its counterparts. Except for the one that connected the East and West wings of the school, that is. This hall (at least 200 hundred feet in diameter) was the vast intersection that housed the Treasure Archives I'd passed by earlier in the week.

Hmm, I never got a chance to finish telling you about those did I? Lady Agnue had interrupted my train of thought at the time.

No worries. I'll remedy that oversight right now.

The Treasure Archives was a collection of the most precious and famous historical objects in our realm. They were the important trinkets that our fairytales were known for, and they were kept in five locked glass cases here at school.

On this night, like every other, they glowed before us in the light of the chandeliers above—all too aware of their unrivaled significance.

Like every other girl at Lady Agnue's, I had the contents of these cases memorized from having walked past them so often. No one could help it really. From the golden magic mirror used in *Beauty & the Beast* to the enchanted water lily that could turn people, like Prince Egot, into frogs, each object on display was intriguing and mystifying.

Of course some of the items in these cases were also relentless sore spots for the Legacies and Half-Legacies at Lady Agnue's. They served as constant reminders of the shadows we lived in, and the expectations we were supposed to live up to.

I knew Blue, for instance, always cringed at the sight of her sister's torn red cloak and, next to it, the tastefully placed axe that the hunter had used to save her. It still had some blood crusted on its edges.

Super classy.

SJ, meanwhile, tried to ignore the objects that haunted her when we passed them. But, every once in a while as we made our way by the Archives to get to class, I knew of at least one that bothered her—that dang ruby red apple. It was perched on a tiny glass pedestal in the center case and angled to show off the small bite taken out of it, which revealed the apple's poisoned white flesh.

Then there was me and my shadow—my mom's infamous glass stiletto.

On the one hand, the delicate treasure made me happy to think of the true love my parents shared and the triumph of their coming together despite the obstacles that had stood in their way. Then again, it was also a symbol of the role my mother and pretty much everyone else in the world expected me to fill. And it was an even greater reminder that no matter what I did, I probably would never be able to fit myself into it.

As Blue and I passed the Archives on the way to the

ballroom, I saw the fragile shoe sitting in the center case as usual. The glass shimmered from every angle—beautiful, transparent, and unforgiving, like so many things about this place.

After a few more minutes, we arrived at the back entrance of the grand ballroom. It was a humongous space—large enough to fit four stables—decorated with gold-encrusted walls and glistening chandeliers. The centerpiece was a massive chandelier seven times the size of all the others that hung over the middle of the dance floor. This one's pastel crystals numbered in the thousands and twinkled like clouds of gorgeous confetti high above our heads.

Far below the chandelier's glittering enormity, I spotted SJ—one of only a few other students in the vicinity. She was the head of the ball planning committee and, as usual, she and her team of student volunteers, along with Madame Lisbon, had gotten here early to go over their final checklists before the main doors opened.

While Blue and I generally preferred to be late rather than early to these types of functions, we had decided to come down early to help our responsible friend with her final preparations for the first ball of the semester.

SJ was scurrying about the great room in her strappy, scarlet dress—its small train intercut with streaks of sparkling navy that swayed behind her as she saw to the orchestra, the food, and the ice sculptures. She made the work appear effortless, and retained a distinct aura of fabulousness all the while. The color of that gown was perfect on her, and I wondered if she noticed just how many people's heads turned to admire her as she passed by.

Hers was not the only remarkable outfit this evening. Blue was looking lovely in her gown too. It was a simpler dress—

the same rich shade of blue as her trusty cloak, which set off her eyes beautifully. The edges of the skirt were trimmed with a jaunty, black lace design that mirrored the single strap draped across her right shoulder. And she paired the ensemble with an assortment of dazzling onyx bracelets that gleamed on her wrists like the afterthoughts of dark magic.

While I knew she didn't really like dressing up, I imagined she had to feel relatively pleased tonight wearing an outfit that made her look so naturally radiant.

I gazed down at my own dress for a moment and considered what I looked like to the rest of the world.

Did anyone ever see me as being that pretty?

And did I really care whether or not they did?

To be honest, I was not sure on either count. All I was certain of was that I was just as proud to be wearing this shimmering, silver ball gown as I was sporting my untamable, long hair and the combat boots beneath my skirt. Was it a contrasting look? Sure. But would I have had it any other way? Absolutely not.

A few minutes later, right as Blue and I finished helping Madame Lisbon set up the check-in table, SJ came over grinning excitedly to tell us that it was time. Our professor gushed with enthusiasm and gave the guards the signal to open the grand doors on the other side of the room.

In the next instant a sea of glittering fabric and fine designer suits came pouring in.

I watched our classmates enter one pair at a time. Almost all of them were coupled off like that—one well-dressed penguin for every extravagantly feathered lady peacock. It was kind of cute in a nausea-inducing sort of way. All of Lady Agnue's' girls and Lord Channing's' boys looked like the exceptional people the world expected them to be.

Music started moments later and a formal dancing circle formed in the center of the room. Dozens of couples began waltzing perfectly in tune with the rhythm of the forty-piece orchestra.

From dancing to punch sipping, our schools' balls were traditional to the letter—with regulations to no end. I had always been able to get away with disregarding most of these rules, but some were harder to avoid than others. Take, for instance, the aforementioned dancing circle. Formal etiquette dictated that whenever any gentleman asked a lady to dance, she had to accept. She could only stop dancing when her suitor deemed their dance over, or if the pair had been dancing together for at least ten minutes and someone else cut in.

So unfair it's best not to even get me started.

Typically, though, this was not something I had to worry about. No one ever asked Blue or me to dance, so the two of us (plus Jason) usually hung around the snack table people-watching and making sassy commentary throughout the evening. SJ, on the other hand, spent the night running around making sure everything was progressing smoothly.

Since she was technically working in doing so, she was the only girl allowed to refuse a dance request. And SJ got *a lot* of dance requests.

Lucky.

I mean in regards to refusing dance requests of course, not the getting them part.

Around half an hour into the dance, Jason found Blue and me over by the buffet. He was looking fairly fresh this evening in his dark gray suit. His tie was the same color as Blue's gown so the two of them could've totally passed for a matching pair when standing next to each other like that.

I shoved another miniature quiche into my mouth as Blue pointed out the girls who were clearly wearing helper bras. Jason, in return, pointed out which guys were wearing lifts in their shoes.

As they went on like that, I smiled to myself. Those two were like a couple of peas in a pod. Like Jack and Jill, only more hardcore and far more entertaining.

An hour into the dance, it was turning out to be a perfectly normal and pleasant evening until his highness, Chance Darling, showed up and added an unexpected twist to my night.

Ah, Chance Darling.

What could I possibly say about Chance Darling?

Let me start by asserting that I think every girl has a different idea of what a "totally hot guy" is. But, I also think that there is a certain level of attractiveness a guy can reach that, no matter what a girl's specifically into, she will agree that he is by definition a good-looking fellow.

Chance Darling was one of these good-looking fellows. He was the Prince of Clevaunt, grandson of King Midas, and most girls considered him to be the hottest thing since two-wheel-drive carriages. To put it in its plainest terms, he was a charmer, a ladies' man, and a perfect young royal by all traditional standards. In addition, his physical appearance could've best been described as a cross between a fairytale's ideal prince charming and a well-toned personal trainer.

So did I personally think he was handsome? Of course. However, despite his outward immaculateness, he definitely did not cause me or my friends to swoon on sight like so many of the other girls at Lady Agnue's.

Why?

Because you could give a dirt-bag a pearly white smile and a fancy suit, but he'd still be a dirt-bag.

This punk, as Jason referred to him, was snide, conceited, and more self-absorbed than a kitchen sponge. Holding a conversation with him was like talking to a mannequin in a store window—if mannequins were endowed with a sense of self-importance and an impressive dose of narcissism, that is.

Appropriately, Chance was Mauvrey's man. With their similar levels of superficiality, attractiveness, and their horrible personalities, the two of them had been a natural couple for years. So, knowing all of this, you can understand why the following surprised me so much.

"Good evening, Crisanta," Chance said.

He bowed formally as I used the back of my hand to wipe the residue pastry crumbs from my face. "Uh . . . Hi, Chance," I responded.

"Crisanta, would you do me the honor of joining me on the dance floor?"

I glanced over at Blue and Jason with a *"What the heck?"* expression on my face. They shrugged in confusion.

I cocked my head at Chance, but he didn't seem to be joking.

"Seriously?" I asked.

"Completely," he replied.

Chance extended his hand and I stared at it apprehensively. Out of the corner of my eye, I could see Mauvrey and her cronies across the room. Her face was so red with anger as she glared at me I thought steam was going to start pouring out of her ears.

As much as I really didn't want to dance with Chance or create any more animosity between Mauvrey and myself, there were rules. I had to accept Chance's invitation. Not because I didn't like breaking rules. That was sort of my nature. But Lady Agnue and Madame Lisbon both happened to be within earshot at the moment, so if I chose to go rogue then and there, they would've surely gone ballistic. As such, I unfortunately had no choice but to accept the prince's inexplicable offer.

I sighed, extending my own hand. "Sure, Chance. Why not."

He took my palm in his firmly and twirled me onto the dance floor with great pageantry.

The couples were currently in the midst of a Viennese Waltz so Chance put his right hand around my waist and took my right hand in his left. We danced in silence for several minutes and I was shocked that his highness did not correct me on the mistakes I made with my footwork.

Finally, I decided to ask what anyone who saw us together was undoubtedly thinking.

"So, uh, Chance, just out of curiosity . . ." I began. "Why exactly *are* you dancing with me and not Mauvrey like you usually do?"

"Mauvrey grew over the summer," Chance replied bluntly.

"Come again?"

"She is nearly as tall as I am now. If we were to dance together, she would block people from seeing my face."

"You're dancing with me because I'm sufficiently shorter than you?" I asked.

"Yes," he responded without emotion. "Though do not let that bother you; you should still enjoy this time with me and be flattered I asked you nonetheless. Trust me, there are plenty of petite princesses at Lady Agnue's who fit the bill.

But, despite your impertinent nature and slightly masculine nose, I find you, Crisanta Knight, to be uniquely attractive. And as an added bonus, your hair and eye colors do not clash with my own. Therefore, I have decided that we are perfect together and you shall be my new heart's desire from hereon out."

I stared at Chance open-mouthed, processing the unbelievable levels of shallowness his answer had managed to achieve. Then, with every proceeding twirl, in the next several seconds my angry feelings began to boil for the idiot who was forcing me to twirl for him.

At that point I was ready to kick Chance in his crown jewels when, luckily, someone tapped me on the shoulder to cut in.

Thank you, thank you whoever you are for saving me from the second-most irritating person . . .

I turned around.

Excellent. The number one most irritating person I'd talked to today was here too.

"Can I cut in?" Daniel asked Chance rhetorically.

The prince seemed a bit annoyed to have to give up his carefully selected dance partner, and for a second he and Daniel had one of those silent, macho stand-offs. Reluctantly, after a slight hesitation, Chance did concede though.

With another overly stiff bow he thanked me for the dance and gallantly strode away like the impeccable prince he thought himself to be.

Daniel did not wait for my permission and took my hand, continuing the dance as if nothing of particular peculiarity had happened.

"Hey," was his opening line.

"Uh, hey," I responded.

Daniel quarter-turned me and smirked. "You looked so angry I thought your head was going to explode."

Our dance escalated as the melody began to pick up, causing a problem for me. Between the size of my dress, the added speed of the tempo, and the uncomfortable nature of being so close to Daniel, mistakes became a lot harder to avoid.

I almost tripped on the hem of my dress at his latest comment. When I recovered, I gave him an expression that was two-thirds repulsion and one-third confusion. Based on that look, he explained himself.

"Blue, Jason, and I were watching you dance. I don't know what Chance said to you, but whatever it was, you seemed angry enough to pop. Kind of like how you looked earlier today when you couldn't handle the fact that I beat you so easily. Anyways, they thought you needed a lifeline so when Chance's ten minutes were up I decided to do you the favor and cut in before you completely lost it."

I rolled my eyes. "Well, thanks a lot."

"You're welcome."

"I was being sarcastic."

"Shocker."

I would definitely have to thank Blue later for letting this jerk make me his dance partner. She and Jason were probably in hysterics right now. I glanced over my shoulder toward the buffet.

They weren't there.

Scanning the room, I finally saw them on the far right side of the dance floor . . . *dancing*.

It was weird. Blue hated dancing. But they seemed to be having a good time so I figured maybe he dared her to or something.

Daniel and I waltzed for a few minutes without saying anything more to one another. I would've liked to have said that at least this went smoothly, but that would have been a lie. Daniel stepped on my feet periodically. And he turned me the wrong way on more than one occasion, causing me to spin right into the line of dance traffic. Not to say that I was exactly Miss Fancy Dancey either. Despite a decade of training, I still made mistakes and tripped every now and again.

What can I say, if you don't have rhythm, you don't have rhythm. Of course—

Ow!

What was that, like, the fiftieth time he'd stomped on my toes?

"Geez, Daniel. You couldn't take five minutes away from sword fighting practice at Lord Channing's to learn how to dance without trampling your partner?"

"No, I suck at dancing because this is my first week at Lord Channing's," Daniel replied stiffly. "My book appeared nine days ago. I barely had time to pack, let alone take waltz lessons. What's your excuse for being such a bad dancer?"

I didn't retaliate. For one, I was a bad dancer and I knew it. And two, Daniel had just brought up a far more interesting topic of conversation.

So here's the thing, for royals, protagonist books appeared when they were born because every prince and princess was destined to be the main character of his or her own fairytale. For all other chosen main characters, though (the common protagonists, as it were), books typically came into existence during early childhood.

Every once in a while a common protagonist's book

would emerge in their pre-teen years, like it had for Blue for instance. (Unlike full Legacies who were royal, Half-Legacies that weren't were not guaranteed to be main characters themselves.) But I had never heard of a protagonist book appearing for someone old enough to be in their second to last year at one of our schools. That was just not a thing.

"Your book just appeared a week and a half ago?" I repeated.

Daniel nodded. "Yeah, and so did my prologue prophecy."

Whoa, back-up. Now that was intense.

Remember how I told you earlier that, while people in Book know they'll be main characters when their books appear, there is no telling when the Author will begin writing their fairytales?

So that's true. But the thing of it is, we are aware when she actually does begin to write them.

You see, the first thing the Author pens in a protagonist book is its prologue. We refer to it as a "prologue prophecy" because those vague, succinct, and obnoxiously rhyming lines prophesize what that person's story will be.

When these prologues appear, we protagonists sort of feel it. A powerful jolt hits our bodies, leaving us with a temporary spiral mark burned into our foreheads and a feeling akin to being struck by lightning. As such, this sensation has been nicknamed the "prologue pang."

I can't really explain what one feels like past that, given that I haven't gotten mine yet. Truth be told, the only one of my friends who has is Jason. His prologue appeared about a year ago. But he never talked about the experience. To this day we still didn't even know what his prologue says.

In respect of personal privacy the only people with permission to view prologues are the Scribes, our headmasters (Lady Agnue or Lord Channing), and the students whom they are about. Thus, whenever a new one emerges, a Scribe will magically transport it to the respective school and the headmaster of said academy will read it to the named protagonist privately.

Of course, if protagonists wish, they can tell whomever they want, or invite others to listen in on the reading; it is their prerogative. But this choice depends on the person. Some people like to brag about their prophecies while others (like Jason) prefer to keep it to themselves.

I couldn't believe that Daniel had gotten both his book *and* his prologue within the last two weeks.

It was weird to put it mildly, and no doubt super overwhelming. Maybe that was why he was being so irritating. It was an understandable reaction. After all, I would've probably done the same if my life had changed so dramatically without the slightest warning. I loathed the idea of prologue prophecies, but at least I'd known my entire life to expect one.

Then again, Daniel could've been happy about it. He had been a common before this. (One of Book's many ensemble characters that weren't assigned by the Author to play any specific, or important role in life. They're only foreseeable mission was to help make up the masses that lifted up the people—the main characters—who were.)

Now he was a protagonist—one of Lord Channing's esteemed, chosen "Young Heroes." His status, his life, had just gotten a serious upgrade. So I supposed this jerky attitude of his could've just as easily been a reflection of his newly developed sense of importance.

I realized then that I had been staring off into space and dancing on autopilot for some time. Daniel was still waiting for my response to his massive revelation.

Alas, I honestly didn't know what to provide for one. Just because the idea of prologue prophecies made me queasy, didn't mean that was how he felt. Although, either way, I conceded that it was probably a lot for the guy to process and, jerk or not, the right thing to do would be to cut him some slack.

You know, try and empathize.

"Wow," I finally said. "Um, a lot to handle. I'm sorry, I guess. That sucks."

He nodded in agreement. "Yeah. It does. I take it you're not a fan of prologue prophecies either?"

"Why would I be?" I replied. "They turn people into puppets. Look at everyone here. They've all totally accepted that they will live their lives like marionettes—dancing around following the instructions of some unknown master without question. It sickens me as much as it disappoints me. Frankly, it's all I can do not to just—"

I abruptly stopped myself when I realized that I'd been letting an uncensored stream of babble pour out of my mouth.

It was true I did actually feel that way. Nevertheless, I usually wasn't that forthcoming about my innermost feelings with other people, especially people like Daniel—who I didn't know well, but knew I didn't like.

"It sickens you," Daniel thought aloud in reflection. "But you still participate in it."

The inherent allegation immediately sucked me the remaining way out of my internal monologue.

"What are you saying?" I asked defensively.

Daniel and I bumped into another couple. They shot us a glare before twirling away to the music like pros. Interruption over, my attention went back to Daniel.

"What I'm saying is that you're a hypocrite," Daniel accused bluntly as we picked up the tempo again. "The idea of prologue prophecies, the Author, and all this supposedly 'sickens' you; yet, you're still a part of the show. A good little puppet—dancing along like all the rest of them."

I began to miss dancing with Chance. At least his insults were less intentional and *far* less personal.

"That's not true!" I snapped. "I'm not a hypocrite, nor do I willingly go along with all of this. I just haven't figured out a way to break free of it yet and until I do I'm just . . . trapped."

Daniel gave me the same cold look he'd given me when we'd first met—like he knew something about me that I didn't and, whatever it was, he clearly didn't like it.

"I know what you mean," was all he said.

The unexpected iciness threw me for a beat. However, in the next three quarters of a second it took for him to spin me, the seriousness in his tone faded away. When I came back around to face him, I found that his cockiness and smirk, both of which I was now growing familiar with, had returned to his face just as suddenly as they'd left.

"It's too bad," Daniel went on then. "Based on what I'd heard about you I thought you'd be a bit less submissive."

"Submissive?"

"Yeah, you know—obedient, weak, unwilling to fight."

Oh, that is it. Rules be darned; I was not dancing with this guy for another second.

I dropped, rather, pushed his hand away and squared him off.

"Daniel," I steadied my voice. "You don't know anything about me. But allow me to enlighten you a little. I am not so obedient that I will keep dancing with someone who insults me. I am not so weak that I won't stand up for myself. And I am definitely not so unwilling to fight that I won't drop-kick you in the shin right here if you don't back off."

He smirked again.

I hated that smirk. Even though I was feeling, like, lion-status angry, that smirk made me feel like nothing more than a perturbed kitten.

After a long pause, Daniel shrugged.

"All right, Knight; fair enough. Look, I'm sorry okay? Just forget it," he said.

I opened my mouth to respond but then Daniel raised his eyebrows and lifted his chin, gesturing behind me.

I glanced over my shoulder. Lady Agnue was headed toward us—no doubt on her way to reprimand me for breaking the rules. I turned back to Daniel and he offered me his hand again. I glared at it reluctantly at first, but since I didn't feel like getting yelled at or sent to after-hours detention, I eventually conceded.

Irritably, I took Daniel's hand and we resumed our waltz just in time.

Foiled in her attempts to publicly punish me, Lady Agnue stopped short in her beeline, huffed, then walked back the way she'd come as my partner and I danced on.

"Knight," Daniel said plainly, "it's clear you don't like me."

"Obviously," I agreed.

"And that's fine because I don't like you either."

I mirrored his smirk. "Yeah. I got that."

"But since Jason's my roommate and Blue's yours, I'm guessing we're going to be seeing a lot of each other. So . . . I propose a sort of truce."

I raised my eyebrows as I waited for the punch line. But,

much to my surprise, it didn't come. He actually seemed serious.

"Go on," I said.

"Plain and simple," Daniel stated. "If you try to be less irritating, I will try to insult you less on your irritating qualities."

"You think *I'm* irritating. Well, isn't that the pretzel calling the cracker crunchy," I scoffed.

Ugh, what a jerk.

Still, he had a point. Blue was my best friend and she and Jason loved hanging out together. So Daniel and I probably were doomed to see a lot of each other.

It would suck to be forced to spend time with him in any capacity, but if we weren't arguing, his presence might've at least been somewhat tolerable. Which meant it really was in both our best interests if I agreed to play nice with the insufferable boy.

For now anyways.

The melody began to change as the orchestra subtly moved into a new song. With a sigh I at last looked up and responded to my partner's proposal.

"Fine, Daniel," I said. "A conditional, half-hearted truce it is."

I gripped his hand a little tighter and locked my eyes with his as our new dance began. "But I give you fair warning. Watch your step."

CHAPTER 6

The Change

 wonder why birds aren't influenced by what day of the week it is?

I mean, today was Monday. It was my understanding that everyone hated Mondays, at least a little bit. Yet, there they were at ten o'clock in the morning, outside in the blinding sunshine singing like they couldn't have been happier.

Singing with Nature class was definitely not my favorite subject. Usually I would just lay low and hang around with SJ and her huge animal entourage for the duration of the period, but today we had a quiz.

A quiz in Singing with Nature basically involved going up to the front of the class and belting out a melody of your choice with the intention of calling a specific animal to your side. Of course, for me this typically resulted in no animals responding to my banshee-like voice and me standing in front of the class looking like an idiot.

Why did I have to be the one princess in the history of the universe with less-than-impeccable vocal chords?

Today was the first exam of the semester and we had to call blue birds to our sides. Bonus points if we could get them to harmonize with us. SJ had helped me practice all day the day before but, other than drawing the attention of a couple of crows and a lone deer, the practice was not successful. And, personally, I think the deer just showed up to see what all the racket was about.

Needless to say, I was dreading the performance ahead.

At least our teacher, Madame Whimsey, was really nice about my singing inabilities. Whenever we had tests, she kept a pained, but sympathetic smile on her face for me. And she was compassionate enough to give me extra credit for feeding the birds three times a week. SJ, however, had offered to do the job for me that particular morning so that I could get some extra practice time in before the exam.

Our Singing with Nature class was held outdoors in an area of the garden next to the forest, allowing our vocal projections to be easily heard by the animals nearby. At present, Madame Whimsey—a relatively buxom woman with dark skin, a warm smile, and kindly brown eyes—was shuffling through some sheet music over by the crystal fountain situated amongst the azaleas. Most of the other princesses, meanwhile, were a good distance away either getting in some vocal warm-ups of their own, or giggling over their time at the ball.

I did not join them in their reminiscing of last Saturday's event, or their shared rehearsals. Instead I opted to stand within the relative concealment of the portion of forest that fell within the boundary of the In and Out Spell. Only in its seclusion did I feel at ease belting out my scales. Practicing in front of the other girls was about as comfortable for me as going to dinner in nothing but my sports bra and pajama pants. I was already anxious enough without having to worry about their judgment prematurely. Thus, for now privacy was my friend. Or at least it would've been if it wasn't for Mauvrey.

To add to the unpleasantness of the barely started day, my nemesis chose that particular moment to seek me out and confront me about the whole Chance-dance thing from Saturday's ball. She'd obviously decided this was the best place to do it since she was naturally superior to me in the subject. Mauvrey was as gifted with animal communication as SJ. Which, honestly, I didn't understand, seeing as how SJ was so kind and Mauvrey was so toxic.

Apparently animals weren't the best judges of character.

Filled with extra confidence because I was alone, Mauvrey sashayed over to me with only Jade in her wake. Girtha wasn't in this class (being non-royal and all).

I sighed as they approached.

Might as well get our teenage girl stand-off out of the way early in the week, I suppose.

"Crisa," Mauvrey hissed.

"Mauvrey," I said just as confidently. "So, what's on the agenda for our rivalry this morning? Rehearsed, unoriginal insults on your part followed by me rolling my eyes? Or are we mixing it up today?"

"Like I would need to insult you. Look at yourself, you have already done my job just by wearing that outfit."

"Wow, real clever. And now cue my eye roll," I responded dryly as I obligatorily rolled my eyes.

"Show some respect, Crisa," Jade chimed in, trying to defend her friend. "You know, Mauvrey had to get a massage *and* a face peel at the school spa yesterday to calm herself down after you attempted to steal her boyfriend on Saturday."

Mauvrey shot Jade a poisonous look. Evidently the evil princess did not want me to know just how upset I'd made her.

"A face peel, huh?" I said, shaking my head. "You should be careful, Mauvrey. Even for a royal those can get pretty expensive when a girl has two faces."

KO!

Mauvrey's eye twitched for a second, but the eerie calm she normally emanated returned almost instantaneously. She tossed her hair back and stepped into my personal space.

"Contrary to what my little friend here has suggested, Crisa, I was not intimidated by you. Like anyone ever could be. You want to talk about two-faced? How about the girl who pretends like she does not care what anyone thinks, but secretly wishes she could fit in like all the rest of us?"

Mauvrey lowered her voice to a malicious whisper and leaned in even further. "You and I both know that if you could fit into that transparent slipper and become everything you are not, you would not hesitate to do so. That is why you wear those stupid earrings every day, is it not? A secret hope that maybe the stumpy gourd will surprise everyone and transform into something beautiful? I hate to break it to you, sweetie, but the clock struck midnight for you a long time ago. So honestly, I would just get used to being exactly what you are—a lousy princess who has deluded herself into thinking she is strong, but in reality is just as helpless in influencing her identity as the rest of us. It is unavoidable. And no amount of Fairy Godmothers or magic is ever going to turn you into something else . . . *Pumpkin.*"

I truly didn't know what to say then, so I focused on trying to conceal the nerve-rattling effect of Mauvrey's comment as she stepped away from me. Regrettably, I swallowed my feelings a moment too late. She knew she'd gotten in my head.

This wasn't because she was right about me wanting to fit in. She'd been wrong on that count because I genuinely had no desire to be like Mauvrey's brand of snooty princess or Lady Agnue and her highbrow traditionalists. I liked who I thought I was.

No, the reason her vicious words had shimmied their way inside my brain was because she'd hammered at a notion that had been simmering in the back of my mind since my confrontation with Lady Agnue. What if who I *thought* I was wasn't an accurate reflection of the truth?

I went around every day talking the talk and walking the walk of a girl who thought she could be strong enough to be a hero, unique enough to decide her own path, and confident enough to still represent as a princess even if her own version of the role was unorthodox. But what if this wasn't really the case? What if—in spite of my best efforts—I didn't have any such control over who I was? What if, in the end, my parameters were already set in stone by Lady Agnue, the Author, and everything and everyone else in this world whose regulations and ideas for my identity seemed to take precedence over my own?

I couldn't help but self-consciously touch the silver, pumpkin-shaped accessory on my left ear.

While I was always skeptical about the somewhat cheesy double meaning my mom had placed on the earrings—as Mauvrey had so accurately narrowed in on—there was a small part of me that had always hoped there was some truth to it. That I, in fact, could change into something more despite how the world saw me now.

Whether that hope was a foolish or a fair one though, I was never entirely sure.

"I'm waiting," Mauvrey said tersely—interrupting my moment of introspection.

She was clearly expecting me to attempt some sort of

zinger to top her comment. But, for once I didn't have one. I was at an absolute loss for any such sass as I was still recovering from the blunt coldness of her perfectly targeted hit to my self-esteem. Of course I couldn't very well let her know that.

"Umm, well . . ." I stalled, as I waited for a retort to dawn on me.

Think. Think. Come on.

Ooh, got one!

"Truth be told, Mauvrey, I'm going to have to get back to you on that. How 'bout I mull over comebacks with Chance next time he asks me to dance at a ball and then give you my response? I'll just look for you over on the sidelines with all the other girls who couldn't attract dance partners."

Mauvrey's face reddened and she opened her mouth to retaliate. Although, before she got the chance to voice her own comeback, Madame Whimsey blew on her harmonica to get our class's attention.

"Ladies, ladies," she sang in perfect pitch. "Let us all take our seats and begin this morning's examination please."

"This is not over," Mauvrey spat as the other students began to migrate through the expansive garden toward its epicenter.

I shrugged coolly. "I didn't think it was."

She shook her head at me, amused. "It is 'did not,' Crisa. Princesses, even wannabe princess like you, do not use contractions. Or are you so beyond help that even that itty bitty rule cannot get through your head?"

"Maybe I just like breaking the rules. You should try it sometime; it might make Chance like you better. Worked for me."

I gave her a cocky wink at that, which infuriated her even more. With no time left to continue our verbal sparring match, Mauvrey angrily turned on her heels with another hair toss and headed toward her seat with Jade close behind.

Pleased to have effectively thwarted my nemesis's attempts at further harassment *and* ticked her off in the process, I smiled and went to take my seat as well.

I gotta say, while I don't necessarily encourage having archenemies, foiling them can be pretty darn fun.

Returning from the forest where she'd been feeding the birds, SJ joined me on the white marble bench that served as our shared desk. "I saw you speaking with Mauvrey," she whispered as she sat down.

"Speaking is a loose term," I whispered back as I swatted a bee that appeared to be confusing the pleated red dress over my black leggings for a large flower. "It was more like the teenage girl equivalent of a grenade battle."

"She did seem quite angry," SJ agreed.

"I gave her a reason to be. She came over to try and mess with my head so I rubbed in the fact that her super shallow prince charming dumped her like yesterday's fairy dust for me at the ball."

SJ shook her head disappointedly. "Crisa, that was not very nice. Mauvrey might actually have real feelings for Chance."

"SJ," I moaned under my breath. "*She* started it."

"Yes, but *you* finished it. Crisa, I know you do not like to back down from a fight, but perhaps next time you should try lowering your guard momentarily so as to give Mauvrey a chance to be something better. Taking a pause to display restraint like that is not showing weakness; it is showing strength."

"Maybe so, but if you lower your guard that way and end up being wrong about a person, you've given them a free a pass to take you down."

"Good morning everyone," Madame Whimsey sang, halting our conversation. "Quiz day is upon us and as per tradition I shall now pick from a hat the name of the princess who will be going first on this beautiful day. I am so looking forward to being soothed by the sounds of each and every one of your sweet singing voices."

She dipped her hand inside of an obnoxiously yellow beret and drew out a name.

"Crisanta Knight . . ."

"So much for soothing sounds," Mauvrey commented intentionally loudly.

A few girls in the class snickered and I wrung my hands uneasily. Madame Whimsey hushed them as I took a deep, calming breath.

SJ patted me on the shoulder for support. A moment later I took take my place in the spot of shame at the front of the class. Everyone was looking at me, some with amusement like Mauvrey and Jade, some with sympathy like SJ and our professor. I grimaced.

Oh, this was going to suck.

As it would happen though, the fates took pity and chose to save me from the embarrassment of damaging my classmates' eardrums. A common protagonist, Lisa Taylor (a friend of Blue's actually), suddenly came running through the garden calling out to Madame Whimsey.

Lisa was out of breath when she reached us. We had to wait for her to stop panting before she could explain what was so urgent.

"Madame Whimsey. SJ and Crisa are wanted in the infirmary," she finally said. "It's Blue. She got her pang. It was bad."

SJ and I burst through the infirmary doors.

The room we entered was beige and lacked character of any kind. Frankly, the smell of anti-bacterial soap that filled the air was probably the space's most charismatic quality.

I spotted Blue lying on one of the far cots that lined the wall. The nurse was attempting to put a cold compress on her head, but Blue kept swatting her away, refusing to be tended to. As we approached, the nurse huffed indignantly and stomped away, muttering something about foolish pride.

When Blue saw us her scowl faded into an expression of defeat that I had never seen on her before. Her eyes were foggy and warbled like a pond hammered by rain, and her face looked completely drained of heart and soul. This morbid appearance did not give any cause for elaboration on her part, though. One look at the spiral mark temporarily burned into her forehead and we all knew what had happened. Her prologue prophecy had appeared.

Several moments of silent understanding passed between the three of us before SJ gathered up the courage to ask Blue the question hanging in the air.

"So . . . has Lady Agnue read it to you yet?"

"Yeah, you just missed her," Blue responded distantly.

Our friend slowly began to sit up and tuck her hair behind her ears. As she did so, I noticed that her cloak was splotched with mud and that she had several large scrapes on her arms as well as the bluish beginnings of a bruise on the right side of her head.

When SJ and I inquired about the injuries, Blue told us

that she had been climbing one of the large magnolia trees by the practice fields when her prologue pang had occurred.

As noted, neither SJ nor I could really describe what the onset of such a pang felt like, having never experienced one for ourselves. But, based on what we'd heard and seen from our classmates who had, it was supposedly very rough, physically draining, and uniquely intense to the protagonist receiving it. When Marie Sinclaire had gotten hers, for instance, she'd described it as a shower of hammers hitting her various limbs all at once while her heart jolted her about like a possessed rag doll.

Lovely, right?

Anyways, that explained Blue's injuries. Having a spasm like that when you were climbing a tree was way less than ideal.

As it turned out though, Blue actually considered herself lucky. She was only about twenty feet up in the tree when it hit her, rather than all the way at the top. And, while the pang had been fairly strong and knocked her out of the tree, she'd been able to rally enough consciousness to claw and grasp at its branches to break her fall on the way down.

Still, despite the fact that she described the experience as fortunate, she was clearly banged up pretty badly. Then again, I gathered that with someone like Blue, the bruise on her ego from being taken to the infirmary was a lot more upsetting than the actual bruises she'd received.

After some awkward silence I got the nerve to ask her what SJ and I were subsequently dying to know.

"Well, what did it say?"

Blue sighed lengthily. "Well, as expected it was pretty vague. But the general gist is that I am going to go on a really dangerous adventure with a lot at stake. I'll be involved in a monster fight at some point, and am supposed to unite some people. My varied skill sets will be useful along the way. I, uh, will make certain decisions that will either save or destroy a few people, and . . ."

Blue's eyes darted away from us and I saw my friend's face twist into another unusual expression for her character. It looked like pain.

"Blue, what is it?" SJ asked.

"Jason . . ." she said sadly.

Then, suddenly, she shook off whatever burden had been plaguing her and a scowl crossed her face. "I'm supposed to end up with Jason," she said angrily as she banged her fist onto the cot's bedside table. "I can't believe it. I mean it's him and only him, non-optional and non-negotiable. What in the heck am I supposed to do with that?!"

Blue started to rant about how enraged she was, how her identity was no longer hers to define, that it was unfair she really couldn't do anything about it, and—most importantly—how she would love nothing more than to wring the Author's neck right about now.

I could totally sympathize with how she felt. Moreover, I still couldn't believe this had actually happened to one of us. It was real now. The thing we'd each been dreading, but ignoring our entire lives had claimed Blue. Her fate had been taken out of her hands.

I was sure she was at least a little relieved that her prophecy was not a ridiculously dull or passive sentence. It did say she would have an intense adventure that would utilize her skills, and a monster fight (which I was sure she was already looking forward to).

Even so, the rest was of it was way more than unsavory. Making decisions that would save or destroy people was a lot of pressure, sure. But no longer having a say in who you would end up with was an absolutely awful notion. Jason was a good guy and everything, and a friend, but no one should've been forced to spend their lives with someone they didn't pick out for themselves.

Furthermore, Blue was Miss Independent! She prided herself on the fact that she didn't need to rely on others. She was feisty and untamable and an adventurous free spirit. So the Author telling her that she had to be with one specific person forever was as intolerable an idea as it was a depressing one. Because, not only did it mean she was virtually shackled to the boy for the rest of eternity, it also implied that no matter how hard she'd worked to define who she was on her own terms up 'til now, she was still at the mercy of pre-ordained destiny. None of her fighting had made a difference in the fate she'd been assigned.

And if that was the case for a girl as strong as her, what hope was there exactly for someone like me?

"I'm so sorry, Blue," I managed to muster after some time had gone by. "I wish . . . I wish there was something we could do."

"Me too," she said bitterly. "But wishing doesn't change anything, now does it?"

CHAPTER 7

Snow White & The Seven-Minute Study Break

*P*rincesses should not have to be stuck doing homework at ten o' clock at night. That's my humble opinion, at least.

Barely a month into the school year, the pile of required reading books on my nightstand was so tall I could've constructed a city for SJ's bird friends outside. It was like our teachers had a bet going over who amongst them could obliterate the most of our free time.

I had a research paper on Thumbelina due Thursday for my Fairytale History class. Friday I had a presentation on "How Saying Less is More" in D.I.D. (that oddly enough had to be at least twenty minutes long). Even my Animal First Aid elective, which I'd actually been doing fairly well in, was kicking it up a notch.

I mean, how was I supposed to learn how to suture a wound on a deer's leg by next Monday? It's not like I could very well go shoot one in the forest and get it to hold still while I tried.

Presently, I was sitting on my bed leaning against the golden headboard with a textbook open to some miscellaneous chapter on my lap.

Past the recollection of a few random terms like "Stiltdegarth" and "Shadow Guardian" though, I couldn't have told you what the pages of said text covered. Honestly, I'd stopped reading around nine o'clock and, despite the masses of homework I had to do, was now far more interested in the pile of darts sitting beside me.

We had a dartboard taped to the back of our bedroom door because practicing throwing darts relaxed me. SJ thought it was a constructive way to let out aggression and work on focusing my mind on accomplishing my goals. But she insisted we cover it with a poster of a scenic meadow during the day, lest someone catch us with it. Blue, on the other hand, thought it was just a good way to practice aim and suggested that if anyone caught us with it and tried to take it down we could throw the darts at them instead.

As I continued to send one dart after another at the target board, my roommates immersed themselves in far less procrastination-based activities.

Blue was flopped down on her bed pouring over a scattered pile of open literature. If the girl's prologue prophecy was bothering her, it was difficult to tell. Aside from the day it actually appeared, she hadn't shown any signs of dismay. In fact, Blue hadn't mentioned it once since receiving it several weeks ago, and rather seemed to be pretending like nothing had changed in the slightest.

It was a weird reaction for her to have. She was so distraught about the prophecy the day she'd received it that I would have thought she'd be complaining about it nonstop. Even girls at school who were happy with what their prophecies said, tended to speak of nothing else in the weeks immediately following their bestowment. But, for whatever the reason, Blue was staying silent.

Naturally, SJ and I had followed her lead by not bringing up the matter either. We weren't about to rub salt in the wound. Still, the behavior bothered me as I truly didn't know how she could suppress such agony. Out of the corner of my eye, I studied my friend from across the room with both curiosity and concern.

At the moment Blue seemed perfectly content to be absorbed in her plethora of books. Her eyes were currently scanning excitedly across a particularly large, fancy copy with weathered pages and a shiny bronze cover.

To each her own, I guess.

On the other side of the room, meanwhile, SJ was deeply focused on reading her special potions book. Unlike Blue, whose hair resembled a bird's nest the way it was bunched up on top of her head with a large scrunchie, SJ's hair was still tightly and intricately woven behind her. She literally didn't have one hair out of place—even after a full day of school. And while Blue and I had long changed into our pajamas and were spread out on our comforters like cats, SJ remained in her gold-colored day dress and sat with such perfect posture at her desk it would have made statues feel self-conscious.

At that point my unceasingly ladylike best friend got up from her seat and made her way across the room to retrieve a fresh jar of ink from our shared bookshelf. Once she'd passed out of my firing zone I continued to launch dart after dart at our target board. Although, when SJ turned around to head back to her desk, she stopped in her tracks and properly took notice of how I was spending my study hours.

"Crisa," she sighed at my lollygagging. "You are wasting time."

"SJ, I'm working on my aim. That is most certainly not a waste of time," I said, throwing another dart at the board.

It landed just barely outside the vicinity of the bullseye and I scowled at the target in frustration.

"Well, I suppose you do need more practice . . ." my friend said with a hint of teasing in her tone.

SJ walked over to my bed, picked up a dart, and gave me a *"watch and learn"* look. Then she threw it across the room and it landed right in the center of the bullseye. My eyes widened in shock.

"How did you do that?"

"What?" she shrugged. "Can a girl not have other hobbies besides singing to animals?"

I opened my mouth to ask another question, but SJ waved me off before I had the chance. "On to more important matters, Crisa. Practice needed or not, you really should be studying," she chided as she went back to her desk.

"I *am* studying," I retorted as I fired off another dart—trying to replicate SJ's surprising accuracy. "I am studying the art of doing nothing of particular importance. Frankly, I think Madame Lisbon would be terribly impressed; it is very damsel-in-distress behavior. She may even give me extra credit."

SJ was not amused; she took studying, no matter how silly the subject, very seriously. Blue, however, laughed at the remark and seemed to think the budding conversation was worth breaking her homework concentration for.

"You're so right, Crisa," she grinned. "Your level of purposelessness right now is downright exemplary. Madame Lisbon and damsels in distress everywhere would be proud."

SJ's mouth curved into a smile as she shook her head at the both of us. Then she noticed the big, bronze book that Blue had been focusing on so intently.

"Blue, what are you reading?" she asked.

"Oh, um, it's a collection of *Snow White* adaptations from some of the other realms," Blue said as she picked up the text proudly and held it up for SJ to see.

Contrary to what might be expected, Blue was actually a huge fairytale history nut. The irony of it was pretty funny really. While my rebellious friend hated the limitations and absurd consequences fairytales and fairytale life imposed on her, she was absolutely fascinated by them nonetheless.

I guess maybe it was a "knowledge is power" kind of motivation?

Seriously though, you could ask her any question about any version of any fairytale and she would know the answer. With all the research and readings she'd immersed herself in over the years, she probably knew more about the combined trinkets in the Treasure Archives than the majority of the school's staff put together.

"Blue," I chimed in. "Haven't you read *Snow White* about a million times? How interesting could so many adaptations be?"

"Actually, a lot more interesting than you'd think."

"Yeah, okay," I scoffed.

"No really," Blue said eagerly as she sat up and pulled the fat, fancy book onto her lap. "For starters, did you know that, like, all versions of *Snow White* mention the poisoned apple, but only a couple mention the poisoned corset and poisoned comb that the witch tried to use on her first?"

"Well, can you blame them?" I asked sarcastically. "Death by a fashion appliance or a grooming tool is not nearly as exciting as death by fruit."

SJ put the jar of ink on her desk and crossed her arms.

"Ha ha, Crisa," she chided. "Judge while you can, but

one of these days the Author might just write a story where some enchanted knickknack gets *you* into a great deal of unwarranted trouble."

I smirked and hopped off my bed in response. "Yeah, you're probably right. I'll probably get taken down by something really lame, like a poisoned toe ring or a magic paperweight." I picked up a paperweight from my desk, feigned a fainting spell, and dropped to the floor dramatically. "Total ka– ka– karma," I choked as I pretended to die.

I opened my eyes and grinned at my friends.

Blue was laughing openly, snorts and all. SJ had her hand to her mouth—trying to stifle her "unladylike" guffaws. But after a moment she couldn't hold them in any longer either and laughter burst from her like water from a dam.

"Knowing you, you won't need the Author to write you into trouble, Crisa. You're fully capable of getting into it on your own," Blue joked, shaking her head.

I picked myself up from the floor, dusted off my fluffy, green pajama pants, and plopped down on my friend's bed beside her. "Thank you, Blue. I both appreciate and resent that. Anyways, sorry I interrupted. You guys both have my total attention now. Tomfoolery aside, SJ, what does your mom have to say about this whole comb-corset-poison business?"

"Well," SJ began, "my mother told me that, like the apple, the corset and the comb were both products of dark magic. But more than that, they were each enchanted via a potion to look so beautiful and appealing that, if you got close enough, they would make you want to use them even if common sense dictated otherwise."

"Like high-heeled shoes," I suggested.

"Exactly," SJ continued. "However, while the effects of the apple could not be reversed because she had ingested it, the deadly magic of the other objects could be. The comb's venomous, magical powers easily wore off when it was removed from her hair, and the corset's poison shut down when it was unfastened. So unlike the apple, which required true love's kiss to reverse, these were all relatively easy spells to break. Bear in mind, though, my mother was still lucky to survive them."

"Why's that?" Blue asked SJ, her eyes as big as croquet balls with excitement. She was a sucker for a good story. And this was, after all, a classic.

"Well, simple to break or not," SJ said reluctantly, "a person only has so much time to be saved from that kind of dark magic. If a spell's window of opportunity closes and no one has come to the rescue, the poison finishes the job and . . . kills them."

The atmosphere turned ominous and somber then. No one spoke for a few minutes as we reflected on the seriousness of SJ's story.

In retrospect, it was easy to joke about seemingly silly things like death by an apple, a shoe made of glass, or hair so long you could climb it. But, the truth was that ridiculously impossible things happened all the time in life (especially to people like us) and a lot of it really was no joke.

SJ's mom was almost killed multiple times by her crazy, jealous, former beauty-queen stepmother. Blue's sister was swallowed up whole by a wolf and would have spent eternity in his digestive tract with her grandmother if that hunter hadn't come along. And my mother—my kind, patient, couldn't hurt a fly mother—lost both her parents by age nine and, protagonist or no, was treated like an abused shut-in for the majority of her teenage years. Pretty intense stuff when you thought about it.

Meanwhile, here we were. For now, we were just three girls sitting in a room doing homework. But we didn't know how our stories were going to turn out. Blue had already gotten her prophecy and was trying to process the loss of control she had over who she was. And any one of us could've been next.

In truth, none of us knew what travesties or tragedies would shake up our lives in the years to come, or even when. Sitting here, waiting for some higher power to tell us what came next—it felt like we were all just biding time.

Thoughts like this hung in the air a little while longer as we temporarily allowed the fears of the future we normally suppressed to creep from the corners to the forefronts of our minds. Thankfully though, SJ abruptly broke the silence a minute later—forcing back the depressing atmosphere like sunshine driving away an embankment of fog.

"Blue, did you know that not one *Snow White* adaptation gets the names of the dwarves correct?" she stated matter-of-factly.

"No way," Blue countered, her mind snapping back to the present as she started flipping through the bronze book like a madwoman.

"No, really," SJ went on excitedly. "Their real names are: Fred, Joe, Jamie, Mike, Bill, Stan, and Alejandro."

"You're making this up," Blue insisted as she kept turning the pages in her book— frantic at the possibility of not knowing everything about everything.

I couldn't help but smile as I listened to them argue.

Only Blue was bold enough to literally challenge Snow White's daughter on *Snow White*—a challenge she seemed to be relishing by the way. And as SJ lectured her on how ludicrous an idea it was that anyone, even dwarves, could have adjectives for first names, my fears and worries were once again pushed to the back of my mind where they belonged.

It was good to have friends.

CHAPTER 8

Something Fishy

reedom!

Well, temporary, restricted freedom . . . but freedom nonetheless.

Midway through fall semester the cumulative student body of Lady Agnue's and Lord Channing's customarily took a joint field trip to one of the two kingdoms by the sea. It was a week-long venture intended to be an opportunity for our schools to bond and for us students to learn about diplomatic relations.

That was all fine and dandy by my account, but what I was looking forward to was a few days away from this ivory-towered prison.

It was quite a sight really—the dozens and dozens of carriages lined up in the school's driveway. The In and Out Spell had been lowered earlier in the day and now our entire school entranceway was more clogged than rush hour in Century City.

Pairs of horses in armor so intricate you'd think they were war heroes stood in front of each vehicle. Unlike the richly colored carriages, the horses were all white—standard issue for protagonists. In the distance I also saw several massive livestock carriers following our parade along with sixty armed knights on black horses spaced out amidst the whole fleet.

Overkill much?

SJ, Blue, and I patiently waited for our carriage to arrive. Mauvrey and I had already exchanged insults that morning. And, while she had probably won that round, the three of us were now being thoroughly entertained by the embarrassing scene my nemesis was causing on the front lawn. Evidently her carriage was the wrong shade of pink and clashed with her luggage.

From across the crowd, Jason and Daniel spotted us and started to make their way over. This was the first time Blue had seen Jason since receiving her prologue pang, so SJ and I watched her steadily as they approached, waiting to see how she would react. Surprisingly though, there was no measureable reaction at all. She greeted him like nothing was different and the two exchanged their typical high five.

Hm. I guess if she can keep it together with her new boyish-obstacle, so can I. Daniel and I did have some kind of truce going, right?

"Hello, Daniel," I said when he reached us.

Daniel nodded his head toward me. "Knight."

This seemingly ordinary exchange actually got more of a rise out of Blue than her meeting with Jason had. Her eyebrows shot up with curiosity.

"Whoa, whoa, whoa," she interjected. "What's going on? What happened to this great rivalry I've been hearing so much about? Crisa said you guys couldn't stand each other."

"Blue!" I objected.

"Oh, come on. I was super stoked to see the two of you duke it out."

"Well, sorry to disappoint but Daniel and I have declared

a truce," I said, although it came out as more of a question than a statement.

Daniel confirmed it with a shrug—apparently still as surprised as I was that it had managed to last even this long.

"I give it a week," Jason chimed in.

"I give it a day," Blue countered.

On that note, a guard with the roster called out Daniel and Jason's names. Their carriage was ready and it was time for them to go. They said their goodbyes and departed, planning to meet up with us when we'd arrived at our destination.

To my displeasure Chance Darling chose that moment to detract from my day even more than my awkwardness with Daniel or snaps of spite with Mauvrey had. The prince headed toward us—strutting with confidence like a peacock that was all too proud of his feathers. I gagged and braced myself for whatever condescending, annoying dribble was about to come out of his mouth.

Chance smiled and bowed his head to acknowledge me and my friends. "Crisanta, you look lovely today," he commented.

True that. Between my gray, lace-up heeled boots, matching leggings, and long-sleeved mint dress with silver sparkly belt accentuation, I did look pretty poppin' this morning.

But that was aside from the point. Any compliment out of Chance's mouth was a waste. And I'd put money down that it was just a jump and a skip away from an irritating follow-up comment.

"What do you want, Chance?" I asked bluntly.

"Crisanta, my dear, it is your lucky day. I have decided to give you another opportunity to be mine. There is an empty space in my carriage. Please join me."

Aw, there it is.

I rolled my eyes dramatically and both my friends gave Chance a look that said, "*Seriously?*"

Well, that's what SJ's look translated to at least. Blue's was probably something more akin to, "*Just give me one more reason and I will punch you between the eyes.*"

"Thanks," I responded dryly. "But I think I'll pass."

"Crisanta, dear, my request was not intended to be optional."

"Chance, *dear,*" I chirped—mocking his tone. "My response was not intended to be negotiable. Yet here we are."

Frustration did not suit Chance's chiseled features very well. His brow wrinkled and his mouth scrunched up like a disturbed clown. After a beat he seemed to realize my position on the subject was unmovable, though. In response, he took a deep breath and bowed again.

"Very well," his highness remarked. "But you should know, Crisanta, I *always* get what I want. Eventually even you shall succumb to my charms."

Chance turned on his heels and we watched him walk away just as unapologetically and ever-confidently as his former girlfriend—Prissy Princess Mauvrey—always did. Who, by the way, I noticed out of the corner of my eye was currently giving me another one of her world famous death glares from the other side of the driveway.

I paid my clearly jealous mortal enemy no mind. Instead my attention was re-captured by Chance. Or rather, by Blue's gagging at the sight of the girlie sycophants that soon surrounded him anew—drawn to his sea foam green eyes like moths to a super obnoxious flame.

"Please let me throw a rock at him," she huffed in disgust.

I laughed and patted her on the shoulder. "Maybe next time."

An hour later, we were heading west through the scenic countryside.

It was an absolutely gorgeous autumn day. Most of the forests we passed through were oblivious to the changing season and retained the lush evergreen colors they were known for in storybooks. My friends and I kept the side windows of our carriage open to fully admire this scenery we so seldom got to enjoy, and to take in the fresh, chilled air along with it.

For most of the journey the three of us chatted and played carriage ride games, including Enchanted Forest Bingo and, SJ's favorite, Name That Potion.

To her dismay we had forbidden Blue from playing her favorite game, Punch-Carriage. This may have seemed mean on the surface, but it was a justifiable course of action. When we'd made this trip last year she'd picked the color beige and whenever a carriage of that color had driven by, she'd responded by jabbing one of us in the arm without exception or delicacy.

Let me tell you, there are a lot of beige carriages out there.

Ergo, a veto of the game seemed appropriate unless we wanted to arrive at our destination covered in bruises. Again.

Thankfully, Blue got over our, quote, "fun-sucking decision" relatively quickly and enjoyed the ride with us nonetheless.

We had a fairly pleasant time for the majority of the trip, until the peculiar incident that occurred when we were crossing the border into the kingdom of Adelaide that is.

SJ was in the midst of going over last spring's copy of the *Century City Summit Review* for the eightieth time, which, personally, I thought was a complete waste. This year's second summit was in about a month, so a new issue would've been coming out soon anyways.

Did she really have to be so darn responsible *all* of the time?

While my overly studious friend perused her totally outdated periodical, Blue was busy showing me how to weave a net large enough to catch a bear. Some girls packed books or games for road trips; she packed rope. That was Blue for you.

I had to say, it was pretty cool. Her ropes class had lent each of its students a ball of enchanted yarn that, when activated with three tight squeezes, instantly transformed into forty feet of climbing rope.

Awesome, right?

I guess my instincts had been spot on—that class really would have been more fun than Singing with Nature.

Unfortunately, my net lesson with Blue was interrupted by the abrupt halt of our carriage just as we were about to enter Adelaide. Something had cut across our path and the driver had barely had time to stop—leading me to slide off the edge of the seat I'd been precariously perched on.

I popped back up and joined SJ at one window while Blue peered out the other.

We were separated from the stream of traffic on the other side of the road's intersection. The quick stop had thrown off the vehicles behind us too—causing horses, passengers, and drivers alike to become extremely disgruntled.

After looking out the window for a beat, the three of us realized the reason why the border's crossing guard had not permitted our vehicle to continue. A prison carriage was passing in front of us.

The prison carriage was starkly different from our own method of transport. It was gray and plain. The windows were barred with thick steel poles and the doors had heavy padlocks on them. The whole eerie thing was being pulled by several horses that were black as night and perfectly matched the colors of the sheaths and crossbows worn by the knights riding them.

Our fleet of protagonist-wielding carriages was being escorted by similarly colored knights, weapons, and horses; it was true. But these seemed different somehow. The prison knights practically emanated intimidation—weapons gleaming like dark glass, helmets reflecting inky blackness like holes in space, and horses whose hooves clattered against stone like crackles of lightning.

I studied them and the portable prison they were charged with—no doubt on the way to Alderon to permanently deposit its passengers within the boundaries of the kingdom's one-way In and Out Spell.

"Magic hunters," SJ whispered in my ear as she, too, eyed the foreboding spectacle.

I nodded in agreement as I watched them go by.

Magic hunters were dangerous, to say the least. Vicious and relentless, they were an ancient group that had been around as long as magic. Each one possessed a crazy sixth sense that allowed him to detect the scent of magic, and a gift for tracking it as well. And they used these abilities whilst traveling the realm to hunt creatures and objects that carried any form of enchantment they could steal.

I was not exactly sure how they went about taking the magic once they'd cornered their targets, but I imagined it couldn't have been pleasant. That, after all, was the reason magical objects were typically kept secret, pixies were always in hiding, and Fairy Godmothers lived at a headquarters that floated somewhere in the sky—constantly concealed in the clouds and always changing location.

From our window, I could see that there were two magic hunters riding inside this particular transport. The farther one was more difficult to make out, but the hunter closest to the window had a long, crooked nose, leathery, tan skin, and wisps of gray hair hanging in his ragged face. I squinted to try and see him more clearly, but when I did it was like he sensed me watching him.

His head spun so quickly in my direction it should have snapped his neck. But it didn't; it only elongated its appearance like an old rooster mid-crow. The hunter immediately locked his cognac-colored eyes with mine. Then he leaned closer to his window so that his face was pressed up against the bars as he inhaled in a deep, disconcerting fashion.

I fidgeted in my chair, reminding myself that he couldn't get out of his carriage.

SJ noticed the hunter's strange behavior and glanced back at me to make sure her eyes weren't deceiving her.

Yup, he was definitely looking at me.

My heart sped up a bit and I felt an odd hole form in the pit my stomach.

The hunter continued staring at me even as his prison transport began to move out of the way. When it had finally gone, and our own vehicle moved forward once more, Blue pointed out the window.

"Was he . . .?"

SJ nodded hesitantly. "Yes."

Blue shifted toward me. "At you?"

Both my friends stared at me now too, waiting for my confirmation. But I didn't give it to them.

"Come on guys, of course he wasn't," I said.

My eyes darted around for an explanation and spotted the enchanted rope on the seat next to Blue. "It must've been the ball of yarn. It's magic, and he probably sensed it," I reasoned.

"He wasn't looking at the carriage in general," Blue insisted. "He was looking at *you*."

I knew she was right. But acknowledging it would have been way too weird. Plus, if I did admit it, she and SJ surely would've used their supersonic, best friend powers to deduce that I was freaking out about it. Which I definitely was, but didn't want them to catch on to. I mean, what kind of aspiring hero gets all flustered because some creepy guy looks at her funny?

Can you say, damsel behavior?

There was no need to come across that way to my friends. As it stood, they were pretty much the only people who *might* believe I could be something more than that. Giving off the impression that I was so easily rattled would certainly not help the situation.

As such, I swiftly decided that it would be best to shrug off the incident, sweep the matter under the rug and pretend like nothing was wrong in the slightest.

I faked a bemused smile and shook my head. "Please, Blue. Don't be ridiculous. It was the yarn. What other explanation could there be?"

Blah, blah, blah, yak, yak, yak, blah, blah . . . blah.

I didn't know about the rest of my classmates, but that's what I heard while our guest speakers were talking.

It was a few hours later and all Lady Agnue's and Lord

Channing's students were crammed inside of a massive amphitheater at Adelaide Castle. We were supposed to be taking notes and taking advantage of this great lesson in diplomacy, but this lecture had gone about an eternity too long and my attention span was wavering.

Every year our schools' diplomatic field trip was hosted by either Adelaide or Whoozalee (the two kingdoms by the sea) because they represented a perfect model of diplomacy. The reason? Their relations with each other, and their relations with the rest of Book and Mer (the city under the sea) were critical to our realm.

Since these two kingdoms were the only ones with uninhibited oceanic borders, they alone shared the responsibility of fairly controlling the fishing trade for our entire realm. Meaning they had to indefinitely respect borders, regulate fishing restrictions, and maintain peaceful relations with the mermaids of Mer who were apparently super temperamental, and none too pleased about having to share their ocean in the first place.

Basically to sum up, these guys were experts in diplomacy.

I knew I really should've been paying attention. Understanding that kind of political mumbo jumbo was a key aspect of being royal. Then again, how many hours could a human being truly listen to a lecture about fishing?

"Lara, Lila, Lonna, Lita, Lindsey, Lauren," the speaker in the seashell necktie on stage continued to lecture.

"What's he going on about?" I whispered to Blue, who was sitting between me and Jason.

"Langards," Blue said under her breath.

"Man guards?" I repeated back.

"No," Blue whispered a bit louder this time. "*Langards.* Mer's royal family."

I nodded and pretended like I knew what she was talking about.

The guy on stage with the seashell necktie suddenly bowed and people began to clap. I clapped too—thankful the speech was over and that we could go to lunch. I assumed we would be having fish. I liked fish.

A little lemon, some tartar sauce, maybe a side of bread . . .

My stomach made an audible rumbling noise at the thought. SJ, who was seated to my left, evidently heard the noise and glanced at me in shock. My face turned red and I clapped louder to drown out the embarrassing, un-princess-like sound.

When the applause died down I readied myself to get up but, instead of dismissing us, our headmistress introduced someone new—a woman in a royal blue jacket and matching pencil skirt. This woman who proceeded to take the stage was Sarah Steinglass. She was the Adelaide Ambassador and the Book government official in charge of preserving and updating the realm's Sea Silence Laws.

"Thank you, thank you," Ms. Steinglass said. "The Sea Silence Laws were enacted before most of you were born. However, I am proud to be here and discuss specifically why, in the years since their passing, Whoozalee and Adelaide's diplomatic relationship with Mer and the entire realm has improved so dramatically."

Ms. Steinglass had a conflicting air about her. I would've described it as the type of aura a person gave off when they seemed nice, but you couldn't help but feel like they were holding something back. It was as if she had a secret coldness in her nature that she didn't want people to catch onto, so she overcompensated with smiles slightly too big for her face.

Aside from her hollow perkiness, another distinguishing factor about the Adelaide Ambassador was her size. She was pretty short—even from the back of the room that was obvious. Equally apparent was the fact that her voice inherently boomed like it belonged to a person twice her height, allowing her to project even to the farthest corners of the amphitheater.

Despite her generally off-putting persona, I actually wanted to listen to this particular lecture of hers. I didn't know the full story behind the Sea Silence Laws and was truly curious about them.

Sadly, the introduction Ms. Steinglass had given was misleading. Her talk about the aforementioned set of regulations was fairly generic and a lot of those basics I already knew.

A long while back the Mer-people became very difficult and uncooperative with us land folk. They used their undersea magic on humans that made them upset, entranced sailors with their siren voices to sink ships for sport, and cut fishing lines whenever they felt like it. As a result, over time the Sea Silence Laws were put into place in order to separate us from them as much as possible.

Basically, it worked like this. The ocean was divided into certain sections that we humans could not sail out on and sections that the Mer-people could not swim into. Simply put, the sea was divided in two parts: the area within fifty miles off the coast was traditionally ours and the deep waters—anything past that—was Mer-people territory.

The other key aspect of the Sea Silence Laws was that Mer-people and humans were forbidden from speaking to one another. *Like at all.*

It was kind of harsh if you asked me. Honestly, I couldn't

believe the Adelaide royal family even tolerated it. The queen, after all, was the famous little mermaid princess who once fell in love with, and eventually married a human prince—her husband, the present king of Adelaide.

I supposed the two of them must've caused quite the scandal back in the day when they first got together, since there were literally, like, a zillion government-mandated laws against it. Although, given that they'd managed to stay a couple I figured that true love really could conquer all.

Anyways, more to the point, after their union our hydrodynamically designed heroine and her prince lobbied for years to try and get the Sea Silence Laws overturned. But to no avail. With the endorsement of the Fairy Godmothers, the ambassadors of the other kingdoms voted against repealing the laws time and time again.

Nevertheless, the king and queen valiantly continued to fight the good legal fight over the years no matter how many times their efforts were shut down. Well, until their daughter disappeared, that is . . .

It was super tragic really, and it remained the greatest unsolved mystery of our realm. Princess Ashlyn had been a Legacy at Lady Agnue's—a royal and the eldest daughter of everyone's favorite aquatic protagonist. She was a few years older than me, so I'd never had a class with her at school and had only ever seen her in passing. But people said she was the sweetest girl you'd ever meet on land or sea. Not only that, but she was also quite gifted. Due to the genetic combination of her parents, she was born with a special set of powers—breathing underwater and the ability to swim at incredibly fast speeds.

Like a mermaid with two legs instead of a fishtail, or just a super cool, ocean-oriented human.

However you see it, it's a pretty epic princess power. Unlike my own princess powers of sass, snark, and screech-singing. Which (let's face it) are far from being worthy of admiration.

Sadly, this princess's story did not end as magically as her abilities or bloodline would have suggested. One night about a year and a half ago when she was home from her final year at Lady Agnue's for Spring Break, Ashlyn vanished without a trace. No clues, no witnesses, nothing. She just flat-out disappeared.

Both the entire realm and the entire ocean were searched for months on end. But she never turned up. Nor did any solid evidence of what had happened to her. All the Godmothers in charge of the investigation found were a fanny pack with Ashlyn's name embroidered on it at the bottom of the ocean thirty miles off the coast, and a trail of footprints outside her bedroom that disappeared when they reached the edge of the cliffside. Beyond that, though, absolutely nothing. Whatever must've happened to Ashlyn that night at sea was shrouded in as much mystery as it was morbidity.

Everyone had their own theories about what fate had befallen the princess in the depths of the ocean. Personally, my money was on a shark attack. Which I felt bad even thinking, seeing as how that would've been a pretty awful way to go for such a nice person.

I couldn't even begin to imagine what kind of affect all this had on the king and queen.

My eyes wandered over to the far left side of the stage where the rulers of Adelaide and Whoozalee were seated.

The human queen of Adelaide sat in her throne—no longer a mermaid, and certainly no longer little. Instead she seemed old, tired, and more mortal than most. Her formerly bright, flowing hair was pulled back tightly in a restrained up-do with a tiara constructed of gold and seashells. Her facial expression was blank. And even from my nosebleed seat in the amphitheater I could see the emptiness in her deep blue eyes.

No. It was clear she was never the same after losing Princess Ashlyn.

She and the king did have another daughter—Princess Onicka. The young princess was seven years old now and apparently had the same powers as her older sister. Of course, it was not like she was ever allowed into the ocean to use them. This was partly because of the Sea Silence Laws, but anyone sane knew that it was mainly because her parents would never let her out of their sights.

The tiny, auburn-haired Onicka presently sat in a mini-throne next to the queen. She fidgeted relentlessly and was clearly bored and wishing she were elsewhere. I could relate.

I shifted my attention back to center stage.

Good grief, was this women really still talking?

I just had one of the longest mental tangents ever and the end of Ms. Steinglass's speech didn't seem to be anywhere in sight. As a consequence, my vision and mind began to grow blurry.

Yes, in retrospect it was a bit rude of me to nod off in the middle of someone's presentation. But in my defense, I had held on for as long as possible.

My ill-timed nap was short and filled with choppy dreams. I kept seeing all these small, different-colored Xs popping up against a white backdrop. There were blue ones, yellow ones, and red ones, and their numbers were multiplying quickly—eliminating the empty areas across the washed out background of my subconscious.

The space of my dream was almost entirely filled with their various colors when one, sole black X appeared in the center of the dreamscape. It was the same size as the others at first. But then it began to grow larger and larger, moving at an angle that made it seem like it was headed straight toward me. In fact, I was almost certain that the now giant, black X was about to crash into my metaphysical face when suddenly—

SMACK!

No, the X in my dream had not actually hit me, but someone else certainly had. I woke up from the jolt of the impact at the back of my head and discovered that people were beginning to file out of the auditorium. My friends stood around me with bemused, surprised expressions on their faces. I looked at them, perplexed, rubbed the base of my skull where I had been struck, and turned around to find its source. Daniel was standing in the row behind me with his eyebrows raised and his smirk aimed in my direction.

"Did you hit me?" I asked in disbelief.

"You were asleep and it was time to go. Somebody had to wake you up."

"I can't believe you hit me in the head!" I hopped up from my seat—my cheeks hot with anger and embarrassment.

"Calm down, Knight. It was more like a friendly swat."

"Oh yeah? Well in that case, come here. Let me give you a little friendly swat in return."

"I told you their truce wouldn't last a day," Blue said to Jason. "I win."

"It only counts if she hits him back," Jason clarified.

"Fight, fight, fight," Blue chanted under her breath, egging me on.

SJ, however, swiftly intervened before the situation could

escalate to that. "Relax, Crisa," she said as she patted my shoulder. "He did not mean anything by it. Besides, you can get him back later. It is lunchtime."

Lunchtime?

My stomach growled again and I decided that for now I would practice restraint for the sake of my hunger.

"Fine," I huffed as I walked past SJ and into the aisle. Then I glared at Daniel. "But smack me again and you're gonna need a whole lot more than a row of chairs to ward off what you've got coming."

I ended up being wrong; we had chicken-fried-steak for lunch, not fish.

Go figure.

When mealtime was over, my classmates and I were escorted out to the cliffside for an outdoor lecture on Adelaide's economic structure.

It was a bit messed up that we didn't get to go down to the actual beach, but the guards insisted that it was against Sea Silence Law policy for any unauthorized personnel or fishermen to be that close to the ocean.

Which to me, of course, translated as a challenge to find a way to get down there later despite that.

SJ hung out with me at the back of the group during this particular portion of our itinerary. It was unusual for her to sit so far away from an instructor. Just as it was unusual for Blue to be sitting toward the front with Jason and Daniel. The only classes she ever sat up front for were the fairytale history ones. Yet, there she was.

I watched her pass a note to Jason, which he read quickly when our teacher wasn't looking. He tried to suppress a laugh at whatever joke Blue had shared with him and then scribbled something back to her in return.

SJ leaned close to my ear. "Crisa?"

"Hmm?"

"You know I am not the type to pass judgment on others, but does Blue's behavior strike you as odd?"

I figured she must've been observing Blue too. Which was a bit of a relief to be frank, because I was beginning to wonder if maybe it was just me who was weirded out by how our friend had been acting.

"Yeah, I know exactly what you mean," I whispered back. "Nothing against Jason, but I thought she would loathe him now, or at the very least be distancing herself from him. The idea of prologue prophecies in general ticks her off. Now that she has a specific one of her own to hate, you'd think she'd be rebelling against it."

"I agree," SJ stated slowly. "Jason is a wonderful boy, but knowing Blue, it is a wonder she has not broken his jaw with one of her right hooks by this point."

I shrugged. "Maybe your nagging has finally gotten through to her and she's replacing her anger with kindness."

"Do you really believe that?"

"Not even a little. But it's all I've got. Anyways, I would think you'd be proud of the way she's handling the situation. Why do you seem just as worried as me?"

"Crisa," SJ muttered. "You, Blue, and I may disagree on a lot of things. But you have known me for many years and are well aware that, despite how it may appear, I too wish our lives were different. That we were not forced to live these . . . assigned roles."

I blinked like a startled deer caught in carriage headlights.

I recalled SJ having expressed sentiments like this once

or twice before. Even so, it was kind of easy to forget that she felt that way. She was such a natural princess. And she did such a good job of embracing her designated identity and what was expected of her that, to most people, it would've seemed like she loved every bit of it.

Truth was though, if you got close enough, and paid enough attention, behind her gray eyes you could detect something quite contrary. You could sense the same sadness about our fates that I'd known my entire life. The difference was that she concealed how she felt about it nearly all of the time.

I didn't know if that was bravery, denial, or a bit of both. Either way, in rare moments like these it was nice to be reminded that—despite my extreme lacking in the princess department—my best friend and I still had more important things in common. And, bearing that in mind, I should have always been able to trust her . . .

CHAPTER 9

Mermaids Like Taffeta

O n behalf of all female-kind, I would like to say that a great majority of the most fabulous outfits in the world are super uncomfortable.

At present, SJ, Blue, and I were on our way to attend Friday evening's ball at Adelaide Castle. Ordinarily such occasions did not make me feel particularly excited. However, after a week of fishing talks and dreary guest lecturers that attempted to make up for their lack of charisma with ocean-themed business attire, I was ready for at least some kind of semi-stimulating activity.

Moreover, since neither Blue nor I were given the chance to sneak away and get any combat practice in this week, sashaying about in our epically aquatic outfits was all the action we had to look forward to at the moment.

Which brings us to our ensembles for this evening.

The dresses that had been delivered to our suite earlier this afternoon were both gorgeous and sea-themed. They were also too tight around the waist, long enough to trip on, and itchy in places you didn't want itched. But, in spite of their lack of comfort, the fact remained that they looked nothing short of spectacular.

The gown SJ wore was crème-colored and had a seashell pattern sewn into the lace at the top of the corset and at the bottom of the skirt. It also had a layer of shimmering gold fabric underneath the lace, which made the whole thing glitter like it was made of pure stardust.

Tonight my elegant friend had her hair in a bun, which allowed her to show off the dangling golden earrings she was wearing to perfectly accent the dress. And her graceful, matching crème-colored shoes—well, they almost made me rethink the boots I was wearing.

Almost.

Blue's dress, meanwhile, was bright turquoise and strapless. It was lovely, but the real stunner was the hairstyle she was sporting. Earlier that day SJ had somehow convinced our rebellious friend to set her hair in curlers. How SJ had managed to accomplish this, I did not know. Blue once said she'd sooner rip out a raven's uvula with her bare hands than go all "salon-girl." Yet, there she was—her natural, dirty blonde waves transformed into such radiant curls that she would've given any princess a straight-up run for her money.

Since we were on the subject, I did concede that my ensemble wasn't half-bad either. The drop-waist, dark seaweed-green gown I had on was beautiful. Its bodice was soft and slimming. The single strap over my right shoulder had black jewels that matched the sparkles on the cuff bracelet clasped to my left wrist. And the flowing skirt cascaded around me with such grace that for a moment it made me question if the dress had been sent to the right girl. Of course, one look at the back of the dress and I knew that it could only be meant for me.

Last week before we'd departed on our trip I had gone to the seamstresses back at Lady Agnue's per usual and requested a dress with a zipper to prevent death via corset strangulation. Alas, I feared whatever comfort had been secured by this month's alteration was counteracted by my dress's fabric.

The stylish gown's remarkable skirt was constructed of several layers of bustled taffeta. As a result, it was extra huge and heavy and completely messed with my equilibrium. Adding to that lack of balance, I was already being a semi-good sport by wearing my fancy, high-heeled ankle boots for this evening's festivities instead of my standard combat ones.

That's a major commitment on my part just so you know. I mean, taking on heels while handling ten tons of taffeta—can you say accident waiting to happen?

As impressive as the dresses were, the ballroom where tonight's main event was being held was even more magnificent than all of our outfits combined. Walking in with my friends twenty minutes later, its grandeur absolutely took my breath away.

I had never seen so many candles in one place. They filled the room with a warm glow that made everything feel as if destiny, or true love—or better yet, fresh pastries—were in the making all around us.

But even these innumerable burning lights could not compare to the ones right above our heads. With an entire ceiling constructed of glass, Adelaide Castle's ballroom offered a crystal clear view of a thousand twinkling stars that gleamed in the night sky like silver confetti strewn across a deep navy tablecloth.

For a moment—just a moment—I breathed in the intoxicating atmosphere.

Countless Legacies at our schools had parents whose fairytales had begun in rooms just like this. Myself included.

As ridiculous as such ideas were to me—love at first sight, wishing on stars, Prince Charming's, and other such nonsense—I would admit that there was something in the air. Something that felt like . . . Oh, what was the right word?

Magic?

I paused and thought on the word.

Hmm. Yes, magic.

That was it.

It felt like magic.

So much so, in fact, that I started to wonder if maybe it wasn't entirely our predecessors' faults that they'd succumbed to stereotypes when trapped within the environment of a classic ball. The glowing energy in the room was clearly having a stronger effect on my classmates than if somebody had spiked the punch. Each one that entered seemed more entranced than the last.

The setting was even making *me* feel all warm and fuzzy inside. And warm and fuzzy were so not two adjectives I used to describe myself. Like ever.

But that's what was happening. At least, that's what I figured was happening given that I was getting a bit dizzy and my hands were becoming hotter the more I thought about the magical atmosphere of this place.

Wait.

Maybe it's not the setting. My hands are actually really hot.

I came out of my ballroom-induced trance in that instant when I realized my fingers felt like they were three thousand degrees. More disconcertingly still, when I turned my hands over, I discovered that my palms were actually pulsing red as if burning from within.

Perhaps I would have (and should have) lingered on this

peculiarity a bit longer, but Blue's nudging me on the arm just then snapped me away from the subject.

"Look's like the she-lion's cornered herself a lone gazelle over by the watering hole."

"What?" I stammered.

"Duh, it's a safari metaphor." Blue shrugged. "Mauvrey's cornering Marie over by the punch bowl."

I turned in the direction that Blue was indicating. Sure enough, my nemesis seemed to be closing in on Marie Sinclaire. It didn't take me long to understand why. Marie was wearing the same purple dress as Mauvrey. Not exactly the same mind you, but similar enough to throw a self-absorbed, spoiled royal girl like Mauvrey into a tizzy.

Unfortunately, our friend Marie appeared oblivious to this oncoming conflict and wandered out of the room without noticing that Mauvrey and her villainous posse were right behind her.

No, gazelle. No!

"I'll be right back," I said as I moved to exit the ballroom.

"Crisa," SJ interceded. "Maybe you should let this one go."

I stopped short. "Come again?"

"Getting involved may not be the wisest thing for you to do here. I mean, do you truly want to get into it with Mauvrey *right now*? Lately, the two of you have been at each other's throats more than usual. Perhaps it would be best if you just kept your distance from her for a while."

I glanced over my shoulder and pondered the idea. But then I shook my head—sure of what I was doing.

"SJ, I can handle Mauvrey. I'm practically conditioned for it. But you know how some of the other princesses are. Marie, for example, is super sensitive. I'd rather it be me that absorbs whatever venom Mauvrey expels rather than someone like Marie, who she might actually hurt."

SJ and Blue looked at one another for a second—both of them clearly confused by my statement.

"The things Mauvrey says don't hurt you?" Blue asked, genuinely curious.

I considered saying no at first, but then flashed back to Singing with Nature class a few weeks ago and remembered Mauvrey's awful words:

"I would just get used to being exactly what you are . . . no amount of Fairy Godmothers or magic is ever going to turn you into something else, Pumpkin."

The statement had rattled me. Moreover, it hadn't been the first time. Mauvrey had been taking shots at my self-esteem for years. And had it not been for my sassy overconfidence and capacity to retaliate with effective zingers, I would've for sure had some kind of nervous breakdown by now.

Even so, none of that seemed to matter at the moment. If anything it was all the more reason to go and help Marie.

"Okay, yeah, the stuff Mauvrey dishes out may sting a bit," I half-heartedly admitted to my friends. "She's been out to get me for a long time, so I ought to know better than anyone. But that's the point. If I can keep anybody else from feeling that way, even if it means putting myself in the line of fire, then I'll do it. I may not be able to stop her from coming after me, but I sure as heck can stop her from going after someone else. And I think that means I have a responsibility to, right?"

I paused and waited for SJ's response. I assumed it would be some sort of lecture about my reckless, self-destructive tendencies, or how un-princess like my behavior was. Much to my surprise though, instead all she gave me was a small, sort of proud smile and a nod of approval.

Huh. Alrighty then.

"So do you want us to come with, Crisa? You know, help you out?" Blue asked as I turned to leave. "I've got a few throwing stars in my bra."

"Nah, I can handle this on my own," I replied. Then I hesitated. "Wait, your dress is strapless, how did you . . . On second thought, never mind. I don't wanna know."

"Oh, wait. I've got something else!" Blue said.

"Blue," I grunted under my breath. "I don't want any weaponry from your bra."

My friend raised her eyebrows. "My dress has pockets too, Crisa." Blue reached inside the folds of her turquoise gown and pulled out a ball of yarn—the enchanted one we'd been practicing with on the carriage ride over. "Remember, three squeezes turns it into rope. Then wrap one of the ends around your pinky finger and it will instantly become a ball of yarn in your hand again."

"I got it, I got it," I assured her as I took the ball of yarn and shoved it inside my left boot. "Thanks, Blue."

"Be careful and hurry, Crisa," SJ added. "Lady Agnue is not here yet and people are still arriving, so you remain permitted to enter and exit the ball freely. But it will not be long before the event officially begins and you know perfectly well that you do not want Lady Agnue to catch you wandering about without permission after that."

"Noted," I said.

And on that piece of advice—with yarn in my boot and feistiness brewing in my gut—I took a deep breath and marched across the ballroom toward the grand west doors.

My hand was inches from their handles when I felt someone's fingers graze my arm. Without logical reasoning, I cringed from the touch and pulled away. Although, when I turned around, I realized that my first instinct had been spot on.

"Chance."

"Crisanta."

I didn't know what was more irritating—the prince's relentless pursuit of me, or his inability to look anything less than perfect.

Shouldn't there be some kind of cosmic rule that says if you're that *annoying you at least have to have a bad hair day every once in a while?*

I guess not. Because Chance Darling had been getting on my nerves something fierce as of late, yet in an all of our exchanges he'd never looked anything less than a ten.

Make no mistake; verbally kicking him in the shin was as natural to me as it was vaguely enjoyable. Nevertheless, I would have been lying if I'd said that it was not slightly more difficult to do when the prince—dressed in his sleek tux— was so close to me. His eyes alone were a force to be reckoned with, especially in the entrancing glow of this ballroom.

And I think he knew it, too.

"Leaving so soon?" he asked as he leaned against the door, blocking my exit.

"Getting some air," I replied.

"You shouldn't wander the castle unescorted, Crisanta. Might I join you?"

"If I wanted to warm up maybe," I said. "Sadly, it's already too toasty in here for my taste, so I don't need any extra *hot air* following me around."

Chance crossed his arms. He looked more smug than

insulted, which perturbed me. I tried to mirror his detached stance. Marie was in trouble and he was blocking my only exit. I needed to terminate this little convo swiftly and the only way to do that was to outmatch him. Verbally, that wouldn't be hard. If shrewd eloquence was a weapon, I felt sure I could have bested any of the heroes and princes here.

Regrettably, what Chance lacked in that department he more than made up for with his self-assured demeanor. Comparing his confidence with mine felt a lot like comparing a house made of bricks to a house made of sticks. Both looked theoretically sturdy from the outside, and could hold up equally well to certain conditions. However, while the former was unshakeable to all assaults, the latter was flawed. If someone found the right weak spot—the hidden, but ever present shortcomings in its design—a strategically placed huff and puff could very well blow it down.

Chance stood up straight and stepped closer to me. "You know you're only prolonging the inevitable," he said.

"Really?" I responded. "Because I think you're only extending the uncomfortable. I don't like you, Chance. Why do you insist on continuing to bother me? Haven't you had enough?"

He sauntered around my left side and leaned his face so close to mine that I felt his breath on my neck.

"Would I be here if I had?"

I turned my head to look him directly in the eyes. His princely charms were strong, but my conviction in this instance was ten times stronger. And I wanted him to know that beyond a shadow of doubt.

While I may not have been as fearless as Blue, as flawless as SJ, or even as self-secure as Mauvrey, the part of my character that knew the difference between something I wanted and something I didn't was as unyielding as steel.

"I'm not like the other princesses, Chance," I said with a slow, hypnotic fluidity to my voice.

"I know," he replied just as slickly.

"Good. But there is still one other thing you need to know about me . . ."

I reached up steadily, grasped his bowtie, and gingerly brought his face so close to mine that there could be no mistaking in his mind ever again that he had any power over me. I leaned in and lowered my voice to a whisper.

"You *can't* have me."

I released him and motioned toward the ballroom behind us as my glare narrowed. "*So. Pick. Someone. Else.*"

At first, Chance seemed a bit flustered by my tactic and my comment. The bemusement in his expression had hardened ever so slightly, and his cheeks were tinged with a touch of redness.

But, a second later he straightened himself, held up his right hand, and casually snapped his fingers. When he did, for a moment his pupils sparked gold like a beautiful, angry reflex.

The flash caught me off guard, so I didn't react in time to pull away before his other hand made contact with the cuff bracelet on my wrist.

The instant it did, the bracelet began to change. Within the blink of an eye the magic that was his inherited birthright spread, causing the accessory to increase in both density and weight as it turned to solid gold. I yanked my hand away protectively—feeling strangely violated, irate, and kind of jealous.

Stupid King Midas. Why couldn't my genetics be laden with magical awesomeness? All I had to show for my fairytale bloodline was a fondness for pumpkins and a talent for cleaning my room that I was ashamed of.

"Nice trick," I commented, rubbing my wrist now that I'd gotten past the initial shock. "Overcompensating for something?"

"I could ask you the same thing," Chance countered. "You're trying too hard to deter my advances, Crisanta. Meanwhile, I can see the classic truth residing behind your stubbornness as clear as glass. I'm a prince; you're a princess. The math is simple; the outcome as novel as, well, a world called Book. Whether you want to admit it or not, our inherent destinies together are a lot like the gold in this bracelet—solid, resistant to corrosion, and a surprisingly strong conductor of *electricity*."

He moved to touch the accessory on my arm again, which felt more like a handcuff now than a bracelet, but I held up my hand to keep him back.

"Except this isn't real," I said.

"What?"

"It's fool's gold," I stated bluntly.

Chance took a slight step back in surprise. I couldn't tell if he was more confused or offended by the accusation. "No it isn't," he replied earnestly.

"It is if it came from *you*," I said.

With that, I unclasped the heavy bracelet and shoved it back at him.

"Here," I continued. "You keep this. I'll keep my heart. And we'll call it even. I don't care what classics you believe in, Chance. But I do know they have no place here. I'm not saying they don't matter at all. Goodness knows we're reminded of their shadow every day. I'm just saying that I'm not going to live in it. Not now. Not ever. And certainly not with you."

I moved for the nearest door and grasped its handle.

"Where are you going?" Chance asked, looking more dumbstruck than I'd ever thought possible.

I glanced back. "Long term? Hopefully forward. For now, this way will do just fine."

I turned my back on the prince and stepped out the door, my heart flushed with satisfaction and my mind sharp with resolute clarity.

Unlike the beautiful place I'd just emerged from, the western hallway connecting to Adelaide Castle's ballroom was dark and deserted.

The students and staff had entered the party through the east wing. Even if they hadn't, anyone with any sense was inside by now—drinking in the room's energy and the complimentary tropical punch—versus out here walking through empty pockets of the castle. The likes of which were kind of creepy if I was being perfectly honest.

To start with, there were the suits of armor. They weren't that different from the ones at Lady Agnue's—shiny, tall, and each holding a weapon of some sort. Nevertheless, at night in the shadows they loomed over the hallway and practically threatened to turn animate should you make a wrong move.

Then there were the curtains. Framing enormous windows, each set was navy, super thick, and some twenty-five feet in length. They hung to the floor—only a good tug away from collapsing like haphazard sandcastles. I kept myself from walking too close to them as I made my way down the corridor, concerned that one might abruptly come down and bury me beneath ten pounds of velvet.

Despite their intimidation, even these droopy drapes could've been considered pleasant in comparison to what they adorned. The blue stained-glass windows lining the pathway before me were vast and iridescent. The cold wind blowing in a few open ones sent a shiver up my spine. And the moonlight streaming through them cast strange, aqua-colored streaks across everything in sight, making me feel like I was the sole fish in a really posh fish tank. A really posh, mildly ominous fish tank with some super unsettling décor . . .

Perhaps in broad daylight, bronze sculptures of coral and a fountain in the shape of a buoy surrounded by seagulls may have been quaint and delightful. But at night they were precisely the opposite: just plain eerie.

I proceeded relatively slowly in the direction of the freaky-looking fountain at the end of the hall, passing each twisted, coral-inspired piece of artwork with precaution.

Weirded out as I was, I kept my eyes and ears peeled for any sign of Marie or Mauvrey. At least until I was about twenty feet away from the fountain and my hands curtly began to burn up again.

For the first few seconds I tried to ignore the feeling. After all, I'd felt the same strange burning sensation in the ballroom just a couple of minutes ago and it had dissipated as rapidly as it had begun. So, naturally, I hoped that it would do the same now. Alas, I was swiftly proven to be very, very wrong.

After ten seconds I had to acknowledge that my hands truly felt as if they were on fire. And it was *not* going away.

Hot!

Hot! Hot! Hot! Hot! Hot!

I ran the rest of the way to the fountain and sat on its edge when I got there—dunking my hands into the pool as fast as I could.

Ahhhh!

I winced as the water attempted to cool the invisible flames emanating from my fingertips. But, regrettably it didn't seem to be helping. To make matters worse, I suddenly lost my balance and slid off the edge.

I would've completely fallen into the fountain had it not been for my quick reflexes. I grabbed hold of one of the bronze seagulls before I hit the water.

Ugh, come on. Get up, get going, and go get Mauvrey, I grunted to myself as I clutched the seagull forcefully—using it as a boost to pull myself up.

On my feet again, I noticed that the water from the fountain had stopped streaming out at some point during the embarrassing episode. Looking around, I discovered that this was because my foot was pressing down on the valve beneath the carpet that connected the fountain to its exterior water source. Consequently, when I lifted my boot off of it a second later, the spouts of water burst with three times more force than they had before.

I jumped back to avoid the geysers, which thankfully did not project at that magnitude for very long since I'd only been standing on the valve for a few moments.

Well, that was close. If I'd still had my hands in the fountain I would've totally gotten—

It dawned on me then that the burning sensation had completely stopped.

I studied my palms, confused. There was not a single sign

of a burn, a cut, or even a leech that would've explained the horrifying feeling that I'd just experienced. It made zero sense. It was just like that first day back at Lady Agnue's. One minute—crazy, nonsensical fire pain. The next—nothing.

The thing was though, if I had to admit it, that day we all came back to school wasn't even the first time this had happened. The same phenomenon had occurred on two separate occasions during the past summer alone—once when my family was visiting the Fabbro Mountains and got attacked by a giant rock monster (*don't ask*) and then again when I'd befriended that disoriented gnome wandering through our castle in late July.

Yeah. Living in an enchanted realm is never dull, is it?

Anyways, if I really thought about it, I could actually remember this whole deal with the short, strange bursts of burning on my hands happening several times in the last few years.

But, while in the past I'd just shrugged off the odd episodes, now that the periods between them were getting shorter I was being forced to concede to the truth. That truth being that this was totally bizarre, definitely not normal, and was seriously starting to freak me out.

Maybe I should tell SJ and Blue . . .

Actually, on second thought bad idea.

It's like with my nightmares. There's a reason why I don't tell my friends all of the details. The less kerfuffled logic behind that being, well, some things about yourself are just better left ignored.

Aren't they?

"Eeep!"

My head spun in the direction of the short-lived cry.

Marie.

I scurried down the rest of the corridor and made a

sharp right turn into a high-ceilinged library. In front of me now was the back side of a much larger fountain with three dolphin statues spouting steady streams of water out of their mouths into the pool beneath them. Directly beyond that structure was Marie, backed up against the edge of the fountain. And some twelve feet across from her was the enemy I sought.

Mauvrey and her two disproportionate lackeys were glaring down at Marie—the massive window behind them casting their faces in villainous shadow.

"Am I interrupting something?" I asked, tearing the trio's attention away from Marie.

Mauvrey seemed a bit startled to find me there, but flipped her hair and accepted my bid into the showdown nonetheless. "Not at all, Crisa. In fact my friends and I were just having a few words with Marie."

"Yeah. Sure you were," I said as I quickly surveyed the area. "Were those words 'self-centered, self-righteous narcissist,' by any chance? Because those are typically the words that come to my mind during any conversation with you."

Spotting what I was searching for, I moved slowly around to the side of the fountain, stopping just at the edge and strategically planting my foot down in the desired location. Marie shot me a nervous expression as I approached. I gave her a subtle, reassuring smile in return before crossing my arms and readying myself to be disparaged by Mauvrey, who'd been silent for way too many moments now.

"Mauvrey," Jade said, also noticing my enemy's hesitation. "What are you waiting for? Crisa just insulted you. Say something."

"I do not have to," Mauvrey responded coolly to Jade.

Then she focused her line of sight on me in the way a shooter would a bullseye.

"You see, this is merely a game between Crisa and myself," Mauvrey went on. "And while she may enjoy the occasional pull ahead, at the end of the day we both know that she cannot possibly hope to win."

"And why's that?" I countered as I noticed the suit of armor holding a bow and arrow two feet to my right.

Mauvrey curved her lips into a confident grin. "Because I do not play fair." She nodded to Big Girtha, who responded by reaching into her size-a-million dress and pulling out two sets of brass knuckles.

Okay, did I miss the memo on battle-ready bras tonight or something?

I mean, how does that even work?

"I am going to ask you one time out of courtesy," Mauvrey continued as Big Girtha slipped her fingers into the brass knuckles. "Go back to the ball, Crisa. I promise I shall deal with you later. But, for now, this is none of your business."

"See, that's where you're wrong, Mauvrey," I said, unshaken by the threat. "Any time you go too far and cross that line, you make it my business because it falls to me to push you back over. So *I'll* ask you one time out of courtesy. Leave. Marie. Alone."

Mauvrey rolled her eyes. "Oh, please. There are no teachers, no heroes from Lord Channing's, and no annoying friends around to protect you. If I stuck Girtha here on your tail right now, you would need all the luck in the realm to save your callused skin."

Big Girtha crinkled her massive Sasquatch eyebrows as she pointed at me. Then she menacingly punched her right, brass-covered fist into her left palm suggestively.

I glanced again at the adjacent suit of armor and then up at the window immediately behind my nemesis. It sported the same giant, meaty curtains that hung heavily from the windows in the hallway.

"Actually, Mauvrey," I replied, turning my attention back to her. "I don't need protecting, or luck, or saving. All I need is this," I said as I reached under the skirt of my dress and pulled out Blue's ball of yarn. "And just a little more time for build up."

"What is she talking about?" Jade whispered to Mauvrey.

"Good question, Jade," I interjected. "You see, I've been standing on this valve for a couple of minutes now, and I thought it was important that I give it as much time as possible so that the reaction would be big enough when I let go."

Mauvrey tilted her head in confusion. "Wait, what?"

I whipped my head toward Marie. "Duck. Now."

Marie didn't question the command and dropped to the floor as I lifted my boot, which had been forcefully pressing down on the fountain's water valve for some time.

My nemesis and her friends hadn't noticed that the fountain had stopped running for the last two minutes. And now the residual pressure built up from the blockage created an explosion rivaling the biggest geysers of any valley. Each of the three dolphins released enormous bursts of water, which shot straight in the direction of Mauvrey, Jade, and Big Girtha and knocked them completely off their feet and against the window behind.

The immense pressure of the aquatic explosions lasted long enough for me to grab the bow and arrow from the adjacent suit of armor and rapidly tie one end of Blue's yarn to the arrow portion of it.

I hastily squeezed the squishy ball three times—transforming it into rope—and then fired the arrow just as the fountain's water pressure died down.

The arrow pierced the top of the curtains. I grabbed my end of the rope and pulled as hard as I could to rip the sagging drapes from their hooks. Too busy hacking up water and trying to reorient themselves, Mauvrey and her friends did not have time to react when the curtains subsequently fell down on top of them.

My enemies temporarily buried beneath the damp, velvety mess, I wrapped my end of the rope around my pinky finger. A split second later, the ball of yarn reappeared in my fist.

I raced over to Marie and extended my hand to help her up. "Come on. We gotta go."

"Is this the part where we run away?" Marie asked as I yanked her to her feet.

"Marie," I responded as we dashed out of the room. "We are not running away. Running away is for damsels in distress."

We sped around the corner and hastily headed down the hall I'd just come from.

"So what exactly do you call this then?" she panted as she tried to keep up.

"Retreating with purpose," I called back. "Duh!"

"Yeah, but—Ahhh!"

I spun around just in time to see Marie toppling over. Her heel had broken and she was now sitting on the ground in a purple, mushroom-shaped compression of her massive, floofy dress.

I helped the fallen princess up again. Marie took off her heels and held them in her right hand as we made our way back toward the ballroom. Alas, when we arrived at the west doors I'd exited from, I jiggled the handles only to discover they were locked.

"Now what are we supposed to do?" Marie whimpered.

"We'll have to find another entrance. Let's try this way," I said, gesturing to my right. "I think this other corridor might lead to the east wing. We can enter through there."

Marie nodded and followed my lead into the next hallway.

Several staircases, a foyer, and a sketchy wax figurine exhibit later, Marie and I eventually found ourselves in a small observatory. It was pretty dark, but the circular ceiling was glass just like the one in the ballroom so we had the glow of the moon to illuminate our way.

Unlike the ballroom, however, instead of candles, this room was filled with maps of stars and cloud formations. And, in lieu of a spacious dance floor, in the middle of the space sat a large, copper telescope that gleamed in the moonlight like lost treasure.

The metallic, majestic thing was magnificent. But what really caused my eyes to light up was the sight of a very different discovery just beyond the beautiful instrument. On the other side of the room was a door with an actual castle directory!

I cantered up to the helpful, unexpected door hanging and learned we only needed take that door, two flights of stairs, and a hard left turn to arrive at the east wing entrance of the ballroom.

Perfect! I thought to myself as I swung the door open.

"Crisa!"

Not perfect.

Mauvrey was standing at the opposite end of the observatory atop the staircase we'd just ascended. Her blonde hair was a straggly mess and her purple dress dragged soggily on the floor. The seriousness of hatred and—no doubt—thirst for revenge in her eyes was only detracted by the droplets of water that comically dripped off her nose and onto the floor.

She appeared to be alone, but I stepped in front of Marie protectively all the same.

"Hey, Mauvrey. Where'd your hench-girls get off to?"

"We split up to find you," she answered.

"Well, you found me," I said firmly. "Now if I were you, I would turn around and pretend like you didn't."

"Or what?" Mauvrey hissed.

It was actually an interesting question. I didn't have my wand. And even if I did, I wasn't about to *battle* Mauvrey. That would've been ridiculous. We may have been mortal enemies, but I would've never actually hurt her. I drew the line of our rivalry at combat as I assumed she did. That is, when she didn't have Big Girtha around to do her bidding anyways.

"Or . . ." I started to say as I rubbed the back of my neck and stalled, scanning my brain for an idea.

But, as it turned out, for once I didn't need one.

From behind Mauvrey a seagull suddenly bolted up from the stairwell toward the dome of the observatory. He was dark in shade (aside from his bright, golden eyes) and his abrupt appearance startled Mauvrey just as much as it did me and Marie. The only difference was that my nemesis's surprise was greatly extended when the seagull swooped back around and dive-bombed in her direction.

"ARGH!" Mauvrey screeched.

She swatted at the seagull with one hand and tried to protect her head with the other. But it was no use; the bird would not leave her alone. He pecked at her hair, her arms, her dress—eventually causing her to flee back down the stairs shrieking as she attempted to escape its torment.

Now that *I really didn't see coming.*

Marie shot me a shocked expression. "Did you do that?"

I snorted. "Please. I'm good, but I'm not that good."

We both took advantage of this stroke of luck and proceeded on our way. Soon after (thanks to the directory's guidance), we arrived at the set of grand doors we'd been pursuing.

I began to go for their thick, brass handles, but Marie grabbed my arm before I could reach them. "Crisa, I am not sure I can go back in there."

"What are you talking about?" I asked.

Marie plopped down on a bronze bench nearby and let out a weary sigh. "My shoes, they are broken. And just look at my dress; it is bustled in the front so you can completely see my bare feet. You know the rules of female protagonist gatherings—no skirt, no shoes, no service. Lady Agnue will put me on princess probation and kick me out of the ball on sight. That is, if the other princesses do not turn on me and toss me out themselves first."

"Marie, I think you're being a bit overdramatic. The other princesses aren't going to throw you out because you don't look the part."

"How can you be sure?"

"Well, I'm a princess and I don't care."

"Yes, but you are not a *good* princess, Crisa."

I stopped for a second, surprised by the bluntness of her statement. I was a tad insulted and slightly taken aback but mostly, I felt sad because a part of me realized that she might've been right. Whether she was or not though, no sooner did the comment escape her lips did remorse and realization streak across Marie's face.

"Oh, Crisa! I am so sorry! I did not mean that. I was not thinking. I am—"

"Marie," I said, cutting her off. "It's fine. Really. I'm over it."

I forced a smile and gestured for her to hand me the ruined heels. Her face was still rosy with embarrassment from being so candid, so her eyes darted away from mine. Nevertheless, she obliged and gave me the damaged footwear.

At first I considered breaking off the second shoe's heel and fashioning a makeshift pair of flats. Although upon further inspection I understood that there would've been no way to even out the broken heels and prevent a twisted ankle. Maybe if we had been in one of the other hallways I could've used a sword from one of the suits of armor to file it down. But there were no suits of armor in this hall; just more of those stupid, coral-themed art sculptures.

Then I had a thought. Before Marie could object I sat beside her, lifted the massive skirt of my dress, untied my fancy, heeled boots, and then set them on her lap. "There," I said. "One pair of heels. At least technically anyways."

"What, what about you?" Marie stammered.

"I've got other boots in my suitcase upstairs. Don't worry about it."

"No, I mean, what about you *right now*. If you give these to me then it will be you who does not have shoes for the rest of the ball."

"Oh, please. My mother once danced on glass. I'm sure I can handle a few hours in bare feet." I shrugged.

She stared at me, still processing. "Crisa, are you sure?"

"Marie, take them. My dress is long enough to cover my feet so Lady Agnue will never be the wiser. And if any of the other princesses give me trouble, well, I'll see if that seagull's still flying around here somewhere and get him to pay them a visit."

Marie put the boots down and paused for a moment. Then she gave me a huge hug that I didn't think such a fragile-looking girl was capable of.

Never underestimate the infinite power of a good pair of boots, I guess.

I let Marie re-enter the ball a few minutes ahead of me so that we wouldn't draw attention to ourselves by sneaking back in together.

As a result, I found myself alone again and absentmindedly fiddling with the thank you present she'd just gifted to me. Marie had felt so guilty about taking my boots that she'd insisted upon my taking a small token of her gratitude in return. That token had been a pearl bracelet she'd been wearing. It was a bit too fancy and delicate for my taste, but it was lovely, and it was nice of her to offer.

Truth be told though, as I toyed with the accessory my mind wasn't so much reflecting on the sheen of its pearls as it was on what Marie had said:

"But you are not a good *princess, Crisa."*

Marie was sweet, and harmless, and my friend. I knew she hadn't meant to hurt my feelings and was probably going to be beating herself up about it for the rest of the night. Even so, that didn't change the fact that her comment had struck a chord. I found myself still trying to shake off the feelings of self-doubt it had caused as I re-entered the ballroom several minutes later.

I supposed it was silly for me to be upset about the remark. I mean, sure I was not a good princess in the traditional sense. I couldn't sing or dance well, or curtsy unsarcastically. Princes repelled me. Balls bored me. My hands were covered in calluses from sword fighting. And my candor was frank, brass, and without restraint.

But does that really mean that I am not a good princess at all?

I sincerely hoped it didn't. Contrary to what some of my rebellious protests might have indicated, as I'd told Lady Agnue at the start of the semester, I was not opposed to being a princess. I was simply against the idea that it was the only thing I could be. I was fighting to be something *more*, not necessarily something *else*.

But, at the end of the day I was as unsure whether or not that obstinate fighting would make a difference in my chances of becoming something more—of becoming a true hero—as I was about whether having the title, birth right, and a decade-and-a-half of breeding made me a true princess.

According to my headmistress, Mauvrey, Marie, and the rest of the world, it seemed there was a pretty good chance that it didn't.

"Something wrong?" SJ asked as I rejoined her and Blue.

I swallowed the internal conflict for another day and shrugged. "No more than usual." Then I saw Daniel making his way over to us with Jason and I grimaced. "On second thought . . ."

Daniel and Jason snaked their way through the crowded ballroom. As they approached, I had to admit that they both looked fairly dapper this evening. That is, Jason did at least. Daniel, well, he was Daniel. So I really couldn't say the same about him without adding an eye roll or some other hint of snark.

We all exchanged hellos when the boys reached us. Everyone except Daniel and I of course. The two of us just exchanged nods of acknowledgement.

"You look . . . nice, Knight," he added afterwards.

"Um, thank you," I said suspiciously.

I presumed that he couldn't say anything nice about me without adding his own brand of snark either. However, when he didn't add any more commentary, I cautiously garnered that he was being for real. As such, I forced myself to choke out the necessary—not totally untrue—reply.

"You look nice too, I guess," I said, rubbing the back of my neck sheepishly.

I avoided Daniel's uncomfortable gaze then and turned in the direction of the dance floor. In doing so I spotted something—or rather someone—more unpleasant. Chance. He was barely twenty feet away and headed straight toward me, no doubt intent on asking me to dance.

Oh, heck no.

I really was not in the mood to humor his ego a second time tonight.

He was getting closer.

My eyes widened and in panic I averted my gaze from Chance to the nearest available human person who might've trumped his company.

"Daniel," I heard myself say before common sense could stop it. "Ask me to dance."

He smirked. "What?"

"Just shut up and ask me to dance." I glanced behind him and saw Chance picking up speed. "Now, please."

Daniel turned to see what was freaking me out so badly. When he saw Chance, he struggled to conceal his laughter. "Ah, got it. Fine then," he said as he proceeded to bow overdramatically. "Crisanta Knight, will you do me the honor of this dance?"

My friends snickered. But I nodded quickly, grabbed Daniel's hand, and pulled him onto the dance floor—shooting the frustrated prince a triumphant grin.

Ha! Not today punk!

"So I guess I'm not your least favorite person in the realm," Daniel said as we began to move to the rhythm of the music.

"No," I responded flatly. "But you're a solid third."

He turned me.

"Dang, coming in third sucks," he countered. "I guess I'll have to step it up then. Now you've got me curious though. If that tool's number one, who's number two?"

"Do you know who Mauvrey Weatherall is?" I asked.

He rolled his eyes. "Everyone knows who Mauvrey Weatherall is. Whether they want to or not."

"Very true." I nodded in agreement as I box-stepped backwards. "Well, anyways, I really didn't feel like spending more time with Mr. Prince Alarming over there. So, well, I guess, um . . . uh. . ."

Daniel smirked at my flusteredness. "Are you trying to thank me?" he asked.

"Thank you?"

"Yeah, for saving you back there."

I felt like a small blood vessel burst in my brain at the insulting words.

"Let's not make a habit of it," I grumbled.

"Agreed," Daniel responded, not noticing the fury I was holding back.

"Why did you ask *me* to dance anyway?" he wondered aloud as we swayed. "I mean, why didn't you just ask Jason?"

Dang, that's a good point. Why didn't I just ask Jason?

I tilted my head, confused by the lack of logic in my own choice.

"Honestly, I don't know," I replied. "What can I say, Daniel. I guess I freaked and now I'm stuck with you."

At that point, I noticed Blue and Jason (having decided to dance with one another, it seemed) starting to twirl over to us. They moved well together, and Blue actually appeared happy, which was confusing on more counts than one. To begin with, there was her whole natural dislike of the formal dancing thing. That aside, I still didn't see how she could be so calm around Jason when she knew she was being forcibly shackled to him for the rest of her life.

"Hey guys," Jason said as he and Blue glided up next to us.

"Just thought we'd give you a heads up, Crisa," Blue piped in. "SJ offered to dance with Chance to help you out. Now you don't have to worry about him cutting in when your ten minutes are up."

"Really? Oh, that's awesome! I'll have to thank her later."

"That's what she said," Blue responded with a wink. "Well, see you guys later."

With that, the two danced away in perfect synchronicity.

Daniel and I managed to dance together without fighting for a few minutes. Of course, we weren't saying anything to one another at all so that was probably why the peace lasted so long.

Surprisingly, our toe-stomping percentage had also significantly decreased since our last ballroom pairing. I thanked goodness for that, because if it hadn't, the bare feet I was concealing beneath my dress would've seriously gotten injured.

Cordial new relations aside, we avoided eye contact as much as possible. It was just too awkward otherwise.

My sightline lingered on the ballroom floor instead. Although, in doing so something caught the light and turned my attention back to Daniel. It was the same golden pocket watch I'd seen on him the first time we'd met. I tried to get a better look at it, but found myself unable to as it was dominantly concealed within the innards of his pants pocket.

The idea occurred to me to simply ask him about the watch, but inevitably I thought better of the notion. Holding a conversation with one another without insults flying about was not one of our shared skills. So talking to him at all—let alone asking him about something private, like this watch— was probably just an all around bad call.

Unfortunately, it seemed Daniel had not made this connection yet, as he chose to interrupt our momentary peace with his own attempt at small talk.

"So . . ." he began benignly enough. "Are you going to the tournament tomorrow?"

"By going, do you mean watching?" I asked automatically. "You know that us 'damsels' are forbidden from actually participating."

He rolled his eyes again. "Oh, here we go. I should've known that you were the type."

My hand clenched in his. "Type of what?" I asked.

"The type of overly self-righteous girl that turns century-old traditions into civil rights issues."

"Oh, please," I scoffed. "You make chauvinism sound so noble. Guys not allowing girls to participate in some sport is just another stupid way they have of trying to keep us in our place. And it makes no sense. We can be just as fast and just as strong as you are."

Now it was Daniel's turn to scoff. "Yeah, okay." He glanced away from me and I saw the corners of his mouth turn upwards.

"Don't give me that smirk; I'm serious," I snapped.

"I'm sure you are," he said. "But that doesn't mean you're realistic. You've got gumption, Knight. And you're a half-decent sword fighter; I'll give you that. But you and your dainty classmates wouldn't last five minutes in a Twenty-Three Skidd tournament with a bunch of *actual* heroes. Girls can be fast and strong, but amongst each another, not in comparison to guys who have spent their whole lives training to be as fast and strong as physically possible."

"You're a jerk, Daniel," I said plainly. "And you're wrong."

"And you're delusional, Knight," he responded. "And you'll never get the chance to prove me wrong."

I abruptly stopped dancing and glared at him dead on. "You know what, Daniel? Truce off." I started to storm away then, but turned back to add one final comment. "And *I will* get the chance to prove you wrong."

I successfully managed to make a break for the back exit of the ballroom without any of the castle or regular school staff catching me.

I knew it was extremely unwise to forgo the most major of school rules—ditching a dance partner and leaving a ball without permission. And, frankly, if Lady Agnue had caught me, I seriously would have been toast.

But Daniel had been the last straw. I was used to dealing with the condescending snide of people like our headmistress and Mauvrey, who'd known me for years. Daniel, however, had barely known me a month; yet he talked to me as if he already knew me inside out.

Such overfamiliarity really pushed my buttons, especially since I didn't understand how he did it, or how to push his back.

Ergo, ditching this dance was well worth the risk if it meant getting away from him baiting me with more such provocation, or any other stereotypical, princess-belittling nonsense that would fill me with rage like his most recent comments had.

I was so angry at that point that part of me just wanted to punch the wall, or him, or anything really. Although since he wasn't here, and slamming my fist into the wall would've just added physical injury to the list of things already upsetting me this evening, I conceded to leaning against it for a second—closing my eyes, and taking a deep breath.

And exhale . . .

Sigh.

All right. That's a little better, I guess.

Some level of calmness having returned to my mindset, I was now able to properly take in my new surroundings. The back door I'd slipped through had let out into a spacious, pale yellow corridor that led to the men's restroom. Anger no longer impeding my clarity, I began to notice the pictures of the royal family decorating the area. They lined the walkway in parallel lines and tempted my interest sufficiently.

I began to slowly wander past them, studying each one in turn. The first was of the king and queen on their wedding day. The celebratory scene of matrimonial bliss was set on a pier that stretched into the sea and was surrounded by hundreds of gleeful Mer-people who watched the spectacle expectantly.

From there the pictures continued to follow the timeline of the royal family's life. And it was through these pictures that I saw Princess Ashlyn grow from a newborn into a pretty eighteen-year-old with curly, chestnut hair and the big, kind eyes of a well-loved Labrador Retriever. After looking closely at her image, I could see her as someone who seemed genuinely lovely of spirit. Maybe even a person who I could have been friends with in a different world.

I neared the end of the hallway.

The second to last picture in the series had all four members of the royal family present. The whole scene seemed as perfect as possible—united, content, and full of warmth. But then I came to the final image in the series, and it was obvious that the family's happily-ever-after had been shattered in the time between the two portraits.

Ashlyn was not in this one, so it must have been from this last year after she'd disappeared. The king and queen's faces had lost all the color and laughter that had characterized them in previous pictures. And, unlike the others, this one did not have the sea in the background. Instead the family stood lifeless in a stiff, dimly lit throne room that made me depressed just looking at it.

I was so distracted by my sadness for the royal family's ghostly image that I didn't notice Mauvrey sneak up on me. As a result, I jumped slightly when she spoke.

"What is the matter, Crisa, not having fun?" she asked innocently.

Mauvrey had somehow managed to change and redo her hair in the last twenty minutes. It was a shockingly fast turnaround. So much so that, if I didn't know any better, I would have had trouble believing that the soaking wet, frazzled girl I'd left to the mercy of a seagull just a short while ago was the same composed princess-of-darkness standing before me now.

My nemesis had changed into a coral-colored dress with actual pieces of coral around the collar that looked like small spikes. It suited her a lot better if you asked me, as did the overall sharp, twisted shape of her gown.

Mauvrey had an unusually large glass of punch in her hand and an expression of eerie contentment on her face. I took a step back and eyed her cautiously.

"Hardly," I replied. "Why exactly do you look so happy? Destroy some other poor girl's self-esteem when I wasn't around to stop you?"

Mauvrey's smile spread like a disease across her porcelain cheeks. "Very funny, Crisa. Actually, I am happy about what is going to happen next."

"And that would be?"

"This."

Mauvrey threw the contents of her massive glass of punch at me. My hair, face, and upper body were soaked with the sticky, red liquid.

Okay, it was my own fault. I'll admit I probably should've seen something like this coming.

Alas, I didn't. And now I have to decide how I'm going to play this.

Hmm, the way I figured, I had two options here—freak out and give Mauvrey the satisfaction of upsetting me, or remain calm, cool, and collected like it didn't bother me at all.

Freaking out would lead to me punching Mauvrey in the nose, which is what Blue would do. Keeping calm would dissolve the intensity of the situation, which is what SJ would do. The first option would be so much more satisfying—especially since I actually really liked this dress. But the second choice was way wiser in theory.

Dang, the SJ half of my conscious wins this round.

I nonchalantly wiped some of the liquid off my face with the back of my hand. "And what, Mauvrey, did you intend to accomplish with that?" I asked.

She was clearly taken aback by my lack of reaction, but retained her superior, cocky tone nonetheless.

"You are soaking wet and your dress is utterly stained all over," Mauvrey reminded me. "The only way out of here is back through the ballroom. Thus, you are going to look like a fool when you traipse back out there in front of everyone looking like this. Well, more of a fool than usual, I should say."

Don't lose it. Losing it will give her the upper hand.

"Mauvrey, Mauvrey, Mauvrey. And here I thought you were better than that," I said as I casually began to squeeze the punch out of my hair—wringing it like a towel.

My nemesis crossed her arms. "What are you going on about?"

"While your silly prank is a good one by clichéd, teenage girl standards," I explained, "it's still pretty lame for our situation. What's the matter, Big Girtha busy or something?"

Mauvrey narrowed her eyes. "Lady Agnue found her and Jade wandering around the halls. They are grounded for leaving the ball without permission."

"Got it. Well, good effort anyways. It's not your fault, I suppose, that on your own you lack the creativity to execute any interesting form of revenge."

"Well, you still have to go back out there as a dripping wet mess," Mauvrey snapped. "And there is no ladies' restroom back here to even allow you to get cleaned up a little."

"Yeah, but there *is* a boys' bathroom," I countered.

"What?"

"My dress is dark-colored, and the stain isn't that noticeable. I'll just go clean myself up in the boys' bathroom," I said, gesturing to the door behind me.

"You cannot do that," she stuttered. "It is the *boys'* restroom; you cannot go in there."

"Again, Mauvrey, a touch of outside-the-box thinking would do you some good. Now, if you'll excuse me." I picked up the front bustle of my skirt and pushed past her.

"Oh," I added just before exiting. "And have a lovely rest of your evening."

I left my dumbstruck enemy and entered the boys' room without hesitation, admitting to myself that handling the situation that way had been rather satisfying. I would have to thank SJ later for the advice.

For now though, my attention was drawn to the interior of the bathroom, which turned out to be an even brighter shade of yellow than the hallway I'd left behind. This bright paint emphasized the warm glow of the golden, seashell-shaped towel racks and sinks at the center of the room, giving me the overall feeling that it was daytime rather than night.

I proceeded to turn on one of the sink's faucets and clean myself up—splashing water on my face and rinsing out the sticky redness from my hair. After a few moments, I felt a light gust of cold air and the scent of the ocean against my face. I glanced over my shoulder and saw an open window in the corner—its silk curtains fluttering in the breeze of the outside world just beyond. I turned off the tap and walked over to it curiously.

Interesting . . .

Some fifteen minutes later, my dress was dragging on the sand in my wake as my feet were periodically splashed by the cool swell of the rising tide.

Madame Lisbon would've been mortified.

The open restroom window had been too tempting an escape to pass up. So, despite the fact that I hadn't known where it would lead me, I'd chosen to shimmy through it. Not an easy trick, mind you, considering the sheer size of my gown.

As it turned out, my small portal to freedom ended up depositing me in an unmanned dumpster area at the very back of the castle. And—moving quickly and silently in the darkness thanks to my bare feet after that—I somehow managed to sneak over a nearby fence and down an old footpath naturally carved into the cliffside without getting caught. Which, again, I did while wearing this ridiculously poofy dress.

How's that for stealthy?

Having successfully stayed out from under the line of sight of the castle's lighthouse and guards on duty, I was now down on the beach and finally alone. The only reminders of the ball were the faint traces of music that danced in the wind. But soon, even they were drowned out by the sound of the waves and the smell of the sea.

The combination of being out here by myself—away from all the pomp and circumstance—and doing something that was against, like, a dozen rules gave me such a rush of calm and delight I couldn't help but feel elated. I walked along the empty beach in a state of bliss for what seemed like a few minutes. Although I guess it must've been a lot longer than that, because when I turned around to survey the way I'd come, the glowing castle on the cliff was so far behind me it might as well have been a firefly.

The wind was starting to pick up then, causing the few seagulls that had been flying around out here to soar off in search of their nests.

For a second I thought about following their example and heading back to the castle. However, that's when I saw a small stretch of beach that extended out into the ocean about forty yards away. It was a natural path made of piles of sea rocks and stones. And without remorse I soon found myself following the risky, but irresistible impulse to get across it.

It was tricky work, and I had to tread very carefully because the rocks were slippery and it was hard to see. Eventually though, I succeeded in making it to the edge of the strip. Once I did, I put my hands on my hips triumphantly and gazed back at the beach some hundred feet away.

My vision having fully adjusted to the night, from this vantage point I was now able to notice the cliff's idiosyncrasies. For one, its shoreline curved in and out like a hunchback's spine, making it so that only the bluff I'd come down and another on my left could be seen. That second one was nothing like the bluff I had used though. Its edges crept toward the ocean in the form of a plateau with thinning innards that looked like jagged, rocky fingers stretching into the sand.

Even from this distance I could tell it was huge and intricate and one of the most intriguing constructs of terrain I'd ever seen. I considered how deep it went and what lay beyond. But I was unable to ascertain either, as that was where the bluff rounded and caused the rest of the realm's edge to bend out of sight.

I turned my head and focused on the cliffside itself.

At first it looked as if it had been discolored with dark spots. Then I squinted my eyes and realized that what was actually dotting the cliffside was a selection of caves and crevices jutting in and out of the rock that lined the beach.

In no mood to head back right away, I gingerly sat upon my patch of rock and stared off at these caves, wondering if they were all interconnected and, if so, how intricate the resulting tunnel system must've been. Then I wondered if anyone had ever tried to navigate their way through them. And then I wondered about the logic behind leaving a trail of breadcrumbs to help a person find their way back from anywhere. It didn't seem like the best of laid plans in retrospect, as miscellaneous wildlife could've easily just eaten the trail and—

"Well, don't you look like a fish out of water?"

I let out a small squeak of surprise. I hadn't expected to see much of anything out here in the middle of the night. But I especially hadn't expected to see a half-fish, half-human blonde girl pop out of the water and start playing with the taffeta on my hemline.

"Sorry, didn't mean to scare you. I usually go hang out by that rock over there," the mermaid said, pointing to a lightning bolt-shaped formation at the edge of a similar strip of rocks I hadn't noticed before.

"But it's taken tonight," she explained. "Another mermaid

and her beau are sucking each other's faces off. Like, get a coral reef already, am I right? Anyways, hi, I'm Lonna. What's your story?"

Lonna, Lonna . . . Why does that name ring a bell?

Maybe SJ was right and I should've spent less time mocking our lessons and more time listening to them.

Then it hit me. "You're one of the princesses of Mer. Lonna Langard, right?"

"So? What of it?" the mermaid asked.

"Nothing, just . . . I thought Mer-people weren't supposed to come this close to shore. What are you doing all the way out here?"

"Same as you, I would guess," she said. "I needed some space, felt like breaking some rules. Any of that sound familiar?"

I huffed in amusement. "More than you know, Lonna. More than you know."

We both smiled at the similarity. It was always nice to meet someone you had stuff in common with even if, you know, species wasn't one of those things.

"I'm Crisa," I finally said. "Well, it's Crisanta Knight really. But that's not the point. It's nice to meet you, Lonna."

I extended my hand and in response Lonna put down the piece of taffeta she'd been toying with and reached up to shake it. When our fingers were just a few inches away from touching though, her eyes suddenly widened and she yanked her arm away.

"What are you trying to do, kill me?" she barked angrily as she shot back a solid seven feet in the water.

"What? No. What's wrong?" I stammered.

Lonna rubbed her wrist as if it was stinging and eyed me carefully. "You . . . don't know?" she asked.

"Know what?"

"I thought everybody knew."

"Knew what?" I repeated.

"That bracelet you're wearing," Lonna said, gesturing to the gift Marie had given me. "It's made of pearls."

"So?"

"*So* pearls are Mer-people's greatest weakness. They sort of suck the life from our bodies, drying us out like those fish sticks you land folks are so nuts about."

I raised my eyebrows, genuinely shocked. "Seriously?"

"Yeah," Lonna replied. "Why do you think we let you two-leggers have all of our oysters for food? We want those things out of the ocean and eaten before they have a chance to grow their awful pearly by-products."

"Well, I'm sorry," I said. "I didn't know. Honest. But here, look." I removed the bracelet and tossed it aside as if it was made of nothing more than plastic beads and string. "Now we're good, right?" I asked her hopefully.

Lonna twirled her hair for a moment, but then shrugged. "Okay, yeah. We're good."

She swam back over to the rocks and swiftly went back to playing with the taffeta at the bottom of my dress. It was a bit of an awkward way for two people to hang out really. But I had already ticked Lonna off once and didn't want to provoke her any further, so I resigned to let the girl have her fun. Plus, she just seemed so fascinated by the sparkly material that I would've genuinely felt bad swatting her away.

Hmm, I guess mermaids—even mermaid princesses—can't exactly wear fancy dresses underwater.

That sucks.

My new friend's hair was blonde, like I said, but even at

this proximity it was hard to gauge the exact shade due to the fact that it was soaking wet and cloaked in nighttime. Her eyes were bright purple though, of that I was certain, and they matched the seashells she had in her hair and the bathing suit-style top she was wearing.

Finally, after a decent amount of time had passed I decided to try speaking to her again. I wasn't quite sure how forthcoming she'd be. For one, I'd apparently almost killed her with an accessory a few minutes ago. And two, the Sea Silence Laws said we weren't supposed to speak to one another at all. But I had to give it a shot.

I mean, come on, how often does one get the chance to chat with an actual mermaid?

"I like your sea shells," I attempted.

"Duh, everyone likes purple," Lonna replied absentmindedly.

Okay, so I guess mermaids don't like small talk. Noted.

I sat there quietly for a couple more minutes until eventually I elected to give conversation another go. Not that having a mermaid play with your dress fabric wasn't a delightfully strange pastime but, frankly, I was getting bored.

Maybe a more serious topic of conversation would get her to talk to me with sufficient depth. But what could I possibly say to instigate that?

Ooh, never mind. I got it. And it's so obvious too.

"So, Lonna," I started all mischievously. "What are your thoughts on the Sea Silence Laws?"

Oh yeah, I'm controversial like that. It doesn't matter if you're human, fish, or something in between—politics always get some kind of rise out of a person, and Lonna is no exception.

"They're stupid," the mermaid replied sharply. "We used to be friends with two-leggers. Made life more interesting, you know—being friends with another species. Of course, ever since those dumb holes started appearing we've been shunned like they're our fault."

I cocked my head. "What holes?"

"In the In and Out Spell," Lonna responded. "Stupid, lame-o Fairy Godmothers. Dude, just because you can't keep your magic junk together doesn't mean you've gotta be totally rude to those of us who know about it."

"Wait. What?"

Lonna abruptly stopped twiddling the taffeta.

I could see the gears turning in her head as her eyes fogged over and she stared at the wet rock between us. She'd clearly said something she wasn't supposed to and was internally panicking while attempting to figure out how to play it cool and act like she hadn't.

"Lonna," I said, trying to get her to keep talking. "What do you mean by *holes* in the In and Out Spell?"

She didn't move.

"Lonna, what are the holes?" I tried again more earnestly.

Still nothing.

"Lonna!"

Okay, another lesson learned—don't raise your voice to a mermaid.

They offend easily.

Lonna's eyes shot up from the rocks and met mine. Her glowing purple corneas fixated on me so intently, but curiously, that they anchored every bit of my focus.

Then, without warning she tersely huffed and tossed her wet hair over her shoulder. A bit of water hit me in the face, but our staring match at the moment was so intense that I didn't feel the need to even blink, let alone wipe it off.

"You want answers, Crisa?" she said suggestively, as if

posing more of a challenge than a question. "Go and find them yourself."

Although I seriously would've liked to, there ended up being no time to respond to this vague proposition. As soon as Lonna uttered the last syllable of her sentence, she flashed a devious smile, winked at me, and dove back into the water before I could endeavor to get anything else out of her.

She was gone in the blink of an eye. The surrounding world went silent once more except for the sound of the tides. And I found myself alone in the dark with a soggy hemline and way too many unanswered questions.

CHAPTER 10

Twenty-Three Skidd

"This is a bad idea," SJ warned.

I nodded. "You're right. It's stupid, reckless, and could have disastrous consequences."

"I'm so proud of you!" Blue practically gushed as she put on her riding gloves.

Okay, backstory time.

Late last night after I got back from my walk on the beach, Blue'd had the brilliant idea to go undercover and compete in the boys' Twenty-Three Skidd tournament today.

After Daniel's assertion at the ball that girls could not hack it as heroes in such an event, I had been inspired enough to do the same. Furthermore, I'd kind of always wanted to give the game a try.

Twenty-Three Skidd was the most popular sport in our realm. A long time ago, jousting had been the preferred game of choice for Book's heroes and athletes. However, one day some genius was all, "Hey we've got Pegasus horses. Wouldn't that make the game more interesting?" And (since they were obviously right) this adjustment was made to the game permanently.

Following that, one year at the Century City Summit a

Fairy Godmother named Belinda Skidd described a strange, aggressive game that she had observed while visiting Earth on some business. It was called "Lacrosse," and it was said to be the most fearsome sport in all the realms.

This idea fascinated everyone so much that our jousting game was modified even further until it became Twenty-Three Skidd—the competition we knew and loved today.

As part of our little week-long field trip, the boys from Lord Channing's were holding a grand tournament of the sport this morning. The intent: to entertain the damsels.

You know, muscular boys competing in a public arena to demonstrate to the observing girls who amongst them is the strongest, the fastest, and who can take off their shirt with the most pizzazz mid-fight.

Needless to say watching such a spectacle was so not my speed. Moreover, Blue and I hadn't been in the practice fields in days and were getting fidgety. After a week of ballroom dancing and fishing lectures instead of our regular private combat training, we were most definitely not in the mood to spend an afternoon on the sidelines. Even if we hadn't been craving the action-adrenaline rush, we still wouldn't have settled for that. Because, seriously, what sounded like more fun: a fierce athletic battle in the sky, or sitting on velvet-cushioned bleachers clapping every time some prince did a victory lap around the arena after scoring a goal?

"Neither of you should be doing this," SJ nagged, even as she handed us pieces of armor. "Especially you, Crisa."

"Hey, why especially me?"

"Because whether you admit it or not, you barely got any

sleep. You were tossing and turning all last night with your nightmares."

I opened my mouth to object. Not because she wasn't right, but because I wanted to know how *she* knew that. It was true, last night a flurry of agonized nightmares about Natalie Poole had twisted across my sleeping consciousness like a cyclone. My only break from her torment had been tempered gusts of equally unwelcomed presences to my dreamscape. And those had featured the voice of that nameless, faceless boy whose dark essence and enigmatic words relentlessly pervaded my sleep and made me cringe nocturnally.

Between the two of them, I was kept tossing and turning until sun up. Although since I hadn't said anything to SJ or Blue about it this morning I couldn't fathom how SJ had possibly deduced it.

I was about to probe this matter further when she cut me off.

"Do not try and deny it either," she said. "For goodness' sake, the circles under your eyes speak for themselves."

"Gee, thanks, SJ," I huffed.

"I am just worried, all right," she said, speaking in a much softer tone. "Please, just promise me that the two of you know what you are doing."

"You know what they say, SJ," Blue chimed in mischievously. "Don't make promises you can't keep."

SJ sighed and placed her fingers to her temple as if trying to suppress a headache. "I would feel better if you would at least take your wand with you, Crisa."

"Too risky," I replied. "Someone could see it transform. Or worse, it could fall out of my bag mid-flight."

"Besides," Blue interjected, "it's bad enough those poor boys are about to be beaten by a couple of girls. They'd totally die if they knew they were beaten by a couple of girls wielding a magic wand. Why add insult to injury?"

Blue and I rapidly put on the remaining pieces of armor and the rest of our gear. We only had a few minutes left before we needed to report to the arena. As we finished getting ready, SJ fetched the final piece of our disguise from her purse—two tiny glass vials sealed with cork stoppers. They were each no bigger that an index finger and contained a navy-colored liquid.

"Okay," she began, holding up the vials. "While I must remind you once more that I do not like using my potion skills to support your mischief, I did make these for you in the palace kitchen this morning. They should alter your voices to sound more masculine for about one hour."

We each took a vial from her and uncorked it. The liquid inside smelled like grass stains, raw steak, and feet.

Gross.

"Uh, SJ . . . you learned how to make this potion in class, like, a month ago. You sure you got it right?" Blue asked hesitantly.

"Of course I got it right. You know I memorize every potion I learn. Now drink your liquid man-voice so we can get on with this madness."

Blue and I grimaced, then each swallowed down our dose of the concoction in one quick swig. My stomach bubbled and a large belch escaped me. Then one came out of Blue.

"Testing, testing," I said. "One, two, three!" On three, my voice sank four octaves.

Blue tested out her masculine voice then too and was

delighted with the result. "Oh wow, this is going to make smack talk on the field so much more epic!" she exclaimed in her new deep resonance. "Check me, I'm a giant! Fee, Fi, Fo, Fum!"

"Blue, that is racist," SJ scolded.

"Good grief, SJ! Give me a break. That was classic!"

The two of them continued to bicker as I went to retrieve our helmets from under a nearby orange tree.

When Blue had forged this rebellious idea of hers last night, we'd recognized that we wouldn't exactly be able to ready ourselves in the locker rooms along with the boys. Add to that, two girls waltzing down to breakfast in full body armor wouldn't have emoted the subtly or secrecy we were going for either.

As such, after foraging the castle for the armor we needed for the event, my friends and I had spent our post-ball hours sneaking into the Adelaide Castle orchard to hide our gear.

With trees so large and lush, this stretch of land was one of the most secluded and well-protected portions of the castle campus. Plus, it was only a couple miles away from the back entrance to Adelaide's Twenty-Three Skidd arena on the adjacent cliffside. So it had been the perfect place for us to get ready without being found out.

"Ladies," I interrupted as I returned with our helmets, "—and I use that term loosely since Blue and I currently sound like my Great Uncle Leroy. We'd better go take our places."

I handed Blue her helmet and she put it on with some extra sass aimed in SJ's general direction. SJ rolled her eyes, exasperated by Blue, but then wished us both good luck nonetheless as she made to leave the area.

Before disappearing through the trees completely I saw her glance back with an expression of uncertainty. She was worried.

I smiled to reassure her. That was usually my job in our unorthodox adventures. While others would be afraid of what was to come, I never allowed myself to admit such weakness. And because of that, I was typically charged with a role that was quite different in these scenarios—inspiring confidence in our crazy plans and, more often than not, coming up with them too.

"All right then," I nodded to Blue as I put on my own helmet. "Let's go shake things up, shall we?"

The entrance tunnel smelled like seawater and boy sweat.

Blue and I were standing in the underground waiting area just beneath Adelaide's Twenty-Three Skidd arena. We were surrounded on all sides by princes and heroes, but none of them detected our girlish presence. Most of the boys were fully armored up by now—ready to make their journey out of the tunnel at any moment—so beneath our armor, Blue and I blended right in.

In addition to the protection of our disguises, we also had disorder on our side to serve as sufficient cover. Unlike normal Twenty-Three Skidd games, today there was no pre-ordained division of players into specific teams. Yes, Lord Channing's had five different Twenty-Three Skidd teams that competed against one another throughout the school year. However, as this morning's tournament was more of a showcase for the enjoyment of its observers and bore no weight on their teams' internal rankings, it was sort of like a free for all. Any Channing's student who wanted to participate (whether they were officially on a team or not) could do so. Meanwhile those who didn't feel like playing could simply watch from the stands.

Blue and I had learned that all the boys wishing to enter today's event were supposed to meet down here a half hour before the match, armored up and ready to receive team assignments once let onto the field. As such, no one suspected that we didn't belong. We were just another couple of heroes biding their time in the bustling tunnel before the game got underway.

Despite the assurances of these factors, and SJ's potion, we still decided to keep uncharacteristically low profiles and not speak to anyone.

I didn't consider this a great loss. Boys weren't that into small talk anyways.

As we waited, I spotted Daniel, Jason, and Chance in the corner. They didn't have their helmets on yet, so they were easy to pick out in the crowd.

Chance had decided to go without body armor (probably to show off the muscles beneath his tight t-shirt), but was wearing bronze shin and elbow guards that matched his helmet. Daniel and Jason, on the other hand, were both fully armored up like sensible people. Jason's gray armor had a maroon design and a crest with a picture of an ox. Daniel's armor was all onyx black, with a blue lion insignia on the left shoulder, matching the blue feathering on top of his helmet.

Their gear was sleek, no doubt custom-made, and caused me to feel a little jealous. Blue and I had on the plainest of silver armor, which was slightly rusting and carried the odor of mothballs with it. Even our helmets were subpar; they were super scratched up and had withered feathering on top—mine was purple, Blue's was orange.

Overall the suits were as unextraordinary and traditional as you could get. But then the two of us couldn't afford to be picky seeing as how we'd had to "borrow" these off some of the suits of armor in Adelaide Castle's more deserted hallways.

What can I say, you have to work with what you've got.

I twiddled my thumbs in silence next to Blue, but after a while I started to get a bit angsty waiting in the confined, underground space.

Was there like a rule that said we couldn't wait in a place that had proper ventilation, or at least snacks?

Suddenly the gates opened, sunlight filled the tunnel, and we were called forward.

The boys began to march confidently toward the light. Blue and I followed their lead, our ears adjusting to the cheers that grew louder as we made our way outside. When we finally reached the end of the tunnel, there was only one word to accurately describe what I saw and how I felt: *Spectacular*.

We faced a massive, open arena. The field was as green as physically possible and there were two giant goal posts 600 feet in the air on opposite ends of it, projecting high into the powdery clouds. All around us fans lined the bleachers, creating a roar of excitement made even more surreal by the morning mist blanketing the stadium.

I took a deep breath and forced my mind and fluttering heart to stay focused, despite the intoxicating atmosphere.

I knew the rules of jousting perfectly, like everyone did. Nevertheless, Lacrosse was pretty weird and (as mentioned), while I'd seen plenty of Twenty-Three Skidd matches in my time, since it was an all-boy sport I'd never actually played. Accordingly, as we made our way to the center of the arena

I made myself run through the rules in my head just to be on the safe side.

Okay, for starters, rule one: No girls allowed.

Eye roll.

I don't think that'll ever stop ticking me off.

But I digress as that's so not the point right now. I have bigger, more immediate fish to fry.

Anyways, rule two: Every Twenty-Three Skidd player was to be mounted on his (or *her*) own Pegasus and wield a lacrosse sword. That was a five-foot long staff with a grip function that could extend the staff an extra two feet on either side when activated. This weapon had a small netted basket on one end for handling the ball, and the sharp point of a jousting spear at the other end for, well, handling your opponents.

Basically, the net basket was used for catching the ball and hurtling it to your teammates or through the goal. The other side of the staff, meanwhile, was used for offense, defense, scare tactics, bad sportsmanship, and—sometimes it seemed—as a general anger release.

At the start of the match the game's glowing green ball would be launched into the air by a cannon and all players would take off on their Pegasi. The first team to score twenty-three points by putting the ball into the opponent's goal post twenty-three times was the winner. It was that simple. Theoretically anyways.

All right. I have totally got this.

The referee proceeded to separate our group into two teams—odd and even numbers. His associates, in turn, stuck corresponding, glowing red or purple numbers onto our backs so as to identify which team we were on once the tournament began. Blue and I were lucky enough to make it onto the same team (evens/purple). And I was extra pleased to learn that Daniel, Jason, and Chance were on the opposing team.

Yay, general anger release time!

As the ref continued to distribute team assignments, I took another look around the stadium, particularly at the fans. It wasn't just all the girls from our school, the boys who weren't competing, and the staff of Lady Agnue's and Lord Channing's. The stands were also filled with hundreds of Adelaide and Whoozalee citizens.

Huh, I guess everybody loves a good battle-royale.

The cheers were loud and ricocheted across the arena's curved walls. It was magnificent and terrifying— an exhilarating combination of feelings—and I absolutely relished it.

At that point the ref finally indicated that it was time for us to saddle up. The players moved toward the Pegasi that were strategically positioned in inverted-pyramid formation on both sides of the field. Attendants handed us lacrosse swords as we made our way over to them.

Hmm, so this is what it feels like to hold a lacrosse sword, I mused as I twirled the thing easily in my hand. *Not bad— light, versatile. I like it.*

Intriguing new weapon in hand, I chose a pure white steed in the third row while Blue selected a grayish speckled one from the second. She gave me a thumbs-up when she had mounted the beautiful creature, which I returned.

When grounded, Pegasi did not look that different from regular horses. Aside from slightly elongated torsos and silver hooves, they were virtually identical. Their main point of inter-species distinction (their wings) vanished whenever their hooves hit the ground so that they could better camouflage themselves. When they took flight, however, that specialness revealed itself in a form that was as brilliantly functional as it was breathtakingly unexpected.

Pegasi wings were not solid or made of feathers like the illustrations in a plethora of fairytales might've led other worlds to believe. Rather, they were of a more holographic nature—made up of an inherent magical energy that Pegasi produced, which bent the light and wind around them to allow for flight. These wings shifted in color like contained auroras and were not tangible to the touch. Solid objects could pass right through them without interrupting their magical purpose.

The Pegasus I had selected was completely white in mane and coat, but as I sat on her saddle I wondered what specific color her wings would manifest in when they eventually sprouted.

I looked closer then and discovered that there was a bronze nameplate at the top of my Pegasus' saddle with the name "SADIE" engraved into it. I began petting her mane a moment later and then scratched her behind the ears while we waited for the other players to ready themselves and for the game to commence.

Sadie seemed surprised by the gentility at first—shaking her head with a startle—but soon after she started to whinny with delight. I supposed she wasn't used to getting this kind of attention from the boys.

Our bonding was cut short when the ref blew his whistle.

The game had begun.

The other players instantly reacted to the sound, giving their steeds a swift kick with the heels of their boots. The Pegasi whinnied. Puffs of blue and orange smoke came out of their nostrils, which seemed to symbolize the magical incendiary that had just gone off inside them, activating their powers. In the next instant each Pegasus's eyes glowed either bright cobalt or shining silver and their wings exploded from their sides in the form of glittering light.

One after another the boys and their winged battle partners shot into the air with great enthusiasm and aggression. I took a quick deep breath and followed their lead—giving Sadie a light kick as I let out my own, "Hee yah!"

Sadie whinnied excitedly in response and a pair of giant, swan-shaped wings sprouted from her torso.

Magic sparkled as the purple and green wings started to flap mightily. I ran the fingers of my left riding glove through their tightly condensed energy, unable to fully comprehend the splendor. My hand passed right through the magic wings like they weren't there at all.

For a moment, I couldn't believe that such things were capable of producing sturdy flight. But, a second later when Sadie and I jolted into the sky, I was reminded never to judge a book by its cover.

Sadie carried us both into the clouds with such power and ferocity I had to grip the reins with all my might to keep from being jerked off. Then, as the competition-based crazy started to unfold everywhere around us, I had to hold on even harder.

Okay, confession time.

Other than a few times on Pegasus ponies when I was little, I had never actually technically ridden one of these before. Blue had, and she'd convinced me that the experience was no different than riding a regular horse. So, given that I was a pro at that, I figured I would be just fine. Alas, during those first few minutes that Sadie and I sailed through the crowded clouds I realized one very clear thing in regards to Blue's assertion—she lied.

I clutched the reins in one hand for dear life while I tried to balance the weight of my lacrosse sword in the other and, you know, not fall off the flying horse in the process. I hadn't even seen where the ball had gone and was just trying not to scream as I searched for Blue.

Sadie was ascending really fast and consistently bobbing and weaving in order to avoid ramming into the other players and the announcers who were also flying around in order to commentate on the game's proceedings.

Adding to my current non-existent sense of security, I noticed that a large safety net had risen from beneath the field. It was now hanging fifty feet above the arena floor with a medical-assistance tent stationed directly below it.

Real reassuring, I thought to myself with a gulp.

"DUCK!" I suddenly heard someone yell.

My attention shot back up.

A pair of black Pegasus hooves barely missed my head. A blur of onyx armor and blue helmet feathers whizzed past me without further courtesy.

Daniel.

Personal grudge match aside, I decided to steer Sadie high up into the sky to avoid any more hit and runs while I got the hang of this.

After a minute or so the two of us broke past an embankment of clouds and found ourselves in a calm area surrounded by blue and bathed in the sunshine that had thus far been unable to break through. Even from up here you could hear the faint sounds of shouting, cheering, and booing from the game below. But I ignored the temptation.

I needed a minute to figure this out, otherwise I'd have no shot of making it through in one piece.

The first thing I had to master was the flying. I soon realized that the part of Sadie's saddle between the horn and the gullet was equipped with a holster for locking the lacrosse sword into a sturdy angled position when it was not in use. So I secured the staff there for a few minutes as I mastered the basics of riding my new game partner.

To my grateful surprise, soon enough it did begin to feel a bit like riding a regular horse. The difference I needed to adjust for, though, was consistently shifting my weight and balance to be in sync with Sadie's wing movements.

Having accounted for that, it wasn't long before I had the flying aspect down. Once I did, I drew the lacrosse sword from its sturdy resting place and began messing around with it in one hand while I gripped Sadie's reins with the other.

After several minutes of practice I learned that the keys to handling the weapon were mastering fast wrist movements to rotate the staff from basket to blade and (extra elongating function aside) being adept at my own quick extensions for effectively using either end. Having discovered these two basic mechanics, I was stunned at the swiftness with which I began to develop a rhythm for the staff.

Honestly, considering how flustered I'd been just minutes before, I was amazed at how fast I found myself getting good at this. The staff of the lacrosse sword just felt right in my hand. The weight, the grip, the extension that was so much more versatile then a normal sword—I loved it. And more importantly, unlike most things I'd ever tried, it actually seemed to come naturally.

"Hee-yah!" I shouted as I gave Sadie another kick of my heel.

I was ready to return to the match. She clearly felt the

same way because she plunged back through the clouds with way more speed and excitement than I'd expected. The two of us dove into the middle of the arena and I saw that the score was already 12 to 11—odd team ahead.

All right, time to get in this game.

I surveyed the arena's airspace. Dozens of Pegasi were darting across the skies. The players were either charging one another or charging after the ball, which I finally spotted flying through the air off to my left.

That's also when I saw Blue. She zipped right in front of a knight in golden armor and caught the glowing, green ball in her lacrosse sword's basket. Immediately four opposing players flew after her in ready pursuit.

I kicked Sadie into high gear.

Blue was circling far below—unable to get any closer to the goal because players from the odd team were coming at her from all angles.

I had an idea.

While the other players on my team were occupied trying to defend Blue, Sadie and I flew up again. We shot straight above the fighting mass and over my friend, Sadie's white coat camouflaging into the clouds around her.

"Up high!" I called down to Blue.

My friend was startled at first, but soon recognized my manly voice. And when she saw me she did what her opponents were least expecting—she spun her lacrosse sword and lobbed the ball forty feet back, high into the sky.

I zoomed in without interference and caught the ball. Members of the opposing team began desperately chasing after me, but I was far enough away that none of them posed imminent threats. I was already on my descending dive toward the goal.

There were only two odd-numbered players directly in my flight path waiting on defense. One went high and one went low. The low opponent was aiming to plunge underneath Sadie, while the high opponent was rotating his lacrosse sword with the weapon side pointed at me as he charged.

Their play was obvious. High guy was going to attack so that I would be forced to rotate my staff to its weapon side to defend myself. And, as a consequence for the rotation, the ball would fall out of my net basket and the player below me would be in the perfect position to swoop in and catch it.

Come on, guys. Not very creative.

High guy was closing in. However, instead of rotating my staff downwards like he expected, I waited. Then, precisely when he was within range, I released the reins and used both hands to powerfully swing my staff while pressing the extender function on its grip.

The cross-handed haymaker smacked my opponent's staff right out of his hand and sent him veering out of control. As a result, the lower opponent was left confused, empty handed, and, most importantly, in my dust as Sadie and I shot toward our destination.

I shrunk the staff back to five feet and with another fierce swing I heaved the ball through the goal post—evening the score 12–12. The arena filled with cheers and I grinned beneath my helmet.

Game on, boys. Game on.

The competition continued fervently from there without break or lull. If one team had the upper hand at any point, it wasn't for long.

With every passing second I became increasingly enthralled by the heated, relentless nature of the sport. But, more than that, as the tournament went on, there was another aspect of the game that I found to be even more powerful than the intensity of the match itself—the realization that I was actually really good at it.

Oh, let's be real. I was fantastic!

I genuinely couldn't believe it. My whole life I'd felt deficient at everything I'd ever tried—from curtseying to woodcarving. But this . . . this I connected with. The lacrosse sword worked for me. And the feelings of success and ease that came with that skill were unlike anything I'd ever experienced.

In short, it was phenomenal. I was having so much fun that I didn't even get annoyed when Chance Darling took off his shirt after scoring a goal and the dramatic display got more applause from the girls in the arena than the actual point had.

Nearly an hour into the match I'd scored five goals, Blue had scored two, and time was almost up with the game tied at 22–22.

The closeness of the match did not concern me though. For arguably the first time in my life I felt unstoppable. I had the ball in my possession and Sadie and I were plunging through the sky on our way to seal the even team's triumph.

What were the only obstacles keeping us from doing so? Merely two players in charcoal-colored armor (17 and 19) coming into my line of sight with another high and low attack.

Oh, please, I thought to myself as I readied to swing at the high player like I'd done before.

Unfortunately, I never got the chance. This defensive play turned out to be nothing like before. Without warning the low player suddenly dive-bombed beneath me in an arc.

He swung the basket side of his lacrosse sword upwards, pressed the extender function on his grip, and caught Sadie's right front hoof within its trap. The force of the move was so strong and tragically accurate it caused Sadie to flip over—tossing me off her in the process.

No! No! No!

I tumbled through the clouds with one hand clutching the staff of my lacrosse sword and the other hand flailing. I thought I was totally done for until by some miracle I saw Sadie swooping around far below. She was coming back for me.

I adjusted my body to fall at a slant—my trajectory curving as I got closer to her. Amazingly enough, it worked. In fact, it worked perfectly! When I was about a hundred feet from the net that draped across the stadium's floor, Sadie was flying right below me. A few moments later when she was within reach, I grabbed her mane with my free hand and pulled myself onto her back.

Grasping the reins tightly once more, I leveled Sadie off just in time and the two of us zoomed back into the sky to the sound of roaring applause.

The fool that had knocked me off Sadie (17) now had the ball and I was eager to chase after him. It seemed Blue was too because seconds later she pulled up alongside me and joined in the pursuit.

As we followed him, we watched in disgust as he executed one dirty move after another on his way to our goal. He and his cohort (19) knocked so many opposing players off their steeds that it looked like the sky was raining with our fallen teammates. One by one they dropped to the arena's safety net and were taken out of the game.

"I'll ram him on the left!" Blue yelled. "When I knock the staff out of his hand, you catch the ball!"

I nodded and she sped up to fly ahead.

Blue circled down below before brusquely charging back up to cut off 17 from the front. He tried to evade her, but she was right in his flight path and he had no time to move out of the way. Her Pegasus' body-slammed into his, causing both him and his staff to fall.

While he seizured like a maniac on his way down to the net like he so rightly deserved, I set my sights on the ball that had been knocked loose from his lacrosse sword. It was free-falling up ahead and it was totally mine. Or so I thought.

Just then I heard a very distinctive yell coming from behind me. It was Blue. Even masked in manly essence I could recognize my friend's voice, *and* recognize that she was in trouble.

I glanced over my shoulder as Sadie sped forward and saw that 19 had gone after Blue in revenge for taking out his buddy. The rider had rammed Blue from behind with his lacrosse sword, knocking her off her own Pegasus as recompense.

Her armor glinted through the clouds as she toppled downwards—her steed nowhere to be seen.

I took another quick look at the increasingly close ball. It illuminated temptingly against the sky as it fell—the goal right behind it with no opponents to stop me from winning the match and sealing my glorious victory . . .

Without hesitation I yanked at Sadie's reins, swerved her in an immediate U-turn, and we nose-dived after Blue instead.

Placing the lacrosse sword in its holster would have gotten

in my way at that point so—unstable as it felt—I passed it and the reins into one hand while I extended the other. "Blue!" I yelled as Sadie and I got closer. "Take my hand!"

Even with her face hidden behind that helmet I could tell she was surprised to see me. Nevertheless, she steadied her drop as much as possible and reached forward with her free hand as I approached.

When Sadie and I were parallel with Blue, I grabbed her hand and pulled her in with a strong jerk. She settled behind me on the saddle and the three of us changed direction back toward the action.

Blue lifted her visor. "Why did you come back for me?!" she shouted as we maneuvered across the clouds. "You could have gotten the ball and scored the winning goal! Do you know what that would have done for your reputation? You could've taken off your helmet and finally gotten people to take you seriously as a hero like you've always wanted!"

Sadie swerved to avoid running into a disoriented Pegasus that had lost its rider.

"Blue!" I called back as I searched the sky for the missing ball. "You're more important to me than my reputation. If I let you fall, you'd get examined by the nurse on the field like all the other guys who go down. You do that, and everyone will see who you are. So yeah, maybe my reputation improves. But none of the guys—let alone any of the girls—will ever let you forget that *you* of all people couldn't hack it up here with the heroes. There's no way I'm letting that happen!"

Blue didn't say anything. Not that there was time for more conversation. I'd finally spotted the object I'd been after. Two riders who'd been fighting over possession of the ball had let it slip through their grasps and now it was dropping through the air straight ahead of us.

"Get ready!" I ordered.

Blue reached out her right arm, extending her lacrosse sword as far as she could. She was just about to catch our prize when a pair of familiar black hooves sailed over my head. Someone else swung down his own lacrosse sword and snatched the ball before we had the chance.

Daniel had it now. And he took off toward our team's goal with haste—paying no mind to Blue, Sadie, and me as we pursued him. Our other team members attempted to slow his pace, but barely broke his stride. They did, however, give us a chance to catch up to him, and that was something I could work with.

As the distance between us closed, the cogs in my brain began to churn out another one of my classic, unorthodox, and debatably stupid ideas.

There was no way we could flat-out challenge Daniel with two riders on one Pegasus. It was allowed and everything. Frankly, pretty much anything was up here. (*Why do you think we're wearing such sturdy armor?*)

But having more than one person on a Pegasus threw off speed, balance, and the effectiveness of any offensive attack. In other words, there was basically zero possibility we could take the ball from Daniel so long as Sadie was supporting two riders.

Ergo, one of us had to go.

"Fly below Daniel and catch the ball when it drops!" I instructed Blue as I twisted the reins around the saddle's horn to hold them in position.

"Wait! What are you gonna do?"

I kicked Sadie to go faster. "Shake things up!"

I gripped onto Blue's arm for support then carefully crescent-kicked my left leg over Sadie's head so that I was riding sidesaddle. Clutching her mane while still holding my lacrosse sword, I egged her on despite the fact that I was barely able to keep myself steady.

"I'll come back around and scoop you up like you did me," Blue said as we narrowed in on Daniel.

"No, don't," I responded. "Take the shot. It's your best chance. Once you clear the goal and win the game all the riders will descend to the field and won't have to report to the med tent like the fallen do. So all I have to do is hang on until then and I'll be fine."

"He's going to fight you. You could fall like I did."

"I won't," I answered without a hint of doubt in my voice or my head.

I am not a damsel in distress. I can be a good hero and I'm going to prove it to everyone right here and right now.

Sadie charged behind Daniel—wings flapping at maximum power. Our ambitious team got closer and closer until we were flying about eight feet above him on his left side. He glanced at us and pressed the extender function on his staff's grip preemptively, but kept going strong— confident he would be able to counter any strike I threw at him in this unbalanced state.

Still, I could tell he was keeping an eye on my lacrosse sword just in case I decided to try something. My lacrosse sword and not actually me, mind you. So, although he was startled, he was able to respond in time when I hurtled the weapon at his head a second later.

Just as I'd expected, Daniel ducked to avoid the blow. Right when he did so, I released Sadie's mane and jumped— my eyes focused solely on Daniel's staff.

He turned his head just in time to see me coming and reacted as I'd predicted by shoving his weapon firmly into its saddle holster. But, that was *all* he'd had time for. The moments he'd wasted ducking my throw kept him from flying away, which kept him from keeping me from grabbing hold of his staff.

I clung from it now—dangling in the air momentarily before my left foot found its way into his saddle's toehold and gave me the boost I needed to support my body weight.

I looked over my shoulder and saw that Blue had driven Sadie downwards and was flying steadily about thirty feet below—waiting for me to make my move. Of course, that task was easier said than done. Daniel was still headed toward our goal post at full speed and, while I may have been holding on to his lacrosse sword, the basket end clutching the ball was out of my reach. Add to that, Daniel was intensively maneuvering his Pegasus left and right in an attempt to toss me off.

Try as he might though, I held on tightly and refused to loosen my grip or my resolve. Instead, keeping my left foot in the toehold, I leaned out and shimmied my right hand up as far as it would go on the staff. And then, shifting my weight, I began to forcibly shake it.

"Are you crazy?!" I heard Daniel shout. "Let it go!"

"Not a chance!" I yelled back as I kept swinging my weight back and forth, lurching the lacrosse sword as hard as I could.

After a few seconds my mad method triumphed. I was able to knock the ball loose from the staff's basket, causing it to fall. Below, Blue swiftly caught it and took off in the opposite direction toward the other team's goal.

Whoot! Whoot! Go get 'em, Blue!

We'd done it. We were gonna win. More importantly, Blue and I had proven we could totally hold our own amongst the heroes. I was thrilled; on top of the world (or at least pretty close to it at this altitude).

Unfortunately, this euphoria didn't last. An instant later it was unexpectedly replaced with quite possibly the most awful feeling I would ever know.

It felt like someone had simultaneously slammed me on both sides with a pair of really robust, invisible Pegas, but worse. Worse because the pains kept coming like one strike after another with no apparent way of stopping their agony as I didn't even know what was causing them.

My body convulsed so hard that I lost my grip on Daniel's staff. My foot, however, was twisted within the toehold of his saddle. So, rather than falling off the Pegasus altogether, I was now dangling from it upside down.

The position made the helmet fall from my head, which allowed my hair to spill out. It blew around my face erratically as I was dragged through the clouds like a flying rag doll.

In retrospect, I conceded maybe it was a good thing that the invisible blows of pain I kept feeling were causing me to lose consciousness. Because, had I been less disoriented, I probably would have been way more freaked out by the fact that I was hanging just below the rampaging hooves of a Pegasus that was violently plummeting through the air.

Out of it as I was, I did see Daniel staring down at me. His helmet covered most of his face, but his dark eyes more than conveyed how shocked he was.

I figured he probably thought it served me right to be suspended in this precarious position. Yet, instead of letting me continue to be dangerously dragged along, he actually had the nerve to try and help me.

Daniel removed his lacrosse sword from its holster and

swung the basket side down as far as it would reach. "Grab on!" he ordered.

I swallowed my dizziness and eyed the staff Daniel extended to me. But, tempting as it was to get out of this situation, I didn't take it.

How could I?

Let him help me? Save me? Prove he was right about me this whole time? I'd much rather hang upside down like this until we landed than give him the satisfaction.

Sadly, this didn't appear to be an option for me either. Whatever clarity I'd had left after the first round of jolting pains had come on, evaporated at the onset of the second.

They were more intense this time, and my strength correspondingly disintegrated with each convulsion. On the fifth shockwave, my foot jerked sufficiently enough to free itself from the saddle's toehold, allowing me to be completely thrown off Daniel's Pegasus and into the sky.

My hair rippled through the wind as I plunged toward the stadium, which was erupting in cheers as Blue scored the winning goal somewhere in the distance. My world, though, was spinning too much now to see straight, let alone see her. I was beginning to black out.

Lamentably, unconsciousness did not overtake me before I heard the discernable sound of people in the crowd murmuring and interrupting the merry tone of the applause.

"LOOK!" someone yelled.

They'd seen me—my long hair having been a dead giveaway no doubt.

Missing a shot, falling off a Pegasus, and getting eliminated from the game were all upsetting turns of fate. But the idea of losing consciousness just in time for everyone to see that it was me in that suit of armor was absolutely mortifying.

My hands flailed and I gasped for air as I tried to stay awake. Alas, my efforts made no difference. It felt like I was drowning. My vision blurred and my entire body just felt heavier and heavier as breathing became more difficult and everything grew foggy like it did at the end of one of my nightmares . . .

CHAPTER 11

I'm Doomed

 Pegasus licking my face was the most unusual way I'd ever been woken up.

I opened my eyes and Sadie's large pink tongue swept across my forehead a second time. I could hear a chorus of gasps and murmurs accompanying the general blur of the arena, but most of the details remained indiscernible. The few things I did manage to perceive were Blue, SJ, and Jason having some kind of argument with Lady Agnue on one side of me, and Daniel on the other. He was just standing there, looking down on me.

And yes, I do mean in both senses of the phrase.

Needless to say the Pegasus saliva was the best part of the experience.

It was too much to handle, so I was actually thankful I blacked out again. Unfortunately, my subconscious chose to transport me to the nightmarish world of Natalie Poole because, apparently, living through one crushing reality this afternoon just wasn't enough.

Natalie was in a busy hallway that reminded me of my own school, what with its flood of kids, myriad of books being transported back and forth, and general sense of conformity. But this place was also a lot more gray, a bit more depressing, and smelled vaguely of bologna and sneakers.

She was approaching one of the many lockers that lined the walls—desperately clutching an art history book like it was a security blanket. When Natalie reached the locker (her locker, I guessed), she tucked the book under one arm and put in the combination. Just as she was about to open it, though, she stopped short. Behind her the crowds were parting as a small group of individuals began to pass by.

I'd gone to a school for protagonists long enough to detect the air of self-importance that followed around people who thought too much of themselves. And this pack of kids striding down the corridor reeked of it.

The five teens that exhibited the severe, self-endowed case of "chosen one syndrome" consisted of three obvious lackeys and two leaders. The boy leader was starkly handsome, so much so that he may have even given Chance Darling a run for his money. And yet . . . he did not have the cockiness in his expression that Chance did. Instead there seemed to be something like kindness residing in its place.

The other top dog in the group was a blonde girl that had her skinny arm linked through the handsome boy's muscular one. Her appearance reminded me of Mauvrey, as did the venom in her grin and the demon coldness in her piercing eyes.

As the whole group came closer to Natalie the lead boy smiled at her warmly. Natalie's face flushed in response and she absentmindedly continued to grasp at her locker's handle as their eyes met. Regrettably, the second she opened the locker door a booby trap went off inside, causing a balloon filled with red paint to explode all over her.

The hallway echoed with laughter at her expense. The obvious ringleader was the aforementioned alpha-blonde. The only person who didn't laugh was the handsome boy.

He tried to tell the others to take it easy, but the female leech on his arm made sure the guffaws were far too loud for anyone to hear him.

Utterly mortified, Natalie slammed the locker shut and took off running. Eventually she came to a door. As she burst through it, a giant flash of bright white light consumed my perspective.

A series of brief, vivid flashes proceeded to rush across my dreamscape. People ran through the streets screaming as a large shadow passed over them, rocks crumbled like a cave in, a forest exploded with cannon fire, a train plummeted downhill through the night, and then—

"She escaped."

"How is that even possible? She's a princess and she was unprotected."

"That's just it, though; she *wasn't* unprotected."

"How do you mean? You cornered her alone, didn't you?"

"Yes, but she . . . protected herself."

"Well, you're a hunter, aren't you? Adapt. And the next time you find her—"

"I know. End her."

"Exactly. Despite that smirk on your face, I know you understand how serious this is; how important it is to our cause. Why *are* you smiling anyway? It's hardly like you."

"Because I take pride in my work, majesty. And after meeting the girl, I can honestly say that taking care of this one will be my pleasure . . ."

Suddenly glass was raining down everywhere I looked. It was black in shade, but stained in red and gold hues that caused its sharp edges to shimmer. Just as abruptly, from within the downpour the head of an enormous, bronze serpent jolted out. Its mouth was open, and it lunged in my direction. My heart stopped with cold horror as the metallic creature's fangs rushed toward me, about to swallow me whole, until—

Until nothing.

Natalie Poole's tormented world, those strange, but jarring, disconnected flashes, the skin-crawling voices of that ever-present, uncharacterizable boy and the girl he always seemed to be talking to in the epilogues of my nightmares—all of it vanished.

The next thing I knew, I was in a completely different room; this one filled with cots and silence. When I looked around I discovered that I was lying in one of the cots while still wearing the majority of my Twenty-Three Skidd armor.

I'm awake, I realized with a rush of relief.

And evidently in an infirmary.

Adelaide Castle's infirmary, unlike our own, was really something to write home about. There were six beds (mine included) in the room. They were powder blue and their silk comforters had unique, contrasting navy wave patterns weaved into them. Additionally, each bed had a glistening silver headboard, a nightstand made of sea glass, and what appeared to be handmade candles shaped like different types of exotic sea creatures sitting atop the white shelves protruding above them.

It was all super impressive to say the least. Although the most beautiful thing to behold in this place was not so much any of these lovely amenities, but the view of the ocean outside.

One wall of the infirmary was constructed entirely of twenty-foot tall, glass windows that faced the sea. There was a selection of open glass doors interposed between them that led out to a balcony too. So, not only did I have the privilege of looking out at this magnificent body of water, but I could also take in its smell as a light wind passed the distinct scent through the doors—filling the whole room with a sense of complete peace.

Not a bad place to recover.

SJ and Blue were presently facing one of these windows, staring out at the sea and completely covered in afternoon sunlight. The same rays of sunshine also glinted off my armor and helmet, which I found perched on the nearest nightstand along with my dirtied riding gloves.

I blinked hard as I tried to adjust to the light. It was difficult, as was pretty much any other kind of movement I proceeded to attempt. The worst though, was the feeling in my lungs. They felt hurt, heavy, and unusually still—like they were barely working at half capacity. Which obviously was troubling because I kind of needed them for breathing.

Wait; hold on. Breathing . . . Was I even doing that?

I suddenly let out a huge hacking cough and air rushed into my body.

Ah, there we go.

The sound caused SJ and Blue to whirl around. When they saw I was conscious again they couldn't have dashed to by bedside any faster.

"Crisa, you are awake!" SJ gushed, hugging me awkwardly around my armor.

"That was really something," Blue commented, hugging me on my other side. "Even for you."

"Thanks," I grunted as I sat up straighter. The blood rushed to my head and I became all too aware that it was pounding with a migraine. I rubbed the back of my neck and squinted at the pain. "What happened?"

Blue and SJ fidgeted—neither of them meeting my gaze. I was confused as to the reason for this at first, but then I realized what they didn't want to tell me, and what I probably should've already figured out for myself.

"My prologue prophecy appeared," I gulped. "Didn't it?"

"Yeah," Blue affirmed, finally looking me in the eye. "'Fraid so."

I held my breath as I reached for my helmet. Sure enough, in its reflection I saw the condemning spiral mark on my forehead. I pushed a loose strand of hair behind my ear to get a proper look at it.

The mark was nearly gone. All but the faintest traces of it had blended in with my skin. But its soft appearance did not matter. In that moment, I knew I could live a hundred years and the image would never fade from my memory. It was burned into me like a bullseye; a target; a cast iron brand on a cow who'd been marked for slaughter.

Placing my helmet back on the nightstand, I swallowed the sight and the understanding like the sourest of cough syrups. My book had begun. My life, or whatever bit of life I actually had, was over. Now would have been another really good time for a blackout, but alas, I received no such luck. This was my new reality. And I knew I could never go back.

"The Scribes are zapping it over to Lady Agnue. It should be here any time now," Blue said, interrupting the silence.

No sooner did she say this than the infirmary doors burst open. Lady Agnue strolled into the room with purpose carrying a large book under her right arm—*my* book, I presumed, as my name was encrusted in gold lettering on the forest green front cover.

I had to suppress the urge to vomit on sight.

"Glad to see you are awake, Miss Knight," our headmistress

said coldly. "The sooner we get this over with, the sooner we can discuss your punishment."

"Listen, Lady Agnue—" I started to say.

"Not a word, Miss Knight," she snapped. "You have embarrassed me, the school, and yourself above all else with your antics today and there is no turn of phrase your smart mouth can conjure that will change that. What you did was a disgrace. For Blue it was breaking the rules, but most people do not have very high expectations for her anyways."

"Hey!" Blue interjected.

Lady Agnue rolled her eyes and waved off my friend without missing a beat. "But you entering in the Twenty-Three Skidd tournament was simply unacceptable," she continued. "You have brought shame to the very princess institution. Honestly, if it was not for your mother being who she is, I would have you expelled or even . . ."

Our headmistress took a deep breath—obviously trying to rein in her anger. "But I digress," she said after a long exhale. "And as expulsion is not presently a sentence I am allowed to bestow upon you, we had best move on to the matter of your prologue prophecy."

"About that, headmistress," SJ cut in timidly. "What happened to Crisa today? Traditionally when our prologues appear we experience a few brief jolts and a fainting spell—maybe a light headache when we awaken. Crisa has been unconscious for nearly five hours and she looks as though she has been hit by a carriage."

I was tempted to be insulted by the remark, but the truth was I did feel like I'd been hit by a carriage . . . and then nearly drowned, and then trampled by a Pegasus to boot. My head was on fire, my bones felt like giftwrap tissue, and my hands were white as snow.

Geez, what had happened to me?

"Miss Knight's prologue pang was very severe, I agree," Lady Agnue admitted. "Usually the intensity level of the pang corresponds with the intensity of the prologue prophecy that has appeared for that protagonist. If the prophecy has very high stakes and responsibilities, for example, the pang will be more extreme. However, Miss Knight's prophecy is so ordinary and uncomplicated that I truly do not understand why it affected her so severely. Perhaps she is just weak."

Ignoring this comment, I stared at Lady Agnue and then at my book. It was time for me to know. I nodded at her and straightened up—bracing myself for the terrible blow to come.

Lady Agnue opened the book to the first page, but before she began to read she hesitated and glanced over at Blue and SJ.

As mentioned before, there were two cardinal rules with prologue prophecy readings. One: The only times the books that contained them left the Scribes' possession were for these readings. And two: The only outsiders allowed to read them were the schools' headmasters and the protagonists whom they were about. Unless that protagonist authorized otherwise of course.

I nodded again at Lady Agnue, giving her the okay to continue. SJ and Blue were my best friends. I needed them there with me, now more than ever. On my signal our headmistress cleared her throat and began to read me my fate.

"The girl impervious to love at first sight,
Will soon find that Prince Darling is her white knight.

Limited excitement or affect of spells,
Uncomplicated courtship leads to wedding bells.
Obedient, elegant, the exemplary wife,
And destined to lead a Perfect Fairytale Life."

Okay, so I didn't know what kind of thoughts were running through SJ and Blue's heads at that particular moment, but mine went a little something like this: *"Ahhhh!!!!!"*

That's as good as I could describe it to you anyways. Truthfully, in my head it sounded a bit more intense than that. But as I lack the ability to accurately convey the world-shattering, wheel-screeching, explosion-obliterating sound that welled up in my brain right then, "Ahhhh!!!!!" would have to do.

"Lady Agnue," I managed to stutter after the initial shock had passed. "That can't be my prophecy. It just can't be! I mean, it's like . . . and I'm like . . . Well, for starters there is absolutely no way that I'm marrying *Chance Darling*! Everything about that prophecy is wrong. It has to be."

Our headmistress shut my book sternly and glared at me dead on.

"Believe me, Miss Knight, I am as surprised as anyone. To begin with, in order for a lady to accomplish any of the events in this prologue I would have assumed she needed to be a good princess, which we all know is simply not who you are. Nevertheless, it would seem that we were both wrong. Myself in regards to believing that a terrible princess such as yourself could not lead a perfect fairytale life, and you in regards to believing you could be some kind of hero."

"But—" I started to protest again.

"But nothing," Lady Agnue interceded. "While you may not like the truth, Miss Knight, I strongly suggest now, as I have for years, that you stop fighting the inevitable and get over it. This, and nothing more, will be your fate. Who you are has been decided, and it is in no way up for debate."

With that, Lady Agnue nodded goodbye to SJ and Blue and excused herself from the infirmary with a loud slam of the door. When she'd gone, I leaned back against the coldness of the headboard and closed my eyes to the coldness of the world.

For years I'd wondered what my reaction would be when I someday received my prologue prophecy.

Would I yell and scream? Burst into tears? Throw a tantrum? Pretend like nothing was wrong? Take a flame-thrower to my book? Or all of the above?

In truth, however, my reaction was absolutely nothing like that. In fact, it was nothing like I'd expected it to be, period.

At first I sat in silence staring at the swelling sea as I tried to process the news. I attempted to analyze every logical option, reasonable consequence, and inherent domino effect of the different courses of action I might take next—just as I knew SJ would do. Although, in the following moments, the gut feelings and uncensored instinct that were more characteristic of Blue's teachings struggled against such rationale and begged for a more impulsive, ardent response.

Both these forms of influence persisted to pull me back and forth for a few minutes—each competing for my undivided commitment and urging me to make a definite choice between leading with my head or my heart from here on out.

But then, as I stood on the threshold of this crossroads and felt the weight of both paths begging for fidelity, something happened.

An idea suddenly formed within me that was a by-product of both. It was something logical and instinctive, something thought-out and impetuous, and something that my head knew was possible just as surely as my heart knew it was right. Call it a burst of genius or a stroke of utter insanity—it was by far the strongest, most ridiculous, most inspiring thought I'd ever had. And the second it was born I knew there would be no going back or reasoning with it.

"No," I abruptly blurted out.

SJ blinked. "What do you mean, *no?*" she asked.

I sat up straight again, my blood practically boiling from the resolve beginning to burn inside of me. "I mean NO. I don't care what Lady Agnue, or that stupid prophecy, or the Author says. The girl described in that book isn't who I am. I won't . . . I *can't* let it be. There has to be another way, another option. And I don't know how, but I'm gonna find it and I am going to change my fate. I have to."

"Crisa," Blue sighed. "Believe me, I get how you feel; you know that I do. And you know I'm very pro rule-breaking. But defying one of the Author's books isn't about breaking a rule. It's trying to go against life and, like, nature itself. That's never been done."

"Then it's long overdue," I responded without pause.

SJ and Blue looked at me like I was crazy. But, honestly, I would've thought they were crazy if they hadn't. What I was suggesting was unheard of—it was completely insane. Of course, that didn't mean it was impossible . . . Right?

I could see the gears turning in their heads as they tried to wrap their minds around the ludicrous prospect I'd just presented them with.

My friends were loyal, dependable, and usually game for whatever mischief or adventure came our way. However, I wasn't exactly asking them to crash a tournament or play a prank on Madame Lisbon. I was asking them to believe that we could rebel against everything we'd been taught to accept our entire lives, *and* believe that it could work.

Moreover, I was asking them to put their faith in that idea as it came out of me—the girl who'd just thought of the totally bananas plan within moments after receiving life-altering news, and who might've also been suffering the side effects of a partial concussion from a 500-foot drop.

Eventually though, it was Blue who first began to humor the notion.

"Let's say it could be done . . ." she pondered aloud, "changing your fate, changing all our fates I mean. How would we even go about it?"

"The Author," I answered firmly. "Everyone knows that the only person with the power to control fates is the Author. And I figure if she wrote these in the first place, then there's no reason she can't just write us new ones—but this time ones of our own design."

"Okay, so we'd have to get to the Author," Blue continued.

SJ shook her head. "It is impossible."

"Or something very close to it," Blue corrected.

The two of them had a kind of silent conversation with their eyes for a beat as they thought on the notion. After a few moments had passed I let out a deep breath and readdressed them before common sense could cause their conviction to slip away from me any further.

"Look," I asserted. "Blue, you were right before. Wishes don't change anything. But actions *can*. We can change that prophecy the Author gave you and rewrite your destiny to be something that you actually want it to be. And, SJ, we can insure that the one you eventually get is based on your will, not someone else's, and that the only role assigned to you in the future is one that you picked out for yourself.

"The bottom line is this, guys: I know it sounds nuts, but I also know that neither of you are happy with the Author's ability to just up and take our lives from us. *So*, I am simply saying that we shouldn't just sit here and throw in the towel. We owe it to ourselves to at least try and take them back. You know that we do."

I paused and watched as contemplation cut across my friends' faces.

The idea sunk in.

The idea took hold.

The idea was . . . *considered*.

"All right," SJ said after the beat of reflection had passed. "Suppose it *were* possible. To begin with we would need to find a way to escape Lady Agnue's in order to even attempt a journey to the Indexlands at all."

"And more importantly, we'd have to figure out how to break the most permanent, and supposedly unbreakable spell in Book: the In and Out Spell *around* the Indexlands, " Blue added.

I raised my eyebrows hopefully. "Does that mean you're in?"

Blue and SJ looked at each other. I figured they were each racking their brains trying to see if any of the reasons not to do this outweighed how much they knew they actually wanted to.

As suspected, none did. The idea to change our lives, take our fates into our own hands, and decide who we were for ourselves—it was an insane, beautiful, tempting idea that could not be extinguished now that we'd given life to it.

SJ placed her fingers to her temple to ward off a headache

for the second time today. "Crisa, if we are going to do this, first and foremost we will need information."

Blue tilted her head curiously. "What kind of information?" she asked.

I smiled mischievously, leaned forward, and lowered my voice to a whisper to avoid being heard by a passing nurse.

"*Fairy Godmother* information," I replied.

CHAPTER 12

I Hitch A Ride On A Magic Mushroom

rying comes easy for teenage girls. Frankly, I think we're genetically engineered for the vulnerable undertaking.

In my opinion, this sucked. For, no matter how tough or logical we were, if we lowered our defenses at the proper moment all it took was the right emotional rise to get the waterworks going.

I'd lived at an all-girl boarding school long enough to validate this claim, *and* confirm that the innate shortcoming was as inconvenient as it was annoying.

Like thanks, nature. It's super helpful to get all misty-eyed just from reading a sad book or because the banquet hall ran out of chocolate chip cookies.

Sigh.

Emotions are the worst, aren't they?

Anyways, it was because of this inherent ability to turn on the waterworks that the Fairy Godmothers no longer responded to every princess or female protagonist at the drop of a tear like they used to. Now there was a whole routine we had to go through in order to get their attention.

My friends and I were presently in the back garden

of Adelaide Castle just past the orchard where we'd been conspiring earlier. The hour was late, the stars were out, and the odds were not great. But, there we were.

SJ was fixing my makeup (for extra showmanship when the performance commenced) while Blue was standing beneath a weeping willow nearby, talking with Daniel and Jason. She was holding a large purple textbook with *"Damsels in Distress 601"* written on the cover in silver. She was laughing, smiling, and seemed to be having a good time.

"Look up," SJ ordered as she applied my mascara.

I held back my urge to object and obeyed her request, but tried to keep Blue and the boys in my line of sight in the process.

More than ever I wanted to ask Blue why she still remained so amicable with Jason. The behavior she'd been exhibiting was mind-boggling. I mean, not only was he the guy she was unwillingly chained to for the rest of her existence. But the main reason she was game for this little fate-challenging adventure was to fix that very problem.

Despite my longing to probe into the matter further, I forced myself to continue to leave it alone just as I had been doing for the past month. SJ and I had made a promise to each other that as long as Blue didn't bring it up, we wouldn't bug her about it. An agreement I was seriously trying to respect since I could truly empathize with our friend's situation. Now that I had a prologue prophecy of my own, it was totally the last thing I wanted anyone to bother me about.

Hmm. Maybe in hindsight of those feelings . . . I *could* understand Blue's silence on the subject. At least from a practical standpoint.

I'd been devastated to receive my prologue prophecy. But I'd immediately realized in the ever aftermath that allowing myself to writhe in that distress was pointless. The only thing it would accomplish would be me feeling more miserable.

Conversely, if I ignored these feelings of dismay and refused to give them the satisfaction of crushing me and taking away my sense of fight, then I could turn around and try to convert my energy into something useful. And that (like Blue, I garnered) was the course of action I'd elected to take.

It was simply more productive to keep my mind focused on the long, arguably impossible goal ahead rather than get caught up in the despair of the present. Turning melancholy into fire for fueling resolve was a far better use of one's time than sulking in it, after all.

This had always been as much Blue's style as it had been mine. And now, more than ever, I was truly grateful for my tendency to bottle up weaker feelings in this manner. For if I could keep doing that—keep my eyes on the prize and avoid the heartache that common sense or cowering to the odds would bring—it might just give me the inferno-sized fire I'd need to fight what was coming.

SJ finished with my makeup and called the others over so that we could go through our plan once more.

"Okay, Blue," I said when we'd all gathered round. "Read the checklist again."

Our friend opened her textbook to the designated page. "Alrighty," she said. "'A princess or other female protagonist will surely receive help from a Fairy Godmother if she experiences: One: An Unpleasant Confrontation. Two: Insulting/Hurtful Words. And Three: Tears that cause her to run away to a private location, fall to the ground, and bury her face in her hands.'"

"That's so specific," Jason laughed.

"Yup, apparently damsels do it by the book," I responded. "Now then, let's get this show on the road. Come on, Jason. You're on."

"Oh, Crisa, didn't I tell you?" Blue interjected. "Jason's not your co-star this evening. Daniel is . . ."

I was pretty sure my blood pressure went up at the mere suggestion. I held up a finger to the boys. "One second, please," I said brusquely. They gave me a strange look, but nodded as I grabbed SJ and Blue by the wrists and pulled them away.

I lowered my voice so that the boys wouldn't hear. "Blue, what are you talking about? First off, I can't believe you even let Jason *tell* Daniel about this. He's here now, and I'm dealing with it, but there is no way I'm actually going to team up with him for this next part. No way, you hear me? None. Zip. Zero. Just absolutely not—you got it?"

"Crisa," Blue whispered. "Jason is good at a lot of things—axe-throwing, high-fiving, rope swinging. But confronting people just isn't his scene, recreationally or otherwise. I mean, come on, the guy's practically got honest-to-goodness selflessness carved into his DNA. He won't be able to do this even if he is acting. SJ and I both agree that you'll have much better luck with Daniel. He's naturally good at insulting you."

"Besides," SJ said, patting me on the shoulder. "Jason told us that Daniel is apparently just as adamant about changing his fate as we are, so we can count on him. You really should give the boy a chance, Crisa. He is not that bad, you know."

"No, actually. I don't know."

"Well, Jason mentioned that Daniel tried to save you during the tournament. He tried to keep you from falling when your prologue pang hit."

"Emphasis on 'tried,'" I asserted. "More emphasis on the fact that I definitely didn't ask him to."

It irritated me like no other that Daniel had felt compelled to try and save me today. And it irritated me even more that I had put myself in a situation where I needed saving in the first place.

No girl should do that; it's far too clichéd and way too demoralizing.

But it happened. My attempts at trying to prove I could be a hero had (quite literally) fallen to the ground. What's more? My heroic boy nemesis had been given a front seat to the whole spectacle and was no doubt itching to hold it over me.

Still . . . as much as I wanted to avoid spending time with him because of this, I knew SJ was right. Daniel would be way better for the role of confronting and hurting me than Jason. And that's exactly what we needed in order for our mission to get its heels off the ground. So, while I loathed the idea with a passion bordering on detrimental, I reluctantly agreed to the casting change and my friends and I rejoined the others.

Blue cleared her throat as she proceeded to cover the rest of the plan.

She had stolen several Pegasi from the Adelaide Castle stable, which she'd tied to an apple tree in the orchard. She, SJ, and Jason would be hiding with them while Daniel and I did our thing. Then, once I'd "burst into tears," I would run to the nearby riverbank and Daniel would join them until the Fairy Godmother arrived and I yelled the signal. This would subsequently cause the Godmother to realize she had been called there as a trick and make her take off—creating a trail for us to follow right to our desired destination: Fairy Godmother Headquarters.

Fairy Godmothers travelled in the form of shooting stars, you see. So any one of them would've been easy enough to pursue via Pegasi as she flew across the sky leaving a glistening trajectory of light in her wake.

It was kind of a hassle, but this whole routine was necessary because (as mentioned) Fairy Godmother Headquarters floated somewhere in the sky over Book. Not only that, it was always moving to protect its Godmothers from people who would take advantage of them—magic hunters or otherwise.

As such, the only way the Godmothers left themselves vulnerable to outsiders was in the manner I'd just explained. At least theoretically anyways, given that no one had ever made a run at what we were attempting. Only princesses and other female protagonists had the power to call for magical help in this way. And thus far it seemed the majority considered ticking off Fairy Godmothers a risk they'd presumably rather avoid.

I, on the other hand, had already gotten on the bad side of that one Godmother, Lena Lenore, so unlike my protagonist counterparts I figured a second didn't really make a difference.

In retrospect, I knew ours was not the most elaborate or foolproof plan for reaching the Godmothers' elusive domain. But to be fair, since it had to be executed tonight, my crew and I had been forced to work pretty quickly to get it together.

In the morning we were leaving Adelaide to return to our respective schools. Once we were back, the In and Out

Spell around Lady Agnue's would go up again—preventing us from leaving the campus and, ergo, from attempting to get to Fairy Godmother HQ to talk to Emma. Which was the whole reason we were doing this in first place.

In order to reach the Author we needed to find a way past the impenetrable In and Out Spell surrounding the Indexlands.

Since the Godmothers were the ones who'd cast the spell all those years ago, we figured that they'd be the only ones with knowledge on how to break it. Yes, we knew no random Godmother was just going to up and share this kind of powerful information with us; that was a given. However, our thinking—our hope as it were—was that my mother's Fairy Godmother (my own regular godmother, Emma Carrington) might just be the exception to this rule.

Like I said, she used to be a big part of my family when I was little. And despite her withdrawal from our lives a decade ago, the two things I still remembered about her very clearly were how much she loved me, and how she was one of the few people who'd never treated me like a misshapen piece in someone else's puzzle. She'd believed in me. She'd believed I could be more. So if anybody would've been willing to give my friends and I the information we needed and support us with what we were trying to do—I felt certain it would've been her.

A minute later when Blue finally finished with the full recap of our plan, she turned to address me specifically.

"Crisa, I don't know how this Godmother will react to, you know, being tricked down here. But good luck. Assuming she doesn't turn you into a koi fish, we'll have to move fast to have a shot at making this work."

My friend closed the book and pulled up the hood on her

cloak in full mischief mode. We said our farewells and she, Jason, and SJ went to hide while Daniel and I were left alone together to execute the first phase of our mission.

He and I proceeded to stroll across the grounds uncomfortably and wordlessly as we tried to find a nice open spot for our imminent performance.

To be honest I preferred the silence, and was dreading when it would end. I didn't want to talk to him; I didn't even want to look at him. Just seeing his face filled me with anger. Partly at him naturally for, well, being him, but mainly at myself. One glance and everything came rushing back. I could see his face looking down on me as I dangled from his Pegasus—the epitome of a damsel, of weakness.

Maybe Lady Agnue was right; maybe I was as poor an excuse for a hero as I was for a princess. Maybe I really didn't have control over who I was no matter how hard I tried and this was all just a waste of time.

No. Stop it. You're going to prove her wrong. You're going to prove the Author wrong. You're going to prove them all wrong, my inner voice reminded me.

It doesn't matter what that prophecy says. Who I am isn't written yet. And the only person who will have a say in it when it is, is me.

I shook my head as Daniel and I continued to walk—attempting to rid myself of the doubts that wormed their way into my subconscious the more I thought about this afternoon's turn of events.

Eventually we stopped at the top of a small hill overlooking a ravine. The moon was casting a glow over the entire property and reflecting off the water below. My right arm still sore from the fall during the tournament, I took a moment to switch my satchel to the left shoulder. Meanwhile,

Daniel gazed out into the distance all serious-like as if he were thinking about something deep and philosophical.

Like even.

"So . . . um, Daniel, why are you doing this exactly?" I suddenly asked him—my curiosity inexplicably overtaking my better judgment to avoid speaking to him for as long as possible.

He raised his eyebrows—evidently as surprised as I was that I'd been the one to initiate the conversation.

"Done with the silent treatment, are we?"

"Being silent isn't one of my specialties," I replied with a shrug. "Just like being charming isn't one of yours. Now really, how bad is your prologue prophecy that you felt compelled to join our small gang of rebels? I mean, you barely know us for starters. But more than that, most people would say what we're attempting is nuts."

"Yes. They would," he agreed. "But my prologue and why I'm joining your little quest don't matter. They're *my* business. And you of all people shouldn't get involved. Got it?"

His tone had risen sharply just then and I took an awkward step back in response. He seemed to get a handle on whatever weirdness had possessed him though, and his cool, collected swagger returned in the next instant.

"So, on to *our* business," he continued as he began to pace around me. "I can see that this confrontation is already unpleasant enough for you, so I think we can check that off the list. Which means that I guess now I'll proceed to, quote, 'hurt you with my words.'"

I crossed my arms and maintained eye contact with him as he circled around me. "Honestly, Daniel, no matter what our friends believe, I don't think there is any insult you could throw my way that would hurt me. Tick me off, sure. You've proven that time and again. But hurt me? You've got no chance."

"Because you're not like the other princesses," he said. "You're not fragile, delicate, or sensitive."

"Exactly," I agreed.

"Not subtle, graceful, or naturally endearing."

"I suppose not," I said.

"You're rude, impatient, and judgmental."

"Yeah, and so are you," I scoffed.

"True," Daniel continued without missing a beat. "But unlike you, I'm not the self-destructive outcast of my school. I mean let's face it, Knight, you don't really belong at Lady Agnue's, and the only reason they don't kick you out is because of who your mom is."

"Well, I don't know if I'd say—"

"It's too bad, really," he interrupted. "Your mom is one of the most famous fairytale characters of all time, beloved by people in every realm. And *you* are her legacy—literally the worst princess Book has ever seen. Bringing shame to her name and yours one stupid stunt at a time, like at today's tournament."

"Hey, that's not—"

"And the saddest part," he cut me off again, "is that even if you are okay with this, you can't fight what's coming. No matter how much you struggle against it and try to be something more, in the end who you are will never be yours to decide. In fact, that role is already picked out for you. It's sitting on a shelf right now, telling you the same thing that everybody else already knows but you're too stubborn to admit—you'll never be strong enough to fight it, no matter how much you wish you were. All you can ever be is exactly what you are—a sorry excuse for a princess and another damsel in distress incapable of being a hero."

I was wrong.

That had hurt me. At the very least it had gotten under my skin.

My first instinct was to punch him, but then Daniel winked at me and I realized this was my cue. So instead I allowed my legs to carry me quickly down the hill toward the ravine.

I wasn't sure if the moonlight had prevented Daniel from noticing how red my face had gotten, but I hoped it had. While the tears I forced out of my eyes and my dramatic collapse to the riverbank were fake, the doubts he'd managed to hone in on definitely weren't.

How did he do that? I wondered as I knelt in the marsh. *How did he know just the right words to get to me like this?*

I already had to regularly fend off the insecurities about everything I was and everything I wasn't brought on by archenemies like Lady Agnue and Mauvrey. With them, at least I could keep the effect of their words at a minimum by either staying away from them, or dishing back sassy retorts that sufficiently silenced their venom. But Daniel was different. I couldn't push him away like an enemy because he'd somehow slipped his way into my inner circle of friends. Meanwhile, since I really didn't know anything about him (aside from the fact that he had a shocking amount of self-confidence and a blatant disregard for people's feelings toward him), I had no kind of ammo to throw back in his face.

The worst part still was the fact that someone I'd basically known for a month could pick up on insecurities I tried so hard to conceal. Which in turn made me wonder if maybe they were a lot less baseless than I wanted to believe.

I mean I'd known Mauvrey and Lady Agnue forever so it was way more acceptable that they'd learned enough about me over time to discern my insecurities. But with Daniel . . . well, he'd noticed them right away.

Were they—was *I*—really that obvious?

I continued my bogus crying by the riverbank for a couple more minutes but, alas, nothing happened. No magic, no fairy dust, nothing. Absolutely zip. And the previous mental tangent having worn me out already, I was starting to get uncomfortable sitting there. The embankment was cold and kind of damp. Add to that, I didn't know how many more fake tears I had left in me before my supply dried out.

Thankfully, right as I began to get discouraged and think this a failed endeavor I noticed a bright red glow reflecting in the river beside me—rapidly getting bigger.

I turned my head toward the sky and witnessed a ball of fiery glitter zooming across the clouds before plowing into the mud a few feet away. When the flash of light subsided, a woman appeared before me. She was dressed in a luminescent silvery gown with shimmering ruffles that made it look like streaks of lightning were embedded into the fabric. The remarkable ensemble, like her smile, lit up the area around us.

The woman's eyes, too, twinkled just as brightly. They were a deep blue and contrasted with her bright red mane, which was pulled up in a high ponytail with small crystal bobby pins sticking out all around it. The most noticeable characteristic about her appearance, though, was that she seemed surprisingly young for a Fairy Godmother. She didn't appear to be more than a few years older than me.

"Hi!" the Godmother chirped.

"Um, hi," I said, wiping the pretend tears off my face as I got up from the ground.

"So, what's up?" she asked me outright.

I tilted my head, a bit taken aback by her directness. "I, uh . . . need your help."

"Well, duh!" she gushed. "I mean what can I do to help you? Wait—hold that thought. Before you tell me, I should let you know that I can only provide you with a fabulous new gown, give you a ride to a ball, or transform animals into helpful attendants. If you need anything other than that I'm going to have to call my supervisor."

"Come again?"

"I'm new, you see and, well, I'm still in training and that's all I know how to do so far. You know, the basics."

I looked away and rolled my eyes.

Figures that dresses, rides to balls, and animal sidekicks are the basics.

I stared at her a bit longer, which I guess made her feel awkward because she bit her nails nervously and then began fidgeting with one of her ruby-encrusted bangle bracelets.

Upon studying her more carefully I noticed that there was, in fact, a silver nametag pinned to her dress that read: "DEBBIE NIGHTENGALE (Trainee)."

While others might have considered this a setback, the wheels in my head had long started to turn and I realized that if I played my cards right I might actually be able to work this curveball to my advantage.

"Um, Debbie," I began. "I don't need a gown, but I do need a ride. Think you can help me out?"

"Yeah, for sure," she replied. "Just tell me your destination and I'll see what I can do."

I twiddled my thumbs, feigning embarrassment. "The destination is kind of personal actually. Could you possibly just whip me up something that can go anywhere? I'd be ever so grateful."

"I don't know," Debbie said slowly. "We're really supposed to get all the details before we use magic to help our Godkids."

I faked an epiphany-esque expression and gave her a patronizing head nod. "Ohhh, I see. Look, Debbie, if you haven't learned how to cast that kind of spell yet it's no big deal. You don't have to lie to me. I'm not gonna hold it against you for being a trainee."

"I didn't say I couldn't do it. I just don't think—"

"Deb, it's fine," I interrupted. "There's no shame in being new on the job. If you can't do it, you can't do it."

"I can do it," she asserted.

"Debbie, you don't have to. Seriously I can just find someone else to—"

"No really, I can do it!" she stated with confidence. "Just give me a chance. Watch." Debbie pulled out one of the crystal bobby pins from her hair. Instantly it grew into a magic wand. Long, slender, and off-white—it was identical to my own except for the fact that hers travelled in the form of a cute hair accessory while mine had to be lugged around in this old satchel.

Debbie scrunched her brow and closed her eyes—garnering concentration. After a few seconds she opened them again, waved her wand, and pointed it at a mushroom cap growing in the dirt by my feet.

Red sparks flew from the tip of her wand and encircled the mushroom like a tiny, shiny tornado. I barely had time to jump back before the spore inflated to the size of a carriage and sprouted four smaller spores at its base to serve as lopsided wheels.

Leftover sparks dissipated off the fully-grown mushroom carriage as I came closer. Debbie strutted proudly around its right side and patted her creation like a game show prize presenter. I studied the vehicle's magnitude. Debbie's eyes full of hope and eagerness to please, she tilted her head in my direction.

"So?" she asked.

"It's a carriage all right," I laughed happily.

"Yay! I am so glad you like it!" Debbie practically sang as she jumped up and down and gave me an excited hug.

Then, just as suddenly, she recomposed herself and put on the most serious expression she could muster. She waved her wand again, causing a piece of glowing parchment to shimmer into existence in her hand and a pair of bright red reading glasses to appear on her face.

Without hesitation Debbie held the parchment up to the moonlight and read its contents aloud.

"Young Princess, this carriage will take you anywhere you wish to go. It is a round trip ride for one person only, and will expire at the stroke of midnight. Please keep all arms, legs, and feet inside the vehicle at all times. Fairy Godmother Headquarters is not responsible for any physical or emotional injuries obtained as a result of this enchantment. If you are satisfied with the service your Fairy Godmother has provided, please fill out the attached survey on her performance. Once signed, the evaluation will be magically transported back to headquarters for appraisal. Thank you and, on behalf of Godmother Supreme, have a magical day."

All finished, Debbie took a deep breath and grinned from ear to ear—very pleased with herself. She then waved her wand once more, which made the glasses vanish from her face and the form she'd been holding magically reappear in my hand within a sealed envelope.

"By the way," Debbie added, not noticing my surprise. "You can totally fill that out whenever. It's magic paper, so it can't get ruined. And it's enchanted so you won't lose it until it's been signed. But if you can, try and get it in soon. Annual reviews are coming up and I'll be darned if that trick Tami Robinswood wins Godmother Trainee of the Year instead of me."

I nodded and shoved the envelope into my satchel. While I may not have known who Tami Robinswood was, I did know that I was totally going to give Debbie one heck of a review. The carriage was perfect, and it was a way better means for getting to Fairy Godmother HQ than chasing shooting star dust. Plus, I also felt kind of bad about tricking her into helping a human obtain a free ride to her and the other Godmothers' top-secret home base.

Guilt aside though, I knew I'd made the right call. I needed to get to HQ and this was the best way to accomplish that. Furthermore, a Fairy Godmother's whole purpose was to help her assigned Godkids get what they desired, and in this case the Godmother in question was Debbie and her Godkid was me. So, technically, we were both doing what we needed to.

I suppose that's either infallible logic or total bologna. Either way, what's done is done. Might as well just move on, try to make it up to her later, and inspect my new ride.

"Um, Debbie," I said as I looked over the enchanted vehicle she'd crafted and noted a fairly major problem with its construction. "Where's the door?"

Debbie panicked and scurried over to the carriage. She

inspected it and tapped her finger to her lip, perplexed. Then she waved her wand twice in the direction of the creation. More sparks zipped off its point, but they fizzled out when they made contact with the mushroom and nothing happened.

Her dress (which on closer inspection may have actually been made of real lightning) began to grow grayer, stormier. Streaks of light crackled angrily across the darkening, flickering fabric as she stood there with her arms crossed and her eyes glaring narrowly at the mushroom. Then, in a brief moment of frustration, Debbie abruptly scowled and kicked the vehicle.

Upon her heel's impact a door and several windows popped out of the fungus as if on cue. As soon as they appeared, the crinkle in Debbie's agitated expression softened.

"Ah, that's better," she sighed.

Her dress's storm subsided and faded back to its original iridescent shade. After tucking a loose strand of red hair behind her ear, Debbie made a grand, theatrical gesture toward the vehicle and asked me if there was anything else I required. I said no, and thanked her profusely for the help.

On that note, Debbie waved her wand a final time and red sparks appeared in a ring at her feet. They grew around her body until she evaporated into them—becoming one big ball of red, glowing energy. She levitated there in front of me for a second before taking off and soaring across the sky in a massive arc.

I watched in awe as she flew away, lighting up the black night with streaks of scarlet.

Just as her trail began to fade, my friends and Daniel came over the hill behind me on their Pegasi. Blue was mounted on the same gray, speckled Pegasus from this afternoon. And Daniel was on the back of the black steed he'd ridden earlier in the tournament as well.

I was further delighted to see that the third Pegasus (the one SJ and Jason were currently sharing) was also familiar. It was Sadie. Evidently she was as pleased to see me again as I was to see her, for her eyes lit up and she began to whinny excitedly the closer they drew toward me.

"Crisa!" Blue moaned as they approached. "What happened? We never heard you yell the signal and when the Godmother took off we weren't ready. Now the trail is gone and we'll never be able to follow her."

"Relax." I shrugged. "I've secured another means of transportation."

I proceeded to tell them what had occurred in their absence while avoiding eye contact with Daniel and scratching Sadie behind the ear. After my explanation—and a short lecture from SJ about how unprofessional Debbie's Fairy Godmother conduct was in soliciting a good review—I hopped into my one-seater mushroom carriage.

"Um," I said awkwardly once inside. "Take me to Fairy Godmother Headquarters."

Nothing happened.

"Come on, mushroom. Time to go."

Still nothing happened.

I started to feel foolish as my friends and Daniel stared at me through the window. But then I remembered something. "Blue," I called out of the carriage. "Kick the mushroom!"

Blue maneuvered her Pegasus next to my unorthodox vehicle and gave it a good smack with her left foot. At that, the whole thing shook and shot off into the sky like a comet—

leaving its own trail of red sparks and the smell of sautéed shiitake behind it.

Glancing out the window, I saw my friends and Daniel flying in pursuit a few dozen yards behind.

Well okay then. Mission on, I guess.

The carriage climbed higher and higher, ascending so close to the heavens the constellations probably felt claustrophobic. Like a foxhound in the front seat, I stuck my head out the window excitedly—my eyes taking in the spectacular sight and the wind rushing through my hair.

After a bit, the vehicle began accelerating and making sudden turns and small dives through the clouds. On each occurrence I glanced back to make sure I hadn't lost anyone. Thankfully, I never did. While at times the Pegasi did seem to be pushing themselves to keep up with my mushroom's unpredictable flight pattern, they kept on my tail.

The Pegasus with SJ and Jason on it did lag behind increasingly more than the others as our journey continued, though—a price for supporting two riders.

SJ hated flying, at least the Pegasus method of it anyways. This was partly due to her aversion of plummeting through the sky fully exposed. However, the fear was more attributed to the weird way horses tended to dislike her (a fact that I'd always found secretly a little hilarious given the way other animals would do just about anything for her).

In appeasement of these personal obstacles, it'd been necessary to pair our friend with someone for the trip. In my opinion Blue was a much better flyer than either of the boys, but since she enjoyed the occasional loop-de-loop, SJ had instantly opted for a different travel partner. Jason, always happy to help in any way that he could, had been the one to offer up his Pegasus flying services as a result.

His selflessness aside, I wondered if he was now regretting the decision. He was clearly having trouble steering with the way SJ was clutching him in a death grip of panic. She appeared to be violently digging into his sides like a frightened cat—anxiety etched across her face like cracks in a ceiling.

On the total opposite side of the spectrum, Blue was undeniably loving this chase. Her Pegasus's holographic, glistening wings shifted between different shades of royal blue as they flew, which set off the color of her cape as it flapped around her.

My friend was smiling like mad and continuously egging her steed to go faster, causing its wings to change color even more rapidly and her wavy blonde hair to wildly blow in the wind behind her.

Overall, while she may have been far away from me in proximity, I could still see that the thrill of the experience was making her eyes shine with a brightness that rivaled that of the stars around us.

My attention shifted to a different part of the sky then, and as a consequence I found myself observing the final member of our group—Daniel. His steed had produced silvery wings that looked sharp against the darkness of the sky, making him easy to spot.

From my vantage point Daniel didn't seem very happy, but he didn't seem afraid either. He had his eyes glued to the back of my carriage with a really determined expression on his face. Like everything else about him though, it was a look I could not decipher.

As I continued to study him from my safe distance,

I began to feel a tremble of cold remembrance slithering up my spine. I closed my eyes and shook my head in silent protest—trying yet again to ward off the gnawing feelings of insecurity.

But it was no use. The tighter I shut my eyes the more I saw my book, my mother's glass slipper, the sky blurring around me as I plummeted to the ground, and Daniel's stare burrowing into me as I fell. Watching me, judging me, reminding me of all the things about myself I'd rather pretend weren't there but he—more than anyone else—wouldn't let me forget.

It wasn't like Daniel was the first person to ever look at me in a way that I didn't want to be seen. I was totally used to people perceiving me in certain, unfavorable lights. Frankly, my whole existence thus far had been pretty thoroughly characterized by the phenomenon.

Accordingly, I'd grown accustomed to being very blunt and direct when addressing such assumptions about me. Which in turn made for an effective way of getting people to back off.

This head-on, head-held-high method had worked for me over the years—serving as a consistent way to get my opposers to leave me be.

Seriously. In the past whenever Lady Agnue, or Mauvrey, or anyone else made comments about my lack of princess-ness, or hero-ness, or any other kind of assertions about who they believed I was, it had never gotten under my skin that much. The simple reason being that I'd never entertained any delusions about how others saw me. I'd just always assumed they were wrong and simply didn't know me well enough to realize it.

My whole life this had been my strategy, my norm,

and my comfort zone for handling the confrontations and accusations that threatened to tear down my faith in myself. Only now . . . it appeared to no longer be working. At the very least, the strategy seemed to be losing its *oomph*.

Since about the time Daniel had shown up, I'd noticed that the judgments people made about me were having more of an impact—my normal tactics failing to keep them at bay. Maybe it was the appearance of Blue's prophecy, maybe it was my own, or maybe it was just the mounting pressure and expectations that seemed to be growing around me now that I was getting older. Quite possibly it was a combination of all three. But most certainly it was all amplified by the boy currently flying behind my carriage.

Like I said, with Daniel barely knowing me at all, his unprecedented over-familiarity with the person I was afraid I was made me feel as though such accusations were a lot more legitimate than I'd once believed. As a result, I felt an increasing sense of doubt forming in the corners of my mind that was causing me to second guess myself, and a lot of other things too.

To tell the truth it was all beginning to feel a great deal like emotional vomit. I kept sucking the plethora of rattling insecurities back in as best I could, but I just couldn't stop them from rising to the surface. And as time went on, it was only natural that I started to wonder more and more if maybe the reason I could never fully swallow down the thoughts and escape their torment was because . . . I couldn't prove they were invalid.

Stop it, Crisa. Don't be stupid, I heard my subconscious echo in the back of my mind. *They're wrong about who you are. You know they are.*

But then again, I thought to myself in turn, *if that's true then why do I still feel this way?*

My subconscious did not appear to have a response. So my head and heart were left on their own—hurting as they struggled to find some logical or instinctual bit of insight that would answer this question.

Alas, any such clarity seemed determined to elude me for the time being. Which meant that I was stuck with the task of resisting those awful, unacceptable thoughts, and the realization that I did not know how to justify their existence with the way I'd always seen myself.

As I continued to ponder the dilemma I kept staring back at Daniel—the source of my ill-timed insecurities, whom I'd been watching for some time now. All the while I hadn't thought he'd seen me looking at him. However, just then he abruptly pointed in my direction and shouted something that I couldn't quite make out.

My face flushed with a touch of self-consciousness until I discovered that Daniel wasn't gesturing at me, but up ahead. I turned and saw that we'd broken through a bank of illuminated clouds and were rapidly approaching a massive, pink structure.

It was shaped like the most traditional fairytale castle you could think of and was sitting atop a plump cloud like a dollhouse on a heavily stuffed pillow. The full moon was *literally* right behind it—giant, glowing, and slightly golden.

The whole image took my breath away. It seemed to have the same effect on the carriage because the mushroom slowed down the closer we drew to its majesty.

I kept my eyes on the building as we headed toward it—studying its every feature.

Fairy Godmother HQ was constructed of glittering,

pinkish chrome bricks accentuated by towers of lilac-colored steel. Lanterns blazing like small, golden suns hung from every balcony. Dozens of windows mirrored the stars surrounding the castle. And a large, silver door framed in gems marked the impressive main entrance.

My vehicle soon came to a stop in front of that door and floated next to it casually. Before I could assess my next move, the carriage flipped on its side and dumped me out. I screamed for a second until I realized that I hadn't fallen through the clouds, as they were solid as a pile of goose-feather comforters.

I stood up and waved at the others to come closer. The Pegasi were hesitant at first—blowing more colorful puffs of blue and orange smoke out of their nostrils in protest—but eventually they descended and landed on the poofy cloud beside me. When they did, their eyes stopped glowing and their wings vanished from view, returning them to their normal horse-like forms.

Blue and Daniel dismounted first. He stretched nearby while she went to help SJ down. I ignored him and headed for the silver door without delay. It had the words "Fairy Godmother Headquarters" spelled out across it in jewels of various colors. I paused in front of it, which gave the others time to join me. We all stared at the door for a beat before Blue stepped up and knocked forcefully.

"Blue!" SJ squeaked.

"What, you have a better idea of how to get inside?" she huffed.

We really didn't, so we waited there on the front steps hoping for something to happen. Sure enough, a few moments later a buzzing sound went off inside and the door opened on its own. Good fortune aside, it seemed a bit too easy so the others and I entered through the archway with caution.

The five of us stepped into a silvery, circular room with a series of floral landscape paintings hanging on the walls alongside a lone building directory. This directory informed us that the first and second floors of the compound consisted of offices and the "Grand File Room." Floors three and four were training areas, five through nine were the apartments that the Godmothers lived in, and the tenth floor was simply marked "Private Affairs."

On the other side of the room sat a translucent desk. Behind it was a mousy, middle-aged woman with a long nose who didn't look up as we came toward her. The woman's nametag read "Coco La Rue" and she was devotedly filing her nails beneath the counter.

This seemed insane to me. Not because I deplored cuticle care, but because each of her fingernails appeared to be covered in tiny diamonds. Hence I imagined it was a really expensive manicure to shave away at so aggressively.

Since she hadn't acknowledged our arrival, I decided to speak up. "Um, hi," I said outright, approaching the edge of the desk.

"Name?" Coco responded sounding relatively annoyed.

"Um, Crisa."

SJ elbowed me.

"Crisanta Knight," I corrected myself.

"*No*," Coco responded icily, putting down her nail file and glaring at me. "I mean the name of the dolt Godmother you clearly tricked into getting you here."

"Who says we tricked anyone?" Blue replied. "We were just passing through when our mushroom carriage ran out of gas, and—"

A small jolt of electricity suddenly shot out of Coco's intentionally aimed pointer finger, zapping Blue in the chest.

"Ow!" she yelped as she staggered backwards, absorbing the shock.

"Hey!" Jason protested.

Coco flexed her wrists, causing tiny crackles of electricity to sparkle at the tips of her other nine digits. "I'll ask one more time before I have you escorted from the premises and back to wherever it is you came from," Coco responded coolly. "*Name?*"

"Um, Tami Robinswood," I lied quickly, not intending to sell out Debbie.

Coco pressed a few glowing, holographic buttons on the screens that levitated above her desk. Then she picked up a normal quill and wrote something on a notepad beside her.

"Look . . ." I said as she scribbled, attempting to appeal to her compassion in some way. "Coco, is it? I know we're not supposed to be here. But we came to see one of your Fairy Godmothers. Emma Carrington. She was my mother's Godmother and we just didn't know how else to contact her."

"Well, your plan has holes, honey," Coco responded as she kept writing. "Emma doesn't work here anymore."

I raised my eyebrows in surprise and firmly placed both my hands on Coco's desk, squaring her off. "What? No, that's got to be some kind of mistake. She has to be here," I said.

"No mistake. Emma hasn't worked here for nearly ten years," Coco asserted, meeting my stare with a malicious one of her own. "Now then, if that is all, feel free to help yourself to some candy while you wait for security to escort you out."

The passive-aggressive woman coldly pushed a glass bowl filled with gumdrops across the desk with her expensive-looking manicured hand. Then, without even giving us so much as smile, she turned her attention back to her nails as if we were already long gone.

Now I know I did not just travel two hundred miles in a flying mushroom to get turned away by a snooty, self-involved receptionist named Coco LaRue. I need a good, crazy idea and fast.

I rapidly surveyed the room and saw that apart from the entrance we'd come through, the only other door was about a dozen feet to my right.

Actually, you know what, forget good. A straight up crazy idea will get the job done too.

Before SJ, Ms. LaRue, or my common sense could stop me, I bolted for the other exit.

"Hey, wait a minute!" Coco screeched like a terrified canary.

But it was too late. I had already thrown open the door and was running down the hallway. My friends and Daniel—evidently deciding that they didn't want to hang around with Coco either—took off after me.

"Do you know where you're going?" I heard Jason yell as they tried to catch up with me.

"Nope!" I shouted back.

The hallway we raced down was painted white, had white carpeting, and was lined with doors that were all white as well. The fact was, the only things in the area that weren't white were the numbers on each door, which were bright pink.

At first I wasn't sure how I would know when to stop running and pick one of these doors, but then a violent alarm started ringing through the corridor and I realized that the time to choose had come.

Up ahead was the first door I'd seen without a number. It was marked, "Grand File Room." It seemed as good an option as any, so I threw it open and sped inside. The alarm hadn't stopped, but when I entered the room, I did. Unfortunately, I stopped too abruptly and the others full on rammed into me—knocking me over.

I jumped back on my feet without pause and swiftly observed the room we found ourselves in. This place was twenty times as wide and tall as the grand ballroom at Adelaide Castle, and it was also completely white. What was most intimidating about the space though was not its size, but the fact that it was filled with hundreds of rows of platinum file cabinets. These rows were tightly packed together and each column consisted of dozens upon dozens of the cabinets stacked on top of one another like building blocks, stretching to the ridiculously high ceiling.

Out of instinct that this was not a good place to be, we tried to head back the way we'd come. Regrettably the door behind us had swung shut just after our entry and now appeared to be locked.

At the other end of the room I spotted several doors that looked like another way out.

"There!" I yelled above the sound of the alarm.

We raced through the middle of the stacks toward the door in the center. As we did, I caught closer glimpses of the different file cabinets. Most of them just had names or cities printed on their fronts, and they appeared to be in alphabetical order. But when we were about halfway across the room, one very specific cabinet caught the corner of my eye.

I couldn't explain how I'd managed to see it, but I knew that I had. Consequently, I knew just as badly that I had to go back for it. And so, without warning or thinking, I suddenly halted to a stop, changed direction, and sped back down the aisle to the row where I'd seen it.

"Knight, what are you doing?" Daniel called after me.

I didn't have time to explain. I just ran until I reached the row marked: "*ROW N.*" The moment I reached it, the alarm stopped.

I glanced back toward the others, who seemed equally confused. Then an automated female voice filled the room—coming out of what must've been a building-wide intercom.

"Attention staff. Intruders detected. Please evacuate all training areas and report to your designated safety stations. Proceeding to initiate campus-wide lock down. Grand File Room floor evaporation will commence in three . . . two . . . one."

The announcement echoed around us before being cut off by static. It was immediately replaced by a higher-pitched alarm that pierced my eardrums in a way that the first one could've only aspired to. Pairing off this lovely new sound, the lights in the room began to dim and the floor started glowing a deep shade of magenta with pulsating streaks of red like veins in an artery.

A second later the entire floor vanished beneath our feet and we fell into the pinkish wormhole that had inexplicably consumed it.

I dropped through absolute nothingness for about three seconds before plunging into a body of water that was as dark and cold as it was unexpected.

My friends were lost to me; all I could make out were the filing cabinets that hung from above like stalactites in a cave. There was only one set of cabinets from each row down here though. As I swam for the newly formed ceiling they protruded from, I wondered where the rest of them had gone.

This ceiling, which was clear and glossy, showed me the

answer. On the other side of it I could see the file room we'd just been in. And I saw that the remaining cabinets from each row were still piled up there.

I pressed my hands against the barrier separating me from the room above. It felt solid. Nevertheless, I began to ram my left shoulder against it. Hard as I tried though, I couldn't even make a crack. It was unforgivingly concrete and icy like the top of a frozen lake.

I reached my hand into my satchel to try and use my wand as a means of breaking out. Although, before I had the chance, this new ceiling (the file room's floor) began to glow again just like it had right before we'd fallen through.

The light illuminated the strange sea and I caught a glimpse of the others in the distance. When they saw me they started to head in my direction. But seconds later we were all taken aback by an additional set of cabinets that came down from the room above. They crashed into the water around us. Moments after they dropped in, the glow of the ceiling subsided.

The floor portal . . . it's sucking the rows of cabinets down here one level of stacks at a time. That means our way in here is also our only way out.

I readied myself—grabbing onto the highest handle of the nearest set of cabinets. Seconds felt like an eternity as I held my breath and waited in the darkness. My lungs started to hurt as I began to run out of air.

Finally the ceiling lit up once more.

When it did, I looked toward my friends and Daniel and pointed upwards. They followed my lead and grabbed the handles of the cabinets they were closest to, using them to climb back into the file room.

We passed up through the barrier but kept ascending as fast as we could so as not to be taken back down along with next set of cabinets.

It worked. The five of us were barely able to clear the portal before it turned to solid floor once more, blocking the Grand File Room from the watery depths looming underneath it. Thankfully, "barely" was all we needed, as it was more than enough to keep us alive.

I released a deep breath of relief when I saw the others were okay—wet, but otherwise just fine.

"Now what?!" Blue shouted over to me.

I pushed a strand of soggy hair behind my ear and glanced around. The doors we had been headed for at the other end of the room were now some ten feet above the floor. As each set of cabinets sank, the walls of this place were rising higher and higher—taking our exit farther away from us as a result.

"Climb!" I called back to her.

Grabbing one handle of a file cabinet after another, we did just that—continuing to scale the stacks a block of them at a time.

We were up against the clock, as every twelve seconds or so the floor beneath us would glow again and suck more cabinets through. I moved slower than the others due to my natural aversion to climbing pairing badly with the slipperiness of my wet hands. Add to that, each time the floor opened up and more files sank down there was an accompanying tremor that almost threw me off whatever cabinet I happened to be clinging to.

Still, while these room-shaking episodes slowed me down, at least I never fell. I gripped the handles with conviction and resisted the urge to freak out as I hung on for dear life until the shaking subsided each time.

My uncoordinated climbing aside, we were moving relatively fast. And those intervals between the sinkages caused us to gain a decent lead in our race against time. So much so that a minute later, when we'd all made it to the tops of our respective stacks, we were actually above the level of the desired doors by at least twenty feet.

It was good news, as was the fact that I'd managed to climb up this high without slipping and/or dying. But the victory dance had to wait, as we still needed to make it to the other side of the room.

Without any discussion each of us began to hop from one row of cabinet towers to the next—making our way to the distant doors in a manner akin to a grand, life-threatening game of hopscotch. It seemed to be advancing us pretty quickly, but after my third jump I suddenly stopped when I realized something. I'd forgotten about the cabinet I'd been after before.

My friends and Daniel were a good ways ahead and still going forward. I had to make a decision before it was too late and they noticed my delay.

Ok, Crisa. The floor is literally *disappearing. If you go back now, what if you can't make it to the other side of the room before the doors are out of reach and you get trapped below with nowhere to go? Turning back makes absolutely no logical sense here.*

I turned back.

This was not the time for logic; this was a time for gut instinct. And mine was telling me that whatever was in that cabinet was immeasurably important.

I hopped back to the stack adjacent the one I'd originally come for. My eyes began scanning downwards—squinting through the dim light as I read the names printed on each of the cabinets.

"Nye Vanderbelt, Norman Lerman, Nona Sanchez, Neil Diamond . . ."

I looked farther and farther down—reading several dozen more names.

Come on, I know I saw it.

"Nehari Brown, Navara Burell . . ."

Wait! There it was! The last cabinet—the one closest to the floor—was the one I was after.

Yes!

Alas, my triumph was cut short in the next instant when the very cabinet I sought was digested by the floor portal.

No!

What do I do, what do I do?

As it happened, what I did was probably the stupidest, most reckless thing I'd done all weekend. Which was *really* saying something.

I jumped.

My body swan-dived into the watery room below along with the latest stack of cabinets.

When I hit water I immediately started swimming downwards. The cabinet I was aiming for was only one of several to have been sucked down in this latest interval of sinkage. Though since it had been the closest set to the portal it was now only a slight ways away.

Upon reaching it, I pulled the top drawer open and found a single, glowing folder inside.

With no time to spend wondering how the water hadn't already disintegrated the thing, I shoved it into my satchel.

Above me the ceiling lit up once more and I took that

as my cue to swim for it. I had to get out of here before the portal closed again. Which I totally would have managed to do—by the way—had it not been for the unfortunate fact that right at that moment I was distracted by the unexpected sight of another body diving into the water.

Daniel?

He swam over to me, a surprised and angry expression on his face that nowhere near matched the surprised and angry expression on mine. I seriously would've yelled at him then had it not been for the lack of oxygen. So instead I mime-yelled at him before making my way up to the now resealed barrier.

At the next opening we climbed back into the file room and started to scale the cabinets anew. "What were you thinking?" I shouted at Daniel as I gripped one handle after another in ascent.

"What was *I* thinking?!" Daniel scowled. "I saw you fall off the stacks and went back to help you."

"For your information, I didn't fall, I jumped!"

"Fine then. You're not clumsy; you're just stupid!"

I was about to respond when the floor acted up again and unleashed a much larger tremor than usual. The force threw me off the cabinet I was holding onto, but I was able to grasp another handle with my right hand before I fell more than a few feet. I swung from the grip and when I looked up I was infuriated to see Daniel reaching out for me.

"Here," he had the nerve to say. "Give me your hand."

Now it was my turn to scowl. "I. Don't. Need. Your. Help!"

I focused my strength and pulled myself up until my foot found another cabinet to boost up on. Once it was secure, I kept climbing the tower and ignored Daniel until we reached its summit.

The walls around us had grown a lot in our absence. And even though we were as high as we could go, the doors on the other side of the room were no longer far below us. They were now exactly at eye level, yet still a good hundred-foot dash ahead.

SJ, Blue, and Jason, on the other hand, had just reached them. They stopped short at that point, for it seemed only then had they noticed that Daniel and I were missing from the group. When they looked back for us I waved them to continue forward as Daniel and I started hopping from one row to the next in our attempt to catch up.

"Keep going!" I called out insistently.

They seemed reluctant to proceed without us, but since the exits were rising and would soon have moved past them, Blue reached out and twisted the knob of the nearest door. It swung inwards and she jumped in first, followed by SJ. When SJ made it inside however, another layer of files sank and the door rose above Jason's head.

Even with this obstacle he was not waylaid. He quickly responded by backing up and getting a running start toward his target before jumping off the cabinet stack.

Jason's hands barely grasped the bottom edge of the doorframe, but he was still able to pull himself up into whatever room the exit led to. Meanwhile, Daniel and I leapt from one tower of cabinets to the next in a mad rush to get to the other side before it was too late for us to do the same.

Despite our best efforts, we just didn't make it soon enough. By the time we reached the far wall, the door our friends had gone through was a solid twenty-five feet above our heads and counting.

We had no way of getting up there. And it wouldn't have

been long before the rest of the cabinets we stood on were absorbed through the floor and the two of us were trapped inside that inexplicable oceanic chamber along with them. I began rummaging through my satchel—searching for something that might give me an idea.

Let's see. I have my wand, the survey Debbie left me, a dinner roll, and . . . wait a second, Blue's enchanted ball of yarn!

I hadn't gotten the chance to give it back to her after she'd loaned it to me the night before.

Thank goodness this satchel is so deceptively big; there aren't many practical handbags in the world that can hold so much random junk like this!

Small victory aside, the yarn wasn't enough to get us out of our current predicament. While the discovery was helpful, the door we were aiming for was too high up now for me to throw the other end of the transformed rope to my friends. Add to that, the height and angle of the door paired with the flopsy, lightweight nature of the ball itself made it impossible to simply toss it up to them in this form either. No, the yarn alone would not be enough for an escape. But I knew what would.

If only I had a . . .

"Crisa!" Blue shouted from the doorframe above—as if reading my mind. "We searched the room and there was a box of arrows in here! Did you bring your—"

"Yeah, I've got it!" I interrupted.

Blue carefully tossed down one of the arrows. I caught it and removed the ball of yarn from my satchel.

"Tie one end of this to the arrow," I ordered Daniel.

"Why?"

I squeezed the ball of yarn three times—morphing it into the giant pile of climbing rope. "That's why."

As he tied the rope to the arrow, I angled away from him and shoved my hand back into the satchel. My wand was *so* not something I was about to show Daniel. Wrapping my fingers around it, I transformed it inside the bag before taking it out.

Bow.

A moment later I pulled a newly transformed, silver and slightly glowing archer's bow from my bag.

Daniel stared at me in disbelief. "You carry a bow in your purse?"

"Well, with all the lipstick and perfume there was no room for a machete. Yes, I carry a bow in my purse, Daniel. Now give me that!" I snapped, snatching the arrow with the attached rope from his hands.

I drew the bow, aimed, and with a focused exhale, released. The arrow shot expertly through the doorway above us.

Huh, I guess aim really does improve with practice. Thank you dartboard and late night homework procrastination.

A few seconds passed before Jason gave us the signal that their end of the rope had been securely fastened. I handed Daniel our end, which was unraveling as it was pulled upward every time another layer of cabinets sank down and the room it was anchored to moved higher overhead.

"You go first," I commanded.

"No way, you go!"

I refused to take the rope back from him. "Look, I suck at climbing. By the time I get up there, the room will be too high up and you won't be able to reach the rope at all. So just go! Quickly!"

He seemed to want to argue, but knew I was right. Whichever one of us went first would have to scale the rope super quickly for the other person to even have a chance of reaching it when it was their turn.

I was not too proud to admit that it would take me a lot longer to climb up than it would for him, which was why I insisted he go ahead of me.

Much to his displeasure, Daniel was forced to agree with the rationale and wrapped the rope tightly around his hand before swinging off the cabinets. He used his foot to keep from ramming into the wall, and to steady himself as he hung from the rope. Then he pulled himself up one hand after another toward the distant room—walking up the wall like a mountain climber.

I morphed my wand back to normal and stuffed it into my satchel as I waited anxiously and watched my hopes of escaping move farther and farther away.

When Daniel reached the door, the others helped pull him inside and reeled in the rope. Bundling it up, Jason threw it back down to me.

I was at the very edge of the cabinet and stretched out as far as I could, but even before the rope unraveled completely I knew it would not make it. Sure enough, it came down just a couple inches out of my reach. As a result, it swung through the air and—with no one to catch it—straight toward the wall.

Oh boy, here goes.

Before any more time could slip away I backed up and jumped off the cabinets in pursuit of the lifeline.

I hit the wall. Hard. But I was able to grab onto the end of the rope with my left hand. After dangling there for a second, I harnessed a combination of luck and upper-body strength to pull myself up along it.

Stupid . . . climbing . . . why . . . did it have . . . to be . . . climbing . . .

Eventually (*or amazingly I should say*), I made it all the way to the door. Naturally, at the exact instant I tried to pull myself in, the wrath of the portal shook the whole file room again and caused me to be launched through the opening with a lot less grace than hoped for. I was thrown inside—falling forward and knocking a nearby Daniel over with me.

"Get off," I spat as we hit the floor and the room settled. I pushed him away and shuddered like I'd just kissed a frog.

"You knocked *me* over," he said, getting up just as vehemently.

I was about to shout back a retort, but that's when I noticed I didn't have to shout anymore. Just as suddenly as they'd come on, the alarms had totally stopped.

Whatever the reason seemed unimportant for the time being. I just knew that I was grateful for a moment to think things through without that awful sound ringing in my ears. As I wrung the remaining water from my hair, I began to do just that—commencing with analyzing the room we currently found ourselves in.

The place was relatively cold, yet fairly musty. Rafters crisscrossed around the ceiling, supporting strange iron gas lanterns, which emanated the greenish glow that provided the room with its limited, eerie source of light.

These lanterns, along with everything else in the room for that matter, were covered in cobwebs. Sitting in the shadowy corner across from me there was a dirty desk with a filth-covered leather chair. And all around the room—blocking entire portions of wall and stretching up to the rafters—were stacks upon stacks of dusty boxes, some open, some closed.

Not seeing another exit at first, the five of us went over

to the pile of boxes to endeavor to find one behind them. In the process, though, we couldn't help but rifle through some of the boxes' weird contents.

Based on the layout of the room, the professional looking chair, and the desk, which still had a dusty stapler and a stack of withered yellow notepads sitting on top of it, I deduced that this was some kind of office that hadn't been used in ages. What kind of office had it once been, though? Of that I had zero idea. The objects we proceeded to find in those boxes were as perplexing as they were diverse.

One had a bunch of bronze arrows like the kind Blue had thrown down to me. A second contained only a single item: an onyx-colored dagger with a leather handle and a golden, swirly design carved into its base. The third box I opened was filled to the brim with broken hand mirrors that must have once been beautiful before time had shattered their faces and taken their rusting toll.

I picked up one of the mirrors by the handle and turned it over in my hand. There was something engraved in the back. With the damp edge of my sleeve, I rubbed the dust around the letters away until the words "Mark One" revealed themselves.

Intrigued, I picked up a second mirror from the pile and repeated the process. Again I discovered the same words etched into the back of the destroyed mirror. "Mark One."

Huh, weird, I thought to myself as I fingered the aged looking glass. *I wonder what it means . . .*

The five of us continued to rummage through the objects inside the various boxes. As this went on, we found stranger and stranger knickknacks. There were empty bottles, shriveled flowers, surprisingly ripe fruit, and the list only got more bizarre from there.

Jason, clearly as put off by the discoveries as we were, held up one of the ripe fruits (a perfectly yellow, practically glittering lemon) and posed the question each of us was thinking. "What is all this junk?" he asked.

"I don't know," Blue said as she bundled up the last of her rope and returned it to yarn form. "But we better keep moving. Something tells me this isn't a yard sale we want to be caught looting through."

She was right. Prolonging this aimless investigation was not in our best interest. If anything, it was just causing us to lose time and become one step closer to being apprehended.

All of us in agreement, we put down the various knickknacks that had distracted us and continued to work on shoving stacks of boxes out of the way.

Eventually we managed to clear the back wall enough to see the wooden edge of a doorframe. At that, it only took a few more moments of team effort to clear the path for our exit.

The hallway we entered into next was as white as all the others. However, there was one thing about this corridor that distinguished it from the others we'd been bolting down earlier—there were no numbers written on the doors. Rather, every door had a name and title printed on it. Looking back at the door from which we'd just exited, for instance, I saw a semi-disintegrated title that read: "Paige Tomkins: Magical Transfers, Tracking, & Recalls."

My brain made a mental note of the name as we fast-walked down the hallway—anxiety rapidly building in the silence around us.

It was now starting to make me a bit nervous that everything had gotten so abruptly calm. After all, it was barely two minutes ago that we were immersed in ear-piercing alarms and sinking rooms. Going from impending doom to total tranquility without explanation or a hint of logical transition felt super suspicious.

Jason, SJ, and Blue were discussing this very thought up ahead while Daniel and I trailed behind. I didn't get to join in the conversation though, as Daniel once again baited me into one of our own.

"That was a pretty impressive jump, Knight," he said, his voice low so that only I could hear him.

"Whatever," I shrugged.

"What's the matter with you?" he asked. "You're not still upset I followed you when you dove off those file cabinets are you?"

"No," I replied.

"Cuz I only did it because I thought you were in trouble and could use the help."

"I said I'm not upset, Daniel," I insisted. "But for the record, even if I was in trouble—in case I didn't make myself clear before—I don't want your help."

"Yeah, I figured that out when you chose to fall five hundred feet today instead of letting me give you a hand in the tournament."

"Good. Glad the message got across."

"Seriously, that's your response?" he asked in disbelief. "Come on, Knight, what's your damage? If you had just given me your hand back there today, you could've avoided the embarrassment of having everyone see what happened to you. How is that not a better option than what you ended up doing?"

Fair point. Avoiding that humiliation would have been great. But even so, I'd rather live down a blood-curdling embarrassment like that a thousand times than let the likes of Daniel, or anyone really, save me.

"Just drop it okay," I whispered back. "I'm not mad about that."

"Well then, what's wrong?" he probed. "Something is clearly ticking you off. It's written all over your face."

I ignored him and kept moving.

He cocked his eyebrow. "Oh wait, I get it. This is about what I said to you back at Adelaide, isn't it?"

Again, I didn't answer. But it seemed he did not need my affirmation in order to ascertain that he'd guessed correctly.

"Oh, that's definitely what it is," he said matter-of-factly. "Look, Knight, my job was to *hurt you*. What did you expect me to say? If what I said bothered you that much, it's not my fault; it's yours. Either you're too soft and need to get thicker skin, or you believe what I said is actually true, in which case those are some identity issues you need to work out for yourself."

"Daniel . . ." I started to say in retaliation. But we rounded a corner then and I spotted a door at the end of the hallway that better claimed my attention. It had the word "MANAGEMENT" printed on it.

I jogged ahead to catch up with the others and motioned toward the door in question. "There?" I asked them.

They shrugged in concession.

It was as good a bet as any if we were searching for straight answers, so we quickened our pace and headed directly for it. When we arrived I turned the knob and our group barged in. The second we did, though, the third most surprising thing in the last couple of hours happened. We found ourselves trapped inside of a large, pink bubble.

Right when we'd entered the room, a magical booby-trap had been triggered. Now the five of us were encased in a translucent, pastel-colored sphere. Which, despite looking like the kind of bubble a small giant might have blown out of chewing gum, we could clearly not pop or escape from. It was like a transparent force field characterized by the vague smell and color of cotton candy.

Like the bubble, the office around us was dominantly pink—with the exception of the silver carpeting, black crystal chandelier hanging from above, and black leather chair residing behind the glass desk at the other end of the room. In this chair sat a perfectly postured woman wearing a tailored, light pink suit and a pleasant smile on her face.

"Children, welcome to Fairy Godmother Headquarters," she said. "My name is Lena Lenore and I am Godmother Supreme."

Lena Lenore . . .

I felt my muscles tense as Lena Lenore stood and walked over to our bubble prison. When she reached it, she turned to an extremely petite blonde standing in the corner behind her. "Daisy, there is no need for this. Press the release, will you?"

Daisy pressed a green button on the wall and the bubble expanded before bursting into nothingness. Residual raspberry sparkles disintegrated into the air as our all-powerful, magical hostess strode around us.

Lena Lenore was a beautiful woman. She looked around forty years old and had dark skin and hazel eyes. Her black hair was up in a regal bun with a pencil sticking out of it like a schoolteacher. Every part of her—from her glossy fingernails to her chrome-colored pumps—was sleek and polished.

It was strange to be this close to her. I'd spent years picturing the woman behind the name who'd sent me those curt, vaguely threatening letters. However, Lena Lenore didn't outwardly seem as nasty as I had imagined. Her face was soft, her expression curious and full of empathy. So much so that, for a moment, I was inclined to give her the benefit of the doubt.

But then I thought better of it. Well-constructed appearance could hide a lot of things from the human eye, but not from inherent instinct. And mine was telling me what I'd long already believed. I did not like, or trust Lena Lenore. The essence of her personality I'd gleaned from her writings notwithstanding, there was just something about the woman. Her gaze was a little too confident; the way she looked down on us, a little too amused; and the spark in her eyes, a bit too calculating.

Moreover, as she studied us, it became evident that the flowery perfume she wore was as noticeable as the air of self-righteousness she seemed to carry around with her.

When she stepped back, I met her eye line.

At the risk of the floor sinking again or being absorbed into another bubble, I figured I might as well speak up while I had the chance. My feelings about the woman aside, it was time to ask for the information we'd come for.

"Ms. Lenore, my name is Crisa. Uh, Crisanta Knight, that is. Cinderella Knight is my mother. And I'm—"

"That's what you're opening with? Really?" Daniel interrupted condescendingly. "Knight, I think we're a bit past formal introductions since these people just tried to kill us with a watery death-trap."

"It's not our fault you were in the Grand File Room when

our security system kicked in," Daisy—the tiny blonde—said in a sharp, high-pitched voice.

"Some security system," Blue snorted. "You just plunged all your files into water. Good luck drying them off."

"It's magic paper, you dumb-dumb. It *can't* be destroyed," Daisy countered in an even higher octave now that she was angry. "And for your information—"

"Daisy," Lenore calmly interceded as she held up her hand. "These young protagonists are our guests."

Daisy let out a slight huff, but nodded before stepping back into the corner like an ashamed, obedient child.

"Now then," the Godmother Supreme continued as she turned to look at me again. "Please. Go on."

"Uh, right," I said. "Well, like I was saying, we're looking for my mother's Godmother, Emma Carrington. Do you think you could take us to her?"

"I'm aware of what you are after, Crisanta Knight. I have read your numerous letters over the years after all, and subtlety is far from your strong suit. But, while I applaud your . . . shall we say, persistence in this matter, I still cannot help you."

"What's the excuse this time?" I asked sharply. "I know it's not security given that we're way past that."

SJ cleared her throat a bit and lightly put her hand on my arm—warning me to cool it.

"No, Crisanta," Lenore responded. "As Coco already informed you, the simple fact is that I am afraid Emma no longer works here. In truth, she was relieved from duty quite some time ago."

"Fired like a chimney is more like it," Daisy added sassily from the corner.

"Daisy!" Lenore snapped.

Daisy blew her bangs out of her eyes and hung her head in frustration. Me? I just stood there, mouth slightly agape.

I couldn't believe it. We'd come all this way to try and talk to Emma—the one person who might've been willing to tell us how to break the In and Out Spell around the Indexlands—and she wasn't even here. I'd thought Coco had just been, to quote our mushroom-making trainee Godmother, Debbie, acting like a "trick." But she had been telling the truth. After working so hard to find this place, my godmother wasn't even here.

Worse still? I'd just learned she'd been *fired*.

I didn't even know that was a thing. It was my understanding that being a Fairy Godmother was basically a lifelong gig. What could Emma—a woman I remembered as being as kind, wise, and fair tempered as anyone—possibly do to warrant termination of her employment?

"Why didn't you say anything before?" I asked Lenore outright. "All this time whenever I wrote you, you acted like Emma still worked here. If Coco was right, then you've been leading me on for almost ten years."

"The Godmother Supreme does not have to explain herself to the likes of you, Crisanta Knight," Daisy interceded. "And unless you want to get zapped like your friend did outside, I would watch your mouth and start showing her some respect."

I crossed my arms and gave Lenore a glare. "I will when she gives me a reason to."

"Crisa," SJ squeaked.

Daisy took a step forward. "Why you little—"

"Daisy . . ." Lenore interrupted, completely unfazed. "Why don't you go sign yourself up for our People Skills seminar next week? There are fliers in the level eight common room. I can handle things on my own from here."

Daisy's eyebrows crinkled as she gestured at me. "But she—"

"Is a guest here," Lenore responded, eyeing me. "And a particularly interesting one at that. So go, now, before I demote you back to the accounts payable department."

With a nervous look and an irritated huff, Daisy removed a silvery bracelet from her wrist. The second she did, it transformed into a wand like Debbie's, and like mine. With two waves of the wand, the door behind us opened and Daisy dematerialized into a ball of lime green sparkling energy that shot into the hall and caused the door to slam forcefully behind her.

"Now then," Lenore continued. "Where were we?"

"Emma," Blue said. "Are you going to tell us why she was let go or not?"

"It's really not very complicated," Lenore replied. "Personal reasons made it so that she was no longer fit to be a part of this organization."

"Well, can you tell us where she is?" Jason suggested.

"I'm afraid that is classified information, my dear," the Godmother Supreme responded automatically.

SJ came forward timidly. "Ms. Lenore, we mean no disrespect . . . but can you not help us at all? It is really rather crucial that Crisa finds a way to speak with her godmother."

"She already has. In fact, I believe Debbie was assigned to her just this very evening."

"No," I explained. "Not my *Fairy* Godmother. Emma Carrington is my *actual* godmother. And you have no idea how important it is for me to talk to her."

"Oh yes, that's right. I do recall hearing something to

that end. But actual godmother or not, I'm afraid I still cannot allow you to speak with Emma, Crisanta," Lenore said, forgetting her smile for a moment and giving me a look of pure wickedness that made me shiver.

Although it only lasted for an instant, the impression it left was nothing short of substantial. The look reaffirmed what my instincts had been telling me since the start of this meeting. And I knew then that I would never forget that first glance at Lena Lenore's true colors—at the shrewd, patient darkness that was lurking beneath her perfect, shiny surface.

The Godmother Supreme swiftly changed the expression on her face back to a smile so sweet it made my teeth hurt. She walked over to me and patted my damp head as if I were a rambunctious puppy that had gotten into mischief.

"It was a good effort, though. Truly, dear, I am very impressed with you children. Few people have made it this far. So at the very least return home knowing that you gave us a nice surprise as you pointed out some minor holes in our security measures."

"Gaping holes is more like it," Blue started to argue. "I mean, come on, we're kids and we broke in here with a plan we cooked up over dinner. And we did it because it's seriously important we find Emma. So why can't you just—"

Lenore silenced Blue by holding up a single finger in warning, glaring at her threateningly before turning her attention wholly back on me.

"Do understand, I know why you are *really* here, princess," she said carefully. "Why you want so desperately to speak with Emma, and were driven to such lengths to find her on this night. And the best advice I can give you in turn is to leave the matter alone. The rest of you children need not concern yourselves with things that are out of your control either. Believe me, doing so would be pointless and very unwise."

Lenore straightened her suit jacket then and sauntered back over to her desk. "On that note," she said as she casually pressed a large, black button beside the quill holder, "it is nearing midnight and your have a carriage to catch, don't you, Ms. Knight? So, on behalf of all the Godmothers, have a safe flight and a magical day. Francisco and Cederick here will see you and your friends out."

Two surprisingly buff Fairy Godfathers (each seven feet in height and carrying wands the size of guitars) suddenly materialized in the doorway behind us. They hustled my friends, Daniel, and I toward the office's exit.

"It was nice meeting you, Crisanta Knight," the Godmother Supreme called after me as we were being led out. "Do try and keep out of trouble."

I shot Lena Lenore a final glance over my shoulder. She was leaning back against her desk watching me. Her smile was gone and her eyes were cold, causing me to wonder if her earlier characterization of me as "interesting" had been something more to be feared than flattered by.

Francisco and Cederick hurriedly escorted us through the maze-like building. (The time we spent crammed in the elevator with them was by far the most uncomfortable thirty-seven seconds of my life).

When we reached the lobby again they pushed us out the silver, jeweled front door and slammed it behind us with all the formality a prestigious cook showed toward any rats that dared enter his kitchen.

It was over. Wordlessly, I got into my carriage while

the others mounted their Pegasi. "Let's go, mushroom," I sighed.

Responding appropriately, my ride took off into the night without protest. I didn't feel like looking out at the stars anymore, so I resigned myself to solemnly staring at the inside of my slowly rotting vehicle. I supposed the carriage knew it was getting close to midnight and wanted to get a head start on decomposing, because the whole thing was starting to reek as badly as the ending to our evening's disastrous adventure.

My hand absentmindedly wandered into my satchel to pull out my wand. Fiddling with it always made me feel a bit better. But then I felt something else inside the bag . . .

The folder! The folder from the file room!

I snatched my prize out of the satchel with a feeling of excitement and dread. Debbie and Daisy had been right about magic paper. The folder and its contents were not only still perfectly intact, but they were as pristine as if I'd just purchased them from an office supply store.

All I could do was hold up the folder then—hold it and study it and take in its general existence as best I could to make sure it was actually real, and that I really, truly had it.

The verdict: It was and I did.

In my hand I held a file with the name "Natalie Poole" printed on it.

CHAPTER 13

Pay Attention: This Chapter's Important

t had been about a week since our epic fail at Fairy Godmother HQ, and we were once again imprisoned at Lady Agnue's while the boys were back at Lord Channing's.

As none of our classmates or school staff had been the wiser about our little, disenchanting venture, everything had more or less returned to normal . . . with the exception of the dirty looks I'd been getting from some of the other students, that is.

I supposed dirty looks was putting it mildly, considering how much backlash I'd received from my princess counterparts as punishment for my vigilante performance in the Twenty-Three Skidd tournament. Most of them highly disapproved of my actions. And they voiced this disapproval through snide whispers, nasty notes passed to me in class, and snarky eyebrow raises whenever I passed them in the halls.

It was a good thing I had SJ at my side most of the time to keep me from acting on any of these gestures of malice; that was for sure. Otherwise at least one of my snooty princess classmates would've gotten punched in the jaw by now.

Despite all this persecution, there was at least one good thing that had come out of the whole tournament debacle— the new level of respect a lot of the students had for Blue. The common protagonists were widely impressed with what she'd achieved that afternoon in the tournament. They applauded her fearlessness in entering the competition, recognizing that she had been the first one of them to really prove her capacity for heroics.

Add to that, any objections by the princesses of Blue's behavior were a lot fewer in number and a lot more subtle in nature than their objections of mine. After all—as Lady Agnue had so kindly pointed out at our last assembly—Blue's participation in the stunt was less surprising and insulting to them than my actions were because I was expected to be bound by my princess responsibilities whereas she was not.

I mean, even the headmistress herself had acknowledged during our first week of school that Blue had the potential to be a hero. Me, apparently not so much.

Whatever. I had bigger problems to worry about than the opinions of my classmates.

I had no idea how I was going to find my godmother, Emma. Furthermore, even if I did know where she was, I was utterly stumped on how to physically get out of Lady Agnue's now that the In and Out Spell had been reactivated.

Then there was the ticking time bomb that was my prologue prophecy. Over the last several days it had been consuming my thoughts like a virus that was slowly taking me over.

I hated that. And I devoted whatever clear headspace I could muster to trying to think of some kind of plan for fighting against it. Alas, ten days later I still had nothing.

As mounting frustration ate away at me, the only source

of release I had anymore was in the practice fields. While every other aspect of my existence seemed to be in turmoil, there I found the one form of change in my life that I was actually happy to embrace.

After the Twenty-Three Skidd match, I realized that I'd been missing my true calling all these years and there actually was something in the world that I was good at.

The lacrosse sword I'd naturally taken to had given me the idea to transform my wand into a spear. The staff of my new weapon was about the same length as the original tool from the tournament, minus the extra grip function—around five feet. The only alterations I'd made to the lacrosse sword's base design were reducing the size of its blade and scrapping the basket.

The result was a simple weapon, and a much less typical one since I'd never seen any of the boys at Lord Channing's—nor any of our own common protagonists for that matter—employ it. Frankly, I'd never even seen a spear in the weapons shed at our school. That sorry excuse for an artillery was predominantly stocked with second-hand, standard fighting tools like swords, knives, shields, and so on.

I'd certainly never used one of these myself. Heck, the closest thing I'd ever fiddled with that remotely resembled the spear's weight and extension was that broomstick I'd messed around with playing dung hockey an eternity ago.

Yet, despite my inexperience with the weapon, and my tendency to stink at anything I tried at this school, the bottom-line was that it simply worked for me. And since I'd completely refocused my fighting style around it, I'd become, well . . .

You could say that I was no longer what one might call a sucky opponent. Of course you could also say that I was now totally awesome. Which I thought was a much more apt description of my combatant transformation. I worked that spear like Rumpelstiltskin on a spinning wheel—with shrewd decisiveness and skill unmatched.

To say that I relished my newfound skill would've been an understatement. Like a dog learning to fetch or a bird finding it could fly, so was the feeling that came with the discovery of this new and exciting part of myself.

While our practice sessions had become more taxing on Blue as a result of my drastic improvement, she too was very much enjoying the turnaround. The surprisingly high level of skill I possessed with the spear challenged her in a way that most could not. And in this test of her abilities, she also found temporary relief from our shared problems outside the barn.

Today, Blue was fighting with two swords (one in each hand) to push herself even further. I held my wand in my right hand and tapped it against my left as I waited for her to charge. She grinned and came at me a second later—leading with her left sword.

Shield.

I blocked her strike. She'd expected that, and swung around with her right sword toward my head.

Sword.

I mirrored her motion and our blades clashed. Then in the next instant, when she lunged with two low, sweeping strikes, I morphed my wand into the new form I was so fond of.

Spear.

My wand thickened and stretched out in my hand with

a blade protruding at the upper end. I whirled the staff in the same direction as her swords and easily fended off her strikes.

We continued fighting like this for some time. Occasionally I changed the wand back into a shield or a sword, but for the majority of the duel I kept it in its spear shape. It made my strikes so much more powerful, fluid, and unpredictable than I ever could've hoped for. Plus, I had so much reach with it that I was easily able to defend myself from both her weapons—unafraid of the staff snapping since, at its root, it was a magic wand and could not be broken by even the sharpest of blades.

After a while Blue actually looked like she was beginning to get tired. For once I was winning and I was absolutely loving it!

She struck high on the right while jabbing low on the left. Again, both attacks were easy to block simultaneously. The staff twirled forcefully in my hands—one end blocking her left sword, the other knocking the right one out of her grasp completely.

Blue responded by tossing the left sword into her right hand and attempting to charge me once more, but this time I was ready for her. I smacked it out of her grip with another twirl of the staff. Then without hesitation I quickly circled the spear around and swept her feet out from under her before she could move out of the way. Blue landed on her back with a thud and I pointed the blade of my spear at her nose.

Wand.

I smiled and helped my friend to her feet.

"It's a combat-related miracle—a whole new you!" Blue said as she wiped the sweat from her forehead.

"Thanks," I blushed, feeling more humble than expected.

"Seriously, you're fantastic!" Blue went on. "The spear works perfectly for you. And I like that you're mixing it up with the different weapons from time to time to keep me guessing. Very versatile and *super* awesome."

I let Blue's compliment sink in for a second. Sadly, when the moment and the rush of adrenaline from fighting had passed, bitterness and remorse once again tugged at my mind without pause or pity.

"I wish it really was a whole new me," I said as I plopped down on one of the bales of hay. "If it was, I wouldn't currently be doomed to be Mrs. Chance Darling—a girl who fate and the Author would have spending an eternity swooning like a weakling, grinning like an idiot, and picking out china patterns."

Blue kicked at the straw by her feet, trying to search for words to make me feel better. But she soon discovered—just as I had when I'd wanted to console her after she'd gotten her prologue pang—that there weren't any.

We stared at the dirty barn floor in frustration for a minute, breathing in the smell of hay and horse feed. Then the sudden sound of the barn door being opened interrupted our glum moment and filled the musty room with sunlight.

"A little bird told me I might find the two of you in here," SJ chirped as she strolled into the barn.

"Was it that mockingbird who's always hanging around our balcony? Because he is such a brown-noser," I commented.

"No, Crisa. And, by the by, most people would know that is just an expression."

"But most people do not have doves help them make their beds in the morning," Blue countered. "You, my friend, are not most people."

"Okay, okay, so a robin in the rose bushes did tell me you

two were in here," SJ admitted with a smile. "But that is not the point. I am here because I have figured it out."

Blue picked up her swords from the floor nonchalantly. "Figured out what, your highness?"

"The ultimate sugar cookie recipe," SJ groaned. "What do you think, Blue?"

This got Blue's attention. She and I were both a bit taken aback really. We weren't used to hearing sarcasm from SJ. It was like having a bunny growl at you; it just didn't fit. Neither did the spark of mischief glinting in SJ's eyes. Mischief was usually Blue's specialty and, well, I dabbled.

"So . . . what then?" I asked.

"I know how to find out where Emma is," SJ announced triumphantly.

My eyes widened in surprise. "Seriously?"

"It gets even better," she continued. "I believe I know how to get us past the In and Out Spell around Lady Agnue's so that we can get there."

I peered over SJ's shoulder curiously.

She had been working in the potions lab every night for the past week to prepare the special brew she was concocting for our escape. Yet, even with all the hours of labor she'd already put in, this was only the beginning. We still had to break into the Treasure Archives to get the main ingredient she needed to finish the potion.

Oh yeah, did I forget to mention we were planning on breaking into the Treasure Archives?

Were we crazy? Debatably. But was it necessary? Absolutely.

You see, SJ's idea for how to find Emma and escape the

In and Out Spell around Lady Agnue's were linked. And the keys to both were presently locked behind those famous glass cases we passed by every day on our way to lessons.

Our first target: the magic mirror from the beloved tale of *Beauty & The Beast.*

It was brilliant really, and what with Blue's vast knowledge of all things fairytale she was actually a tad miffed that she hadn't thought of the idea first. That mirror was enchanted to show you anyone at any time. All we had to do was say Emma's name into it and we would be able to see where she was. It was so simple I could hardly believe it!

We were planning on breaking into the case that held the mirror, replacing it with a replica, and borrowing it for a few days until we had the information. Now, it goes without saying that when we'd originally put this lovely plot together we had always intended to put the mirror back when we had what we needed.

Ah, the best of laid plans, am I right?
But I'm getting ahead of myself.

The other item we needed was a single petal from the enchanted water lily that induced the tale of *The Frog Prince.* This ingredient was vital for an advanced spell that SJ had come across while studying the special potions book Madame Alexanders had lent her. It was only the final ingredient for this magical concoction she was attempting, though. The rest of the potion needed a lot of prep work and dedication— hence our friend's massive amount of after-school time spent in the lab as of late.

At the moment SJ was surrounded by vials, flasks, measuring cups, and the special potions book. Her right hand was stirring the boiling goopy purple contents of a small cauldron, while her left hand grinded something beige and scaly in a curved mortar dish. She was so focused on the brew she was making, her eyes darting between her various stations and the open-faced book lying between them, that she didn't even flinch when Blue entered the room.

Our cloaked friend made sure the door was closed and the three of us were alone before revealing what she'd brought concealed beneath her cloak. It was a regular hand mirror crafted to look identical to the magic mirror we were after.

I'd sent a message to Jason a few days back via one of SJ's birds asking him to build it in metal shop at Lord Channing's. And, naturally, he had happily agreed to the task. As it turned out, Daniel had also helped. Even though, again, I certainly hadn't asked him to.

Sigh.

It seemed he was fully invested in our mission, whether I liked it or not.

SJ had put several of the deer who inhabited the forest between Lord Channing's and Lady Agnue's on standby a couple of days ago in order to intercept the mirror when it was finished.

As mentioned, our school's version of the In and Out Spell being more basic than its counterparts, it did not hinder animals from passing through it. The lucky creatures could travel back and forth across the forest that separated our campuses at their own leisure.

Blue must've been in the practice fields when one of the deer had delivered the looking glass to her like an honored messenger.

SJ took a momentary pause from her work to examine the beautiful mirror. She approved, I supposed, because she nodded and went straight back to work.

"Oh, and SJ," Blue said—interrupting her concentration

once more. "Jason's note says that you asked him to make you this too?" Blue removed a slingshot from her pocket and put it on the table next to SJ.

"Thanks," she answered absentmindedly, clearly not noticing the puzzled tone in Blue's voice.

"What's that for?" I asked.

SJ waved her hand at us. "Never you mind. Now please keep it down. We only have another hour before curfew and I need to get these snakeskins properly liquefied with the juniper berries before then."

"Do you need any help?" Blue offered.

"No, I just need *quiet*," SJ replied, not looking up.

Blue huffed indignantly and moved for the door. I decided to go with her and leave SJ to the privacy of her lab. There would be no talking to her now, so I figured I might as well return to our room and do some work of my own. It was already Thursday and if we were going to be up all night this weekend robbing the realm's most sacred relics I had to make sure my homework was done before then.

Aren't I just the most responsible?

I was alone in our suite for a long while after that—trying to concentrate on my essay about the history of genies in our realm.

This task proved to be more difficult than breaking into Fairy Godmother HQ though, as I was so not interested. Genies had vanished from the realm, like, forever ago. If they didn't care enough to be around, I certainly shouldn't have had to care enough to document it.

After about an hour of failing to garner enough concentration to write more than my paper's preface, I turned my attention to something far more palpable. As it had been doing relentlessly as of late, the Natalie Poole folder I'd nabbed from HQ was courting my curiosity.

I went over to my desk drawer to fetch it for about the fiftieth time this week. I opened it halfheartedly then, hoping that answers had magically appeared since I'd last flipped through it. Alas, no such luck. It remained as empty as before.

Well, not entirely empty mind you. There were still exactly two items inside—a form and a picture of a teenage girl. The image was a roughly drawn sketch with just touches of color. Nevertheless, I recognized clearly that the girl it featured was Natalie Poole. Everything—from the freckles that brushed her cheeks like a child's, to the sadness in her eyes—was identical to that of the girl who'd spent countless nights filling up my dreamscape.

The document that accompanied the picture contained a bunch of content so plainly laid out it looked like a census. The information included Natalie's date of birth, a bit about her schooling, and some family background (namely that she was the only child of Meg and James Poole).

What I found most interesting, however, was what was listed for Natalie's address. According to it, she resided in a city called "Los Angeles," which was apparently located in our neighbor realm of Earth. Even stranger still was the area at the bottom of the page. This subsection of the paper was blatantly labeled: "IMPORTANT INFORMATION" and had three lines of bullet point text that read:
- *"Magic Classification: Category 1, 2, & 3 priority"*
- *"O.T.L. Candidate: Ryan Jackson"*
- *"Key Destiny Interval: 21st birthday (cross-reference Eternity Gate)"*

Like I said, the stupid folder provided me with way more questions than it did answers.

I mean, honestly, what am I supposed to do with any of that?

It was all so bizarre. It was nonsensical. It was so theoretically useless that I doubted the Godmothers would even miss it. And yet . . .

Although I really couldn't make sense or make use of the information found inside the file, it did give me one marvelous and extremely intriguing realization. The likes of which I was simultaneously grateful for and unraveled by. It made me aware that Natalie Poole was no mere product of my imagination manifested solely within my nightmares. Somewhere, somehow, she was out there. She was real.

The discovery was mind-boggling, and super unsettling too. Every time I'd tried to find some way to fully process the knowledge in the days since realizing it, it felt like my brain wanted to burst with angst.

But, in spite of the incomparable weight this information placed on me (and the fact that it likely would've been ultra therapeutic to talk about), I did not share the revelation with my friends.

For one, I could achieve nothing except more anxiety if I dwelled on the unanswerable questions for too long. The whole thing already caused my head to hurt and my stomach to ache in a post-gumbo-day-in-the-banquet-hall sort of way.

And two, the very idea of trying to explain to SJ and Blue that the girl I had nightmares about was a real person, in another realm, with a file in Fairy Godmother HQ, that I had stolen, seemed an even more unbearable option than keeping it all bottled up inside.

I know, I know, these are my best friends I'm talking about. They would try and understand, they would try to listen, and they would try to . . . try very hard to help me.

But I had already been pushing the crazy card lately with the perilous activities I'd dragged them into (past, present, and future included). So I didn't want to lay an extra, unnecessary dosage of nutso onto our team's already full load.

And besides that. . . Well, I just couldn't tell them. Not just for my own good, but for theirs too.

The information thoroughly freaked me out, so I figured I was doing them a favor by protecting them from assuming its burden. I owed it to them to at least extend that courtesy, especially since a part of me sort of wished that there had been someone to protect me from finding out about all of this.

Sadly, there hadn't been. I now had the truth and along with that came the understanding that a lot of things were about to get weirder and way more complicated. Knowing that, if by keeping my mouth shut I could somehow corral these consequences—only allow them to affect me, and not my friends—then that's just what I was going to do.

To sum up, for the time being there were clearly way more reasons not to tell the others about Natalie than there were to share the revelation. So I kept her folder hidden, kept my internal freak outs to myself, and when my friends asked me about what I'd gone back for during our visit to the Fairy Godmother Grand File Room, I lied and said it was nothing important.

CHAPTER 14

Pearl of Wisdom

n Saturday morning I was awakened by the sound of SJ's screams.

"What's wrong?!" I asked as I bolted upright in bed.

Blue had already jumped to the floor and had her knife in hand—ready for action. "SJ, what's the matter?!"

Our friend was running about the room emptying drawers and throwing things left and right. "The book, I have lost it!" she kept repeating." I have lost the book!"

"The potions book?" I clarified.

Hey, when you live in a world actually called Book, *sometimes a girl's gotta ask.*

"Yes!" SJ confirmed. "I left it in my nightstand drawer before we went to sleep like I always do and now it is just gone!" She moved across our suite like a tornado—clearly not noticing the irritation in Blue's crinkled forehead.

"Really, a book? That's why you woke me up with a heart attack?" she scowled.

SJ ignored Blue and zoomed back and forth in front of us. She was dashing around at such a speed it was almost enough to give you whiplash. I'd never seen her so freaked out. And rightly so, given how important that book was to her, *and* to our plans. Consequently, Blue put away both her anger and her knife, and the two of us didn't waste another second before aiding our friend with the hunt.

"Calm down. It has to be here somewhere," Blue told SJ as we began helping our frazzled friend search the room.

The statement was reassuring in the moment but, unfortunately, proved to be false in the end. After the three of us combed through the entire suite—turning it inside out in the process—we realized that the potions book was not, in fact, here.

I was also stricken with concern when I discovered that something else of value was missing from our room. Something of mine. But I decided not mention this just yet as it would only make SJ even more worried.

SJ sat on the edge of her bed and started to hyperventilate. "What . . . am I going . . . to do?"

"I don't know, but there go our plans," Blue replied.

SJ took a few deep breaths and swallowed hard before continuing. "Well, actually the potions I was making are almost complete and I sort of memorized the instructions a long time ago anyways."

"That's great!"

"But Madame Alexanders is going to expel me when she finds out I lost the book!"

"Maybe not," I thought aloud. "SJ, just how many of the potions in that book have you memorized in the last month?"

"Um . . . all of them, I believe," she said, confirming my suspicion.

Blue rolled her eyes. "Ugh, you really need to broaden the scope of how you spend your free time."

"Hush, Blue, I'm going somewhere with this," I interceded. "SJ, if we can't find your book then we'll copy all of the potions down in a new book from your memory."

"But Madame Alexanders will know it is not the same one," she objected.

"I doubt it; books around here all look the same. Fancy, leather-bound, tinted parchment paper—trust me, it won't be that hard to get the right replacement. Heck, we'll probably find a suitable one in the Lady Agnue's student store."

"But the potions book was really old and worn," SJ objected again.

"Then we'll beat the crud out of the new one until it looks that way," Blue piped in. "Don't worry, girl. It'll be okay. For real."

After some more comforting that she was not doomed, SJ eventually calmed down. And with the help of some of her animal friends outside we were able to put the room back in order within the hour.

Still a little shaken from the trauma, SJ decided to go down to the potions lab when we were done, to finish her work and get her mind off the situation. Blue and I offered to go with her, but she said she'd rather be alone. We didn't object and she departed without us just as the last of the squirrels was dusting off her desk.

The moment she'd gone, as luck would have it, the squirrel in question brushed his tail against one of her glass figurines (the Pegasus one). It fell off the desk and would've plummeted to its destruction had I not been standing there. I was thankfully able to catch the thing in mid air before it hit the floor and broke into a million pieces.

After such a rough morning the last thing SJ needed was to come home and discover one of her beloved collectibles smashed to bits.

It wasn't the squirrel's fault really; SJ shouldn't have kept the shiny knickknack in a place where it could fall so easily. Nevertheless, Blue chased the fluffy woodland creature out of the room as if he were fully to blame. She slammed the balcony doors shut behind him—letting out an aggravated grunt as she did so and ignoring the creature's angry squeaks.

Meanwhile, I drifted back to my own desk and mourned the other object I hadn't been able to locate during our search of the room. Noticing my melancholy, Blue asked me what was wrong and, reluctantly, I told her. One of my pumpkin earrings was missing.

It was the strangest thing. I left the pair on my nightstand every night before going to sleep and one had simply vanished without a trace.

Blue reasoned that maybe it had fallen behind my bed, or was stuck in my clothes from the previous day, or (more likely) one of SJ's dang birds had eaten it. But she reassured me above all else that we would find it. I sighed and tried to believe her as she punched me in the arm affectionately and then marched back toward her bed.

"After all that, you're still going back to sleep?" I asked.

"It's Saturday," she huffed as she buried herself beneath the covers. "And it's before noon."

"Fair enough." I shrugged.

With that, I suppressed the strange unease this morning's disappearances were causing me, cuddled up back in my own bed, and fell asleep to the sounds of the embittered squirrel raging at us from outside.

By seven o'clock the following night, SJ had finally finished preparations for the potions, and for our break-in.

Earlier that day the three of us had also successfully

recreated Madame Alexanders's potions book, so our friend was no longer in panic mode and instead was now delighted to be showing off her newest innovation. At first glance it appeared to be a normal glass marble. However, upon further—extremely close—examination, you could see a kind of colorful gas swirling around inside its translucent shell.

"What is it?" I asked, handing the delicate object back to SJ.

"It is my own creation," she responded. "I call it the Portable Potion."

Blue scratched her head. "Yeah, I'm gonna need a little more than that."

"I have had the idea for some time," SJ explained. "And I started fiddling around with base formulas for it over the summer, which I have now perfected."

SJ held the glass sphere up to the light as she continued. "You see, I brew a normal potion and then make a separate potion that crystallizes it into this form. The original potion is thereby concealed inside of this miniature, easy-to-transport package that will only release its contents upon impact."

"Dang," Blue said as she looked over the tiny orb. "That's brilliant."

I nodded in agreement. "Completely brilliant. So what potion is in this one?"

"Phase two of our plan for this evening," SJ answered. "Now, as per your instructions, Crisa, I have requested that a few finches outside wake us up at two o'clock in the morning. And since we are all ready for tonight, I suggest that we try and get at least a couple good hours of sleep until then."

Yeah, like that's gonna happen, I thought to myself as I rolled my eyes.

Have you ever been in a room that just made you feel uneasy and on your guard?

Maybe it was a dark hallway, a musty basement, an abandoned shed, or an unintentionally creepy puppet store?

That's how I felt when I was in that room.

Well, I should clarify that I was not technically in the ominous room I was referring to; I was asleep and my nightmares had transported my subconscious there.

But I assure you, even in all its blurry dreaminess, this unknown part of Book my spirit presently found itself in felt very, very real.

My dream self was currently following a girl in a richly colored purple cloak. Her entire form and face were hidden beneath it, so the only other thing about her I was able to make out was the fact that she was wearing glittering, black pumps with four-inch, silver-sequined heels.

Hmm, not the footwear I would've chosen for a midnight adventure. But that's just me.

The unidentifiable girl and I were in a grand place with marble floors as black as tar that matched the seemingly infinite number of shelves coiling around the room. These shelves stretched up to the high ceiling, which was being propped up by regal white columns every two-dozen feet.

It was a fairly impressive, intimidating setting. Nonetheless, my attention was captured by something far more intriguing. In the center of the ceiling was a chandelier. This was no ordinary chandelier, though. It looked to be constructed of cerulean glass bottles, and emanated a sapphire blue light that was both beautiful and inexplicably troubling.

The glow was strong and bright—illuminating the whole room with shades of indigo. Although despite the power of its luminescence, it appeared soft somehow. Like instead of pulsating with light as the sun did, the chandelier's glow was more an amalgamation of a thousand delicate threads of blue energy that happened to be conjoined together by a single base.

My subconscious form was yanked away from the entrancing image as the girl in the cloak kept moving.

I guess if you're not the main character in your dreams, you don't really have a say in where you get to spend your time whilst inside them. Bummer.

The girl driving my vision led us to an adjacent room. It was smaller in size, but almost identical to the previous one—aside from not having one of those weird chandeliers, that is.

This new space also had two things that the other did not. On the left side of the entry archway there was a silver statue of a knight holding a black sword. And on the right there was a shining stone statue of a dragon, approximately thirty to forty feet in length.

I watched as the mysterious girl grabbed the black sword out of the knight's hand and proceeded to walk over to the dragon.

What, is she going to try and slay it or something? Uh, news flash, honey, I think it's already dead.

Contrary to my expectations, the cloaked girl went on to do the most peculiar thing. She shoved the sword into the dragon's mouth and turned it clockwise. I heard a clicking sound somewhere in the distance. Then, across the room a bookshelf abruptly made a wheezing sound and swung itself off the wall and to the side—revealing a passageway.

What the what?!

I definitely did not want to go wherever that ominous entrance led. Unfortunately, what I wanted was never a relevant factor in my dreams, so my metaphysical self was, of course, inevitably forced to go through it.

The girl and I travelled down a dusty staircase. As we descended, my already fuzzy dream began to blur even further. Colors began to blend around me and the light was dimming more and more with each step forward. I would be waking up soon . . .

By this point my escort and I had gone through another door, I supposed, because I now found myself standing in an even creepier place than before. It had the musk of a war bunker and a cold, uncomfortable interior design that would've served as an appropriate setting for a cult meeting or a fight club.

This room was packed with people of various dress. The girl in the cloak pushed her way past them in order to reach a group gathered at the front. I squinted to see the hazy image more clearly, but to no avail. By the time she joined her friends or whatever, she had been reduced to a big, purple blob in my eyes.

The audio of the dream was not much better. Cloaked girl was having some sort of heated conversation with one of the group members but, hard as I focused, I only caught the end traces of what they were saying.

"So they believed it?" the black-haired boy she was talking to asked.

"Completely," cloaked girl replied. "No one suspects there was a switch, and our allies have already taken her original one."

"It's not enough that she doesn't know. This one's different than the others. The boss insists that the threat has to be neutralized completely."

Cloaked girl nodded. "I understand. And I already have a plan underway. It will require a few more days to be seen through, but shall allow for a quiet, and unforeseeable elimination."

"It had better," the boy responded. "And by the way, I am still waiting for you to bring me the items you were supposed to acquire in your last assignment; I'll be needing them soon and can't afford a delay."

"I know, and I have them, but I have to wait a bit before taking them off the grounds. The school is already in a panic since their disappearance, so for now I have to play it carefully. Trust me though; I will deliver on that task shortly, just as I will take great pleasure in delivering on this new one. I promise you, Arian, by week's end you will have your treasures and the girl will be but a memory."

Their words were inaudible after that. They, like the room itself, were transforming into an indiscernible blur as the dream grew foggier and foggier. Nearly everything had become a part of this big, murky mess by then. That is, except one thing. On the far back wall of the room there was a map of Book. And on it, there were all of these colorful Xs . . .

If metaphysical dream forms could feel nauseous, mine definitely did. Although I was asleep, my subconscious instantly registered that it had seen those Xs before.

I tried to get closer to them, to the map, but suddenly it was like I was being yanked in the other direction. I struggled to resist, but couldn't. Even more disconcertingly, as I was being dragged away I noticed that one of the Xs had actually lifted itself off the map. It was a black one—the *only* black one—and as I was being pulled away it started to pursue me. Fast.

It was now the only thing left in my dream that was not completely blurred over. Meanwhile, my heart pounding loudly in my chest was the only sound to be heard as it approached. Well, that and the sound of a bird chirping for some reason.

I shut my eyes hard to try and escape. Thankfully, it actually worked. When I opened them again, I was back in our suite.

Immediately I noticed that a little yellow bird was perched on my pillow singing the soft song that had apparently woken me from the confines of my nightmare. The tiny thing blinked at me with curiosity and I patted him on the head. He chirped happily in response and then soared back through our open balcony doors, his job completed.

"I thought I was going to have to wake you myself."

I turned to see SJ sitting on her bed putting on her shoes. She met my gaze in the darkness. "What were you dreaming about?" she asked coolly.

I shrugged. "Oh, you know, typical princess stuff—rainbows, princes, glitter."

"Uh-huh"

I broke eye contact and glanced over at Blue's bed. She was still snoring loudly and there was a plump finch sitting on her forehead.

"Should we—" I started to ask, but SJ smiled and held up a finger, signaling me to wait. A moment later the rotund finch opened his brown beak and sang an off-key, surprisingly baritone note.

Blue's eyes snapped open and she growled and swatted angrily at the bird as he flew back outside. SJ and I laughed as quietly as we could while Blue proceeded to stomp into the bathroom. She was clearly not a 2:00 a.m. type of gal.

A couple of minutes later we were ready. Blue had her knife in its sheath. I'd shoved my wand into my boot for lighter travel. And SJ, with a bag over her shoulder, had begun to walk to the edge of our balcony.

When she reached the railing she cleared her throat and started to sing very quietly. It was a soft, hypnotic lullaby that almost put me back to sleep. But after a few beats, some very alert owls flew over to answer the call (looking so attentive you'd think they'd have just responded to the trumpet sound of a military reveille). SJ—the ever-impressive animal charmer—proceeded to give them their orders. Then without question the owls flew back into the night as we made our way to the door.

Swiftly we exited the room, made our way down the six flights of stairs, and stopped behind the shadow of a pillar when we reached the foyer—sandwiching ourselves within the small gap between it, the wall, and one of the window's flowing magenta drapes.

SJ had instructed the five owls to be individually positioned on trees outside the windows surrounding the school. They were to be our lookouts—monitoring the main hallways that led from here to the Treasure Archives.

We were all well aware that different guards passed through the halls every nine minutes like clockwork, but we couldn't risk the chance that one might've been running slightly late or a bit early. Thus, the nocturnal birds were a necessary precaution. And as it happened, they did not mind, let alone hesitate, to take the opportunity to assist SJ.

Geez, it must be really nice to have animals want to jump through hoops like that for you just because you can sing. I wish I could get a piece of that action; I'd never have to make my bed again.

Silence and shadows everywhere around us, we waited in our hiding place. Soon enough the sound of clanking metal began to echo off the floor tiles as one of the guards went by. A few seconds later came a discernible "Hoot, hoot" as the owl outside let us know that the adjacent corridor was clear. We emerged from behind the pillar and scurried forward.

The three of us travelled that way for the remainder of our trek across the school—concealing ourselves each time we came to another corner and waiting for the owls' reassuring calls before continuing on our way.

Eventually we came to the grand hall intersection containing the Treasure Archives. The area felt more spooky than usual and the three of us exchanged looks before we hesitantly approached the cases. Moonlight was streaming through the windows, illuminating the whole area and reflecting off the many trinkets displayed there.

Blue cracked her knuckles confidently and stepped forward to set our plan in motion.

We only had nine minutes to get in and get out before the next guard came by, so she and I immediately removed a set of bobby pins from our pockets. SJ, meanwhile, retrieved two things from her bag. The first was the small portable potion she'd shown us earlier. The second was the slingshot Jason had made her.

Oh, so this is what that was for.

SJ had said the portable potion would need to impact on something in order to deploy the enchantment condensed inside it. So, I supposed a slingshot was the optimum way to fire such a thing while allowing for accurate aim of its distribution.

"It will last five minutes," she whispered to us, breaking the thick silence. "So we must move quickly."

Blue and I readied ourselves as SJ loaded the fragile object into her slingshot. After a brief exhale, she released it and the portable potion shot across the room. It made a direct hit against the school crest engraved at the top of the center case.

Upon impact, a large cloud of cobalt smoke was released and began spreading over the area where the cases stood. However, the cloud didn't stop there; it kept growing. It speedily made its way toward us and consumed our group and then the entire, massive room within its hazy entity.

"SJ," Blue coughed as lightly as she could. "What's going on?"

"I must have made the dosage too strong," she whispered back. "But do not worry; it should not make much of a difference. For the next five minutes or so we will just not be able to—"

SJ went silent then. Not from shock or anything dramatic like that. It was what she was trying to tell us. You see, the potion she had brewed for this occasion was a *silence* potion.

When SJ had first started concocting the potion we needed to escape from Lady Agnue's, my interest had been peaked. Accordingly, I thought I might peruse her special potions book to see if there were any other recipes inside that could've been useful to our mission. With the trip to Adelaide being so fresh in my mind, I immediately took notice of the page detailing the potion from *The Little Mermaid*—the one that the infamous sea witch had used to steal the sea princess's voice in exchange for turning her human.

I was confused at first because I thought that dark magic was responsible for this enchantment. But then SJ explained to me that (had I been paying attention in class last month) I would've known that the sea witch actually used a potion to silence the former little mermaid and then a separate magic spell to enact the whole flipper-leg swap bit.

The recipe for this vilified mutism potion was detailed in SJ's book. And—given the priceless nature of the objects in the Archives, and the tiny green lights just inside the cases that signified the presence of some sort of security system—I'd requested that my talented friend make us a batch of the stuff in order to silence the impending wrath of their alarms.

Evidently though, it seemed she had made the concoction too powerful and now it wasn't just the Archives' alarms that were incapable of making any noise, it was us and everything else in the room too.

Still, SJ was right. It didn't matter much. Not being able to talk for five minutes really couldn't interfere with our mission in any substantial way. Right?

Wrong.

When the smoke cleared, Blue and I continued with our next step of the plan. The two of us approached the Archives and got to work on the cases' locks.

As much as boys our age naturally tended to irritate me, having alliances with some at least meant the opportunity to learn from them on occasion. During our schools' past field trips and social visits, Jason and Mark had shown me and Blue some of the things they'd been taught at Lord Channing's that we never would have learned at Lady Agnue's.

Over the years, these skills had included: crossbow shooting, plant identification, hog wrestling, lock-picking, and whistling.

Who knew ladies weren't supposed to whistle? Lady Agnue did apparently. When asked about the pastime, she had referred to it as the song of construction workers and suspicious characters. Ergo, the practice had been forbidden from our school grounds since Day One.

Back to the present though, the relevant skill to our current situation was lock-picking. Each case in the Archives had two locks, so Blue and I each took one on and diligently worked to disengage it. After a couple minutes we were successful.

At first we were a bit reluctant to open the case—still nervous that the alarm might be too strong for SJ's potion to completely silence. It was only after Blue tried to yell as loudly as possible that we realized we really couldn't make any noise at all, and thus felt secure enough to proceed.

Blue and I pulled open the glass doors of the Treasure Archives. The tiny green security lights inside turned red, and the whole of the cases began to flash in the same shade of crimson. Thankfully, all remained quiet.

I exhaled with relief. SJ really could brew a mean potion. Maybe for once one of our plans would actually go smoothly.

Ha. As if.

When I reached out to grab the objects we were after, a dark gray force field went up around the trinkets and a puff of surprisingly solid, purple smoke exploded in my face and pushed me back. Suddenly, five side-by-side, tapestry-sized pieces of glittering parchment with the thickness of steel appeared in front of us—blocking access to the case. They were all blank with the exception of the center parchment, which had three words written on it: "Fairytale History Prerogative."

Two smaller puffs of purple smoke appeared then. One produced a glowing, green quill in front of Blue. The second morphed into the shape of a countdown clock above the giant document, which was set at twenty seconds but had not yet started counting down.

It must have been a back-up security measure of some kind. We probably had twenty seconds to pass whatever fairytale history question it was asking in order to gain access to the case.

Easy enough.

SJ and I motioned toward Blue. She was the fairytale history whiz after all, so she was unquestionably our best bet to pass such a test.

Blue nodded at us, stepped forward, and plucked the quill from midair. The moment she did, the three words on the parchment vanished and were replaced with—not a single question—but a *massive* riddle. Like, so big it might as well have been a final exam in one of our honors classes. Glowing red words with letters the size of bologna slices appeared in stanzas across the five magical documents—their brightness contrasting against the formerly dark room.

A second later the smoky countdown clock began to tick backwards.

19, 18, 17 . . .

Blue attacked the riddle as fast as she could, but was clearly worried by its size. Each and every line was missing at least one word (as noted by the silvery, sparkling lines scattered throughout the stanzas).

We wanted to help her, but there was only one quill and none of us could speak. So all SJ and I were able to do was watch nervously as Blue scrambled to fill in the dozens and dozens of blanks before our time ran out.

9, 8, 7 . . .

She was barely a third of the way done when it became obvious that we weren't going to make it. We were going to run out of time and the magic security precaution would inevitably lock us out.

4, 3, 2 . . 1 . . .

The countdown clock vanished when it reached zero, but the tapestry wall remained ever in our way.

Well, that's just great. Now how are we supposed to—

Oh, snap!

An enormous plume of smoke burst from within the unseen depths of the enchanted tapestries. It somehow both solidified and rapidly expanded to the shape and size of a fifteen-foot octopus tentacle, swinging in our direction.

We were knocked ten feet backwards onto the floor.

After a second to absorb the shock, my friends and I jumped up and watched in horror as this smoky limb released six more puffs of purple smoke that rapidly started to change shape as well.

It seemed that the Archives was releasing some kind of defense mechanism. We hadn't solved the riddle in the time allotted, so now the back-up safety measures were kicking in. And boy did they kick hard.

I realized that the giant parchment and the accompanying quill were still levitating in front of the center case, though. So I figured (or rather, hoped) that if we could finish the riddle, maybe we could turn off the security system.

The clouds of smoke had now taken the shape of six solid knights that began drawing swords from the sheaths strapped to their backs.

I grabbed my wand from my boot. It immediately started giving off an off-white glow (which usually happened whenever I utilized it in a dark space).

We still couldn't make any noise, so I gave Blue an *"I got this"* kind of look and gestured toward the tapestry, indicating for her to try and finish it while I bought her time. She got what I was implying, but shot a worried glance toward SJ. Our friend seemed a bit nervous, but waved Blue toward the tapestry riddle just as vehemently.

The knights came at us then. Blue dove left while SJ and I went right. I had to distract the smoky swordsmen away from Blue while she worked on the puzzle, so I morphed my wand into a boomerang and hurled it at the three knights pursuing her. It smacked one of them directly in the head and ricocheted back to my hand.

That definitely got their attention. The knights after Blue switched their focus to me—giving her a chance to return to the riddle and continue where she'd left off.

Spear.

My favorite new weapon elongated in my hand, still giving off an off-white glow. The enchanted attackers began to come at me—swords swinging—and I signaled for SJ to get back.

The first knight swung at my arm and I easily jumped out of the way and stabbed him in the side with my spear. He disintegrated back into smoke, which, for a moment, caused me to believe that maybe this wouldn't be so hard after all. Unfortunately, seconds after dissolving, the living smoke began to re-shape itself into a full-bodied knight again.

All right, that certainly makes things more interesting.

I soon realized that no matter how many times I killed these guys they would always regenerate like the first one had. To say this situation grew increasingly rough as the trend persisted would've been an understatement. I was doing my best to keep them all at bay and keep them away from the Archives where Blue and SJ were now huddled, but they were persistent, and definitely had an advantage over me what with the whole not-being-able-to-die thing.

One took a swing at my head and I ducked—side-stepping him. I twirled my spear to the right, knocking the sword from the knight's hand, then turned to jab a second opponent in the chest.

By then, the knight I'd disarmed had reclaimed his sword so I whirled around to face his charge. He came bearing down on me with an overhead strike. Gripping the staff of my spear firmly in both hands, I shoved it upwards to block his sword. Immediately following, I sent a swift, powerful thrust-kick into the knight's abdominals—causing him to fly backwards.

At that, I brought my spear down just in time to stab a knight approaching me from behind. With another rapid motion I continued to drive it forwards, nailing an overzealous attacker. Then, hard and fast, I swung it back across my right side to hit another knight closing in on my rear.

What a workout.

As the three knights I'd just eliminated reformed, I stole a glance in Blue's direction. By the looks of it she was about sixty percent done with the riddle and probably only needed a few more minutes to finish the job. But I was unable to further verify this, as my assailants did not seem to believe in time-outs. One barely missed me in the next second as he slashed at my forearm while I dove to the left.

As I rolled out of the way, I discovered that I actually

hadn't managed to completely avoid this last strike. The knight's blade had skinned my arm and a small gash by my shoulder was now openly bleeding. Apparently, even though I couldn't kill these things, the limitation was not mutual. They could certainly end me if given the right opportunity.

Shield.

I turned back to block the knight's next blow, but was caught off guard by an additional attacker who'd just popped out of nowhere.

Spear.

I countered his jab as fast as I could, but he was so close that the impact of his blade caused my spear to fly out of my hands. I was now unarmed and out of time. The knight drew back his sword to finish the job.

Luckily, right as he was about to, SJ plunged a sword into the back of *his* head.

In response to my shocked expression she gestured at one of the hollow suits of armor in the back of the room to explain where she'd gotten the weapon.

I let out a sharp breath of relief at the fact that I was, well, not dead. But this temporary feeling of safety drained from my face when I saw a knight charging at SJ from behind. I rapidly kicked my spear back into my hand and hurled it at the knight. It flew over my friend's shoulder and nailed the aggressor in his head. The strength of the throw skewered him backwards, pinning him to the wall until he burst into smoke again.

SJ mouthed a "thank you" in return and I winked at her as I went for my spear.

It was jammed into a high spot on the wall and another knight was running toward it—trying to cut me off. He was fast, but I was faster. When I was just a few feet away from my weapon, I leaped into the air and grabbed the staff with both hands. Like a gymnast using a bar, I swung myself forward to kick the knight in the face with all of my body weight—sending him sailing in the opposite direction.

Wand.

My spear shrank down, dislodging itself from the wall.

Spear.

I stabbed the knight as he got back up, causing him to burst into yet another satisfying puff of smoke.

Just then I noticed that across the room knights were starting to approach SJ—backing her against the opposite wall.

Sword.

I went to my friend's rescue, slashing at the opponents in my way as I did.

Spear.

When I reached her, I shot my weapon into the three that were cornering her and it went through them like a violent shish kabob.

I had appreciated SJ's help, but it was dangerous for both of us if she stayed in the area. We were clearly on the same page about that, as she gave me an understanding nod and ran through the reforming clouds of smoke to rejoin Blue at the front of the room.

Honestly, I wasn't worried about being able to take care of myself while the two of them finished the riddle. They didn't have that much more to go and I was doing pretty well handling the defensive on my own.

Not to toot my own horn, but let's be real; I am a totally boss fighter with this spear. Like so boss I wish that the silence potion would wear off just so I could shout some sort of battle cry, like "Whablamo!"

Alas, all remained silent as I speedily stabbed and disintegrated one knight after another—my friends completely unaware of the epic battle raging behind them as they filled in the riddle's remaining blanks.

It wasn't long before I actually managed to get all six knights disintegrated at the same time. With a moment to breathe as they reformed, I took a look at my friends and discovered that Blue and SJ were almost done with their task. As I did this, though, out of the corner of my eye I suddenly realized that the six individual puffs of smoke were now unexpectedly merging and growing into one, enormous cloud.

Uh, okay. That's new.

The blob kept expanding. It then went on to take the shape of some huge serpent/octopus/kraken thing with six tentacles—three for moving and three for trying to kill me.

Before attacking, the newly formed monster tried to emit some kind of screech that (thanks to SJ's potion) my friends, the rest of the school, and I were unable to hear. However that didn't really matter; I did not need to hear the creature's cry to make me nervous. The sharp snout, fanged mouth, and massive, tentacle-like arms were enough to get the job done quite sufficiently.

I dove aside as one of the arms came crashing down where I'd been standing, then rolled out of the way as another attempted to do the same. When I jumped to my feet, the third arm came sweeping around low to try and trip me, but I leaped over it and kept running in order to lead the monster away from my friends.

I was able to keep this up for about a minute—ducking, diving, jumping, diving, ducking, diving, ducking again, and so on. The problem was, I was so busy trying not to get smashed by the arms that I was unable to have even a second to plot some kind of offensive strike.

Finally, when I gained enough footing to attempt one, I slid under a moving arm and stabbed my spear into one of the creature's tentacles. The monster released another silent screech as the leg dissolved.

I drew my spear back—intending to take out another leg—but as I did, I didn't see one of the other arms coming at me.

A tentacle grabbed my hand by surprise and began to tightly wrap itself around my entire arm before I could pull away. It had been the hand holding onto my spear too, so the monster's grasp now kept me from moving the staff and jabbing my way free.

With my weapon neutralized, a second arm did not hesitate to move in. It entwined itself around my waist then thrust me up against the wall, knocking the wind out of my body. The third arm pinned my free hand while the second arm continued to wrap its way around my diaphragm and throat—tightening its grip in order to squeeze out all remaining oxygen.

"Guys!" I tried to yell.

But it was no use. Despite the fact that I was only about twenty feet behind them, SJ's potion was still active. And the resulting silence kept her and Blue unaware of the action, smoke monster, and throttling of their friend that was currently going on behind them.

Maybe if they can just finish the Archives' riddle this thing will disappear before it finishes choking me, I thought hopefully.

I glanced back at them and squinted at the silvery lines they still had yet to fill in. It seemed they only had one stanza left to go:

"Few weaknesses pertain to the Mer-people's world,
But that which they fear most is all that is _____."
My eyes widened in disbelief.
Oh, geez. I know the answer.
"Blue! Blue!"

Right, they couldn't hear me. So how was I supposed to tell them what to put in that last blank? Neither of them appeared to know, and this smoke beast thing was growing. So not only was I about to be finished off by being wrung out like a flimsy towel, if this monster kept increasing in size pretty soon none of our weapons would've been effective in stopping it.

What was worse? SJ's silence potion was going to wear off any minute. Which meant that the sounds of the Archives' alarm, the creature, and our noisy battle would soon be able to be heard throughout the entire school!

I needed a plan. It was relatively hard to think straight with the way this thing was crushing me. Brains needed oxygen after all, and at the moment I was severely lacking in that department. But I tried my best to focus—analyze the situation, as was my nature even when I did have my back against the wall.

The monster scrunched me tighter and shoved my body harder into the wall behind.

Err, I didn't mean for that to be so literal.

Come on, think, I reminded myself. *Keep breathing and think.*

It seemed that every time one of these smoke creatures got destroyed it took about seven seconds for it to reform. So, if I killed this one then that's about how long I would have to get to the riddle, insert the answer, and shut down the security system. All I needed was one good shot and, well, to get this thing to stop strangling me.

Growing stronger, the smoke monster was beginning to sprout another arm, so I garnered enough gumption to make my move before it could finish.

Knife.

My spear shrank down.

With a struggle, I managed to rotate my hand a few centimeters and plunge the blade of the much smaller weapon into the tentacle holding my wrist. The stab was just enough to cause the beast's arm to burst into smoke. The second it did, my hand was free and I used the knife to stab the other two arms entrapping me. They, too, exploded into smoke and I was released and dropped to the floor.

Spear.

I jumped to my feet and backed away. The monster's arms were already reforming and it was coming after me again.

Okay, I have to get this thing at its center if I want the whole of it to dissolve for the full amount of time. So aim, self. Aim!

I ducked as one tentacle swung at my head. I drew back my arm. Then, with all my strength and focus I hurled my spear at the heart of the monster.

It was a direct hit. But I didn't take time to admire the precision of the strike. The instant I saw the creature burst into smoke I made a break for the display cases.

My friends had obviously not heard me coming, so they were startled when I plowed into them and grabbed the quill from Blue. I looked over my shoulder and glimpsed the blob of smoke—its tentacles already sprouting and starting to move toward us. Quickly I wrote in the final word of the puzzle before it was too late:

"*Few weaknesses pertain to the Mer-people's world,*
*But that which they fear most is all that is **pearled**.*"

When I entered the last letter of the desired word, the whole riddle began to glow. I turned around in a wave of panic and saw that the monster was less than ten feet behind us.

Only now . . . it seemed to be frozen where it stood.

The riddle's tapestry shone even brighter. As it continued to increase in luminance the smoke monster began to disintegrate. One large flash later and they were both gone completely. The entrance to the case was revealed and the force field protecting the treasures vanished from view just as the cases' alarm lights ceased pulsing.

Phew! What a relief!

Thank you, Lonna Languard.

It was pure luck that the mermaid princess and I had met, and even greater fortune that the bracelet Marie had given me had caused the aquatic girl to reveal the information about Mer-people's deep fear of pearls.

Take that Lady Agnue's. See, there are things outside of the traditional princess curriculum that this lovely school doesn't teach us, which could totally come in handy in real life.

I exhaled and put a hand on my chest to try and keep my heart from popping out due to residual adrenaline. "That was close," I heard myself saying.

"Hey, we can talk again," Blue whispered excitedly.

SJ sighed. "And not a moment too soon."

"Fantastic," I panted.

SJ gave me a confused look. "Crisa, how did you know the answer to the last line of that riddle? Blue and I were truly stumped, and you never pay attention to our lessons."

"Does it matter?" I said. "I pay attention to life. Now come on. You two get what we came for, I'll get my spear, and then let's get the heck out of here before we're almost killed again."

"What's the matter, Crisa?" Blue teased quietly. "You're not tired, are you?"

"Who, me? No way. I *love* single-handedly fighting shape-shifting smoke monsters at two in the morning. Who doesn't?"

A minute later my wand was back in my boot, SJ had stashed our two newly acquired treasures inside the shoulder bag she'd brought with her, and Blue finished closing up the center display case.

The Archives looked like they had never been disturbed. The duplicate mirror that Jason and Daniel had made for us was a flawless imitation. And on re-locking the cases, the tiny alarm sensors inside turned green again—resetting themselves.

No one, it seemed, would ever know we were here.

With the help of SJ's owl friends, the three of us called it a night and carefully made our way back to our room. We were exhausted, rattled, and a bit traumatized to be perfectly honest. But now, more than anything, we were curious.

When we'd returned to the safety of our suite my friends and I huddled on my bed with me in the middle.

SJ removed the treasures from her bag—a flower petal from *The Frog Prince's* water lily, and the magic mirror from *Beauty & the Beast*. With great care she handed me the latter. And with a deep breath I held up the beautiful looking glass and said the four words that this whole mission had been aiming toward:

"Show me Emma Carrington."

CHAPTER 15

Frame Job

he Tardy Gods were with us on that particular morning.

SJ, Blue, and I hurried down the stairs in a panic—our morning lecture having already begun. We were horribly late and dreading the scolding we would no doubt receive for the indiscretion of barging into class a half hour past due.

In hindsight, this situation had been inevitable given that we'd been up at all hours of the night with our escapades. After our assault on the Archives, we'd attempted to use the magic mirror over and over again for the better part of an hour. But despite our persistence, it still hadn't shown us anything of importance.

I supposed I should have expected as much. The mirror showed you where people were in real time. So when it displayed Emma last night, all we saw was my godmother sound asleep in her bed. Not much to go on when we were trying to figure out her location at large.

At 3:30 a.m., SJ had insisted we go to bed and try again in the afternoon when we might have better luck. Our hope was that at some point Emma would leave her house and go into town. And, based on what we saw in the background, we could find clues about her geographic position and narrow down the search from there.

In the meantime we had to resume our normal activities. Although given that classes started an eternity ago, I'd have said we were off to a pretty poor start.

When we reached the foyer we executed a sharp right turn to complete our dash to D.I.D. class. But as we made our way, we began to realize something peculiar. The halls weren't quiet.

Usually by this time of day, everyone was already in their respective classrooms. However, as we continued toward class the distant murmurs grew louder and louder until we came to the very area of Lady Agnue's that we'd tiptoed out of just a few hours ago.

That's when we saw it. A large crowd of students, possibly all of the students, was gathered in the intersection that housed the Treasure Archives. The air was full of nervous whispers. My friends and I felt a wave of dread go through us as we slowed down and tried to walk over to the scene as calmly as possible.

I was worried, but mainly confused. The replica mirror that Jason and Daniel had fashioned for us had been perfect. Moreover, we'd hardly left a speck of dust out of place in that glass case, let alone anything that would've set off a red flag to the school's staff.

We approached the swarm, but no one acknowledged our arrival. I strained to look at what my classmates were so focused on.

What in the—?

The perfect, glittering Treasure Archives that we'd treaded so gingerly around last night were smashed to pieces. Gaping holes had been created in the cases' doors and thousands of glass shards were scattered on the floor.

Guards and several of the school's senior staff members were carefully making their first inspections of the area. Meanwhile, another cluster of teachers was off to the side talking frantically in those hushed tones that grown-ups tend to use whenever there's trouble afoot.

Upon examining the destruction closer, my shock deepened at what I saw. Well, what I *didn't* see really. Several treasures were missing from the Archives.

Pretty much everyone at Lady Agnue's had the contents of these displays memorized from having passed by them so many times each day. It was therefore instantly apparent to all of us exactly which four objects had vanished. They were the genie's lamp from *Aladdin*, the pea from the *Princess and the Pea*, the poison corset from *Snow White*, and the mirror from *Beauty & the Beast*.

Of course, the one thing my friends and I knew that the rest of the school didn't was that the stolen mirror was only a replica we were using as a placeholder. The real one was currently hidden safe and sound underneath my mattress.

"What happened here?" I whispered to a frazzled Marie Sinclaire, who was standing to my left.

"We do not know," she whispered back. "It must have been sometime last night. But no one can figure how they did it without getting caught. You would have had to throw, like, chairs through the glass to create holes that big. How did no one hear it?"

It was a good question. SJ's potion had silenced the room for a while, but instructions on how to make it could only be found in that special book of hers. Furthermore, how did the person who did this handle the smoke monster defense system after we'd reset the alarm? And when exactly had they had time to do it? There'd barely been a window of a couple of hours in between when we'd been here and the kitchens had opened for breakfast.

"Ladies, ladies," Madame Alexanders said, emerging from the circle of faculty members and coming over to us.

She cleared her throat loudly and overpowered our chatter with her well-practiced teaching voice. "Children, the staff and I agree that it would be best if you returned to your classes until we get this all sorted out. So hurry on. Quick like bunnies; go, go, go."

We protested a bit, but the other teachers worked together to herd us like frightened cattle away from the crime scene. SJ and I began to merge out of the area with the rest of the group, but after a minute we noticed that Blue was not with us.

It was hard to look around while being pulled along by the moving sea of students, but eventually we were able to spot our missing friend behind us, still by the Archives. She appeared slightly nervous, her eyes glancing around to see if anyone was watching her. When she seemed sure that neither our classmates nor the staff was looking, she bent down and disappeared from sight.

Barely a second later she popped back up again and swiftly forged her way into the migrating group of girls. When she was by our side once more, SJ and I shot her a couple of questioning looks.

"What was all that about?" I asked under my breath.

"Later," Blue responded curtly.

None of us said another word as we continued to shuffle through Lady Agnue's' distraught hallways and into our D.I.D. classroom. That which we had to say could not be discussed here.

You would've thought time was going to fly by for the rest of the day after this morning's incident.

Sadly, it was quite the contrary. Even after what seemed like an eternity we were still captives of Damsels in Distress 601—barely listening to Madame Lisbon go on and on about how to pass out in public without wrinkling your outfit.

I just tuned her out as the seconds ticked by. My mind was too blank to do much of anything else.

You know when you've just had a really rough few days and you're so stressed out and overloaded that your brain just shuts down temporarily as you try to absorb it all?

Well, that was what I was feeling at the moment. I was so out of it. My mouth was hanging open like a frog trying to catch flies and my eyes were glazed over like frosty crystal balls. I was fairly certain that there was nothing capable of snapping me out of such a stupor. Naturally, I was soon proven wrong.

Ms. Mammers (our headmistress's assistant) abruptly burst into the classroom halfway through our lecture. She glanced around the room and glared directly at me for a split second before turning her focus to Madame Lisbon and muttering something in our teacher's ear.

Madame Lisbon's face paled and she nodded.

"Crisanta Knight," she said with slight pause. "Lady Agnue wishes to speak with you in her office. Immediately, please. Ms. Mammers will escort you."

Everyone in the class turned toward me. At first I didn't respond—not because I didn't hear Madame Lisbon, but because I was too shocked to register what she'd said. Blue elbowed me gently—returning me to the present.

I grabbed my bag and headed toward the front of the room. As I passed them, most of the girls stared at me with a look of confusion on their faces.

I tried to keep my expression neutral and nonchalant, like I too had no idea what was this was about. When, in reality, I had a terrible suspicion that this had something to do with the Archives. Why else would Lady Agnue be wasting her time with me (her least favorite student) right now if it didn't?

I figured at least Mauvrey was probably enjoying the spectacle, and no doubt also judging me for the circles I had under my eyes from lack of sleep. However when I glanced over my shoulder to verify this, I noticed that Mauvrey wasn't even here. Her regular seat beside Jade and Girtha was empty.

Figures, the one time I get to enjoy a class without Mauvrey's snootiness and I get excused.

Ms. Mammers waddled very quickly down the corridor. She never looked back to make sure she hadn't lost me, which was a genuine risk considering the speed at which she was going. For a woman with such short, stumpy legs, she sure could move fast.

When we arrived at our destination, she held the door open for me, but obviously didn't take any pleasure in the cordiality of the gesture. I was about to flop down on the couch in the waiting area across from her desk, but she grabbed me by the arm before I got the chance.

"Lady Agnue is ready for you *now*, Miss Knight."

I was kind of taken aback to be honest. I mean, yes Ms. Mammers had given the impression that whatever Lady Agnue had to talk to me about was urgent. But I'd been called into the headmistress's office to be yelled at or lectured before, and even in extreme cases of my misbehaving we usually went through the motions of routine formalities.

Ms. Mammers hastily ushered me into the adjacent office where I found Lady Agnue sitting up straight at her desk. The door was shut behind me and I took a seat in the vanilla colored chair facing our headmistress.

There was one large window in the room behind Lady Agnue's own velvet, magenta chair. It was tall and had its crème-colored curtains pulled back to reveal a view of the school's main entrance. The light outside was so bright it made the entire office feel warm. Except for the area around Lady Agnue that is, which her personality frosted up significantly.

"Do you have anything to say, Miss Knight?" Lady Agnue asked me bluntly as I sat down.

"Um, is that a new plant?" I said, pointing to a small fern on the corner of her desk.

Lady Agnue folded her hands. "Miss Knight, I did not ask you here to talk pleasantries."

"Lady Agnue, you never ask me here to talk pleasantries."

She didn't respond to the comment. Instead, she opened one of her desk drawers and took something out. The object was small and sparkled in the light from the window when she held it up before me. I instinctively reached my right hand to my ear when I realized what it was.

"You found my earring!" I said with more excitement than appropriate for the serious vibe pulsating through the room.

"Yes," Lady Agnue nodded. "Would you like to guess where?"

I blinked.

"This was found within one of the shattered cases of the Archives," she began.

I blinked again.

"One of your classmates, Mauvrey Weatherall, found it. And so now I ask you again—do you have anything to say, Miss Knight?"

Oh crud. She does think I broke into the Archives.

Well, technically I did *break into the Archives. But I didn't* literally *break them. And I certainly didn't steal four of our realm's most sacred treasures.*

Though how exactly do you explain that to your school principle without figuratively hanging yourself? And how in the name of Book did Mauvrey find my earring?!

"Lady Agnue," I said as evenly as possible, "I didn't smash the Archives and take that stuff. I can't explain how my earring got there. It's been missing for a couple days; ask my friends. But I didn't do it. I promise you, I'm not . . . I didn't . . . I just couldn't do something like that."

"Do not make promises you cannot keep, Miss Knight. And for goodness' sake, I thought I warned you about those contractions! You must have used at least a dozen in the last two minutes alone and, frankly, they are causing me to develop a migraine."

Oh for the love of . . .

Calm, Crisa. Stay calm. If you lose your temper now you're only going to get into more trouble.

We kind of stared at each other for a minute then. I didn't know if I would've exactly characterized it as a stand off since there were no tumbleweeds in the background, the songs of the blue birds outside were the opposite of ominous, and, well, we weren't standing. Still though, it was pretty intense.

Usually I was not one to shy away from confrontation, but this was different. There was just not much else I could say here. If the school didn't have any other leads to go on, Lady Agnue was not going to let me out of the hot seat. I was going to get suspended, or expelled, or whatever the princess equivalent of extremely, horribly in trouble was.

I might even get . . . detention.

GULP.

For better or worse, I finally decided to interrupt the silence and face whatever our headmistress's misplaced wrath entailed head on. "So . . . what are you going to do to me?" I asked.

Lady Agnue leaned back in her chair. "For now, not much," she sighed as she glared at me with her narrowed eyes. "I do not like you, Miss Knight," she continued. "As I am sure you have already well realized."

"Yeah," I huffed. "But, heartbreaking as it is, I think I'll get over it."

"Silence," the headmistress snapped, rage escaping her for a second.

All right then. Definitely not the time for sass.

"Crisanta Knight, I would like nothing more than to have you removed from this campus," Lady Agnue went on. "Alas, other members of the school's senior staff feel that we must give you the benefit of the doubt. *They* seem to think that you are simply spirited and naïve, not a volatile troublemaker, and that you would never do anything like this. I, however, disagree and will be keeping a very close eye on you as our investigation continues."

"Um, so does that mean I can go?" I responded.

Lady Agnue nodded and I did not hesitate to grab my earring off her desk and make a break for the door. Tragically,

I was unable to escape the headmistress's lair before she dolled out the very punishment I'd been dreading.

"Just because you are not expelled, young lady, does not mean you are off the metaphorical hook. You will be serving detention in Tower Six everyday after classes for the next two weeks."

The vein in my neck nearly burst from the combined dismay and outrage. "Two weeks! Lady Agnue, come on. That's not fair!"

"Consider it one week for this and one week for the Twenty-Three Skidd tournament. But do look on the bright side, Miss Knight," my headmistress taunted. "Perhaps you can use that time to reflect on your actions, learn to suppress that sense of rebellion in your personality, and practice constructing sentences without those awful contractions."

I was furious, but chose to hold my tongue and bolt out of Lady Agnue's office before my inevitable mouthing off earned me a third week in detention.

Ms. Mammers was not at her desk in the waiting area when I walked out. Which would have made me content had it not been for the fact that Mauvrey was sitting there casually in her place.

"Good morning, Crisa."

"You," I marched over to my nemesis angrily and glowered at her from across the desk. "Where did you find my earring, Mauvrey? I know for a fact that it was nowhere near the Archives."

Her eyes curved into a smile as she calmly uncrossed her legs and stood up from Ms. Mammers' chair. "And how would you know *that*?" she posed in return, squaring me off.

I placed my hands on my hips and mirrored the

confidence she was emanating. "None of your business," I said.

"Maybe not," she continued, "But it *is* Lady Agnue's business. In fact, she has called me in here this morning to discuss the very matter with her further."

"I didn't smash those cases, Mauvrey. And I didn't steal anything."

"Oh, I believe you, Crisa," she replied. "But I would sooner chew with my mouth open and dye my hair brown than defend the likes of you."

"So you're just going to hang me out to dry then?" I clarified. "And try to convince Lady Agnue that I'm guilty even though you know full well I didn't do it?"

"Did not do it," she corrected. "Princesses do not use contractions, Crisa. Remember?"

Oh that is it.

"Mauvrey, I *couldn't* care less if contractions *aren't* princess-like. Frankly, your behavior is way less princessy than mine is anyways. In case you've forgotten, rule seven according to our blowhard headmistress says that princesses aren't supposed to lie either. Yet, here you are, about to go into that office and lie your tail off as a part of your petty vendetta to destroy me."

"Oh please, Crisa. I could run around this school in a pair of short shorts playing the mandolin and I would still be more quote, 'princessy,' than you. And furthermore, if I wanted to destroy you I would think of a much more satisfying way to do it than by framing you with a stupid earring. It is like you said back in Adelaide; I *am* better than that. And as such, I do intend to rise to the challenge you so eloquently put forth to me that evening."

"And what challenge is that?"

"Channeling my creativity to execute a more *interesting form of revenge,* of course," she replied.

Lady Agnue's door swung open before I could come up with a retort. Standing in the doorway of her den, our headmistress glared at me before gesturing to my other archenemy. "You may come in now, Miss Weatherall. As for you, Miss Knight, get back to class. And do not forget to report to Tower Six at five o'clock sharp. For every minute you are late I will be adding an extra day of detention to your sentence."

I stormed out of the office and down the hallway.

As if I was going back to class. I had already been excused from D.I.D. and with the mood I was in I probably would have ripped my textbook in half had I been forced to go on sitting there.

What I actually ended up doing was ditching the remainder of my morning lessons and hiding out in the barn, stabbing at hay dummies with my spear.

When noon came around, I reluctantly headed back toward the main grounds. SJ, Blue, and I had planned on meeting in our room during lunch to try the magic mirror again. By the time I made it back my friends were already waiting for me. Eyes fraught with worry in SJ's case and curiosity in Blue's, I proceeded to tell them what had happened.

"I can't believe Mauvrey!" Blue ranted afterwards. "You should've knocked her teeth in, or gone all Mulan on her butt with your spear."

"Believe me," I said. "I was tempted."

SJ paced the room. "Sorry to change the subject, Crisa, but the events between you and your collection of archenemies aside, I still want to know how whoever broke into the Archives after us went about doing so. I mean, for no one to hear or see them . . . it is inconceivable."

"Maybe whoever stole your potions book cast the same silence spell you did," Blue suggested.

SJ blinked twice and looked confused—as if our friend's statement had been spoken in a different language.

"What? Are we still pretending like the book just got lost?" Blue asked. "We searched this room inside and out. Someone definitely took it."

"Oh, right." SJ bit her lip. "In all our rush this morning, I forgot to tell you."

"Forgot to tell us what?"

SJ walked over to her bedside and opened the top drawer of her nightstand, from which she pulled out a small, very familiar looking text. My eyes widened.

"You found it," I said in shock. "You found your potions book."

"Yes. I could hardly believe it myself," SJ replied. "When I woke up this morning I just discovered it in the drawer. No explanations, it had simply reappeared."

"And you didn't think to tell us until now?" Blue said, punching SJ in the arm.

"Ow, Blue!" she cheeped. "That hurt."

"Well, you deserved it. Keeping something like that to yourself."

"It is not as though I was intentionally keeping the secret, Blue. I was preoccupied with other matters what with our late night ventures, and being tardy for class, and the Archives being destroyed, and Crisa—"

"Guys," I interjected, my brain hurting from the sheer enormity of the day. "Can we focus please?"

SJ glared indignantly at Blue and straightened her dress. "Yes, well, *as I was saying*, even if someone had stolen the book, it would not have mattered. The spell I used last night takes two weeks to construct, and the book was barely missing for two days. So if whoever orchestrated the break-in had intended to use the same spell we did, they would not have been successful. Perhaps that is why they returned it this morning."

"Or maybe they just thought of something you didn't," Blue countered.

SJ furrowed her eyebrows. "Given that the thieves had to smash their way through to get into the Archives, I highly doubt that."

"Well then I'm out of ideas," Blue huffed, flopping onto her bed. "Crisa, anything to contribute?"

"Honestly, I don't really care how they did it," I said bluntly. "I just want to know *why*."

My friends' resulting, reflective silence told me they wanted to know the answer to this question just as badly as I did. There had never been a break-in at school before, and those four items were so diverse. I couldn't think of any one reason to take all of them. None of us could.

Temporarily abandoning any hope of solving this quandary, I decided to change the subject by getting the magic mirror from under my mattress.

It was a lot prettier in the daylight—solid gold with an intricate floral design all around it. I flipped it over in my hand for a second and fingered the words etched into its back. "Mark One," just like the mirrors at Fairy Godmother HQ.

I'd told my friends about the shattered mirrors I'd seen back at headquarters and they'd agreed that the identical words discovered on this one definitely made the situation weirder. Although since none of us were quite sure what that peculiarity translated to (and since it was nowhere near our main concern at the moment) for the meantime we'd chosen to let this mystery simmer on the back burner too.

I turned the mirror right side up again and stared straight into its looking glass.

"Show me Emma Carrington," I ordered.

The glass rippled like it was made of silvery water. When the glistening waves faded to a stop, an image of Emma came into view. She was outside—on her knees in a field of brilliantly colored wildflowers where she appeared to be gardening. The magic mirror also provided sound, so I could hear the flowing waters of the river next to her and a couple of birds chirping nearby. My godmother smiled away, humming some unknown tune to accompany them under the shade of her giant gardening hat.

As upset as I was, seeing Emma's face made me smile. Everything about her was just as I remembered, despite the fact that I hadn't seen her since I was very young.

"Well, we know she is by a river," SJ said, peeking over my shoulder.

"Great," I commented. "That narrows it down to, like, twenty-five kingdoms."

"No wait," Blue grabbed the mirror from my hand and studied the image. "Crisa, she's in Ravelli!"

"How do you know that?"

"Look, there are mountains in the background. But they don't have any snow on them so that eliminates the northern territories."

"Okay, so that means it's either the Lagatta Mountains or the Rangel Mountains," I said. "Still though, together those mountain ranges run through six separate kingdoms."

Blue held up the mirror really close to my face. "Yeah, but only *one* of those six kingdoms has bunniflies!"

Bunniflies?!

I squinted at the mirror and realized she was right. I could faintly see bunniflies hopping and flitting about by the riverbank behind Emma.

Along with your basic enchanted animals like wild Pegasi and the occasional temperamental dragon that roamed the realm and caused trouble, every kingdom in Book had its own special species that was native to that part of the land. And for Ravelli, that species was bunniflies.

Bunniflies were basically normal bunnies—fluffy, big eyes, cottontails, etc. But they had different-colored, big, brilliant butterfly wings sprouting out of their furry backs.

Unique to Ravelli territory, these cuddly, aerodynamic animals inhabited the kingdom's forests and meadows in dense numbers. So if Emma lived in an area surrounded by them, we *had* successfully narrowed down her location.

"Well, that's it then," I said triumphantly. "Emma's in Ravelli. SJ, how soon will your second potion for getting us out of here be ready?"

"I added the petal from the water lily to the preliminary potion this morning," she responded. "The final product should be suitable for ingestion by Saturday."

"Great, that's the first bit of good news I've heard all day," I replied. "Now I guess we just have to find some way to put the mirror back in the Archives before we leave. I want my conscious as clean as possible so that Lady Agnue has no reason to suspect me."

Blue and SJ glanced at each other.

"I don't think that's a very good idea," Blue said.

I raised my eyebrows. "Um, why?"

"Well, someone went through a whole lot of trouble to steal some random, but powerful junk from the Archives. Including that mirror. If we put it back, chances are they'll probably try taking it again."

"Blue is right," SJ said sadly. "And based on what happened this morning, I believe it would be safe to assume that whoever did this would be quite capable of succeeding a second time."

I nodded in agreement. "In other words, we can't put the mirror back if we want to protect it because by stealing it we've already kept it from being stolen."

It seemed like a gray area in terms of good conscious, as SJ was undoubtedly aware. But it did make sense. Whatever the reason someone else had wanted that mirror (based on the means they'd been wiling to go through to get it), I assumed their motives were far from benevolent. As a result, we simply had to hang on to the enchanted object to keep it safe, at least until the school caught the culprit who was after it anyways.

With our lunch hour almost over, I hastily shoved the mirror back beneath my bed, then grabbed a knapsack out of my desk drawer for later.

"Crisa, do you want to hit the practice fields after dinner today?" Blue asked as we headed out.

"I can't," I said with an irritated sigh. "I have detention."

Panic streaked across Blue and SJ's faces.

"Yeah," I said, shaking my head. "That was my reaction too."

CHAPTER 16

Rapunzeled

 hile the hours I'd spent in class this morning
had moved at the speed of a turtle, the time I
spent in detention somehow moved even slower
(like, maple syrup slower).

My stomach growled.

Ugh, why did I have to use a food-related analogy?

In retrospect, skipping lunch even though I knew being
in detention would cause me to miss dinner was a bad idea.
Thankfully I'd at least remembered my knapsack snack
pack. I was always prepared in case I got a major case of the
munchies while I was studying or, more likely, procrastinating
late into the night. So the emergency sack of goodies I kept
in our room was generally fully stocked.

I took a bread roll out of the bag and chewed on it woefully
as I leaned against the cold, stone walls of my prison.

And btw, I'm not being metaphorical here when I use the word
prison.

Detention was the worst punishment a mischievous girl
could get at Lady Agnue's. It was a positively primitive
sentence that was both sad and humiliating.

"How bad could it possibly be?" you may ask.

Well, let me break it down for you.

Princess detention meant being locked in the highest

room in one of the school's tallest towers for five hours at a time, à la Rapunzel.

These tower prisons had nothing but a stone-based interior, a stale cot, and a window to look out unto the world we were being isolated from.

That's me overselling its amenities by the way.

When I finished my roll, I folded my arms and closed my eyes. This was so unfair. It was an inhumane punishment for any teenage girl, but the irony of *literally* being a princess trapped in a tower made it all the more insufferable for me personally.

I wished there was a way I could've gotten out of here, but I was completely stuck. I mean, I couldn't exactly jump out the window or suddenly grow hair long enough to use as a bungee cord for escape. The first option would've led to death via 300-foot drop, and the second, well, even if it were possible, the amount of money I'd need to spend on conditioner afterwards would've been ludicrous.

With no way out of the cylindrical, stone room in sight, I tried to stifle my frustration as much as possible by allowing my thoughts to drift to other topics that might distract me. What I ended up focusing on, however, were my dreams, specifically the one about the Xs I'd had last night. And such ponderings were in *no way* calming.

In all the excitement, anger, and flat out ridiculousness that had occurred within the last twelve hours, I'd managed to avoid thinking about the subject until now. But with nothing else to do up here I couldn't help but realize just how unusual my nightmare from the night before had been.

Other than my Natalie Poole dreams, this was the only other reoccurring vision I'd ever had. And there'd only been a few weeks in between the one I'd experienced this past Sunday and the one about the Xs I'd had while we were on our trip to Adelaide.

Call me crazy, but it felt like that had to mean something.

I mean, if I'd dreamed about Natalie repeatedly and she was real, then maybe that meant those Xs and the mysterious bunker room they'd been housed in were real too. And if that was the case, where exactly in the realm were they?

I knew that if they did actually exist, they were here somewhere. Like I said before, whenever I dreamed of scenes in Book, I was absolutely certain that this was where they were taking place even if their depictions in my head tended to be super blurry. Granted that did not make the most sense. But, really, what part of all this did?

The thing was, even if they were somewhere in this realm—and that was a mighty big if—I didn't know what my dreams about Natalie meant, so how was I to know what visions of a bunch of multi-colored Xs implied?

Putting that brainteaser aside for a moment, the other part of my dream that was bugging me came to the forefront of my mind—the conversation between the cloaked girl and that black-haired boy.

While I was sure the cloaked girl had been a new character to my dreamscape, I couldn't help but feel like the boy had visited it before, if only in the form of brief whispers and flashes. Last night's image of him had been so vague, but even in its foggy residue his voice had been startlingly familiar. It was deep and resonated with me in a chilling kind of way—like the recurring voice I sometimes heard talking to that other girl in the aftershadows of my more vicious nightmares.

It made me wonder then if this black-haired boy had

been the source of that haunting voice all along; and if this had been my first real glimpse of what he looked like, of who he was . . .

Naturally, I couldn't be one-hundred-percent certain that it was the same boy. However as I sat in that tower—closing my eyes and concentrating on the dream—the part of my instinct that regularly courted the highly unlikely found itself believing that it was. This boy—the one the cloaked girl had called Arian—was the owner of those words and that dark, ghost-like presence that had penetrated my sleep for the last three years.

Follow-up questions swiftly began burning in my head in regards to this understanding. Though as many and varied as they were, two quickly stood out amongst them; two questions that I practically ached to know the answer to.

Who was he?

And why did my subconscious consider him so important?

It was all terribly perplexing and rather unsettling to say the least. For, although I had zero idea what he or his co-conspirator in my subconscious had been talking about, their exchange still gave me the shivers. Not in a fearful kind of way, but more like a form of anxiety. It was probably unwarranted mind you, but considering, well, everything, it definitely didn't feel that way.

With resolve, I elected to pick myself off the tower floor then and shake off the morose confliction. That had been more than enough time devoted to thinking about such illogical and unnerving things. And I flat out refused to acknowledge or accept them any further for the time being.

I dusted off my dress and leggings and made my way over to the window to breathe in some fresh air.

While my holding cell couldn't have been any grimmer, the view from it was tranquil and full of the gingered, autumn warmth. The sun was starting to set and it cast the land in a blanket of orange. Shadows stretched from trees, the river reflected streaks of gold, and the sunflowers by the practice fields practically yawned as they bid adieu to the day and retreated within themselves—so much like I often felt like doing.

I could see for miles from up in this tower, even all the way to Lord Channing's. It was quite a distance away and was mostly blocked from view by the forest separating our schools, which spread out over several acres of large hills. Even so, I managed to make out the blue roofing on top of the main buildings. Beyond that, I also spotted traces of stables, an archery field, a regulation-sized Twenty-Three Skidd arena, and a large obstacle course.

I craned my neck to try and see them better, but found it did me no good. As usual, knowledge of Lord Channing's' specifics were out of my reach.

Since our monthly balls were always held at Lady Agnue's, the boys had a much stronger familiarity with our campus than we did of theirs. In truth, the only times we got to go over there were in the spring when they had their Twenty-Three Skidd finals matches. However, even then our exposure to the campus was limited. Whenever one of those matches occurred and the In and Out Spell was lowered, we were taken via carriage to the back entrance of the campus that led to a parking area beside the arena. As such, we were not given the opportunity to see much of anything else.

Staring at the shrouded school from up here made me wonder more than usual what a hero's curriculum looked like in comparison to a princess's. I bet they got to learn all kinds of cool, valiant things like mace fighting and crossbow making. Meanwhile I was stuck here, learning to sing and sew and be complacent with my lot in life.

As I continued to look at the bits of the campus I could see, my thoughts drifted to the boys who lived there. Consequently, I wondered about Chance and how many things at that school he'd turned to gold in order to show off his powers to the other princes. I wondered where Jason was. Maybe in woodshop, or working on his fighting skills in one of the many combat arenas the school was supposed to have? And then . . . Then I wondered what Daniel was doing.

So much for a moment of peace.

Even in my tower's isolation I felt strangely embarrassed by the way just thinking his name made me lose my calm. I couldn't even utter it to myself without filling up with waves of anger over the way he caused me to feel so exposed.

He just got under my skin more than anyone I'd ever met. So much of him was a mystery. Practically the only thing that wasn't was the knowledge that he took an interest in irritating me, and happened to be unusually skilled at it too.

It was true that most boys our age, except for Jason and Mark, had a tendency to annoy me a bit. They couldn't seem to hold intelligent conversations for more than a few minutes, almost always had huge egos, and the majority tended to think of girls as weaker.

But I digress. They're just teenage boys after all. And I've been told that most of them become less obnoxious and far more tolerable as they grow older.

Here's hoping anyways.

Daniel though, did not simply annoy me like normal guys did. I dreaded being around him like cats dreaded water. Every time we had a conversation he unavoidably said something that rattled my confidence and faith in myself in a way that few people could.

It probably wouldn't have been so bad if I could get at him in the same way. But that was a difficult task considering I barely knew anything about him. The boy kept to himself. And no one I asked, not even Jason, could provide me with information that shed light on the enigma of who he was and why he didn't care enough to let anyone see it.

Added to my Daniel dilemma, no one else seemed to have a problem with him. According to my friends, to other people he was a perfectly nice guy and it was simply me that he enjoyed irking.

Given that, it was needless to say that I really wished he wasn't involved in our mission to find the Author. Like, *really*.

But, alas, he was.

As a result, I decided to suck in my pride and preference and—rather than go on complaining about the situation—from hereon out, commit myself to finding some way to put up with him. Or at the very least, finding a way to get past all his mysteriousness so I could bug him in retaliation. This would be quite the task though, considering his level of aloofness (like his obnoxiousness) was thicker than a triple-coated caramel apple.

My stomach growled again.

Dang, I gotta stop making all these food analogies; they're killing me.

I drifted away from the window and back toward my knapsack to see what else I could gnaw on for the remainder of my prison sentence.

CHAPTER 17

The Art of Going AWOL

he next few days drifted by in a blur.

SJ was busy working on our escape potion. Blue sharpened her assorted knives and sent messages via SJ's bird friends to Jason and Daniel to coordinate our plans. And I rotted away in my ivory tower every day after school—practicing defense maneuvers with my spear, and eating non-perishable leftovers I'd saved from earlier meals.

Eventually Saturday night came around and we were at last ready for our escape.

Earlier in the week SJ had actually suggested that perhaps we should wait until the following Saturday to make our move because that was when our next monthly ball was scheduled for. Her logic being that on the night of the ball, the boys would've already been with us so a group escape would've theoretically been simpler.

This was a decent point, but in the end the idea was vetoed because, first, with so many people around for the ball, school security was usually tighter. And second, I really did not want to suffer through one more week of tower time if avoiding it was a feasible option.

SJ, Blue, and I were in our room making sure that we had everything we needed for the mission. Blue was taking inventory of the various weapons she was packing while SJ was filling a small sack with her portable potions. She had certainly been productive in the last week; that was for sure. She was putting dozens of the tiny glass spheres into the pouch hanging from the belt at her hip.

I didn't know what kind of potions were in those spheres, nor what SJ expected to use them for. When Blue had asked, she'd simply shrugged and said that they were contingencies she hoped we would not need.

Part of me wanted to delve deeper into this response, but in the end I respected SJ's genius enough to figure she knew what she was doing. And anyways, I was currently far more fascinated with the other product of her innovation that she'd gifted to us this morning. Around my wrist currently hung the latest fruit of SJ's potion-based inventiveness. She called it: "Soap on a Rope-like Bracelet," or an SRB for short.

Of course, to give credit where credit was due, the enchanted accessory was actually born of both SJ *and* Blue's brilliance.

A couple of days ago, Blue came bursting into our room with a revelation. If we were going on this great journey, which would no doubt take weeks of travel, sweat, and unorthodox adventure, how exactly were we going to remain, you know, clean?

It's kind of a stupid detail, I know. But then again, think about it.

Like Blue explained, it's the sort of thing that is never really addressed in any of our ancestors' fairytales. Which leads me to believe that the illustrations in those books I've grown up reading are totally bogus, since people can't just go on these epically long quests—never showering or changing clothes—and still look fresh as daisies and decent enough to mingle in mixed company.

I mean, it's not like these protagonists carried with them trunks of clean clothes or could freshen up periodically at cozy bed & breakfasts when they were chasing bad guys, or being chased by bad guys. That's just ridiculous.

After Blue's two-minute pitch on the subject, SJ had been completely sold. Our room's resident princess was in no way about to go all grease and grunge for several weeks. Thus, the idea for the SRB was born.

I had to say, I rather liked the premise. The thing looked like a simple rope bracelet. But SJ had laced it with a powerful potion of her own design that made the wearer of the bracelet unable to get dirty. Like, *at all.* You would stay fresh as newly washed laundry 24/7 no matter how much time passed.

Furthermore, if any outside filth got on you—from mud to dragon vomit—after the fact all you had to do was wait a minute and you and your clothes would revert back to normal. You'd be clean as a whistle as if nothing had ever tainted you in the slightest.

SJ had ended up making an SRB for each of us, the boys included.

Thank goodness for that. Boy sweat smells considerably worse than girl sweat. That's just a fact.

As I continued to watch my dainty friend fill her sack with portable potions, I seriously considered suggesting that, should the whole "fairytale princess" thing not work out, she should think about going the small business ownership/ entrepreneurship route with her potions skills. The girl was absolutely brilliant.

When SJ had stored the last of her tiny concoctions, she made sure the pouch was securely fastened to her belt, then slipped the slingshot Jason had made for her inside of her dress pocket. Once done, she gestured for us to follow. I slung my satchel over my shoulder and Blue slid her hunting knife into its holster.

SJ led the two of us into the bathroom and proceeded to open the cabinet beneath our sink. Inside there was a small, iron cauldron filled with bubbling, green liquid. She pulled it out and lifted it onto the counter.

"How did that not set off some sort of fire alarm?" Blue wondered aloud.

SJ ignored the comment and placed the cauldron in the sink. She took out three cups from the cubby behind the mirror and filled each one with the lively concoction. I eyed the stuff and realized I wasn't quite sure how it managed to keep bubbling without any kind of heat source.

Hmm.

Probably best not to think about it.

We each held our respective cups, but hesitated before drinking. We knew this was it. Once we drank, there would be no turning back.

"Well . . . cheers," I said, trying to ease the tension. I chugged down the liquid. SJ and Blue followed my lead. And then we waited.

The formula tasted like mint juleps with extra lime and a hint of rustiness. As it made its way down my throat, it felt like thick, acid-like honey coating my vocal chords. My gut immediately started to feel a disturbance—and not the kind of disturbance it felt after all-you-can-eat-oatmeal day in the banquet hall. This felt like I was eroding from the inside out.

I clutched my stomach in agony while the potion started to take its effect. A vague green mist began to pour out of each of our mouths and encircle our forms. My skin cringed, the veins in my arms flickered silver, and I struggled to breathe as the walls of the room grew higher and higher around me.

If you've never been turned into a frog, consider yourself lucky. I definitely wouldn't recommend the experience.

SJ, Blue, and I were now less than six inches tall, green as ryegrass, and covered in slime. It felt neither pleasant nor attractive. But it was an ingenious plan nonetheless.

In theory, that is.

As we'd learned in class earlier this semester, it was a potion encasing the Frog Prince's water lily—not magic—that made whomever ate it turn into a frog. Consequently, once SJ had found the right recipe in her special potions book she'd realized that if we took a petal from the water lily in the Archives, she could reverse-engineer it to recreate the same enchantment in a lighter dosage. The result would be a much more temporary froggy transformation that could be broken without relying on the shenanigans of true love's kiss.

That exposition aside, you may still find yourself asking, "Well, why did we want to turn into frogs in the first place?"

The answer? One word: loophole.

Our school's In and Out Spell was designed to keep *people* from passing through it, not *animals*. So, in our amphibious forms we would be able to cross Lady Agnue's' magical barrier with as much ease as the woodland creatures that inhabited the surrounding forest. At least, we hoped so.

Everything on the grounds was quiet as the three of us journeyed toward the border of the In and Out Spell. Ever prudent, SJ had made us wait until midnight to enact the plan and get our green on so that, with the exception of the nighttime guards, the school would be deserted and our trek unimpeded.

Since a 12:30 a.m. or 1:00 a.m. departure time would have worked just as well though, I suspected that she was also veering toward fairytale tradition in her decision to make midnight the designated hour of our departure.

Frankly, I didn't care one way or the other. The only thing that mattered right now was that the three of us were hopping to freedom.

Victory getaway music anyone?

No?

Well, all right then, creaking staircases and cricket chirps it is I suppose.

After hopping as stealthily as we could down six flights of stairs, several hallways, and across the practice fields, we were exhausted.

Would it have been easier to walk out of the school in human form and then take the potion when we got down here? For sure. However, would it have been possible? Definitely not.

Sneaking out of Lady Agnue's when you were barely the size of a sandwich was way easier than the alternative option ever would have been. That logic notwithstanding, I was super wiped out from the slog.

Seriously, that was a lot *of hopping.*

When we finally reached the riverbank at the edge of the grounds, I shot my tongue out in exasperation to communicate this sentiment. My amphibious friends mirrored the gesture and then waddled over to that stupid, stone gnome that marked the boundary of our school's campus. Frog SJ and Frog Blue began to blink their big, goopy eyes at me expectantly.

They were nervous about crossing.

It was natural to hesitate. As I mentioned, this whole frog loophole thing with the In and Out Spell was just a theory. We were human on the inside and really didn't know for certain that we could fool the In and Out Spell with our reptilian transformations.

I remembered then just how painful it had been to receive that small shock from the enchanted force field last month when my finger had barely grazed it. If we did not dupe the spell, our entire bodies would soon be violently, mercilessly fried by the magical wall of energy in the same way.

In other words, that old saying, *"Here goes nothing,"* really didn't apply here.

I gulped down some extra slime, and my nerves, and decided to just do it. In the next instant, with a big boost from my hind legs, I leaped forward.

Thankfully, I was not zapped. I landed in the river with a splash and turned around to see a little lavender hole fade and fizzle out behind me—revealing the section of force field I'd just jumped through.

Phew! Okay, this is good. This is very good.

If only getting across the In and Out Spell surrounding the Indexlands was this easy. Too bad that one, specifically, is like a billion times stronger and designed to prevent life of any kind from getting through—human or animal.

Seeing that I remained un-barbequed, my friends followed me and were equally relieved to remain electrocution-free.

A few hundred more hops later, the three of us finally made it to Lord Channing's' border. Jason and Daniel were waiting on the other side of a fence beneath a large apple tree—biding their time until our arrival. Frog SJ, Blue, and I wiggled through the fence and came into their line of sight. Even at this height and in the dark I could tell that when Daniel saw us bounding over he had to try really hard to conceal his bemusement.

"Aw, does someone want a kiss?" he said mockingly as he let a short laugh escape his lips.

I wanted to tell him to shut it or go jump in the river, but my amphibian vocal cords limited me to the trite comeback of "Ribbit!" Which (let's face it) was not my best zinger.

My froggy nerves tightened in anticipation of what inevitably came next.

Ugh, this is going to be so embarrassing.

Remember when I said that SJ's reverse engineering had cured the potion of being permanent or reliant on true love's kiss to break it? Well, the one thing she had not been able to modify was the necessity of a kiss of some sort to end the enchantment.

Now do you see where I'm going with this? No?

Let me spell it out for you: thy name is total mortification.

Jason proceeded to pick up Blue and give her the necessary peck on the head. Once he had, he quickly set her back down. A few seconds later, a flash of silver light enveloped our friend and returned her to human form.

"Whoo, that's better," Blue said happily as she stretched and checked to make sure her hunting knife, cloak, and everything else that had been on her at the time of the transformation had rematerialized with her. "Thanks, Jas."

Next, Daniel carefully lifted SJ off the ground and did the same. After she, too, had shimmered back into herself again, it was my turn. I silently hoped Jason would at least be the one to perform the mercy kiss, but he and Blue had already started to walk off into the forest, SJ not far behind them. I appeared to be stuck with Daniel as my not so charming, not so princely partner for the task.

In hindsight, I reminded myself that this was a small price to pay for everything we were aiming to achieve with the mission at hand. Still, the idea of sharing my first kiss with a boy I barely tolerated while I was a frog was way less than ideal.

I glared at Daniel with my giant eyes and threw in another "Ribbit!" to communicate my disapproval as he picked me up. He smirked in response and gave me a slight, clearly condescending kiss on the head. Then he dropped me like a sack of potatoes right as a magical flash of light returned me to my normal size.

I didn't see why he couldn't have just set me down on the grass gently like he had with Frog SJ. No, he had to dump me in the dirt because apparently Frog Crisa was somehow more unbearable to touch. Human Crisa, as a result, landed on the ground with a thud.

Disgruntled, I got up, adjusted the strap of my satchel, and dusted off the remaining feelings of slime and humiliation.

My friends, of course, failed to notice Daniel's lack of chivalry. So I had no one to lament to as he and I made our way through the woods that surrounded Lord Channing's.

"So, where's our ride?" I heard Blue ask excitedly up ahead.

"Come on, we'll show you," Jason responded.

We walked through a thick forest of trees before coming upon a clearing. In the center stood a simple, crimson carriage with five Pegasi harnessed to it. I thought one looked familiar, and I was right. One of the two rear Pegasi was Sadie. She whinnied merrily when I reached her and nuzzled my hand in greeting.

"Sadie is one of Lord Channing's' Pegasi?" I asked as I petted her mane.

"Yeah," Jason replied. "Adelaide didn't have enough Pegasi for the tournament, so we brought some of our own."

I looked away so that Jason wouldn't see me roll my eyes.

It was so unfair that the boys had a copious supply of Pegasi at their school. The only magical animal we'd ever had at Lady Agnue's was a talking goat a few years back. And he'd been promptly removed from the campus after only a month due to the many complaints received about him eating tapestries and some of the girls' dresses.

So again, I repeat myself: how unfair is it that the boys get flying horses while we get diddly squat?

I didn't recognize the other Pegasi in the line-up. Well, except for one. Also on the team of steeds was the black Pegasus that Daniel had ridden in the tournament. The creature glared at me as if it had been trained by the man himself to do so.

SJ and Blue approached the other Pegasi attached to the carriage. Blue began scratching the ear of the steed in front of Sadie. After a moment, SJ cautiously tried to do the same. However, when her hand came within a few inches of the creature's face, he whinnied abruptly and bucked a bit, stomping his feet and shaking his mane.

SJ jumped back and pretended like the creature's snub didn't bother her, although Blue and I knew perfectly well that it did. How could it not, when every other animal alive treated her like a deity?

"Not that this isn't a great ride," Blue said, trying to change the subject away from our friend's awkward rejection, "but isn't your school going to notice that you took five Pegasi and a carriage?"

"Nah." Jason shrugged. "We've got tons of these for all our tournament training and hero drills. Besides, the kids at our school come and go all the time for quests and stuff so I doubt they'll even notice we're gone. The better question is, won't the three of you be in a lot of trouble when they realize you're missing?"

"Of course we'll be in trouble," I responded casually as I made my way over to the carriage. "But we're in trouble most of time. At least Blue and I are anyways. I hardly think this is the time for us to start feeling bad about it though, wouldn't you agree?"

Everyone but Daniel and SJ proceeded to follow my lead into the carriage. He went to sit up front in the driver's seat to steer our vehicle. She, meanwhile, took a few steps back and drew out her slingshot along with one of her portable potions—an orange one, which she explained contained a levitation concoction she'd brewed specifically for our travels.

While five Pegasi were more than enough to lift a carriage, according to her prior research on air travel, most people also used an extra levitation potion to keep their vehicles airborne. That way the Pegasi's jobs were easier because their main responsibility became steering and pulling the carriage forward, not lifting it and its various passengers off the ground in their entirety.

SJ fired the potion at our carriage and a tangerine cloud exploded around its base. As the gas subsided, we felt the vehicle rise off the ground. SJ boosted herself up on one of the back wheels and Jason offered her his hand, helping her inside.

Using the reins, Daniel signaled the Pegasi that it was time to take off. They all whinnied—their nostrils emitting multi-colored puffs of smoke and their eyes beginning to glow either stunning silver or vivid cobalt. Moments later each produced his or her own set of glittering holographic wings and we were jolted against our seats by the force of their long-awaited rise.

As we sped skywards I looked out the rear window at the school grounds we were leaving behind. Lady Agnue's was still and dark across the river. Its towering shadow stained the gray and purple night almost as strikingly as I knew its walls had stained the majority of my life up 'til this point.

That place had been my home for years. It'd been the greatest influence on my choices and my character development. It, in an essence, had been my whole world—setting the parameters for my path and the lines I was supposed to color inside of for the rest of my story.

Until now that is . . .

Now I was beyond its grasp. Now I was moving out of its shadow. Now—the parameters, the lines, the walls—they were crumbling more with every added meter of distance I put between us. And soon enough, I knew they would never have the authority or the strength to contain me again.

I glanced back at my friends for a second. Then—a small smile easing across my lips—I turned to face Lady Agnue's one last time. With a strange sense of calm I watched it disappear behind the fog as we finally moved on.

CHAPTER 18

My Reluctant Truth

erial road trips were fun at first, but after a couple of hours they were no better than regular ones (especially when you factored in how cold it got that high up in the clouds, and that changing wind patterns could be worse than speed bumps).

Thankfully, Ravelli wasn't too far from our schools; it was only about four kingdoms over.

Most of us fell asleep at some point during the trip. I didn't remember falling asleep myself, but I guess I had because one minute I was staring out at the stars as they whizzed by, the next I was trying to adjust to the light of the oncoming sunrise.

I squinted and rubbed my eyes. Blue, Jason, and SJ were still out. Blue looked really cute with her hood pulled down over her eyes. SJ was sitting up way too straight for someone who was unconscious. And Jason was snoring, but no one seemed disturbed by it.

I turned my attention back to the skyline. It was just ushering in the colors of daybreak. Pinks, oranges, and pastel shades of citrine stretched upwards with the sun rising behind them like a big egg yolk.

Silently, I moved to the seat across from me and peered out the front window. Daniel was as alert as ever with the reins in his right hand. The metallic scabbard that held his sword was hanging from his shoulder and catching the light, as was the golden chain dangling from his left hand.

The chain was attached to the same pocket watch he always seemed to be carrying around with him. I leaned over to try and see it better, but his body blocked its face from view—preventing me, yet again, from taking a closer look at it.

I analyzed the dimensions of the window before me. It was directly behind the driver's seat and took up a good portion of that side of the carriage with the exception of the actual bench area (about five feet by two feet in diameter). An impulse of curiosity getting the better of me, I decided to open the window and crawl out.

Before Daniel could stop me, I had climbed through and sat down next to him. He brusquely stashed the pocket watch back into his jacket when he saw me coming—careful to keep it concealed as he did so.

"What are you doing?" he asked, eyeing me suspiciously. "Gonna push me off the carriage or something?"

"Oh, please," I responded as I slid the window shut.

"That's not a no," he countered.

"Well, I like to keep my options open," I replied.

As I said this I realized that he was smiling at me. Not that normal cocky smirk, but an actual, genuine smile. Stranger yet, I realized I was smiling back. We both seemed to notice this irregularity at the same time though, and immediately buried our grins beneath irritable frowns.

"I just needed to get some air," I assured myself aloud.

He nodded, but didn't add any commentary.

For a while we sat there enjoying the beauty of the

blushing sky. It was nice. The only visible thing beneath us was a valley of clouds so fluffy it could've been made of cotton balls. And the wind against my face was bliss. It was like pure freedom—a sensation that I couldn't remember having felt since, well, ever.

From time to time I glanced out of the corner of my eye at Daniel. He actually wasn't quite so obnoxious to look at when he wasn't talking, causing me to wonder if there was any truth to my friends' claims that he wasn't such a bad guy. Beyond this though, as I studied him, I wondered even more why he'd chosen me of all people to try and prove the opposite to.

"Daniel," I suddenly heard myself saying. "Why don't you like me?"

Wait, did I just ask that question out loud?

What could possibly have possessed me to ask him that?

He broke his gaze away from the horizon and tilted his chin in my direction, perplexed. "Who said I didn't like you?"

Now it was my turn to be confused. *Like, a lot.*

"Um, you did," I said bluntly. "The first day we met. I don't really care or anything; people dislike me all the time. It sort of comes with the territory when you're openly sarcastic and rebellious. But with you . . . I mean, you kind of seem to make it a point to get your dislike across, like it's your own personal vendetta or something."

All right, I am either suffering from severe altitude sickness, or some type of rupture in my head. Because it is definitely not okay for me to be talking to him this openly!

I'm not even sure I can classify that as talking—blabbering on is more like it.

Daniel didn't appear to notice how embarrassed I was over

my forthcoming-ness, though. He seemed too preoccupied with the assertion I'd just made.

He rubbed the back of his neck like he was trying to massage some type of honesty out.

Eventually he made eye contact with me again. Then he uttered the two words I'd least expected to ever come out of him.

"I'm sorry," he said.

I almost fell off the carriage from shock. "What?"

Seriously, what?

"It was messed up of me to just take one look at you and judge you off the bat like that," Daniel continued. "You're not that bad really, and of all people I definitely should've known better."

"Um, apology accepted I guess," I said. "But that still doesn't explain why you've been a total jerk to me since then."

"I don't know what you want me to say, Knight," he said. "I may not dislike you as a person, but being around you isn't exactly my favorite pastime either. I mean you're so . . . you're just so . . ."

He scowled and shook his head. "Look, have you ever met someone who just completely rubbed you the wrong way? Well, it's kind of like that. You bug me. Plain and simple. That's the best way I can describe it anyways. No offense."

Hmm. All this time I'd been so consumed with how much Daniel annoyed me, I hadn't even considered the idea that maybe the feeling was mutual.

To be honest, knowing that it was made me feel a bit better. Like maybe we were more even than I'd originally thought. Or at the very least maybe the unexplainable sense of self-doubt he seemed to instill in me was coincidental, not a reflection of some abnormal ability he possessed to see right through me.

"You know what, Daniel," I finally replied, "for the first time, no offense taken. Mutual irritation I can handle. I did share a room with Mauvrey for a year after all. And if I could get through that . . . Well, maybe there's hope for us yet."

"Yeah," Daniel said, not meeting my gaze. "Maybe."

It was strange. I couldn't believe we'd actually reached some form of understanding. Until that moment I wouldn't have considered that such a thing was even possible between us. Needless to say I should've dropped the conversation at that—called it quits while we were ahead. But no, I just had to go and open my big mouth again.

"I gotta say, Daniel," I found myself commenting after a beat, "it's kind of nice to hear you be open about something for a change."

He raised his eyebrows suspiciously. "Meaning?"

"Meaning you kind of keep to yourself."

"Don't you do the same?" he asked.

"No," I said without even a hint of uncertainty.

"Really?"

"Yes, *really*. I'm pretty open about myself. I'm sure even you can attest to that."

Daniel sort of studied my face as if he was trying to ascertain whether or not to continue. In retrospect, it was definitely the type of introspection that I should've done on myself at least five times in the last few minutes. If I had, maybe I wouldn't be in this situation now—positioned in just the right place of vulnerability for Daniel to drop the hammer that all of my doubts had long been leading me toward.

"You're open about the way *other people* see you," Daniel began slowly, "but, not about how you really see yourself. That's why what I said to you that night we went to Fairy Godmother HQ bothered you so much. I could tell. I'm guessing the same thing probably happens whenever Lady Agnue, or Mauvrey, or anyone else calls you out in a really personal way. Part of you knows they're wrong about who they think you are, and has no problem protesting it. But in the end what they say still upsets you because you're not able to fully convince yourself of *why* they're wrong about you. Am I right?"

Uh, come again?

I was totally stunned. Like, Mauvrey-winning-the-rodeo stunned.

Why would he? How did he? I mean, what?

I was frozen now. I felt utterly infuriated and undermined and unsettled and . . . it was all because of Daniel.

I immediately had the urge to argue with his very blunt analysis of me. At the same time, I found that I couldn't bring myself to do it. Much as the understanding killed me, something in the pit of my stomach suddenly gave way to the feeling that he may have been right.

When he, or any of my other natural enemies tried to tell me who I was, I always felt confident enough to instantly protest their views. However, in the aftermath (especially lately), their words echoed in my head and rattled my insecurities—forcing me to ask myself for a form of self-assurance that should've come naturally if I was as internally sure of my character as my assertions to other people suggested. But, it didn't. Because, I guess . . . I wasn't.

I placed my fingers to my temples like SJ did in hopes of pushing out the merciless self-analysis.

So much for my short-lived hope that Daniel's tendency to read me like a book was merely coincidental phenomenon. For whatever the reason, he really did possess a practically supernatural ability for getting inside my head and forcing me to face parts of myself that I would've preferred to pretend weren't there.

"How do you do that?" I sighed after a minute had passed.

"Do what?" Daniel asked.

I looked away from him in begrudging embarrassment. "Know just what to say to get to me," I admitted.

"Don't flatter yourself," he scoffed. "You're not that complicated."

"Daniel . . ." I said, frustration edging my tone.

He paused. "Knight, maybe we just have more in common than you think, all right?"

"Yeah, okay," was the only sarcastic response I could muster to such an ambiguous statement.

I began to fiddle with the hem of the dark green dress I had on over my leggings. The brown pleats in the skirt matched the color of my trusty combat boots. I tried to focus on counting their twisted laces in an effort to block out the thoughts swirling in my head, but to no avail. Daniel's voice was practically a part of my conscious now—unwanted, but unable to be completely silenced nonetheless.

What had I been thinking, I thought to myself bitterly. *Like he and I could ever be in close proximity to one another without chaos ensuing.*

His assertion that we might have more in common than I thought was ridiculous. Frankly, I sincerely doubted that we had *anything* in common. The very idea that we shared even a single characteristic was absurd. We were nothing alike. Starting with the fact that he was a total jerk-face, and I was not.

Still . . . I couldn't help but ponder what he'd meant. If I truly irritated him in the way he claimed, why would he not only acknowledge, but also confess to such a shameful realization? What did he believe we had in common that could've been important enough for him to deem worth admitting to like that?

One look at him and I wondered if there was even a point in asking. I suppose I had to try but, based on his track record, I garnered my hopes of getting anything out of him were pretty dismal.

Ugh. Why does he always have to answer with those cryptic one-liners? A bit of elaboration from time to time would be nice. I mean, hello, I'm not some kind of oracle.

"Okay, Daniel," I said, disrupting the silence once more with a slight change of subject. "You seem to think you know a whole lot about me. I'm not saying you're right about half the junk you've said. But, I'm going to give you a courtesy you've never given me and actually ask you a few questions before I make any more snap judgments about you. It'll be like a little experiment. I ask you something, and you try to give me a straightforward, non-mysterious answer. Got it?"

He shrugged. "Fine, whatever."

"Alrighty then." I cleared my throat. "You never answered me before. What is so awful about your prologue prophecy that it made you decide to come with us to find the Author?"

"I already told you, Knight, that's none of your business," Daniel responded. "Why are you even so determined to know anyways? Jason's on this quest with us too and you don't seem so obnoxiously compelled to find out this type of personal stuff from him."

"Because I don't have to," I said bluntly. "I've known him for a long time for starters, but, more than that, I respect his privacy because we're friends."

Daniel tilted his head and gave me a look that I did not recognize. "And we're not?" he asked.

Whoa, awkward.

The truth was, I didn't know what to reply because I myself had wondered the same thing before and had never come up with a conclusive answer.

Daniel made me angry in ways I didn't even understand, and in a lot of ways I definitely *did* understand. Still, he was Jason's friend, and Blue and SJ didn't seem to mind him. He'd spent an awful lot of time with us since the school year had commenced. And, to be fair, he'd been more or less a team player since we began this whole future-changing venture. So I supposed he was kind of, technically, by definition, a friend.

Then again, what kind of friend insulted a person the way Daniel constantly insulted me?

Ninety percent of the time we were with one another we were arguing. The other ten percent of the time the only reason we weren't was probably because we weren't speaking at all. For crying out loud, a minute ago he sent me into a massive internal tailspin because, although he barely knew me, he was still able to look through me like glass and say things that, well, that I just didn't want to hear.

To put it simply—it was complicated.

Don't get me wrong, his very presence made me shudder with aggravation. That much was easy to observe. Even so, no matter how hard I tried, I couldn't view him completely as an enemy. He may have said things to me that were hurtful, unnerving even. But I didn't see meanness in his eyes when he looked at me. There was some jaded coldness and traces of shrewdness, as if he was dead set on calculating the best way to keep me at a distance. However, beyond that I saw no ill will. In fact, in those rare moments when we weren't at each other's throats (like when I'd first come out here) I could sense the presence of something else—something ardent and strong, but tinged with a sadness I did not yet understand.

That notion aside, I certainly didn't see Daniel as someone I could count on either. As it stood, I probably would've sooner jumped off a moving train than put my faith in him in that way. This may have seemed like a bit of an extreme statement, but I meant it. I did not trust Daniel. Moreover, I honestly doubted that there was any way I ever could; that our relationship would ever be able evolve past the heated friction we tended to inspire in one another.

Eventually, after taking all of this into consideration, I gave the enigmatic boy sitting across from me the only answer that made sense to his original question.

"We'll see," I said.

Time ticked on without a word from either of us for a while after that. The sun continued to rise and the wind began to decrease as sky welcomed in day.

Truthfully, I thought Daniel and I had nothing left to say to one another by that point and were meant to complete the remainder of our journey in tense silence. However, after a time he cleared his throat—evidently something more on his mind he wished to discuss.

"So . . ." he started to say, wringing his rein-wielding

hands together like talking to me civilly was putting a terrible amount of strain on him.

Like me talking to him was a picnic in the park? Ha.

"So what?" I asked.

"So, why don't you answer a question for me, Knight?"

"'Cuz you were so cooperative with answering my questions? You didn't tell me anything."

"All right, never mind then." He shrugged.

A few beats passed before curiosity got the better of me again. "Fine, Daniel," I huffed. "What is it?"

He straightened up and looked me in the eyes—steel characterizing his expression. "What happens if we find your godmother, find a way into the Indexlands, and then find the Author, but it turns out that in the end there's nothing we can do to change our fates because they've already been written?"

My first instinct was to think he was just trying to get another rise out of me. But the way he'd asked so earnestly, and the way his face appeared to be crinkled with genuine concern, told me that he wasn't joking. I sort of wished that he was though. Because I truly didn't know what to respond, despite how much I wished I did.

I looked away from him and stared off ahead, training my eyes on the horizon.

"Let's just hope we won't need an answer to that question," I replied.

CHAPTER 19

Emma

For the remainder of the journey Daniel and I sat side by side, but we might as well have been in different realms.

After a while the sun lit the entire sky and all traces of night were wiped clean from view. The clouds having dissipated from the intensity of daybreak, I passed the remaining time by counting the number of cottages and streams we flew over as I tried to forget my unsettling conversation with Daniel. The counting began to lose its charm after a few hours though, and I started to get fidgety in my seat as the minutes whizzed by.

Boredom was on the brink of consuming me completely when, finally, I spotted a fairly compact, coffee-colored mountain range in the distance.

We'd arrived.

Daniel landed the carriage in a forest by a river that curved through the kingdom. A few minutes of stretching in the meadow later and we were ready to begin our hike toward the Lagatta Mountains, which crowned the valley ahead.

We didn't know Emma's exact location but, thanks to the magic mirror, which we'd elected to bring along, we didn't need to. The mirror had an extra magical feature that I hadn't been aware of, but that Blue had discovered in one of her numerous fairytale history volumes. When you requested the mirror show you a person, once you were within five miles of said individual, it would glow brighter as you got closer to them.

So, having reverse engineered the landscape behind Emma in the looking glass, we were now close enough to where she dwelled for the mirror's second function to kick in. It gleamed in SJ's hand at the front of our herd—its increasing pulses of light reassuring us that we were going in the right direction.

As we walked, we found it quite difficult not to be in good spirits. The smell of rosemary and other herbs filled the air. The babbling sound of river water and various chirping birds became the soundtrack to our footsteps. And this place was so picturesque it bordered on the unbelievable, what with its endless blue skies, exorbitantly colored wildflowers, bunnies, butterflies, and, yes, Ravelli's famous bunniflies.

The rare creatures were adorable, and I so wished I could've enjoyed their presence as much as the others did while they followed us through the meadow. Tragically, I was allergic to regular bunnies. So, cute or not, having these hybrid ones flying up in my face was a bit of an issue. I was trying my best to retain my composure despite the runny nose and watery eyes the petite, fluffy creatures were inflicting upon me. But eventually I couldn't hold it in any longer.

"Achoo!" I sneezed loudly.

The bunniflies were startled by the sound and scattered in panic.

"Bless you," SJ said on behalf of our group. She took a handkerchief out of her bag and handed it to me as we continued. Once they were certain that they were not in any danger, the bunniflies returned too. Although they kept a minimum five-foot distance from me from then on.

After we'd been hiking for about forty minutes we came across a large, grassy hill. When we reached its summit, our group surveyed the (now much closer) mountains. The sun was pretty strong and the mirror was glowing so brightly I had to hold up my hand to shield my eyes from its glare.

I scanned the valley below.

About three hundred feet ahead of us I noticed a pale blue cottage with wafts of smoke rising from the chimney. It was surrounded by all kinds of flowers and was right at the edge of the river. A little old woman holding a watering can emerged from the cottage and began to tend to the plants.

I didn't need the affirmation of the beaming mirror to tell me that it was Emma; I already knew.

With reinvigorated enthusiasm I headed toward the cottage at full speed. The others were no doubt in pursuit of me, but I was too focused and excited to look back as I raced down the hill.

When I was about a dozen yards away I couldn't hold back my anticipation any longer. "Emma!" I shouted. "Emma!"

She turned around as I closed the space between us, and I put on the brakes to avoid ramming into her.

There she was, my godmother.

Emma was slightly taller than me, and she had a plump, rosy face covered with laugh lines and wrinkles. Her eyes were small and blue and they twinkled behind her glasses like they were filled with secrets.

She let out a gasp of surprise and embraced me with much more strength than you would think capable for such an elderly woman. When she finally pulled back and released me from the hug, she was smiling warmly and her tiny eyes had gotten all glassy with emotion.

The others had caught up with me by then, but Emma had yet to acknowledge their arrival. Her attention was glued solely on me.

She held my arms tightly like I might vanish if she let go. "Crisanta," she said, "it's so lovely to see you."

With the exception of my parents, most of the time when people used my full name it was for formal, royal events, or because I was in trouble. Neither of which I was particularly fond of. But when she said it, it sounded nice. It made me feel like I was home.

"Hi, Emma," I replied happily.

My godmother noticed the others at last and greeted them with a friendly, "Oh, hello there." To which they all responded with their own greetings.

"Emma, let me introduce you," I said, gesturing toward the rest of the group. "These are my best friends Blue and SJ, our friend Jason from Lord Channing's, and, um . . ." I paused momentarily. "He's Daniel."

"It's so wonderful to meet all of you," Emma gushed, going over to shake each of their hands in turn, starting with SJ. "My, aren't you pretty. Snow's daughter, yes?"

"Yes, Ms. Carrington," she responded.

"I knew it! Just as radiant as your mother." Emma pinched SJ's cheek affectionately. "Oh, and a lot more unique than you'd like to give yourself give credit for. I can tell. That will come in handy, my dear; embrace it sooner rather than later."

SJ blushed awkwardly as Emma moved on to shake Blue's hand and then Jason's. When she got to Daniel he held out his hand, but she did not take it at first. Instead she looked him up and down and made a pensive noise like "Hmph."

Now it was Daniel's turn to feel awkward, which (*I'm not gonna lie*) made me smirk a bit with satisfaction.

Eventually, to his relief, Emma shook his hand. Though as she did, she muttered something under her breath that I didn't quite make out.

With bubbling enthusiasm Emma proceeded to usher us inside her adorable house.

Almost immediately I found myself falling in love with the place. The interior of the quaint cottage was painted a light shade of silver. There were tons of knickknacks, books, and dishes lining the walls, but they were all so neatly organized you could never mistake them for clutter.

The windows filled the room with natural light, which reflected off the dozens of glittering wind chimes hanging from the ceiling. And to top it off, the whole place smelled of cinnamon and freshly baked snickerdoodles.

Yum.

Emma scuttled over to her tiny kitchen. "Does everyone like pound cake?" she asked as she scurried back and forth between cabinets. We nodded, and she began fumbling about with placing slices on plates. When she'd finished, she clumsily set cups within their saucers and wobbly filled them with either coffee, cream, or tea—spilling periodically due to the natural shakiness of her elderly wrists.

My godmother was doing everything by hand and I knew we were all thinking the same thing as she headed over to us with the loaded tray of goodies. When she'd set the assorted snacks down on the coffee table, Blue finally spoke those thoughts aloud and asked her what we all wanted to know.

"Uh, Ms. Carrington. Aren't you a *Fairy* Godmother? Why don't you just use magic to do that stuff?"

"Emma, dear. Please call me Emma," she answered. "And I'm not using magic because I don't have any, not anymore at least."

I nearly spit out my coffee from the shock. "Wait, what?"

Emma's eyes dropped to the floor and she sat tiredly on a blue armchair across from a large sofa of the same shade. Following her lead, we sat down as well and prepared to listen to her explanation.

"My dears," she sighed, "I'm afraid your schools do not do the best job of teaching you about magic, do they?"

"Um, we learn about different famous magical objects, and some potions stuff, but that's about it," Jason admitted.

"Well then," Emma said, picking up a teacup from the tray, "I think it's about time you had a proper lesson." She cleared her throat and settled back in her comfortable chair.

"Lesson one," she began. "There is no such thing as *new* magic. Magic cannot be created, nor can it be destroyed. It can only change form or change hands. For example, the magic from that mirror you used to find me could be extracted and put into some other object."

Emma gestured at the magic mirror that was presently in SJ's hand and then to the delicate cup in hers. "Like into one of these teacups for instance. You see, then the cup would become enchanted to show and track people's whereabouts, whereas the mirror would just become an ordinary mirror. The magic of genies, witches, fairies, and Fairy Godmothers works in the same way too; it can be transferred from one person to the next. Of course, Fairy Godmother magic also has some other special qualities to it . . ."

My coffee got cold and the tray of snacks went untouched as we listened to Emma explain the rules and dynamics of Fairy Godmother magic.

The lesson proved to be fascinating, lengthy, and more worthy of taking notes than half the subjects I attended at school.

Emma began by reminding us how Fairy Godmother magic (being all-powerful) needed a conductor to control it, and each Godmother's conductor was her wand. But then she went on to tell us how each of these wands only responded to the specific magical touch of its designated Godmother. Kind of like an ultra-sensitive DNA scanner.

Emma then explained that when Fairy Godmothers retired and moved out of headquarters, they transferred nearly all of their magic into a new Godmother recruit—along with their wand. They were allowed to keep a tiny portion of their magic for basic spells (like levitation, cleaning house, and so on), but around ninety-five percent had to be transmitted into the new hire for realm security purposes.

"So why don't you have any magic at all?" I interrupted, a bit more bluntly than I probably should have.

SJ elbowed me. I glanced over at her and she shook her head and gave me a look that I couldn't quite read.

"Because I did not retire," Emma replied. "I was fired. Well, I was dishonorably discharged, as they would say. But a termination is a termination no matter what type of label you put on it."

Oh. Duh. That's why SJ had elbowed me. We'd already learned from our trip to Fairy Godmother HQ that Emma had been fired all those years ago. Ergo, mine had been a thoughtless question.

Naturally, I was now dying to ask the even more impertinent inquiry—*why had she been fired?* But since I didn't want to push it, I restrained myself from doing so. I hadn't seen Emma in a decade and grilling her with personal questions hardly seemed like the way to make a good impression.

I guess Emma must've noticed me struggling with the thought though, because she smiled sadly and volunteered the information herself.

"Crisanta, children, there are things I fear you will soon learn about the Godmothers. Flaws, if you will, in the ways they have handled matters and neglected others over time. I, along with a few others in recent years, have fought for change within the agency. But such disobedience is not looked upon favorably by the Godmother Supreme or by the rest of our realm's leaders. As a result, many Godmothers such as myself have been relieved from duty."

Emma's voice grew softer, as if the weight of the truth became heavier as she unveiled it.

Fairy Godmothers who were fired, she told us, were not treated kindly. They were forbidden from contacting anyone from their old life, especially former Godkids—like my mother—under the threat of being sent to Alderon. This explained why Emma had cut herself off from my family for the past decade.

In addition, fired Godmothers did not get to keep any of their magic. Nor were they allowed to pass their magic and their wands on to new Godmothers. They were simply stripped of their powers entirely. All that magic was reallocated into fueling the realm's outer, protective In and

Out Spell, and the Godmothers' wands were permanently deactivated as a result.

I hadn't realized it, but while Emma had been talking I had been unconsciously fingering my own wand inside my satchel like I typically did whenever I got anxious. Conversely, Emma had noticed my fidgeting, and accurately guessed what was inside of the bag.

"Is it in there?" she asked.

I didn't question how she knew; I just nodded and took out the wand—presenting it to her like a proud jewel. Emma's eyes shone like they were seeing an old friend for the first time in far too many years. She picked it up and held it delicately, cherishing the object.

Suddenly I understood. This was *her* wand. She had given it me on my birthday nearly ten years ago. Right about the time she was fired . . .

"A dear friend of mine, Paige Tomkins, used to head the Magical Transfers, Tracking, and Recalls Department at headquarters," Emma said. "That was the department in charge of overseeing and managing all transfers of magic between people and objects."

"I saw her name on the door of an office when we were at Fairy Godmother HQ," I abruptly remembered.

Emma blinked. "When were you children at headquarters?"

"Oh, that's sort of a long story," I said quickly. "Sorry to interrupt," I added as I tried to redirect the conversation away from telling my godmother about our recent breaking-and-entering exploits. "You were telling us about your friend. Paige, was it?"

"Well, yes," Emma continued as she looked at me

skeptically. "As I was saying, all magical transfers used to have to go through Paige. We were very close, she and I, and when I got the feeling I was going to be fired I asked two favors of her. The first was to enchant my wand, but of course not catalog this transfer.

"As I said, a wand is useless without that unique Godmother's power to operate it. However, by relocating some *other* enchanted object's magic into it—like I explained with the example of the mirror and the teacup—a wand can potentially conduct magic in other ways if proper criteria is met by the wielder."

Emma turned a bit so that she was looking directly at me as she continued.

"With me no longer able to protect you when I was stripped of duty, Crisanta, I wanted you to have something you could use to protect yourself—something versatile and powerful, but that no one would suspect you had. And since I knew that once my own powers were removed no one would come searching for my wand because it should've been useless by that point, it seemed like the best choice.

"Paige ended up finding the perfect magical object for us to use for the transfer. In one of her trips around the realm cataloging and collecting unauthorized enchanted objects, she came across a special dagger that hosted a unique and very intriguing, weaponry-based power. After presenting it to me, we decided to transfer its enchanted abilities into my wand. From there we simple faked some paperwork, smuggled the wand out of headquarters, and that, Crisanta my dear, is the short version of how your wand came to be."

Jason raised his hand awkwardly. "Clarification, please," he said.

"About what?" Emma asked.

"The wand," interjected Daniel. "What does it do exactly?"

"Would you like to show them?" Emma said as she handed it back to me.

I wasn't quite sure how I felt about it at first; I'd never considered revealing the wand's hidden abilities to anyone other than Blue and SJ. But the way Emma looked at me reassuringly and with full approval helped diffuse some of the uncertainty.

Dissuading my nerves and disinclination as best I could, I took a deep breath, held the wand up before the others, and transformed it.

"Spear," I commanded aloud.

The staff expanded in my hand, its sheen catching the light pouring in from one of the windows. Jason and Daniel were stunned.

Emma proceeded to explain on my behalf how the wand was enchanted to take the shape of absolutely whatever weapon I willed it into.

"I suppose the spear is your favorite form since that is what you chose to show them first," Emma commented.

I nodded. "It's surprisingly user friendly and, even more surprisingly, in the brief time since I've been practicing with it I've gotten pretty good."

"Good? She's great!" Blue said supportively. "Her fighting skills have been totally epic since she made the switch."

I smiled slightly at Daniel. "Yeah, well, sword fighting was never really my thing."

He smirked in return, remembering our first meeting.

"Can we have a go with it, Crisa?" Jason asked.

I raised my eyebrows, unsure of how to respond. "Uhhh, well . . ."

"It won't work for you, dear," Emma interceded. "The wand will only respond to Crisanta. Go ahead and see for yourself."

I was hesitant. That wand was my most treasured possession. I may have grown up with two older brothers who'd forced me to learn how to share, but this was one thing I'd definitely never wanted anyone else to become privy to.

Still, I acknowledged that circumstances had changed. The boys now knew about my wand and what it could do, so I no longer needed to keep it a secret. In addition, I was genuinely curious to see if Emma's assertion was true. Could the wand work for no one else but me?

For the first time I conceded to placing the wand in the hands of someone other than Emma and myself. Having morphed it back to its original state, I decided to hand it off to Blue first. She grasped it eagerly, but carefully, and focused all her concentration on it.

"Knife," she commanded.

The wand did not change.

"Knife," she said again.

Still nothing.

They all passed it around and tried. I flinched a bit when it came into Daniel's hands, but allowed the experiment to continue nonetheless. In the end, just as Emma had claimed, it didn't work for any of them. Once the wand came back to me I tested it to make sure it hadn't broken.

Shield.

Sure enough, it transformed into a thick handle that went on to sprout the round, silver shield I was so familiar with.

Wand.

Returned to its normal form, I looked over my magical weapon as if seeing it for the first time. I then tried to hand it back to Emma so that she could have a proper go, but she refused to take it.

"I'm afraid it won't work for me either, dear," she said. "I don't have my Fairy Godmother magic anymore and, enchanted object or not, that is all my wand will respond to. It's the same reason why it does not work for your friends."

This time it was Blue's turn to raise her hand in confusion. "Hold up a sec," she said. "So why does the wand work for Crisa exactly? I mean, if your wand can only respond to your magic, and all your magic was put into the In and Out Spell, then even with that dagger's abilities transferred inside of it, it shouldn't be able to work at all, right?"

It was a good question. The wand was just another enchanted object and I was just another human. If it didn't respond to Emma or any of the others because of its inherent Godmother restrictions, why should I have been any different?

Instead of answering Blue's question right away, Emma picked up her teacup and took a long, pensive sip—clearly parched from so much exposition. It was only when she sensed the silence had become too severe to endure did she furrow her brow and set the cup back within its saucer.

I tried to read her expression, but it was an enigmatic one. From what I could gather, she was trying to decide how to tell me something important and not freak me out in the process.

"Crisanta," she said slowly. "Bear in mind that I could have asked Paige to enchant *any* object. But aside from the reasons I've already mentioned, I picked this one because

I wanted to make sure it would only work in the hands of someone I trusted completely."

I didn't follow. After all, how could she have made sure that the wand would only function for me?

Her glasses had almost slipped off her nose by then, so I was able to look straight into her eyes. When I did, I found the answer I was searching for—my heart finally registering something that my brain was having trouble admitting.

You know when a small part of you figures something out, but the rest of you is too weirded out to say it out loud because that would make it real? It's like that.

"The second favor you asked of Paige," I began hesitantly, "it was me. You asked her to transfer some of your magic . . . into me? So I could make the wand work?"

"Yes, Crisanta." Emma nodded. "I did."

"That's so cool!" Blue gushed, totally dissolving the tension in the room. "Crisa, you have magical powers!"

"No way," Jason said, doubt infesting his tone. "If she had magical powers I think she would have noticed by now."

"But she's been using magic to operate the wand; she just didn't know it. If she can do that, she can totally do other stuff too," Blue countered.

SJ cleared her throat loudly to get them to stop bickering. Blue and Jason relinquished the argument and turned back toward my godmother, hoping she would set the record straight and settle their disagreement.

"Any amount of my magic will allow someone to operate my wand," Emma told them. "I had Paige transfer a sole spark of it into Crisanta—enough for her to sustain a single power. That is all it would take, and all that I could afford to give without the other Godmothers noticing."

"So what is it then?" SJ asked. "What is Crisa's power?"

"To be honest, I don't know," Emma admitted. "Magic, particularly Fairy Godmother magic, takes to people in different ways and I'm not sure how hers ended up manifesting. There aren't really finite ways to figure it out either. All I can say is that when she discovers what her power is she'll just sort of . . . *know*."

"Wait, hold on," I said firmly. "Emma, there's gotta be some other way to find out besides, well, time and gut instinct."

"Yes, in theory there might be."

"Great."

"But I am not going to tell you. For the same reason that I'm going to discourage you from pursuing the matter on your own after you leave here today. Holding magic is dangerous, Crisanta, in more ways than you currently realize. Therefore, I believe that for your own sake it is best that you not find out what your power is until it is absolutely necessary."

I was frustrated with my godmother's response, and the others seemed just as disappointed. We continued to pry Emma for information about my power for a while longer— pleading with her and attempting to appeal to her reason. Alas, she remained unmoved. Despite our persistence, she refused to change her mind no matter the argument, saying that it was for the good of my own protection.

She reminded us then that the reason Fairy Godmother HQ was always moving and so well hidden was to protect the Godmothers from magic hunters. And she also had us recall that magic hunters tracked magic by its scent.

We already knew both of these things. However, then Emma informed us of something we didn't. Apparently people that had magic gave off a much stronger scent than objects with magic. Even with my small dose of Fairy Godmother power, Emma warned that in close proximity both it and I would be detectable to magic hunters.

As recollection washed over me, I knew she was right. I remembered that magic hunter in the prison transport we'd run into on our way to Adelaide last month. I'd tried my best to reassure myself and the others at the time that he truly hadn't been looking at me. But, deep down, I think we all knew he had been. And now we understood why. He must've sensed what I'd only just learned—that I had magic.

Sitting there, the memory of his intense, cognac-colored eyes—studying me through the bars of his transport as he inhaled what I assumed must've been my magic scent—gave me the shivers. As such, I began to take Emma's warning more seriously.

My godmother went on to tell us that a person's magic scent was considerably weaker when the holder was unaware of the power they possessed or how to use it. So a hunter would, in fact, have to be fairly close in range to pick it up. On the contrary, when a magic carrier did become aware of their abilities and how to use them, their scent would be amplified tenfold.

In other words, once I discovered my power and began using it intentionally, my magic scent might as well have been a red flare because magic hunters everywhere would subsequently be able to sense me from a great distance.

Based on this understanding, while I was still itching to know the nature of my mystery magical ability, I finally agreed not to pursue the issue for now. I definitely didn't want to worsen my already unfavorable fate by painting a large target on my back. Magic may not have been able to be destroyed, but I sure as heck could, and sure as heck would if one of those hunters ever got a hold of me.

Furthermore, if it wasn't necessary to know what my power was in order to operate my wand, I supposed it didn't matter for the time being anyways.

I placed my wand back within my satchel, putting a close on the subject.

Emma got up from her chair and picked up the tray of used cups and nibbled snacks from the coffee table. She carried it back to the kitchen while the others and I got up from the couch and followed her there.

Without being asked we began to help her clean up. Blue started washing dishes as Daniel and Jason dried. SJ opened one of the windows and sang a short melody to call for more assistance. A few moments later, three robins flew inside and aided her and I with putting away the adorable china.

Our conversation having been so stuffed with information, I'd nearly forgotten why we'd come there in the first place. This didn't matter though, because Emma, somehow, already knew that too. When the last cup was in the cupboard and the final bird had flown away, my godmother put her hands on her hips and readdressed us.

"So isn't someone going to ask me how to break the In and Out Spell around the Indexlands so you can go and visit the Author?"

We all looked at one another.

"How'd you know?" Daniel asked.

"Because I know Crisanta," Emma said, winking at me. "So I knew this visit was only a matter of time."

She walked over to the counter and found a loose scrap of paper and a quill and began to write. "Now in good conscious, I must say that for your own safety I truly do not recommend you take this journey. That being said," she continued, "if you really insist on going, know that the only way to get past the In and Out Spell around the Indexlands is to use a potion made from three special ingredients.

"You see, my dears, the In and Out Spell is a shifting enchantment, which means that the ingredients required to break it change every few years. Although—as with all shifting enchantments—the theme for these ingredients remains the same. In this case that would be: *'Something Strong, Something Pure, and Something One of a Kind.'*

"Now, normally there would be no way of knowing what specific three objects the spell would accept to fill this theme's requirements on a given year. But luckily, my friends who remain at the agency still keep me in the loop so I am up-to-date on such important matters. Be warned though. There is, of course, a reason that these particular items were chosen. So believe me when I tell you that attempting to acquire them will be extremely dangerous and nearly, if not utterly, impossible. I am not even sure how to go about gathering them myself. But . . . here they are nevertheless."

She held up the paper she'd written. Blue accepted it and read the contents aloud:

"A Quill with the Might of Twenty-Six Swords,
The Heart of the Lost Princess,
And a Mysterious Flower Beneath the Valley of Strife."

My friend grimaced as she folded up the tall order list and stuck it in her pocket. A gust of wind came through the window at that moment and blew several of the chimes around like a well-timed signal for us to depart.

"Well, at least we know where we're going next," Daniel

said as he wrung his hands together with uncharacteristic apprehension.

"Where?" Jason asked.

SJ and I looked at each other.

"Century City," we replied in unison.

CHAPTER 20

An Hour in Century City

 etting into our realm's capital was easy enough. Unfortunately, it wasn't until later on that we realized getting out would be the tricky part.

We'd said our goodbyes and thank yous to Emma and flown straight to Century City, the beautiful metropolis that was our realm's capital. I myself had only ever been there a couple of times on official royal goodwill tours with the rest of my family. But seeing it from the sky as we approached was an entirely new experience.

Unlike most kingdoms, which were populated by quaint cottages and traditional architecture, Century City was a majesty of incredibly mighty, glistening skyscrapers. Their compilation was a geometry teacher's dreamland. Tall tetrahedral compounds sat around the city's outer limits like enormous spikes. Apartment complexes in odd, almost fluid shapes twisted into the air like giant, metallic pieces of seaweed. Huge high rises with translucent dodecahedral offices interspersed within them like bubbles were everywhere in sight. And shooting up like contradicting reminders of the past amongst all this modernism were fairytale-esque, cylindrical towers that came to a swirl at their tops like freshly whipped cream.

Equally varied were the shades the buildings came in.

Powder blue, bright yellow, lime green, pink, even orange creamsicle could be found decorating the city's rich, rainbow-colored skyline. In addition, these colors were made even more surreal by the metallic structures in their midst that reflected their pigmentations in the striking rays of sunshine.

When nearing our arrival of the utopia, we agreed to park the Pegasi and carriage outside the city so as not to call any unnecessary attention to ourselves.

In terms of species, Pegasi were not all that common. Typically they were only used for Twenty-Three Skidd tournaments and their players, royalty, and important diplomats. So, five teenagers with five Pegasi flying into midtown during rush hour would have been a bit more conspicuous an entrance than what we were going for.

Having landed within the concealment of a small forest just outside of the city, a few dozen downhill slopes, alleyway shortcuts, and cobblestone pathways later and our group was making its way through the streets of the capital—navigating northward toward the city center.

It was pretty easy to find our way; all the streets of the capital were designed to rotate traffic in a counterclockwise direction that matched the circular shape of the metropolis's overall layout.

Even so, the physical trek was nothing if not slow-moving.

Every part of town we journeyed through was packed. Horses and the elaborate, colorful carriages they pulled flowed in a constant stream down the roads. And on the sidewalks, people of every ethnicity in equally bright garments hustled and bustled along with their daily business.

I almost got whiplash as I fluctuated between looking at them, straining my neck to see where the buildings touched the sky, and snapping my focus back to the tantalizing smells of food coming from everywhere around us.

Shops, restaurants, and salons of all fashions lined the walkways. My stomach growled as I smelled freshly baked bread wafting from the quaint cafes in the area and the distinct aroma of hard meats coming from the fancier steak houses interspersed amongst them.

On more than one occasion I considered suggesting that we stop for a quick snack, but thought better of it each time. The traffic was growing increasingly heavy, so we would have to keep going if we wanted to reach our goal in time.

As we continued our migration to the city center, it occurred to me that while the slog was arduous and winding, at least one thing we didn't have to worry about along the way was being spotted.

I assumed Lady Agnue's had dispatched notification to our parents that we were missing by now. But if she'd only sent word this morning, our realm's normal postal service would take at least three days to deliver the news.

Even if she'd employed the use of bird messengers like some of the other princesses at school did when writing home, it would take a day and a half at minimum. Ergo, for the time being our AWOL exploits remained off the radar of anyone official who might have caught us otherwise.

Add to that, none of the commons in the city would've ever guessed who we were either because young, future protagonists were almost always at one of the academies or in their home kingdoms. We weren't really allowed to go anywhere else until we graduated. So, unless someone here knew to be specifically looking for us, we were as safe in these crowds as we were undetectable.

At that point we finally began to close in on our destination:

the Capitol Building. The prestigious site had been well-concealed by the skyscrapers thus far, but now that we were much nearer I was beginning to see the mighty structure's cupola peaking out over the rooftops of some of the smaller-sized buildings.

One look at its grandeur was enough to substantiate the reasoning for holding the Century City Summit here every six months. And today, as it happened, was the date of one of those Summits.

The ambassadors from all twenty-six kingdoms (not including Alderon, of course) would be present at the Capitol Building for their bi-annual meeting this afternoon. These ambassadors were second in power and command only to the kings and queens of their individual kingdoms. As such, they were the sole dignitaries chosen to attend this event since the royal families' foremost responsibilities pertained to looking after their lands.

My friends, Daniel, and I had been thankful that it had only taken a few hours to fly here from Emma's cottage in Ravelli. Although, given the way traffic was delaying us, we hoped that there were plenty of issues for the ambassadors to discuss this time around, which would postpone the signing of the Summit's treaty at the event's conclusion.

You see, we were after the quill that all twenty-six ambassadors would be using to sign their treaty. That's right. *"A Quill with the Might of Twenty-Six Swords."*

Figuring out the first ingredient for Emma's In and Out Spell breaking potion had been easy. But—past the ticking clock deadline already working against us as we tried to get there in time—we knew getting to it would be anything but simple.

For starters, a bunch of kids trying to sneak into the

Capitol Building on one of its highest security days of the year was super risky. Century City may not have had a palace or a royal family to protect, but the guards and soldiers who resided here took their jobs beyond seriously. Like, make a wrong move or even look suspicious and you could be thrown in the public stockades for a week, seriously. That is, assuming the guards didn't just crossbow you down in the street first, which they'd apparently been known to do when pursuing high threat, volatile suspects.

To sum up, these guys meant business.

Even animals were no exception to their strict persecution of the unruly. Last time my family and I had been here, a wild griffin from the neighboring forest had flown in and landed on one of the stalls in the city's outdoor marketplace. Less than seven seconds had passed between when its tail hit the awning and six guards shot it down. My mother had failed to cover my eyes in time as I peered out of our carriage. And, as a result, twelve-year-old me had been left with a very real, very visceral image of exactly what these guards were capable of.

In addition to the danger posed by its security, the Capitol Building was also the only place in the city where we could actually be recognized. Well, where SJ and I could be recognized anyways. The two of us knew the ambassadors from our kingdoms well and saw them frequently at our palaces when we were home from school. Thus, however remote a possibility it was, there was still a chance they could see us.

At last the internal crust of buildings gave way to a clear view of the city center. We approached the roundabout at the front of the Capitol with great trepidation.

In our defense, this was an effect the giant statue in the

midst of the traffic circle seemed to have on every person that entered its vicinity.

It was the most massive statue I had ever seen—a solid gold dragon that stood on its hind legs and stretched to the sky like a beanstalk. The beast had its massive wingspan open, the length of which must've been over three hundred feet alone. It stretched out before us—casting the surrounding streets in shadow.

I stared up at it and felt an inexplicable sense of dread forming in my throat.

Out of instinct I tightened my satchel's strap around my shoulder.

I knew the dragon wasn't real. It was pure metal, a city ornament that had been here for at least the last two decades.

Despite this logic, the beast's eyes triggered something strange inside of me. I could no more explain it to the others than I could to myself. But as best as I could characterize it, it felt like even as the statue stood still—permanently frozen in time—I could almost sense the fire burning inside of him. Waiting to get out.

In the end I chalked this up to the dragon's inherent purpose of signifying the city's power, *and* freaking out any potential troublemakers who might try to challenge it.

The statue's intimidation factor alone was definitely a good way to scare off people who even considered bringing trouble to the Capitol Building. And if the dragon didn't do it, the several dozen guards positioned around the statue's platform, the steps leading up to the Capitol, and the building's rooftop and parapets surely would have.

The guards looked decked out and stoic as ever on this day. Their silvery metallic armor and helmets glinted in the sunlight—cobalt plumes sticking out from the tops.

Each one had a knife sheathed at his side. And, while the ones positioned at higher vantage points all held crossbows trained on the city, the guards on street level brandished an assortment of weapons ranging from maces to swords to really sturdy machetes.

"Ideas?" I said after we'd been staring at the enormity of our task for a minute, calculating our highly improbable odds.

"Well, we definitely can't go straight in," Jason said—gesturing at the steps where one guard was handcuffing a civilian who'd attempted to sneak inside.

"Or up," Blue added, pointing to the roof where eight guards had their bows drawn and were ready to fire at even the slightest disturbance.

Daniel pushed past me. "How about down?" he proposed.

Daniel led us to a manhole a couple of blocks away hidden in an alley.

One ladder and several rats later, we were wading through the filthy water and grime of the sewers below the streets. I could sense SJ cringing from time to time whenever the slush grew particularly murky or stank, but (ever the good sport) she did not complain or protest our chosen route. It was our best option after all. Moreover, assuming her genius remained consistent, the muck wouldn't matter very soon anyways. The second we stepped out of here the enchantment of her SRB's should've kicked in and returned our dirtied shoes to their former crisp and clean states.

Other than the filth, the five of us made our way under the city with no setbacks. In fact I was so distracted by the uncharacteristic lack of problems that I didn't even think to ask Daniel how he knew the way.

Okay, that was a lie. I did think to ask. But when I opened my mouth to do so, a moth flew inside and I almost choked to death. When the blasted bug finally flew out of my windpipe I took it as a sign that maybe it was best if I just kept quiet for once and went with the flow.

After some time, the tunnel came to an opening that was an intersection for eight other tunnels. Daniel pointed to a ladder against one of the walls. I started to make my way toward it, but stopped when my ears picked up something akin to muffled voices.

"Do you guys hear that?" I whispered.

"Hear what?" Jason asked.

I held up my hand to silence him as I tried to pinpoint which tunnel the noise was coming from. It was getting fainter, but I was pretty sure the source of the sound was one of the western tunnels.

It didn't matter though; a second later the supposed voices vanished completely. Whoever had been down here with us had gone in another direction and now all I could make out was the sloshing of the sewage water.

"Never mind," I said, joining them at the ladder. "I thought I heard something."

The others gave me a confused look, but ascended the ladder without any further ado. Daniel climbed up first and gave the sewer hole on the ceiling a good shove. Daylight dropped into the tunnel and we squinted as we climbed out.

The instant our grimy shoes hit cobblestone, a light, silvery glow flickered around them. In turn, I glanced down and discovered that the stain of sewer water on my boots had disappeared. The SRB had worked. My boots looked good as new.

SJ smiled as she inspected her own newly freshened footwear, clearly pleased with herself as she had every right to be.

I've said it before, and I'll say it again; that girl is absolutely brilliant.

We were now behind the Capitol by a bunch of dumpsters. Nearby, I spotted an entrance to the building through its kitchen. Servants were presently coming in and out of it—busily unloading catering carriages.

"Wait here," Daniel ordered as he headed in that direction.

Naturally I was inclined to protest and do the opposite of what he wanted, but before I could pursue him SJ grabbed my arm.

"Give him a chance," she whispered quietly.

I huffed and shook her hand off me. But I waited nonetheless.

A few minutes later Daniel returned with a young female member of the kitchen staff. She was small and freckled with a scrunched-up nose like a possum. Strands of brown hair had escaped her hair bun and hung in her face as she bowed to us excitedly and introduced herself as Kim.

"Daniel says you guys need help sneaking into the Capitol's meeting hall," she squeaked.

We nodded in agreement and she gestured for us to follow.

Somehow—I didn't know how—but somehow Daniel had convinced this girl, this Kim, to fully cooperate with us. And it wasn't just her; the entire kitchen staff she proceeded to introduce us to was more than happy to help us break into a room full of the realm's most powerful VIPs. They ushered us into their domain like we were family, shook Daniel's hand, and patted him on the back like a hero at his homecoming. It was *super* bizarre.

After some discussion, the staff figured the only way we could gain entry to the meeting hall unnoticed was by hiding under the tablecloth-draped dessert carts.

Not the classiest or most original plan, I know. But assuming none of us sneezed, it would get the job done.

There were three large carts. Blue and Jason hid under the first and I was expecting SJ to join me under the second. However, as I positioned myself beneath it—making sure neither me, nor my satchel, would protrude out—I saw she had already been concealed within the third and was being wheeled away. Daniel, instead, crawled in next to me. Before I could argue, the tablecloth fell around us and our cart was in motion.

"What was all that about?" I whispered to Daniel as we rode along, crouched way too close to one another for comfort.

"What?" he whispered back.

"Well, for starters, I wasn't aware Lord Channing's offered classes in sewage topography. Second, what was that back there in the kitchen? Everyone acted like they liked you."

"Stranger things have happened, Knight."

I felt the cart turn and I grabbed onto one of its sides so I wouldn't fall out.

"I mean," I tried again, "it seemed like they *knew* you."

"They do," he said flatly. "I used to work here."

"Wait, what? When?"

"Before I came to Lord Channing's."

I stared at him, not fully processing the statement.

Daniel shook his head and released a short, frustrated sigh. "Knight, I'm *from* Century City. This place used to be my home. I know it might come as a shock to you, but I did have a life before all this, one that *I* had complete control over."

I broke his gaze and didn't pry any further. I'd never really put much thought into what Daniel's life had been like before he was chosen as a protagonist. Most of the kids at Lord Channing's and Lady Agnue's had been at protagonist school since they were little. And many of us (myself included) had known that it was to be our destination long before then. As such, we'd never really lived any kind of life of our own choosing.

In that moment I found myself both envying and pitying Daniel. He'd had what I'd always dreamed of—a life that was his. A chance to be whatever, *whoever*, he wanted. But one day, without warning, it had been taken away from him completely.

I couldn't imagine what that must've been like.

Suddenly I heard the sound of doors being opened, and our carts were pushed into the room that was to be our journey's endpoint.

I didn't need to see it to know the meeting hall was enormous. The ambassadors' voices amplified and echoed off the tiled expanse when they spoke, as did the sound of the carts' wheels rolling along the peach marble tile beneath us.

Several dessert orders later, the sound of clanking dishes and silverware came to an end. The massive doors shut once more and I knew we were now on our own. We tried to remain as still as possible while the Summit continued.

"Back to business," said one ambassador with a particularly hoarse voice.

"Yes, well, we were finalizing updates to put in the next *Century City Summit Review*," replied a woman with a deep voice that sounded way too much like a man's.

"Ambassador Langley," said hoarse voice. "Are there any developments with Princess Annabeth?"

"I'm afraid not," Ambassador Langley responded. "As you all remember from our last Summit, the king and queen of Eebi gave birth to their daughter Annabeth in early spring. But I've spoken with The Scribes and her book has still not appeared."

"The king and queen are getting restless. We can't keep the girl a secret much longer," man-woman interrupted. "The child is nearly seven months old and her birth must be announced."

"Then we fake her book like we did with Prince Jonathan's last year," another female ambassador stated.

I recognized this last voice. It took me a moment to realize from where, but the source of that overly perky, booming tone eventually wormed its way through my memories. It was the Adelaide Ambassador—Sarah Steinglass. I was certain of it.

"Ambassador Lunus," said hoarse voice. "How soon can a fake book be prepared?"

"By the end of the week," Lunus replied.

"Very good," Ms. Steinglass said. "Notify Lena Lenore and her team right away of the adjustment. And as always, remember, everyone that discretion is of the greatest importance in these delicate situations. Every royal has to be a protagonist; it's tradition. If word got out that some were not being chosen and their books were failing to appear automatically at birth, it would result in confusion and chaos throughout the realm, anarchy even. It is as the Godmother Supreme always says; the system only works if it is consistent. No room for mistakes or outliers."

I blinked hard like a surprised deer. I couldn't believe what they were saying. Daniel seemed equally weirded out. I gave him a look that said, "*Are you hearing this?*" He responded with one that read something like, "*Shhh, I'm trying to listen.*"

We went back to attempting to make sense of what the ambassadors were talking about. But as their conversation continued, it just kept getting stranger.

"Very well then," Langley concurred. "We shall announce in the *Review* that the child was born this past Tuesday. Oh, and that reminds me. Argon, have you had the Scribes remove the extra books yet?"

"Yes, Ambassador Langley. They will never be found," Ambassador Argon responded in a low-baring voice.

"How many was it this time?" Ms. Steinglass asked.

"Three this past month, a total of eleven since our last meeting," Argon admitted. "There have been four from Whoozalee, three from Midveil, two from Ravelli, one from Harzana, and . . . one from Alderon."

"They're coming from Alderon now too?" gasped man-woman.

Langley sighed. "I'm afraid so. New protagonist books are being generated for commons in all the kingdoms more frequently than ever. Some of the books are appearing when they are born, while others are turning up for commons who are already in their mid-teenage or young adult years. It's unheard of."

"It's unprecedented."

"It's unfathomable."

"It's troubling is what it is," Argon summarized.

"Well make sure the Scribes keep monitoring the teleportal closely and letting us know each time another common's book appears," Lunus instructed. "We will give them approval to announce a new book only if it does not interfere with this year's main character quota. All non-approved books will continue to be destroyed. It is unfortunate, but it is critical for protagonist population control."

That matter having been settled, the ambassadors cleared their throats—and consciences—and went on to discuss farm reports and new construction projects for the better part an hour.

My back was beginning to hurt from crouching underneath that dessert cart for so long when, finally, one of the ambassadors announced it was time to close the Summit with the signing of the peace treaty. I perked up at that and strained my ears to hear the sound of them signing the document.

When the last ambassador had provided his name, they all applauded their amicable behavior and the Summit was officially ended. We readied ourselves under the carts as the dignitaries began to shuffle out. My heart pounded faster as the sound of conversations dissipated.

Eventually the final ambassador exited the room and we heard the sizeable doors swing shut. I slowly peeked my head out from under the tablecloth to make sure the coast was clear.

It was.

"All right, we're good," I called to the others.

Blue, Jason, and SJ peered out from their carts and then the lot of us fully emerged from our hideouts.

The meeting hall was as vast as I had imagined. The blue-tablecloth-covered desks formed a large semicircle around the room with one huge, golden desk at the center. That was where they had signed the treaty, and that was where the quill they'd used was waiting for us. It lay there forgotten—pretending to be unimportant.

But we knew better.

Blue grabbed the quill. "I guess we can check our 'Something Strong' off the list. That's one down and two to go, folks," she declared triumphantly as she stuffed our first piece of the In and Out Spell puzzle into her boot for safekeeping.

"Well, that was easy," Jason shrugged.

"I wouldn't relax just yet," Blue said. "Trust me, I've read enough of these stories to know that no win is ever this simple. If you ask me, we should get out of here fast before the other shoe has a chance to drop."

"Guys . . ." Daniel suddenly interrupted. "Did you get what the ambassadors were saying about the books?"

The five of us exchanged a solemn look. We'd all heard what the ambassadors had said. There was no denying it. But did we *get* it? That was another matter entirely.

These were twenty-six of the people our realm trusted the most. My own family had an ambassador in there who was meant to be representing our kingdom and its people's best interests. Wrapping our minds around the idea that they were conspiring together to do something so despicable felt unnatural. It also felt an awful lot like betrayal, *and* the very kind of malevolence that they and the Godmothers were supposed to be protecting us from.

"They're working with Lena Lenore and the Scribes to

forge books for royals who don't have them and destroying commons' books when they are too frequent," I summarized bluntly.

SJ shook her head. "This cannot be true," she said.

"You heard them," Daniel asserted. "It is true."

Blue crossed her arms. "They can't be allowed to do that. It's not right."

"No, they can't," I agreed. "Every person in Book has the right to know who they really are, even the people of Alderon. They all deserve a chance to be protagonists if that's what they're meant to be."

"So then it's up to us to stop them," Jason said. "Stop the ambassadors and Lena Lenore somehow. We have a responsibility to, now that we know the truth about what they're doing. Don't we?"

We halted our discussion when we heard the sound of footsteps on the other side of the door. Fully on alert, we waited for the noise to pass and completely subside before continuing.

"You're both right," Daniel said once the sound had gone. "But for now we need to get out of this place before someone finds us. I've worked here long enough to know what they do to trespassers. Come on, we'll deal with this later."

Swallowing our confusion and anger, the rest of us concurred. This was not the time to go yelling at twenty-six of the realm's most powerful people. There would be time for that in the future. I hoped.

With our business done in the meeting hall, we slowly opened the epically large, gold-encrusted doors and crept out of the room.

The Capitol's fancy corridors were pretty deserted by

then, with the exception of several staff members and a few guards here and there. We hid from them with relative ease as we made our way back to the kitchen. Daniel led us there, so thankfully it didn't take very long to navigate across the building.

We'd just hustled behind another corner to avoid being seen by a guard and were waiting for Daniel to give us the all clear when I made the fateful mistake of taking a look back at the elegant hallway behind us.

That's when I saw it. A door at the far end of the hall we'd just run down was open a crack. And streaming out of it I could see a strange, blue glow that called to me like a lost memory. Without thinking, I started moving hypnotically in its direction.

I guess the others hadn't seen me take off, because several beats passed before I heard my name being whispered urgently.

"Crisa? Crisa!"

I shouldn't have ignored them. I mean, it was fairly inconsiderate given that we were kind of on a deadline, kind of not supposed to be in the Capitol, and it was kind of my crazy idea that had gotten us here in the first place. But I couldn't help it. That light, it was almost like . . .

I was about to reach the door when I was yanked backwards unexpectedly.

"Are you out of your mind?" Daniel practically barked.

My friends were right next to him and seemed equally upset. I cleared my throat and emitted an assortment of incomplete words as my response.

They were very articulate and went something like:

"I . . . um . . . er . . . uh . . ."

SJ glanced behind me at the doorway I had been headed

toward. She noticed the bright blue light emanating from it and crinkled her eyebrows. "What is that?"

"I . . . I was trying to find out," I stuttered. Then I turned away from them swiftly and grabbed the doorknob before they could stop me. "I have to find out."

With that, I threw the door open all the way and entered the room of my dreams. Well, *from* my dreams anyways.

The five of us stepped inside the room with the black marble floors, the sleek shelves that wound around the perimeter like an anaconda, and the fifty-foot tall ceilings held up by white Corinthian columns.

There, hanging from the ceiling in the middle of it all (right where I remembered it being in my dreams) was the source of the blue light—the incredible chandelier.

As majestic as it had been in my dreamscape, seeing its magnificence in reality all but made me stop breathing. The chandelier was constructed entirely of tiny, blue, bottled-shaped sapphires. The numerous bottles not only sparkled like the millions of dollars I was sure they were worth; they also glowed. Not concurrently though. Rather, each bottle's light seemed to be flickering with its own pace and consistency like a weary heartbeat—giving the impression that whatever luminescent force was inside them was individually alive.

"It is beautiful," SJ said in awe.

"It's fantastic," Blue agreed.

I walked right toward the center of the room, keeping my head back and my eyes fixed on the light. "But what is it?" I murmured as I stared upwards like I was asking the ceiling itself.

After a minute of silence, SJ came up behind me and put her hand on my shoulder. "Crisa, it is just a chandelier. It is like nothing I have ever seen but—"

"We have to go," Blue finished.

Despite the fact that my gut was telling me that this was somehow more than just a decorative light fixture—I knew she was right. It was best if we left now while we were still ahead, and undiscovered by Capitol security.

Just as I was about to call it quits on this little rendezvous though, the tip of something shiny and silver caught my eye.

"Hold on," I said abruptly.

I scurried across the room. The sound of my boots against marble echoed in my wake. I made my way under an open, arched doorway toward the object I'd seen.

The small extension of the room I now found myself in had more bookshelves and columns, but it also had something extra. Directly to my right was another dragon statue—composed of dark gray stone and scaled to a tenth of the size of the one in the roundabout outside. The tip of the creature's snout had caught the light at precisely the right moment to capture my attention. And, gazing at its magnitude head on, my dream from the beginning of the week began to come back to me with more clarity.

I whirled around and saw the silver knight statue. In his hand was the black sword that the cloaked girl in my dream had been wielding.

I was no longer in control of my actions. I had found the puzzle pieces and needed to put them together. My friends and Daniel, as a result, no doubt thought I was losing it as I ran to the knight, ripped the sword from his hand, and then dashed back toward the dragon. But I didn't care. I had to do this. I had to know.

I stopped in my tracks in front of the creature—staring into its large, black stone eyes and turning the sword over in my hand.

Was it really going to work? I mean, was I insane? I was standing there, holding a sword, and what, I was going to shove it into a dragon statue's mouth and something miraculous would happen?

It was likely that the others were only going to tolerate my crazy behavior for a few more seconds, so a decision had to be made.

To heck with it. What have I got to lose?

With a burst of gumption I plunged the sword into the dragon's mouth and rotated the handle. I didn't know if I was more worried that something would happen or that something wouldn't. Regardless, after a couple of mortifying moments, something did.

A spine-shivering creaking noise filled the room. I turned around slowly. My friends, Daniel, and I watched as a bookshelf against the wall moved forward and to the side—revealing a hidden passageway.

Hmm. Freaky déjà vu or not, you've gotta love the classics.

"Did you know that was going to happen?" Jason asked, clearly shocked.

I didn't respond. I just allowed my subconscious to continue guiding me as I made my way over to the opening.

The passage contained a stairwell that stretched downwards. How far, I didn't know. I just knew that I'd been through it before. It was dimly lit by torches spaced out along an old brick wall, and it smelled of mortar and bad judgment. I placed my hand against the wall for a second then—still having trouble accepting that it was truly there.

"How is this possible?" I whispered to myself as my fingertips grazed the worn clay and I gazed down at the uneven stairs.

The sound of Blue clearing her throat drew my attention

away from their depth. I glanced over my shoulder and back toward the others. They were standing a dozen feet behind me with their mouths agape.

"You coming?" I said as I gestured to the mysterious stairway.

This time it was their turn not to say anything. They simply pursued my lead and we began the descent into the shadows together.

About ten feet down the stairwell we found a metal lever with the word "Open/Close" written on it, which looked as if it controlled the door to the passageway. Jason put his hand on the lever and glanced at us for approval. We nodded our consent. We definitely didn't want anyone following us.

He pulled the handle down and we heard the bookshelf above slide back into place.

Aside from the sound of SJ's portable potions clinking together in the pouch at her waist, all remained silent for the rest of the journey. That was okay by me; creepy hidden stairwells weren't exactly great places for casual conversation. Moreover, I was so spellbound by the surreal nature of what was happening that I doubted that I could've articulated anything of value.

After what seemed like an eternity, the stairs came to an end in front of a rugged, wooden door. Which, upon jiggling the handle, I discovered was locked.

"Blue—"

"I'm on it." Blue drew her hunting knife out of its holster and approached the door.

A few expert lock-picking motions later and a loud clicking sound echoed through the stairwell. The door creaked ajar and we timidly pushed it open the rest of the way and stepped inside.

Ok, you're familiar with that old saying, "Curiosity killed the cat," right?

Yeah, well, I used to think I was too. As it turned out though, I wasn't taking the "killed" portion of that statement as seriously as I should have.

But then, how could I? Right now my fellow cats and I were just far too consumed with curiosity over checking out the room we'd stumbled into.

This room (which was really more like a bunker) was lit up solely by a rickety, bronze chandelier dangling from the ceiling. The atmosphere of the place felt pretty damp; the floor even had some thin trickles of dirty water stretching out from the area beyond its walls. There were several dozen wooden chairs stacked against one wall, as if in anticipation of a small town meeting. And a few gray filing cabinets resided in the corner by the door we'd just come through.

Blue and Jason immediately took it upon themselves to work on unlocking these cabinets.

Meanwhile I stood in front of the podium at the head of the room and looked up at the wall behind it. Because, of course, there was the map with the colorful Xs I'd envisioned—hanging right where it was supposed to be.

Even as I stared at it in all its non-fictitious glory, there was something strange about the image. Like, despite the fact that the map was right there in front of me, it still felt like I wasn't completely seeing it for everything it really was.

It was a normal map of Book. As in my dream, different colored Xs were littered all over it—marking miscellaneous locations across the realm in a pattern that I couldn't understand, but sensed I desperately needed to.

Then there was that inscrutable black X. It was the only one of its kind on the map, and inexplicably made me swallow with apprehension just from looking at it.

In real life this black X wasn't as huge as the one in my dreams had been; it was actually the same size as all the other, more colorful ones. Even so, it still intimidated me. What surprised me more though, was the fact that it seemed to be purposefully placed on the far left side of the map in the area of Book where Lady Agnue's and Lord Channing's were located.

This was a daunting realization to say the least. Unfortunately, its meaning also remained unclear. While I yearned to know the significance of the black X, as well as that of all the others, the map's lack of a key kept both a mystery.

Nevertheless, I continued examining the whole picture—hoping I might be able to uncover some scrap of a clue to help me solve the cipher. Whether such focus would've been fruitful, however, I'd never know. As Daniel chose that particular moment to interrupt my thoughts.

"Knight. How could you possibly know this was down here?" he asked.

"I don't know," I admitted hesitantly. "I just did."

"Oh, come on," he said as he stepped into my personal space. "You shoved a sword into a statue's mouth and opened a secret passageway. Girls—even weird girls like you—don't just do things like that out of the blue."

I rolled my eyes at Daniel and walked away from him. He grunted in frustration and went to join Blue and Jason at the other side of the room. SJ, on the other hand, came over to me.

"Crisa," she said softly, "was this what you were dreaming about the other night?"

My face turned green. My blood went cold. I grabbed her by the arm and pulled her aside as inconspicuously as I could.

"How . . . How did you know that?" I asked her in a sharp whisper.

SJ sighed. "I know that in the aftermath you do not like to talk about what you have been dreaming, Crisa. But sometimes you do talk *while* you are dreaming. Last week, on the evening of our entry into the Archives actually, I heard you muttering something as you slept. It was about a blue light on the ceiling and unlocking a dragon and . . ." She paused and motioned toward the map on the wall, "the room with the master map."

I scratched my head trying to figure out something to say.

It seemed like SJ wished to probe the matter more, but before she could say anything else Blue signaled for our attention.

"Crisa," she called from across the room. "You might want to take a look at this."

Daniel and Jason were holding several folders that they'd removed from the filing cabinet they'd broken into. Blue, however, was holding only one folder in her left hand and, I assumed, a page from said file in her right.

She had a freaked out expression on her face, the likes of which I'd never seen before, not even when she'd received her prologue prophecy. When SJ and I reached her, she handed over the piece of paper without a word.

Geez, ominous much?

What could possibly be on this that would make her—

My mind froze when I took in the contents of the document.

It was me.

Well, it was a page of information *about* me. Most of it was basic stuff—my name, date of birth, height, weight—

Hey, I'm at least five pounds lighter than that!

Focus, Crisa. Focus.

Aside from the basics, the second half of the sheet had a brief summary of who I was, my history at Lady Agnue's, and even a short description of my friends and family. It was *super* creepy. What was worse, though, was what I found at the bottom right hand corner of the page. There, I discovered a picture of myself beside a black X with the words "Priority Elimination" printed beneath it.

I took another glance at the map on the wall behind us, now realizing precisely what that black X over Lady Agnue's indicated.

"Crisa, what . . ." SJ started.

"I don't know," I cut her off.

I glanced around as my mind started to race again. This was not the time to panic (although it seemed like an appealing option given the circumstances). No. This was a time for something quite different: order and action.

"Blue, give me that file," I commanded. "I want to see who else is in there. The rest of you guys, go through the remaining folders. Find out what the other colored Xs mean."

Without hesitation they followed my instructions. As Blue, Jason, and Daniel began pawing through the files, I opened the folder my page had come from and began to look through it while SJ hovered nearby.

There were exactly two other pieces of paper in the

folder. Both were information sheets like mine. And each was also marked with a black X, which I thought was strange considering there were no other black Xs on the map.

The first profile meant nothing to me initially. It featured a middle-aged woman with a heart-shaped face; navy eyes; five feet tall; 125 pounds; no living relatives.

While the information and picture of the woman did not trigger any familiarity though, her name certainly did. "Paige Tomkins" was printed at the bottom of the form.

The Fairy Godmother friend Emma was telling us about.

A sense of urgency sweeping over me, I quickly went on to the second page in the folder. Unlike the first document, this one definitely registered an immediate reaction from me. I almost dropped the folder from shock when I saw the picture of the girl staring back at me beside her own black X notation.

It was Natalie Poole.

The picture of her in this document was identical to the one I'd gotten from the file at Fairy Godmother HQ. The information about her printed on the page was the same too. All that stuff about her "Key Destiny Interval," her birthday, that "Eternity Gate" thing, and . . .

Suddenly I became very aware that SJ was peering over my shoulder. I tried to shut the folder before her eyes could get to the bottom and read the name printed there, but I didn't move fast enough.

"Crisa," SJ stammered. "Natalie Poole? She exists in—"

"Hey, what'd you find, Blue?" I interrupted as our friend approached us with an odd look on her face.

"Green Xs mean 'possible ally,' blue Xs are labeled as

'compromised,' yellow Xs say 'possible threat,' and um . . ."
Blue trailed off. She took a weary glance at Jason and he
finished the sentence for her.

"Red Xs mean 'threat neutralized,'" he said.

The statement was a lot to process, especially since the
folder with the red Xs Jason was holding up was relatively
thick. The way he'd said it though—with a coarseness in his
voice and a shadow in his eyes—gave me a sense that there
was something else too.

He pulled a document out of the red X folder and showed
it to us. It was a page featuring Mark—Jason's old roommate
and our long absent friend.

There weren't any appropriate questions to ask at that
point because there were no answers that would change
what this piece of paper indicated. According to it, Mark
wasn't on a temporary leave of absence from school for
personal reasons. In reality his absence may well have been
. . . permanent.

Blue put her hand on Jason's arm with unusual delicacy
before continuing. "Jason, Daniel, and I have pages in the
yellow folder, the one marked 'possible threats,'" she said as
she held up the papers with each of their own facts and faces
imprinted on them.

"What about me?" SJ asked. "Do I have one?"

Blue shook her head. "No. There are a few other kids
from school in here, though. Seven in total by the looks of it,
which means—"

"Which means we've got to warn them," Daniel said.

"And talk to Mark's family," Jason said.

"And inform our headmasters," added SJ.

They went on like that for a while longer, but I tuned

them out. I turned my attention back to the map behind SJ and began studying it and the pages from the folder I still held on to.

"What is all this?" I muttered to myself absentmindedly.

I guess I'd spoken louder than I thought, because when I looked at the others again each of them was staring at me. They all seemed confused and concerned but, more than anything, they looked like they wanted to know the answer to that question just as much as I did.

Sadly, this was not the time to find it. At that moment our tense, reflective silence was replaced by the sound of massive stones grinding against one another. My friends' faces paled in response and I spun around to discover the source of the noise and their alarm.

The folder dropped from my hands.

There were five people standing in the tunnel that had just revealed itself in the stone wall across the room. The first was a girl dressed like a member of the kitchen staff. Beside her stood three armed Capitol guards like the ones we'd seen outside. And in front of them, was a boy. He was a few years our senior and seemed familiar, though initially I couldn't work out why.

His build was strong and gallant like the heroes of Lord Channing's, but the darkness in his eyes suggested he was anything but. Like his wavy hair, those striking eyes were pure black and radiated a sense of malevolence, confidence, and (at this particular moment) also a hint of surprise at having found us here.

For a second, the group stood there as puzzled as we were—the only sound being the steady drip of water coming from the tunnel behind them. The black haired boy swiftly overcame his initial shock though, and smirked in my direction. Unlike Daniel's smirks however, which just made me annoyed, his made me a very specific kind of nervous.

"Crisanta Knight . . ." he said thoughtfully.

I didn't bother to ask how he knew my name. I was far more stricken by the vague familiarity of his chilling voice and his appearance.

"Well," he continued in a bemused tone to no one in particular. "They do say that when you've lost something—or in this case, *someone*—to look in the last place you'd expect to find them."

I began to slowly move my hand toward my satchel, preparing to grab my wand. SJ (who was standing in front of me and had her hands behind her back) rapidly glanced at me and then subtly pointed her index finger upwards.

She was gesturing to the chandelier above us—the sole source of light in the room. I got what she was saying and continued to sneak my hand into my satchel. Meanwhile, she slipped her right hand into her dress pocket while her left one casually found its way into the small sack hanging at her side.

Out of the corner of my eye, I saw that the guards behind the black haired boy had started to draw their weapons. Jason, Daniel, and Blue had begun to as well.

"And here I was told that you would be a hard one to catch, princess," the black haired boy went on—reaching for the sheath strapped to his shoulder.

I verified that SJ was ready.

She was, her slingshot hot in her hand waiting for my signal.

I gripped my wand tighter.

"It's too bad, though—"

My eyes rose to meet the gaze of the black haired boy.

"—I was looking forward to a little bit of challenge," he said with a disappointed shrug. "Ah well, that's just how it goes isn't it?"

Had another second passed, he surely would've given the order to attack. But we beat him to the punch.

"Now!" I shouted.

SJ fired a portable potion in the direction of the opposing group. I morphed my wand into a boomerang and hurled it upwards. It cut through the rusty chain holding up the room's chandelier, causing the whole thing to come crashing down.

A half moment later I caught my wand and reverted it back to normal as the chandelier smashed into the ground—blackening the room.

In that same instant SJ's potion erupted at the feet of our new enemies. It emitted a great cloud of pink smoke that was barely visible through the darkness, but was clearly spreading our way.

"Hold your breath!" SJ ordered as we dashed for the exit.

We ran out of the room, Daniel slamming the door behind us as we raced up the stairs.

"What was that?" he hollered at SJ.

"Portable potion!" she yelled without looking back.

Jason threw the "Open/Close" lever on the wall in reverse as we passed it. The bookshelf ahead slid open, allowing us to speed back into the cursed room we'd started in.

"That was a highly concentrated sleeping potion," SJ explained as she drew another portable concoction from her bag. "It should have knocked them out immediately, but will only last for a couple of minutes. We have to close this door and get out of here before they awaken and come after us. Stand back."

SJ fired a reddish orb down the stairwell straight toward the lever. Unlike the others, this potion did not release gas. Instead, it caused a small explosion.

"What in the—" Jason started to say.

Regrettably, when the smoke cleared a second later we saw that although the lever had been obliterated, the passageway remained unaffected and was still completely open.

"Plan B," Daniel said as he tried to push the bookshelf back into place. We joined him in the effort, but the shelf would not budge. I looked around desperately and saw that the dragon statue still had the sword in its mouth.

That's it!

I rushed over to the statue, gripped the sword in my hand, and tried to pull the weapon out of the creature's stone larynx. But it was no good; it was stuck.

I put my free hand on the head of the dragon to steady myself while I pulled harder. *Come on, come on! Let's go!* I thought to myself, pressing so intensely on the statue's face that my hand started to feel like it was burning, no doubt from the friction.

Thankfully after a few moments the sword gave way and was released from the beast's mouth—causing the bookshelf to close the passage.

Our group sped out of the room as fast as our legs could carry us. Within minutes we'd raced across the hallway, past the kitchen and its confused attendants, and back into the alley. Then we were in the sewers again, barreling through the tunnel we'd originally come from.

At first the only sound echoing around us was that of our feet stampeding through the dirty water. But then I began hearing voices like I'd heard when we were down here earlier. They were much louder now—taking the form of shouts not whispers, and growing more audible as we proceeded farther into the tunnel.

I suddenly remembered the damp feel of that bunker; the trickles of murky water stretching out from behind its stone walls.

Realization hit me like a hammer.

"Stop!" I yelled as I came to an abrupt halt.

My friends and Daniel skidded to a pause.

"Don't you see?" I said. "They came through a tunnel into that room; they came through the sewers!"

No sooner did I explain this than our pursuers rounded the corner and came into view. Needless to say we decided to change course.

"Don't let them get away!" I heard the black haired boy call out.

We ran back down the sewer tunnel, ascended the ladder to the alley once more, and dashed through the kitchen—knocking over several trays of desserts and a few disoriented caterers.

As we rushed through the halls we'd just been in, I held my wand tighter and tighter, understanding that I definitely wasn't done using it for today.

Daniel led the way again. He was taking us up some stairs, down other stairs, through room after room in an obvious attempt to throw off our followers.

This time I actually *was* too preoccupied to think to question his guidance. Nor did I think to question the pieces of scorched hallway carpeting we kept coming across that definitely hadn't been there a couple of minutes ago.

"Our best bet is to go out the front. It's three floors down," Daniel said as we kept pace with him. "Those guys won't expect it, and the guards are concentrating on stopping people from getting into the Capitol, not out."

Of course the guards that had been with our pursuers were trying to stop us in general. So that did pose a problem when we ran into a couple of them in the adjacent hall. They had their bows drawn and pointed at me.

Shield.

My wand spiraled out just in time to stop two arrows from piecing my sternum.

Blue ripped two throwing knives from her belt and hurled them at the guards. Each knife hit one of the guards directly in the hand—piercing them a bit too graphically to describe.

Their maimed palms dropped the bows they'd been wielding and prevented them from reacting in time to Jason when he came at them in the next instant.

Our friend whipped his axe from its sheath and swung the flat side at the first guard's head like a steel bat, taking him out. He ducked a blow from the second guard before blocking and countering with several vicious strikes, swinging his axe around, and buckling the knee of his opponent. With formidable force Jason proceeded to punch the man in the gut, elbow him in the jaw, then finally send him toppling over like the first guard, throwing in an extra blow to the ribcage for good measure.

Jason flipped the axe back into his grip as we joined his side.

Blue retrieved her bloodied knives and reattached them to her belt, which I thought was a bit gross, but didn't comment on.

"There's a shortcut through the main library," Daniel

said as our group hurried past the now unconscious guards. "Through there."

He pointed at a brown door on the other side of the room. When we reached it we plowed through and found ourselves in a seven-story, cylindrical library—three floors beneath us, three above.

The bookshelves wrapped around the room in an ascending spiral, mirroring the design of the glass ceiling above, which cast a shadow that reminded me all too well of the spiral marks we received when our prologue pangs hit.

Every level of the library had two sides to it—one that ran against the bookshelves and one that faced the wide open space in the center of the room, which separated staggering floors by at least thirty feet of distance.

Given that falling off one of these floors could've gotten you killed, every level of the library walkway was lined with a smooth silver railing designed to keep visitors from going over the edge. Which—at the speed we barged in at—I might have just done.

Jason promptly spotted our exit on the ground level. He had just begun to lead the charge for it when suddenly an arrow came out of nowhere.

My heart stopped for a moment. Time slowed.

The shot was close, and it almost seemed to move in slow motion as we watched it barely miss Jason's body. Had he been another inch forward it surely would have killed him. Luckily, he wasn't, so it didn't. The arrow plunged into one of the bookshelves behind him and we in turn whipped our heads in the direction the shot had come from.

The person who'd fired the arrow was the third guard from the group that'd been chasing us. He was on the opposite side of the room, about one and a half levels beneath us on the spiral walkway. He started to run up and ascend to our level.

We readied to attack and raced to meet him, but Blue did not follow. Instead she dove underneath the railing.

Blue grabbed the edge of the floor with her hands, dropped over its rim, then released her grip—causing her to plunge through the air ten feet until her hands grasped onto the railing of the level directly below.

Immediately she hoisted herself up and used her body's momentum to swing under the new railing. She landed with a gymnast's grace on the library floor a mere six paces before the guard reached that portion of the spiral.

From across the library the four of us watched her finish the fight.

I had to say, for a girl who often embodied the head-on force of a runaway freight train, Blue's combat movements could be as fluid as a ballerina's. From the moment her boots touched the ground, her next three moves were already in motion.

As Blue spun up from her knees, her right leg thrust upwards and she kicked the guard squarely in the chest. Her right foot was still in mid air at that point, but she twisted her body around so quickly and strongly that she was able to throw a spinning back kick with the other foot sans the support.

This second kick buckled the guard's knees. And in the instant it took for the pain to register across his expression, Blue whirled back toward him and drove her fist straight into his head—sending him slamming against the bookshelf behind.

Evidently her summer break village fight club stories had been accurate. Because she continued to attack the guard so powerfully then, that professional boxers would have winced. Even from the other side of the library her searing aggression was noticeable, making me wonder if during all those times in the practice fields we'd fought each other she secretly *had* been holding back.

With a final head-butt, Blue's opponent collapsed. Despite the fact that he was already down and out, she kicked him purposefully in the gut one last time before letting out a grunt of satisfaction and turning back around to face us.

"Dang," Jason said, his eyebrows raised.

"Yeah, well, I do a lot of cardio," Blue said with a shrug.

Our group began to make its way to meet her on the lower level. I brought up the rear. However, unbeknownst to the others, I came to a stop a moment later. A book on one of the shelves had unexpectedly captured my attention—causing me to hang back.

I took a quick step toward it to read the title printed on the spine:

"Shadow Guardians—Origins, Dangers, & Weaknesses."

I didn't quite know why that particular book caught my interest. Maybe I'd seen those words in a textbook at school, or in one of SJ's piles of periodicals; or maybe it was just the fact that the title was written in really shiny print. Whatever the reason, something inside of me was definitely drawn to the book in the same way it had been to that bunker.

Although since not even my dreams could rationalize this feeling, I forced myself to shrug it off and continue on my way. As it stood, inexplicable instinct had gotten me into enough trouble today. And my friends and Daniel were already a whole floor beneath me and I needed to catch up with them.

"Seriously though, you really laid into that guy," I heard Jason say as he and the others reached Blue.

"It was no big deal," she responded. "He tried to hurt you and I. . . Wait a sec. What is . . . Crisa, look out!"

Spear, I thought without hesitation.

I spun to my left and blocked the sword that Blue had seen coming at me from behind. Then I jerked my elbow into the enemy guard's chin, twisted my spear to knock the sword out of his hand, and right-kicked his shin. With one sturdy side-thrust to his ribs and a reverse swing of my staff to his head later, the guard was out for the count.

Wand.

I realized then that a bookshelf on the wall a few feet back had been pushed aside and was now revealing another passageway. This one led to a meeting hall that lay beyond this part of the room. When I turned around again I found Daniel at my side—evidently having run back up here to collect me.

"I thought there were only three guards with that group," Daniel said, staring at my wand.

"And I thought you used to work here. What, did you never take a look at the floor plans?" I said as I gestured toward the gaping hole in the wall.

"You're blaming me for this? You're the one they're trying to—"

"Um, guys," Jason interrupted.

We both whipped our heads toward him. "What?"

Jason didn't say anything; he just pointed upwards. In response Daniel and I tilted our heads and saw that about ten bookshelves on the higher levels of the library were beginning to slide forwards and to the side.

Oh, darn.

Daniel looked over my shoulder then grabbed his sword. "Duck, roundhouse, over the edge," he said curtly.

"What?"

"Now!"

In the periphery of my sight I saw another guard rushing through the opening behind me and I got what Daniel was saying. The second the guard raised his sword to bring it down upon me, I ducked. When I did, Daniel had his sword at the ready and clashed it forcefully with the guard's. His strike pushed the attacker off balance. I spun around the guard's side and roundhouse-kicked him toward Daniel.

The wobbling guard sailed forwards and when he was within range Daniel hammered him in the face—sending him back to me to finish the job by grabbing his right arm and throwing him over the railing.

He landed with a thud somewhere below, out cold.

"Nice work," Daniel said.

"Back 'atcha," I replied. "I . . . hold that thought."

Spear.

With the dull end of my staff I slammed an overeager guard in the side of the neck as he came charging through the doorway like a crazed bull. Then I rapidly rotated my arm to hock his leg out from under him.

He flipped like a pancake and landed with a splat on the floor beside me.

Wand.

I looked back up and saw that the bookshelves had now been fully pushed aside and guards were starting to pour out of them. Some began to run the library's coiling floor to pursue us on foot, while others drew their bows and started to take aim and fire at will.

"Move!" I commanded Daniel and the others.

Arrows nipping at our heels, we raced downwards.

By miracle, a few dozen yards of descending spiral staircase later and the five of us piled through the library exit without being hit.

The guards were still on our tails so there was no time to catch our breaths. But, thankfully, we appeared to be in the home stretch. We were in the foyer of the Capitol now and the main entrance to the building was right in front of us.

Our fortune did not last though. When we reached the giant doors we all pushed together, but they refused to budge even an inch. They either weighed a thousand pounds a piece (which would have been highly impractical), or they were locked.

I glanced back and saw the first couple of enemy guards run out of the library and skid into the foyer. Wand clutched tightly, I lunged to go and meet them. But Daniel put his hand up to stop me. "Figure out how to open the doors," he said. "I got these guys."

Daniel grabbed his sword and charged the two attackers. When he met them he immediately parried the first guard's strike and then punched the opponent in the throat with his free hand. The guard stumbled back, disoriented, and Daniel took the opportunity to swing his blade around and trap the arm of the second attacker.

Leveraging this guard's weight against him, Daniel brought the base of his sword down on the rear of his opponent's neck for a powerful blow—causing the trapped arm to twist, snap, and drop its sword.

At that point Daniel forcefully kicked the first guard before following up with a cross-handed strike to the face that sent the assailant straight to the ground.

Hmm. I had to say, if there was ever a time that I disliked Daniel the least, it would've been right then. The boy could fight.

Confident that he had things under control, I turned my attention to the door problem.

"There has to be a key or a lever or something," Blue said, kicking the door angrily.

"Up there!" I said, signaling to an area across the room.

About sixty feet away there was a balcony with an unmanned guard pedestal—probably the gatekeeper's post. There was a small red button on the wall next to it that must've been what unlocked the doors.

Blue rolled up her sleeves. "Maybe I can climb some of those tapestries and—"

"No need," SJ interrupted.

Before Blue could ask why, SJ had fired her slingshot. One of her portable potions hit the red button like a bullseye. The moment it did, pink smoke exploded and we heard a deadbolt inside the doors slide down—unlocking them.

"Was that another sleeping potion?" Jason asked.

"I believe so," SJ answered. "But it is not important. We just needed the impact so I picked one at random. Now come on, before something else goes wrong."

"Daniel!" I yelled. "Let's go!"

Daniel took out his fourth guard and then bolted to catch up with us. He did so just in time too because as skilled as he was, he surely would have been overwhelmed by the seven more guards that poured from the library in the next second.

With one final burst of strength, the five us pushed the doors open and sprinted outside to freedom.

Just kidding.

We didn't make it halfway down the stairs before every member of outer Capitol security turned their attention and their weapons in our direction. If that wasn't enough, the guards that had been chasing us came through the doors then and honed in on us as well. We were frozen on the stairs like statues. From every angle we were clear targets and had no plausible means of escape. That is, until we heard the roar . . .

From behind us, a deafening, high-pitched noise that sounded part lion, part demon pierced the air. The entire city stopped in cold blood to see what had caused the disturbance and discovered it was neither lion nor demon, but a silver, medium-sized dragon. The monster soared over the Capitol's cupola—coming from somewhere behind the building. His shadow darkened the stairs that led up to the main entrance until he plowed into the street just ahead of the roundabout.

Great. As if we didn't already have enough to deal with. Some rando dragon just had to be in the area and drop in on us too?

Carriages were barely able to swerve in time to avoid being squashed.

The dragon's landing had been wobbly. He'd collided with the hind legs of the giant, gold dragon statue, causing a big clanging sound to echo around us. When the sound subsided all remained still and quiet for a moment. Then the silvery beast howled again and everyone else joined in.

Screaming people took off running every which way as they yelled in violent alarm. Meanwhile the regular Capitol guards forgot about our group and began firing at the dragon in immediate, aggressive response.

For a crazy split-second I felt kind of bad for the creature.

It was like that griffin incident all over again. Poor guy wanders out of the forest into the city and gets pulverized for no reason.

But then I caught a look at the size of the dragon's teeth as he violently thrashed his tail—shattering chunks of building and nearly killing a half dozen people in the process—and I felt less bad.

Regrettably, the murderous guards that had been after us—while momentarily distracted by the dragon—lost no such interest in us as the commotion progressed. In fact, it almost seemed like the chaos heightened the resolve of their chase. Luckily the confusion unleashed by the dragon still created the perfect opportunity for us to lose them though, which we immediately took advantage of.

We sped down the stairs with me naturally falling behind to bring up the rear again. (*Evidently running away was not my thing in more ways than one.*)

The dragon began bounding across the traffic circle as he tried to evade the guards' fire. His weight sent shockwaves across the street like baby earthquakes, causing me and countless others to falter.

He roared again just as I was about to duck under the golden tail of the dragon statue. I glanced up and saw the creature's distant face reflected in the metal just as he released a burst of flames from his enormous mouth.

I looked back over my shoulder and saw that in the dragon's attempts to defend himself he'd just roasted the stairwell of the Capitol.

He was getting closer. So we moved faster.

When we got to the section of the roundabout that poured into one of the city's inner streets, we merged into the sea of frantic people trying to evacuate the area.

It felt like everything was one noise now. The dragon's roar, the people shouting, my heart pounding, Daniel up ahead yelling something about meeting at the carriage—it was all a blur of sound. But I was shocked back to reality when from within the crowd someone reached out, grabbed me by the wrist, and pulled me backwards.

Spea—No!

A civilian running by knocked my wand out of my hand before it had the chance to transform. As I watched it fall beneath the stampeding footsteps of a hundred terrified people my back was thrown against the wall of an adjacent alley.

The force of the grab had been so strong and sudden that I lost my footing when I hit the wall—sinking to the floor upon impact. Not a full second passed when I landed on the ground, and when I looked up to find the blade of a sword an inch below my throat.

The black haired boy from the Capitol was crouched at my level. He was leaning forward with one hand pressed against the wall behind my head and the other grasping the sword beneath my chin. He seemed a bit out of breath but just as confident as before.

His face being so close to mine, I discovered two things.

First and foremost, I finally knew where I recognized him from. He was without a doubt the same boy I'd envisioned in the bunker speaking with that cloaked girl during my fateful nightmare of days past. Which, I garnered, also meant that he was the same long-pondered-over, living, breathing source of the voice that had tormented my dreams for so many dreadful ages.

Second, while such dreams had long been characterized by a wish to know the face of this source with more finite clarity, I now realized that this had been a foolish desire. Seeing him so vividly brought me no peace or closure. Rather, as I stared at every inch of his face, my heart sped with trepidation.

This feeling was only surmounted by the painful sense that the nightmares I'd had of the boy thus far hadn't even begun to scratch the surface of the real ones he might be capable of bringing to my world.

As I drew these conclusions I found myself unavoidably sucked into his deep, piercing eyes. They were far darker than I'd originally assessed. I mean, yes I'd already noticed they were black. But seriously, *dang*. Looking into them was like looking into two black holes or two really, really strong cups of coffee.

But I digress, given that his dramatically dark eye color is not nearly as important as the fact that he is currently holding a sword to my neck.

"Crisanta Knight," he said.

His voice at this proximity made the hairs on the back of my neck stand up. Hearing my name on his lips only made me feel even more creeped out.

I gulped. "Um, yeah, hi there. Pleasure to make your acquaintance," I replied, my eyes darting back and forth between him and the blade. "And you are?"

He smirked. "Arian. And the pleasure is mine."

I glanced around the area. The alley was deserted and littered with a lot of broken bottles and crumpled, forgotten fliers. To my right was an empty grocer's stand with an awning held up by two wooden poles. Next to it was a horse whose rear end faced our direction and whose body was tied to an empty produce cart.

To my left were the streets. There were so many hundreds

of distracted people gushing through them that no one took notice of us. My friends probably hadn't even realized I was gone yet.

Then I saw something catch the light a few yards away. My wand! It had rolled next to several bales of hay and was lying on the cobblestone street some eight or nine feet over. I began to slowly feel my left hand around on the ground behind me in search of a lifeline.

If I can keep this guy distracted a few more seconds I might have a chance here. I've just got to keep stalling until I find what I need.

"So. Based on the context I'd say you were about to try and 'eliminate me,' am I right?" I asked, trying to keep him talking.

"Unfortunately," he replied. "It really is a shame though."

I kept my eyes locked with his as my fingers found what they'd hoped to on the floor of the alleyway. I grasped the object carefully. "And why's that?" I asked Arian as I tightened my grip around it.

"For one, it was pretty entertaining to chase you around like that. After all, half the fun of the kill is the hunt, right? And second, well, you're pretty easy on the eyes."

I smirked. "Poor choice of words."

At that, I swung my hand around and smashed Arian in the temple with a half broken glass bottle that my fingers had found on the alley floor.

The blow was fast and powerful enough to knock him out of his crouched position. The second it did, I scrambled to my feet and dove for my wand. I picked it off the ground and spun around as Arian got back up. He was holding his face, which had a large cut carved into its right side around the area of his eye where I'd hit him.

Spear.

"Still think I'm easy on the eyes?" I asked him as my wand morphed.

"You . . . you have a wand?" he said.

"Correction, I *had* a wand." I aimed the blade end of my trusty weapon in his direction. "Now I have a spear. Which I'm not bashful about using by the way, so I'd highly suggest you answer my next two questions. Who are you? And why are you creeps after me?"

"You want to know who I am, princess?" Arian replied coolly. "It's really very simple. I am the lucky antagonist charged with decreasing the number of problematic protagonists in the world. Now as to the reasons why I am after *you* specifically, they're irrelevant. My team and I have our orders—we monitor for threats and eliminate them when they occur. It's not my business to know the exact details. The simple fact is that your book's prologue prophecy appeared a few weeks ago, Nadia gave the order, and here we are."

"What are you talking about?" I asked. "Who is Nadia and how could *my* prologue prophecy possibly be seen as a threat? It's as lame and docile as they come."

"Oh, you poor, dumb princess," he laughed. "You really have no idea, do you?"

I wanted to ask him what he meant, but my attention was drawn away from his patronization. In my peripheral vision I saw a pack of cobalt helmet plumes making their way through the crowds toward us.

The guards we'd been running from were almost upon me. I had to get out of here, now. But what was my strategy? If I ran, he would chase after me. If I fought him, the guards would get here in time to help him and they'd overpower me with their numbers.

Once again I took stock of my surroundings to reconfigure

my options. At my feet there were a couple more broken bottles. And above Arian there was that awning, which cast the alley in shadow.

However, I now realized that on top of the awning was an extremely large amount of produce—clearly intended to be loaded into the cart of the horse behind Arian. A horse that, based on the way he was jolting around, was clearly getting restless and increasingly perturbed by the chaos in the surrounding streets.

I smiled. "I wouldn't say I have *no ideas*," I said in response to Arian's snide remark.

Before my newfound foe could lunge at me, I spun my spear downwards—catching its end on the inside of one of the half-smashed bottles. With another twirl all too reminiscent of the one I'd attempted back in Lady Agnue's stables with the horse dung at the start of the semester, I flung the bottle at the rear end of the disgruntled horse.

When it hit him, he whinnied and released a powerful back kick in protest, which snapped one of the wooden poles holding up the awning directly above Arian.

Arian raised his eyebrows—obviously thinking I had intended for the horse to kick him and not the awning. "I hope that wasn't for me," he said mockingly.

Wand.

"No." I shrugged and pointed upwards with my trusty weapon. "But this is."

The weight of the fruit being too much for the second wooden pole to hold up on its own, it snapped under the pressure of the awning and the hefty inventory came raining down upon my new enemy.

I didn't linger to enjoy the sight. The moment that first cantaloupe hit Arian's head I turned on my heels and made a break for it—leaving him to be buried in the avalanche of fruit alone.

For the next few minutes after that I just ran. I ran and I didn't look back.

Bobbing and weaving through the panicked crowds, I tried my best to concentrate on the direction I was going and ignore the screams around me and the distant dragon roars coming from somewhere behind. Of course, the latter became a bit harder to ignore when a giant shadow glided over the streets.

Everyone and everything paused as the body of the flying dragon cast the city in darkness. He was circling over the capital now—letting out periodic roars, but not actually attacking. Honestly, from the way he was behaving, if I hadn't known any better I would've said he was simply searching for something, not intending to terrorize the general public as our collective responses would've suggested.

The brief interlude of silence was cut short an instant later when one civilian lost his nerve and screamed bloody murder. Everyone else joined in and the panic escalated tenfold. Consequently it became even more difficult to move through the mass of people.

Still, I kept going. And eventually I pushed my way through the crowds into the alleyway where my friends, Daniel, and I had originally entered the city.

I barreled down its path until I came to the fence at the other end.

Reversing the shortcut we'd used to get into our realm's capital only an hour ago, I climbed onto the nearby dumpster and leaped for the fence. My fingers grasping the wire, I proceeded to climb over it and jump to the other side.

From there it was a straight shot up a handful of grassy hills until I came to the forest where we'd parked. A few dozen pine needles stuck in my hair from plowing through the trees later, I found the others with our levitating vehicle. They all seemed both relieved and notably angry as I jogged up to the side of our carriage and leaned against it to catch my breath.

Blue punched me in the arm "Where the heck were you?!"

"Oh, you know, the city gift shop," I panted.

"Crisa!"

"Look, does it matter? I had some trouble getting out of the city, but I'm here now so I suggest we get a move on while we still have the chance."

The sound of the dragon's screech tore their focus away from me and back to the distraught capital.

Century City's infantry had taken to the skies on some of their reserve battle Pegasi. They were firing flaming arrows in their attempts to ground the dragon. But the arrows just seemed to bounce off the beast's sturdy wings as he kept flying around in circles—letting out the occasional puff of smoke from his nostrils in protest, but mainly just smelling the air like a hound dog.

Escaping all that mess being more pressing than grilling me with questions, my friends hurried into the carriage. Daniel hopped into the front seat as he had before and picked up the reins. I put my foot on the front wheel and hoisted myself up next to him.

"What do you think you're doing, Knight?"

"I'm not taking the back seat anymore, Daniel," I snapped. "Get used to it. Now drive."

For once he didn't argue and just gave the Pegasi the signal to take off. I leaned back against the seat as we were pulled into the sky with a jolt.

The lot of us kept looking back at the city after we'd taken flight—nervous despite being airborne and in retreat. This anxiety only escalated when, all of a sudden, the dragon stopped circling the capital and stared off toward the forest area we'd just vacated.

This distraction was long enough for a flying soldier to fire a well-aimed arrow at the dragon. The shot hit a portion of the monster's deep underbelly near the armpit (apparently one of the creature's only soft spots not protected by scales). The dragon seizured with pain, letting out an enormous roar. Then, in retaliation he flapped his wings mightily and zoomed above the mass of guards. It was there that he hesitated and his silver belly began to glow orange.

Oh no.

The guards seemed to realize what I had and began to fly out of the way. It proved to be not a moment too soon. For in the next instant the dragon let out a burst of twenty-foot flames that would've barbequed them all.

When the dragon finished releasing his fire he swiftly turned and began flying in our direction, disregarding the remaining guards, and the city completely.

No one wanted to say what they were thinking at that point. But as the gap between our carriage and the creature began to seem less and less massive, the tension became sufficient enough for someone in our group to speak up.

"Guys . . . " Jason said. "Is that thing headed toward us?"

The dragon's distance was now closing in on three or four miles. His eyes practically seemed locked on our carriage.

And in that moment, as if to prove a point, he emitted another roar and began flapping his wings even faster.

Oh, dang.

I pivoted around to the open window separating Daniel and me from the inside of the carriage.

"SJ," I called back, "please tell me you have another sleeping potion in that bag of yours."

My friend grimaced, looking ashamed. "I am sorry, Crisa. But I may have used my only other sleeping potion to unlock the Capitol doors."

"May have?"

"Okay, I definitely did."

"You only had *two* of those? You've got, like, fifty potions in that sack!" Blue exclaimed.

SJ narrowed her eyes. "Well I did not set out to make sleeping potions when I brewed the rest of these, Blue. I do not like sleeping potions. I simply made a couple with the extra ingredients I had so as not to be wasteful with the potion lab's inventory."

"SJ," Blue growled.

"Oh, calm yourself, Blue," she responded as she pulled three silver orbs from her pouch. "These should work just fine too. But—"

"But what?" Blue asked.

"But you have to get them inside of his mouth."

Daniel had increased the speed of our carriage to its capacity and the Pegasi were flapping through the skies like their lives depended on it—swerving back and forth and up and down as they tried to shake the dragon off their trail.

SJ looked out the rear window and then at Daniel and me through the front one. "Good luck," she said.

"Wait, you've got the best aim. You should do it," I asserted.

"Are you mad? I may have the best aim, but I am terrified of flying on Pegasi. I can hardly do it even when someone *else* is driving, let alone on a direct course for a dragon."

"What are you talking about?"

"The speed and erratic way the dragon is moving make it impossible to get a clear shot from this carriage," SJ explained. "Someone would have to get fairly close to him to have a chance of getting the potions into his mouth, and the only way to do that is by being on Pegasi."

"You heard the girl," I said, grabbing the portable potions from SJ and stuffing them into my pocket. "Jason, Blue—we're on."

Jason didn't move. "You guys go," he said.

"Dude, are you kidding me?" Blue asked in disbelief. "Isn't annihilating a dragon, like, one of your lifelong dreams?"

"Yeah, but taking three Pegasi away from the carriage will slow it down too much. And I saw you guys in the Twenty-Three Skidd tournament; you and Crisa are better shots than I am. You two should do it."

Dang, that's pretty big of him to say. Seriously, way to take one for the team.

"Good call," Blue nodded in agreement. "Crisa," she turned to me. "Let's go."

I shoved my wand into my boot and tossed SJ my satchel. Then I helped Blue through the window and out onto the driver's perch. There was barely enough room for the three of us. Nevertheless, Blue and I stood there alongside Daniel— holding onto the roof of the vehicle to steady ourselves as we prepared to jump.

We surveyed the five Pegasi before us. Their holographic wings were shifting in color a lot more erratically now that they were going so fast. And the colorful, smoky exhaust coming from their nostrils was way more intense too, like the billowing stacks produced by the front end of an old locomotive.

With SJ's levitation potion at work, removing two of them wouldn't cause the carriage to lose any altitude. But, as Jason had noted, it *would* cause the carriage to slow down. So this had to be done quickly and it had to be done now.

The wind was intense and the whole vehicle was shaking from the turbulence, both of which we'd have to take into account when we made our leaps of faith.

I gestured at Blue. "After you!"

She tightened the cord of her cloak around her neck and turned to Daniel. "Keep it steady," she told him.

He nodded and strengthened his grip on the reins. Blue took a deep breath, released her fingers from the roof, and pivoted toward the Pegasi. Without the slightest hesitation, she jumped off the driver's perch.

Her legs and arms outstretched, she landed with a thud on the saddle of the nearest Pegasus to our right.

I watched her work rapidly to unlatch the Pegasus from the reins—freeing him from the rest of the group. When she'd unhooked the last buckle, she and her steed carefully eased out of the line-up and began flying adjacent the vehicle.

All right, my turn I guess.

I peered out over the edge of the carriage at the stampeding hooves below. Vivid memories of the Twenty-Three Skidd tournament suddenly flashed through my head like a horrid flipbook. I remembered what it felt like to be dangling upside down—thrashing in the air; my prologue pang hitting me like a recurring thunderbolt and causing the world to go black.

"Problem?!" Blue shouted, calling me back to the present.

"No; I'm good!" I lied in response.

Deep breath, Crisa. It's all in your head. You've got this.

I exhaled and jumped—my eyes locked on Sadie, the closest Pegasus to the left. I landed on her a split-second later, but nearly slipped off the saddle from the force of the jump. My hands grasped desperately at her mane as I resisted the urge to scream. Thankfully, I grabbed hold just in time and was able to pull myself upright.

My nerves rescinding, I proceeded to follow Blue's example and unhinge the latches strapping Sadie to the rest of the herd. Soon enough, she too was free and the two of us flew around to meet Blue and her Pegasus.

With the carriage out of the way, Blue and I now had a perfectly clear view of just how critical the situation was. The dragon—scales glinting in the setting orange sunlight—was some 700 yards away and gaining. He was snorting puffs of smoke, and his dead-on eye contact with us confirmed the notion that our shared flight path was no mere coincidence. For whatever the reason, he was definitely following us.

Blue and I kept pace with the carriage—flying directly behind it as we tried to come up with some sort of plan.

"So how do we do this?" Blue shouted through the sound of the wind and the dragon's roars. "Except for that part of his armpit, arrows and spears just bounce off that thing! Which means—"

"Which means we need a distraction!" I suggested.

"Are you offering?" she asked.

"Uh . . ." I glanced back at the dragon—scales sharp like ice picks, incisors the size of lawn chairs, and eyes fervidly glowing gold. "It wouldn't be the worst thing I've had to deal with today!" I finally answered.

"Good!" Blue said. "It'll be just like the Twenty-Three Skidd tournament!"

Yeah, if that Twenty-Three Skidd tournament had involved an enormous monster trying to kill us.

"I'll distract him; you go underneath and hit his weak spot!" I told her. "Then I'll take the shot!"

Blue nodded, then she and her Pegasus pulled off—dropping and disappearing into the clouds to get into position. I gave Sadie a little kick and turned her around as well. She and I headed straight for the dragon. When we were within forty feet of the monstrosity, I maneuvered her to abruptly swoop up right in front of the beast's face like an irritating pest.

That certainly caught his attention. The dragon halted to a stop as fast as a gargantuan creature could halt to a stop in mid-air, and took off after me. Diving, swerving, jettisoning in every direction—from there he kept on my tail no matter what I did. I guess I had ticked him off something fierce, because he sure was committed to pursuing me. Much more than I'd thought he'd be anyways.

I finally saw Blue some one hundred feet below and climbing. In response, I began to level off my flight pattern while reaching into my boot and pulling out my wand.

Gee, I hope this works.

Lacrosse sword, I semi-confidently commanded.

Sure enough, my wand morphed into the spear I was so used to handling now, but then sprouted a small basket at its lower end and an elongated blade on the top. Even buttons to operate an optional extender grip function appeared beneath my fingertips.

I was relieved.

Honestly I hadn't been positive that my wand would change into the lacrosse sword since it was only meant to turn into weapons. But I'd figured, hey, if it had a sharp blade, technically it *was* a weapon, right?

Apparently the wand's enchantment and I were on the same page because it hadn't fought the transformation in the slightest.

Sadie and I continued flying—waiting for my opening—and I couldn't help but note that it did feel a lot like the tournament again. Well, except for the understanding that there was a significantly higher chance that I'd be barbecued if I missed my shot this time around.

The unorthodox Twenty-Three Skidd weapon in my hand, I removed the portable potions from my pocket and loaded them into the basket of the lacrosse sword. I then signaled Sadie to change course and we made a beeline directly for the dragon.

In the distance I saw Blue doing the same; only she was about twenty feet below our target, creeping closer to his skin with every passing second.

Sadie whinnied as we headed for the monster, obviously asking me if I really meant to be literally entering his line of fire and, if so, was I nuts? Regardless of her protests, I egged her on. For the truth remained that there actually was a method to my madness.

The distraction was working. At that moment, the dragon's attention was completely locked on me—his giant, golden eyes so focused on my trajectory that he didn't notice Blue coming up underneath him. He was barely fifty yards from me when she flew right below his armpit.

For a scary beat I didn't see her while she and her steed

were blocked from sight by the folds of the dragon's wing. But then the dragon seizured in agony again. She'd done it; Blue had managed to get close enough to the dragon to give him a good jab in the armpit with her hunting knife.

I saw her and her Pegasus barrel out of the precarious spot just as the dragon roared with unbridled rage. The instant he did, I activated the extender grip function on my lacrosse sword.

The dragon's stomach began to glow orange again, but his fire never came to fruition. I gave my weapon a powerful swing and launched the portable potions from the basket. The glass orbs soared straight into the beast's open mouth while Sadie and I did another sudden swoop upwards to avoid colliding with him.

Blue flew up to meet me then, and the two of us watched as the potions rapidly took their toll. The orange glow on the beast's gut died out. Silver smoke escaped his nostrils just before ice crawled out of his throat and speedily encased his entire being.

The creature struggled—thrashing about to fight the potions' effects—but before long his whole body was a solid ice sculpture. Then, since ice sculptures couldn't levitate, he plummeted through the clouds below and fell completely out of sight.

Blue wiped a bead of sweat from her brow as the last of the dragon vanished from view. "Dang," she huffed. "Remind me to pay more attention in potions class from now on."

She glanced behind us at the carriage. It was a decent ways off and was quickly approaching the dimming horizon. "Come on," she said, her face cast in shadow and her hair caught in the autumnal glow. "We have a lot of ground left to cover."

I stared down at the hole in the clouds through which the creature had fallen, then back in the direction of the city.

I couldn't believe how far we'd come in a day. Moreover, I couldn't believe how much had *changed* in a day.

Within the last twenty-four hours I'd learned that I had magical powers, the boy who'd haunted my dreams for years was most definitely real, and that he and some group of antagonists wanted me dead. It was a lot to process, especially when you added other factors like forged protagonist book conspiracies and the priority elimination of Paige Tomkins and Natalie Poole to the mix.

With all that had already unfolded, it was really anybody's guess what else the five of us would find on our way to collect the other items on Emma's list and reach the Author. Our quest was a shifting road. Pretty much everything about it felt indeterminate now—up in the air as it were.

And yet . . . there was one thing I did know for sure. One understanding that was so powerful it was enough to compel me to forge ahead despite all hindrances, odds, and uncertainty working against us.

I was hooked.

Yes, feelings of dread and doubt pulsed through me about my own shortcomings, the mysteries surrounding us, and the people who were trying to kill me. But even so, part of me just didn't care. Since the moment I'd first taken off toward the sky in that mushroom carriage, we'd been moving forward. And even with the growing weights on my shoulders I knew then that it didn't matter what antagonists or monsters stood in our path; that was the direction I had to keep going.

The collision course I'd set myself on with my fate might

very well have been a perilous, or even fatal one. But I would continue moving forward on it regardless. For I was as adamant about seeing where it would go as I was about seeing how far I could go.

My mother had always told me that I'd be a great protagonist one day. And I still didn't know if she was right, let alone what it really meant to be one. Nevertheless, I concluded now that the only way to find out was to press onwards like this—keep going and embrace, not fear whatever changes might happen along the way. Because while change could certainly be negative, its very existence was a beautiful thing.

And, furthermore . . . it gave me hope.

I'd spent my whole life corralled inside a world that tried to make me believe change was impossible—that we were stuck with whatever lot we'd been given and couldn't do anything about it.

But, if I'd learned anything in recent months, it was that those beliefs were wrong. Change *was* possible. I'd seen it. I'd lived it. And darn it, I was going after it.

That fire that had ignited in me the day I'd gotten my prologue prophecy had only grown in the last few weeks. The more I moved forward, the stronger it burned, inspiring me to keep going and keep fighting for the kinds of change I wanted. The likes of which, in my truest heart and clearest mind, I knew were all possible.

I *could* find the Author. I *could* rewrite my story. And I, Crisanta Knight, *could* become something more. I only needed be brave enough to see it through.

On that note, as I thought on all these matters of strength and story, I took a deep breath. Then, that fire ever burning inside of me—rebellious, ardent, and firmly resolute—I looked back at Blue and smiled.

"Yeah," I said. "I suppose we do."

End of Book One

About the Author

Geanna Culbertson adores chocolate chip cookies, watching Netflix in pajamas, and the rain. Of course, in her case, the latter is kind of hard to come by. As her dad notes, "In California, we don't have seasons, we have special effects."

On the flip side, she is deeply afraid of ice skating and singing in public. Although, she forces herself to do both on occasion because she believes facing your fears can be good for you.

During the week Geanna lives a disciplined, yet preciously ridiculous lifestyle. She gets up each day at 5:00 a.m. to train. Goes to work where she enjoys a double life as a kid undercover in a grown-up world. Then comes home, eats, writes, and watches one of her favorite TV shows.

On weekends, however, Geanna's heart, like her time, is completely off the leash. Usually she'll teach martial arts at her local karate studio, pursue yummy foods, and check out whatever's new at her fav stores like Banana Republic. To summarize, she'll wander, play, disregard the clock, and get into as many shenanigans as possible.